REALMS OF EPENOCHT

The Binding of the Crypt

Realms of Edenocht The Binding of the Crypt

D.S. JOHNSON

A Young Adult Fantasy Fiction Action Adventure Novel

DS JOHNSON
2019

First Printing: 2019

ISBN 978-1-7352859-1-7

Illustrator -DS Johnson

Rosecrest Printing
Herriman, Utah 84096

www.dsjohnsonbooks.com

Dedication

I want to thank my family for the love and support they have shown me through this journey. For the fun dinner time story building moments to the 'feed-yourself-tonight' nights. To the fans of Realms and the drive it gives to keep moving forward. To the characters that want their story told and the fun times in a marvelous fantasy world.

I thank you all!

Contents

Realms of Edenocht

Night of the Velshari

105 Rotations before The End of the Realms
How May I Serve Thee?

The late-night light through the majestic windows faded from the deserted library. The day had been full of tests and interviews on ancient runes, alchemy, and druidic arts. The school of the mages was an elite academy for those gifted with the abilities of elemental magic.

"Gavin wake up. What are you doing? It's after curfew," Dresden said his voice hushed.

Gavin stirred and found small eyes that popped out from under thick glasses.

"Studying. Why?" Gavin said blinking.

"Well if you call snoring and drooling, studying,"

Gavin wiped the evidence of sleep and drool from his face and stuffed his books into his bag. Gavin scooted his chair and cringed as the screech the pad-less feet made against the polished stone ripped open the silence. Dresden crouched almost in half and pushed his thick glasses back up his nose and closed his eyes.

"Just because you can't see them, doesn't mean they can't see you," Gavin jeered.

Dresden peered out from under his eyelids and straightened his robes. Gavin left the chair in its place and rounded the table as he slung his satchel over his shoulder. Gavin led them through the maze of tables and sitting areas until they reached the large solid wood doors. Gavin stopped and put his ear to the cool wood and listened. Dresden slid in behind him and placed his ear on the door and sniffed while he wiped his nose. Gavin rolled his eyes and reached for the long thin iron handle.

He pulled the door open a crack and peeked down the corridor and when he didn't find anything, he opened the door. He found the darkness soothing and was confident they were alone and slipped through the opening and allowed the door to close softly. Their pace was swift, as they moved down the halls they crossed daily, since they were young. Dresden ran to keep up with Gavin's long strides. His short legs and slightly pudgier midsection presented more of a challenge to maneuver as Gavin did.

Gavin detected faint voices coming from around the next bend in the hall and not wanting to spend the next moon cycle on kitchen duty, he rushed against the cold marble wall in time for Dresden to bump into him. Gavin scooted to the edge of the next corner and listened.

"Shhh," Gavin whispered.

Gavin peeked around the corner. A once tall monk clasped his hands in front of his hunched and aged form and addressed two others.

"Meet at the cave, now," said the monk.

"Is that Stralazar the Headmaster?" Dresden mouthed.

Gavin nodded.

"Thelius and Ponchet too," Gavin said.

Gavin could tell because Ponchet was a short round man and even though his hood covered most of his head and face, a slight blondish mustache and beard poke out. Thelius was obvious because his bald head reflected the dim lights and his scar which ran from his left ear down his neck and passed his collar showed through the darkness.

"The incantation?" asked Thelius.

"Not yet, he's still not found the scroll," Stralazar said.

"Then why the sudden meeting?" asked Ponchet.

"It is not for us to question," Stralazar said.

"You can count on us," Thelius said bowing deeply.

Thelius elbowed Ponchet who nodded and bowed. They turned and slipped their hands into their robes and hurried down the polished corridor. Gavin shuffled away from the corner keeping in the shadows as they passed. A tickle in the pit of his stomach lurched upward and his curiosity leaped out of his chest. He shifted his bag on his shoulder and quietly followed the two men.

"What are you doing? It's after curfew. You're going to get caught," Dresden said.

He grabbed his cloak to stop him.

"Go back if you want," Gavin said and yanked his cloak from Dresden's grip.

Dresden shook his head but followed his childhood friend. The monks made their way through the long corridor and down the vast staircase at the front of the entryway of the academy but turned sharp at the bottom of the stairs and into the shadows out of sight and into a side entrance of the fortified gray stone walls of the school. Gavin followed them staying as far as possible behind them but close enough to indicate where they were going. His heart was beating heavily, and a tingle of energy rang in his head giving him a satisfactory sensation of thrill. He turned the corner and found the door they used and pulled on the handle. The door hadn't quite latched shut, making it possible for him to open. The coolness of the night hit his lungs, and he sucked in a deep breath. Dresden covered his mouth with his sleeve and coughed as his lungs adjusted to the moist air. Gavin searched the surroundings and found the monks slipping into the edges of the forest.

"Come on, this way," Gavin said.

Gavin half-shuffled-and-half-hobbled over the school's side yard of mixed flower beds and garden boxes. Dresden was doing his best to keep up but had fallen several paces behind. The further they traveled under the heavy tree cover the harder it was to see, and a thick layer of clouds began to roll over the three moons which caused the temperature to drop a few degrees. The new cold stung their eyes as Gavin kept what he thought was a good distance behind them. At one point he thought he lost them, but he found them emerging from a grove of trees on the other side of a clearing. He was never allowed to be this far into the forest and now the cover of the trees shaded any light the stars or moons might have given off. He kept to the edge of the clearing. Closing the gap, Gavin tripped on a branch sticking out of the ground and almost lost his pack. He froze instantly hoping the monks wouldn't pay attention to the noise.

"Careful," Gavin said shooting Dresden a glare as he stumbled on the same spot.

Dresden glared back with his hands out and his mouth open. Gavin shoved his hand over his mouth to cover his impending speech on equality. It was a good thing this year as sixth-year students their robes were midnight blue. Gavin hesitated for a moment then scurried along a less-traveled path. His eyes darted around frantically trying to find the monks. His blood beat faster, he feared they might have moved around to the back of him, and he was about to be caught, and then he found them near the cliff edge of the mountain range which flanked the backside of the school.

"Do you hear that?" Dresden asked in a whisper.

"Yeah, it sounds like drums," Gavin said.

"But where is it coming from?" Dresden asked.

A soft padding of drums escaped the rock surface which confused their senses. The closer they came, the louder the noise became. Gavin and Dresden slipped behind a tree and witnessed the two monks engage a third. A stranger to them, and they exchanged curious glances and a shrug. A heavy gust of wind picked up and blew against the rock face causing a growling hiss to echo through the trees. The tops whipped around letting a faint glow from the moon shine on the three men. Gavin paid attention to how the men touched a small platform under a ledge in the cliff and the rock wall dematerialized and allowed them to walk into a secret passage. Another man came out of the shadows and Gavin caught a glimpse of his features before the veil closed behind Ponchet.

"It's Breckum, my mentor," Gavin said, in less than a whisper.

"What are they doing?" Dresden asked.

"No idea," Gavin said.

The tickle in his stomach became a hot heat and settled in his core. Gavin could hardly breathe as the excitement now swelled in his chest. He didn't understand, but the insatiable need to learn more overcame him. Thelius raised his hand and let a ball of orange magic escape his palm. He spoke words Gavin wasn't familiar with and Gavin gasped. Dresden put his hand on his friend's shoulder and squeezed. The darkness opened like a curtain and let out a dim cast of light which must have been from a burning lamp on the inside. The man disappeared as the veil of darkness closed behind him. Ponchet followed in the same manner.

Gavin knew if he was going to make the opening he needed to move quickly. Without giving a second thought, he leaped out from behind the tree and slipped into the darkness behind Breckum. The black veil closed tightly behind him and snagged his robe. Sweat crept across his forehead and his heart raced in his chest. He knew if he got caught, he would lose his spot on the student council. The misdeed exhilarated his senses, and he was oddly pleased as this suddenly gave him more satisfaction than anything before.

Gavin moved against the sidewall and held his breath for several minutes until he no longer sensed the instructors near, and then he moved forward with caution while scanning the surroundings for any places to hide in case he needed to. The carved-out hallway was small, with a gradual decline as he crept along the edge and guessed he was going deeper into the mountain. The damp air clung to the hairs in his nose and his breathing began to labor in his chest and the drums grew louder giving his nerves a ridged dull ache. He was always curious, only this time a sensation within his chest propelled him forward.

After several moments, the narrow hall widened and at the end leading into three more hallways. Gavin listened with intent as the monks said more of the strange words, bowed to each other and each went down their own hallway. Gavin wasn't sure what to do now and thought he could go back. But he wanted to learn the secrets. The monks he knew and revered were not what he thought, and for some reason, he wanted to be a part of it. A moment later two returned and waited for the third. Gavin hadn't realized he was now out of the shadows. When the third monk returned, he nodded to the others, and they turned to Gavin.

"Ah, so we did have a follower," Breckum said.

Breckum pulled the deep blood-red hood from his head. His head was shaved and had a dark black marking on his skin. The mark covered the left half of his head and came just short of his left eyebrow. The mark resembled a dragon-like figure, but narrower and sleeker with large spikes on the tail. This mark was unknown to him, even when he studied the art of alchemy with him. *This must be from magic, or maybe*...he realized them staring at him. Sweat poured down his cheek as he froze in terror.

"What shall we do?" asked Ponchet.

His eyes glassed over with a sinister taint.

"We shall take him with. I think he is old enough. He certainly wants to know what is going on, otherwise, he would not have come all this way," Breckum said. With a whisk of his robe, he moved toward Gavin and wrapped his arm around him. "Come; let us take you to Arte-bus," He said with a hint of an evil laugh under his breath.

Gavin Rill's sense of curiosity now stung his body with fear and exhilaration. A realization he'd never understood before. An intoxicating and addictive sensation began to form in his soul. They walked through another black veil. A cold rigid prickling ate at his flesh as he passed through.

Gavin didn't dare speak. The cavern was vast and dim, the drums echoed in his head.

"This is one of my prized pupils," Breckum said.

"I sense greatness from this one," Ar-te-bus said, peering out from under his cloak.

Gavin's pulse was close to choking the breath from his throat.

"How may I serve thee?" Gavin managed.

"Come, let's talk," Ar-te-bus said.

He led him to the center of the room. A cold wind swirled around them.

****

30 rotations later

Long red capes flowed in strides as the Velshari marched in rhythm to their chanting. The leader worked his way down long hallways carved into the mountains unforgiving pressure. Ar-te-bus called the final gathering. Deep in the darkness of the lair, small plumes of smoke swirled toward the damp rocky ceiling. The cavern stretched deep into the darkness of the mountain. Small bursts of stale air tainted with a tart hint of ash and iron heaved from its bowels. Clerics assembled bringing with them the dark secrets and practices of the shadow magic. The scroll was found and was now the time to perform the incantation to give them eternal life.

The clerics now in rows faced the raised platform. They swayed and chanted the needed ancient words. Plumes of smoke puffed and sifted through the air as the chanting grew louder and then softer. Ar-te-bus stood at the altar in the center of the large square room.

"You may begin," Ar-te-bus said.

Gavin Rill set his long spindly fingers strategically on the orb. Pulling his magic from his core, he sent the gray mist into the orb. The ball glowed bright white. Several clicks sounded as the ball opened. Gavin removed the smaller orbs and rested them on the silver platter at the center of the altar. He ran his hand over the balls, and they popped and sizzled. Soft hues of colors sifted gently from the orbs as the stolen magics escaped. He removed the hood of his robe. Deep sunken eyes peered out from under sliver-thin black brows. Ar-te-bus clasped his hands in front of his withering frame.

"Secret forces deep below, send your warriors full of sorrow. Take this offering as payment," Gavin said.

With a loud voice Gavin said the incantation, he performed many times for himself, only this time he left out the words that would allow anyone to return. The black marking on the left side of his head began to darken in color and a bright orange glow radiated from around the edges. A black creature of the night magically etched into each member's skin.

Gavin Rill raised each orb and uttered more of the incantation. Each time the magic glinted and hovered in the air for a split-second and then vanished. After the last orb was emptied Gavin Rill took Ar-te-bus's hand. He poured a thick liquid into his palm burning the skin. He then threw up his hands and uttered the last words.

A loud crack split the air sending the clerics gathered in the room ducking to the ground. A bolt of bright orange light pulsated through the air with a loud reverberation. A sucking noise from the darkness opened and Ar-te-bus was sucked into the fiery beyond. Gavin Rill's helpers, two creatures he found in the underworld, the Sqwall and the Jaduuk emerged. Then he bound the door to the underworld shut, leaving Ar-te-bus in the underworld forever.

The new incantation comprised one more element, he whisked around and shouted more words, no one had ever heard, which bound all the clerics of Velshari to him and him only, and they now were forced to obey his commands. The members of the Velshari fell to the floor with horrid cries and writhed in pain with the new demands of loyalty. Gavin shrieked with the strength of thunder and then silence ripped through the blackness.

1-It Wants to Kill You and Peck Your Eyes Out

Long shadows crept along the dirt path as the sun slipped behind the rigid mountain pass. Serin tightened her cloak and cinched her hood around her face as the cold sting of the oncoming night chill stung her cheeks. Ladtwig and Turkill huddled as tightly as they could to Jagwynn's warmth, but the cold still brought out the purple in their dark bronze lips. Shaz tightened his cloak and huddled close to the side of the mountainside as he rounded the last peak of the Bairr Tiornecht mountains.

Riddick followed in the rear using his earth magic to erase their tracks. The path from the Minca's village had taken them toward the southeast in a wide circle which then switched backed several times until coming to the other end of the mountain range, where instead of climbing straight up the cliff as they had the first time, they would take the steep but manageable pathway. This way was, however, several days longer and the mountain range was much higher in elevation.

"Won't be long until we reach the portal, and then we'll be back in the realm of Ebassia," Shaz said.

"Thank goodness," Serin said through chattering teeth.

Riddick nodded and the Minca managed a slight half-smile. Shaz called the fire element to his hands and took Serin in his arms and pulled her close. The heat quickly surged through her body and gave her the needed relief, and then he warmed the Minca. Riddick shook his hand and Shaz hugged him anyway in which the others chuckled. Riddick grinned with the relief and rested with a small smile.

"Come on," Shaz said.

Riddick waved his hand across the rocks asking them to fill in their footprints and followed the others. After, a few more turns they came to a dead end.

"This must be the portal," Serin said.

Shaz scoured the rock wall for any grips or places to rest his hands or levers or signs. A slight glow illuminated under a glassy surface and Shaz read the marks. He touched the corresponding glyphs around the edges and the rock face fizzled and popped. Shaz stepped aside and let Serin step through, but before she reached the door a tingle caressed her skin, and she hesitated.

"What's wrong?" Shaz asked.

"I'm not sure, this is different from the others," Serin said.

Shaz reached toward the door and could sense a different kind of energy as well.

"What is it?" Riddick asked.

"Not sure," Shaz said.

Shaz searched his mind for anything he might have forgotten to do and placed his hands on the stone again. The glyphs lit up the way they had before.

"Do we enter? We can't go back now," Ladtwig said.

"I suppose so," Shaz said.

"Wait, isn't there supposed to be some kind of tracking spells on these things?" Riddick asked.

"How do you know?" Shaz asked.

"Crolos was talking about it with the Minca he worked with in the Realm of Yune," Riddick said.

"Yep, your right, this one is the symbol for reading one's magical imprint," Shaz said.

"But, how come the portal with Tomos didn't have this?" Serin asked.

"Because, he wouldn't have allowed it to be placed on the portal," Turkill grunted.

"I suppose only the unguarded ones have them," Shaz said.

"I don't recall the one in the waterfall being like that, but again I was swimming for my life at the time too," Riddick said.

"So, what do we do?" Serin asked.

Shaz shook his head. He searched for several minutes but found nothing to clue him in on what he could do to remove the alert.

"I guess we take our chances. Gavin Rhill's going to find out where we are sooner or later if he hasn't already. I mean we just eliminated Semias, I'm sure he's been made aware by now," Shaz said.

"I guess you're right. But we need to stay low and out of sight as much as possible from here on out then," Serin said.

She stepped through the passage with a shudder followed by Jagwynn and the Minca, Riddick and then Shaz.

"Well it still looks like the same mountain," Riddick said.

"What did you expect?" Serin asked.

"Perhaps a valley, the ocean, or a barren wasteland," Serin gave him a sideways glance, "Well, that's what happened the last time I went through a barrier," Riddick said.

She smiled and patted his arm. Shaz closed the barrier behind him and scaled behind the others until they found a ledge sturdy enough for him to maneuver to the front where he and Riddick traded places.

Riddick once again covered their tracks by touching the earth and telling the dirt to remove their footprints. The sun was now shining on their side of the mountain, and the air was warmer than on the dark side which they were all glad for. As they rounded a corner of the highest peak, the trail narrowed and the fear of falling off the ledge became real. Shaz noticed birds soaring through the sky still several hundred lengths below them and figured they must be quite sizable for him to be able to see them from this distance. He pointed them out to the others, but they couldn't see them yet. The terrain was much too steep for Serin's wind-walk, so they had to move at a snail's pace and the travel took for what seemed like forever, in which Ladtwig grumbled every chance he got.

"So how do you suppose Yerild and the others got back to Turob?" Riddick asked.

"Beats me, what did the Earth say to you?" Shaz asked.

"She only said she would return them," Riddick said.

"I hope things are alright back home," Shaz said.

Aye, me too, the commissioner is a real daft head, and he's gonna make for some trouble if he's not careful," Riddick said.

"How's that?" Shaz asked.

"With the new Islands popping up, who's to say what's going on, and your father hasn't been anywhere to be found, no one is around to keep the reef in check, things are going to be real messy," Riddick said.

"Where's my father? Why hasn't he been around? What happened? How come you never told me," Shaz said stopping dead in his tracks.

Serin nearly ran into him and Jagwynn hissed.

"Sorry mate, I thought your Grandfather told you,"

"Told me what?"

"He went missing after we sailed to Ebassia," Riddick said.

"I have no idea how much time has actually passed in Turob. With all the time-shifting, I can't keep it straight," Shaz said.

"Oh, your map does," Ladtwig said.

"What, show me!" Shaz said.

Shaz slung his pack off his shoulder and pulled out his map as Ladtwig jumped off Jagwynn's back. Shaz unfolded the map and waited as the little balls of glittering particles that represented towns and villages or landmarks and barriers jumped off the page. Ladtwig scooted against the wall and pointed to a little compass at the bottom corner of the map. Several discs popped up and barely hovered off one another and spun like a time ticker each at their own rates. The bottom of the map had three circles in which represented the day, moon, and annual rotation as a reference in determining the time differences.

"Here, this is your realm, this one is mine," Ladtwig said.

Shaz studied the disc's and calculated how much time had passed. He closed his eyes and sighed heavily.

"What is it?" Serin asked.

"It's been all most a full rotation's time since Riddick and I left Turob," Shaz said.

Riddick whistled. Serin rested her hand on Shaz's arm.

"I'm sure your family is alright. We'll find an explanation, let's keep going, I bet Inelius will have some insight, the sooner we reach your castle the better," Serin said.

Shaz folded up the map, tucked the old parchment into his satchel, and they continued down the mountain. The air became warmer the lower they went, and the birds finally came into view, in which the others marveled at. They tried to guess what kind of birds they were which only sparked an intense argument between the Minca and Riddick who still hadn't learned not to engage. The sun was now overhead but still over a day's journey until they reached the bottom of the mountain.

"Do you have any idea if we'll find any caves or shelters on this mountain?" Serin asked.

"I don't think so," Shaz said.

"I can make one," Riddick said.

"Good, because I don't think I want to sleep here on the edge of the mountain," Serin said.

"Me either," Ladtwig said.

"You've been awfully quiet Turkill," Serin said.

"I got nothing to say," Turkill grunted.

"Alright, grumpy," Serin said.

"I think he's missing his lady friend," Riddick said.

Serin nodded, she thought he might, but hoped he would adjust alright.

"We'll stop in a bit and make camp for the night, Riddick why don't you move on ahead and scout a suitable place to make us a shelter," Shaz said.

Riddick nodded and scooched passed them and hurried down the pathway. Several minutes later he returned with the location he had selected where he would have the easiest time moving the rocks around to make a shelter big enough for them all to fit into. After reaching the spot Riddick gripped the earth with his hands and stomped his foot and the mountain shook and trembled as it opened. Shaz sent a burst of fire through the cavern and burned any gaseous fumes and Serin sent a gust of air to sweep out the odor, and they made their camp for the night. The makeshift cave was warm and comfortable, and they were happy to rest.

Shaz and Riddick talked about the details of Turob and the new Islands and how Yerild had told Riddick about the sea creatures and making notes as to what to talk to Inelius about when they arrived at the castle. Jagwynn had left to scout out the terrain and Ladtwig organized his rations and ate as much food as he dared knowing they still had a substantial journey before they would be able to eat the Wispmother's magical meals. Turkill sat in the corner gnawing at his dried meat and Serin laid her head on her satchel and watched the massive birds circle outside the cave until her eyelids were too heavy to keep open.

Evening turned to night and a loud screech ripped through the cave. Everyone startled awake and each reached for their weapons. Shaz ripped the sword from the sheath and leaped up toward the black creatures before the grotesque animal landed on the ledge.

"Blast, a sqwall!" Shaz growled.

"I guess they know where we are for sure now," Riddick said.

"I really hate these things," Serin said.

Serin stepped back figuring between the guys she wasn't needed when a thought came to her mind.

"Shaz, I think it might talk to us," She said.

"Are you for real?" Shaz asked.

"Call it a hunch," Serin said.

"How do we capture it?" Turkill asked.

"I have no clue, that's up to you," Serin said.

The guys rolled their eyes. Shaz scooched to the edge of the cave and Riddick followed.

"Serin, lure it into the center, and we'll surround it," Shaz said.

"What, are you insane?" Serin said.

"It was your idea," Shaz said.

"Fine," Serin said annoyed.

Serin stepped into the center of the cave into a ray of moonlight and put her bow on the ground. The black crow-like bird side-hopped onto the ledge a few feet and stopped. Serin backed up toward the back wall of the cave. The black beady eyes of the mangy creature searched the cave and the guys scooted toward the entrance hiding themselves.

"I'm over here, you nasty creature," Serin said.

The sqwall narrowed its sight on Serin and side-hobbled a few more steps. Shaz stepped out from the darkness and with the end of the hilt whacked the bird on the head. The creature fell to the ground with a thud and Riddick grabbed a roll of rope and tied the wings together and Turkill pulled a piece of cloth from his backpack and shoved the fiber into its beak.

"That felt good," Turkill said.

"I'm glad you're feeling a bit better," Shaz said.

"Now what?" Riddick asked.

"We wait until it comes to, and find out what it is doing, I guess," Shaz said.

"Can they even talk?" Riddick asked.

"Well, if not, we kill it and be on our way," Shaz said.

"We're not safe here, so we better wake it up and be on our way," Serin said.

"Can you splash it with some water?" Shaz asked.

Serin nodded and gathered a ball of water and dropped the liquid on the creature who sputtered and gagged. It squirmed and wriggled and sputtered for several seconds.

"I don't think you're going to make it very far," the creature eyed him and understood what Shaz had said. The tooth on Shaz's chest hummed and heated up, and he knew the creature had understood. "Now we understand each other, I am going to ask you some questions, you are going to answer them, and we'll decide whether you live or not," Shaz said.

The sqwall squirmed and tried to shove the gag out of its mouth with its long deep-red tongue.

"I guess we give it a minute to decide to cooperate?" Riddick asked.

"Only one, we don't have time for this nonsense. I'm running out of patience," Shaz said.

The sqwall stopped moving and laid still.

"I guess that's a yes," Riddick said.

Shaz reached down and pulled the cloth from its beak.

"Now, what are you doing here?"

"Searching for you of course," the creature said in a raspy gurgling voice.

"Why?" Shaz asked.

"Gavin Rhill wants you," the sqwall said.

"How many of you are there?" Shaz asked.

"Just me," the sqwall said.

"He's lying, there's several," Serin said.

Shaz shot her a surprised glare. The sqwall's eyes darted to Serin and back to Shaz.

"How can you tell?" Shaz asked.

"I just can, almost as though I can tell what the true intentions are," Serin said.

"Which are what?" Shaz asked.

"It wants to kill you and peck your eyes out, but forbidden, they all are," Serin said.

"Sounds a bit grim," Riddick said.

The creature's beak rounded into as much of a grin as possible and a glint in its eyes flashed. Shaz gripped his sword and shoved through the creature's heart. Panic raced over the face a second before its body sank lifeless into the cold stone.

"We're moving, *now*," Shaz said.

They all picked up their packs and Riddick closed the cave entrance, and they started down the narrow pathway once again.

2-Are We Good?

The image of the sqwalls thoughts swirled around Serin's mind for hours, and she found it hard to sort through all the emotions she received from the encounter. They traveled the rest of the night and into the day to reach the bottom of the mountain and in time the weather warmed up to the degree they pulled their cloaks off and put them back in their packs or were wearing them around their waists. Jagwynn had caught up and was padding softly next to Shaz who rubbed her head between the ears.

"Do you think we can use Serin's wind-walk now?" Turkill asked.

Shaz pulled his map out and laid it on the soft grass. He ran his finger along the markings of the map.

"There's a small settlement not far from here, and then quite a distance over the grasslands to reach the castle. I think we will want to ride horses this time and buff them. There won't be any cover for quite a distance, so we will need to have something we can go as fast as possible in case we're tracked by any sqwalls. Jagwynn, will you be able to keep up with buffed horses?" Jagwynn yawned and licked her paw. "Yes then, since you don't want to use your words today," Shaz said.

"No, we can't, we can't lead the sqwalls right to the people, what if they become prey to them?" Serin said.

"We need horses, we can't outrun sqwalls over the grasslands without them," Shaz said.

"Are we going to use the five-finger discount?" Riddick asked.

Riddick wriggled his fingers with a slight maniacal grin.

"Are you suggesting we steal them?" Serin asked.

A flash of mock surprise crossed his face, and he put his hands behind his back.

"Well, yes, you want to be stealthy, don't you?" Riddick asked.

"I can. No one will ever see me, I'm the smallest plus I blend into the darkness," Ladtwig said with a big grin.

"We are not going to make Ladtwig into a criminal," Serin said.

"We're not making him, he volunteered," Riddick said.

Serin shot him a glare and Shaz grabbed her hand and gave Riddick the '*I wouldn't go there,*' look.

"I don't like this either, but we're not the ones who asked for all this to happen. Bad things are going to happen to a lot of people. Besides this way we won't be here long enough to even leave a trace for the sqwalls to find," Shaz said.

"Fine," Serin grumbled.

Serin threw her arms up and cast her air spell on everyone, and they hurried through the thick forests until they reached the edges. Shaz and Riddick checked the map and calculated the distance and determined how much time they would need to cross the small distance of grasslands and arrive at the outskirts of the village before nightfall. The time came for the sun to hit the right part in sky and Serin buffed again, and they hurried out from the underbrush. The village came into view as they hurried over the small rolling hills which now encompassed the landscape. Ladtwig and Turkill, atop of Jag, crept quickly through the grass until they were only several lengths from the nearest log cabin.

Ladtwig slipped off Jag's back and Turkill leaped off her side with a soft thump, and they scurried to the side of the building. They crept around to the edge, peeked around the corner and searched for a stable or corral. Riddick lowered close to the ground as he hurried toward the next shadow and Jagwynn padded several lengths ahead of

Shaz and Serin who followed in the rear. Shaz, Serin, and Riddick made their way to the other side of the village and waited. Turkill and Ladtwig moved quickly from house to house but came up with nothing until Turkill spotted a small corral across a little clearing.

The stable stood alone with no protection, so they would have to risk being noticed. Turkill held up his fingers and counted down, and they bolted across the partial-dirt-partial-grass area. Several dogs started to bark the closer they came, and a small firelight came on in the nearest wood cabin. Turkill scurried behind a thick post sticking out of the ground and Ladtwig somersaulted into the cover of a table that was used to secure iron shoes to the horse's hooves. A loud burly man hollered at the dogs from the house and then the light went out. Turkill waited a few minutes for the dogs to calm down and hurried to the horses with Ladtwig right behind.

"How long do you think this will take?" Serin asked.

Shaz shrugged and listened to the sounds of the night. Serin wrung her hands together and held her breath.

"They're fine," Riddick said. He lifted his ear off the ground and gave her a big grin. Serin tried to smile back but her nerves made her too anxious, and she paced back and forth. "Not long now, they're on their way, send up your signal," Riddick said.

Shaz threw up a small flame ball in the air and hoped no one else saw the sizzle, before it popped, and faded into the night breeze. Several minutes later Turkill and Ladtwig rode on two horses with a third trotting behind.

"Did you have any trouble?" Shaz asked.

"Who do you think you are talking to?" Turkill asked.

"Sorry, we couldn't fetch any saddles, they were too heavy for us to shove onto the horses and the dogs were becoming restless," Ladtwig said.

"Don't worry Ladtwig," Serin said.

Shaz climbed onto his horse and Riddick his and the Minca climbed onto Jagwynn. Serin buffed Shaz, Riddick and Jag and the horses didn't like the magic and whinnied and pranced until the guys were able to steady them.

"What about you?" Shaz asked.

Serin boosted herself onto the horse and buffed her and her horse, gripped the mane and kicked the animal hard in the side. The animal didn't have time to think about the magic and bolted into the night. Shaz and Riddick gripped the mane of their horses in time for the animals to lurch after her. Serin's air magic didn't only help them move faster, but the force helped everyone stay on and padded their seats as if sitting in saddles. The Minca settled into their usual riding positions and Jagwynn found her stride.

A long time had passed since she'd really stretched her legs last and it was satisfying. Serin lowered close to the animal and allowed the horse to run as fast as it wanted, unless it started to slow then she kicked it to keep its speed. She knew with the sqwalls hunting them, and the distance they needed to cross without cover, crossing in the dark would be the best. The three moons high in the sky gave them plenty of light and the wind in her face refreshed her energy.

Shaz was surprised Serin pushed her horse so hard and wondered what the matter was. A few times he tried to ease up to her, but he could sense she wasn't in the mood, and he let her be, besides with moving so fast the wind wouldn't allow her to hear him anyway. Twice Shaz whistled and pointed to show her the direction, and she readjusted her horse. Based on the position of the moons, several hours passed, and she wondered why her air spell had lasted so long. She wondered if her extra nervousness for the safety of the people boosted her casting.

The horse's hooves hit the hard ground with a thud, and she pulled the horses' mane bringing the animal out of its trance. The horse jerked as the sudden shift caused the hooves to make contact with the solid ground.

"Whoaa," Serin said.

Shaz and Riddick came up behind her and slowed their horses as they regained control of the solid surface once again. Jagwynn and the Minca came to a stop next to Riddick, and they sat up.

"Are you alright?" Shaz asked.

"How much farther?" Serin asked.

Shaz pulled out his map. The little balls bounced and Shaz studied the moving parts of the time dial.

"At this pace, we should be another day and a half, but I don't think we can drive the horses this hard the whole time. Another couple of hours in this direction we should find a settlement where we can rest the horses and hide out during the day, then we can ride again at night," Shaz said.

"We have to go as fast as we possibly can to the next settlement before the sqwalls catch our trail, we can't lead them to any settlement," Serin said.

"Serin, we might not be able to do anything, we have no indication on how they track us in the first place," Shaz said.

Serin scowled and rebuffed everyone who started out as soon as the magic casting completed. Serin dug her heels into her horse and laid close to its neck, within a few minutes she caught up to Shaz and Riddick, and she guessed her horse wanted to be the lead horse. The impression was the horse wanted the magic and understood how much faster it was. Another few hours and the three moons began to fade into the now lightning sky and Serin pulled back the horse and let Shaz take the lead. Small smoke plumes drifted in the early morning mist, and they knew they were drawing closer to the settlement.

One nice thing about the air magic was a buffer of the pounding of the hooves against the ground was created, and they hardly made a sound. Shaz found an outlying of trees and steered the crew toward them. The horses began to pull against their riders as the air buff kept them lifted off the ground. Serin could tell they were tired from the long ride and patted her horse's neck. Jagwynn and the Minca padded up, and she let them off. Shaz dismounted and patted his horse gently and grabbed a handful of grass and began rubbing the cool stems on the back to brush it. The horse yanked a mouthful of grass and chewed delightfully as Riddick and Serin dismounted their horses. Serin pulled water from the air and made a small puddle for the horses to drink.

Ladtwig fell on his hinny as his legs were numb and Turkill almost fell but caught himself and grumbled. Riddick stretched his long legs and wiped the wind made tear crusties from his face and shook out his long wavy red locks.

Shaz watched Serin take several long draws from her water bag and finished rubbing down the horse. He moved around the horse and took Serin's pack and set the bag down and gripped her hand and pulled her away from the others.

"Serin, you're quite upset about something, what's wrong?" Shaz asked.

"I can't shake that disgusting creatures' thoughts out of my head. What if they followed us?"

"I don't sense any sqwalls near us," Shaz said.

"Yeah, but you didn't at the mountain cave either," Serin said.

"True, I didn't think of that, I wonder why not," Shaz said.

"They have always had the upper hand on us. What about them allows them to sneak up on us like they do?"

"Good question," Shaz said.

"They aren't allowed to peck *your* eyes out, but they can anyone else. Shaz if they attack these people, it will be *our* fault. Plus, we stole poor farmers' horses, probably all they had," Serin said.

"I won't let that happen," Shaz said.

"What are you going to do?" Serin asked.

"Give me a bit to think, maybe the others will have an idea, but as soon as we are far enough away and when we can, we will find someone to return the horses and even pay them for the trouble," Shaz said. Serin nodded and Shaz leaned in to kiss her. He hesitated and moved her chin, so her eyes met his. Her soft green eyes sparkled in the daylight, but her brows were pinched tightly. "I'm sorry you had to see what that evil creature was thinking, I can't make that go away, but I will do what I can to stop them and keep the people safe," Shaz pulled her tight to him in a hug. Serin relaxed in his grip and sank softly into his embrace.

"I'm amazed at how you do that," Serin said.

"Do what?" Shaz asked.

"Make me feel better like you do, and deal with all the evil things," Serin said.

"You make *me* feel better but thank you. Now I need you on your best game, for the people's sake, for my sake," Shaz said.

Serin's mixture of unrest and determination rippled across her face.

"What do you think is going to happen?" Serin asked.

"I have no answers, but things are different here, the shadow magic in these parts are more significant than in the Minca realm," Shaz said.

"That's lovely," Serin said.

"I need you at your best, I'm going to have to sift through much more than before," Shaz said.

"Alright, let's go," Serin said.

Shaz kissed Serin, their lips met with a familiar fashion. Their bond began at their first meeting and started to grow with trust and understanding, and through the power of Synmagic, now because of love. Shaz pulled away and smiled at Serin and took her hand and led her back to the others.

"Are we good?" Riddick asked.

"Aye," Shaz said.

"Good, because I found a tavern at the end of the settlement, we can maneuver the horses to the other side through the gully, then when night falls, we can head out again," Riddick said.

"Sounds good," Shaz said.

He grabbed his pack and Serin slung hers over her shoulder. They mounted their horses and galloped in a wide arc into the gully where Riddick had scouted. The sun made its way half-way to center and the heat warmed the grass sending a pleasant mixture of nettle weeds and fresh dirt into the air. Riddick pulled out a length of rope and tied the horses to a tree and Jagwynn slipped into the shade and turned around in circles several times before she laid down in the soft cool grass.

"We'll be back in a bit," Shaz said.

3-We're Just Passing Through

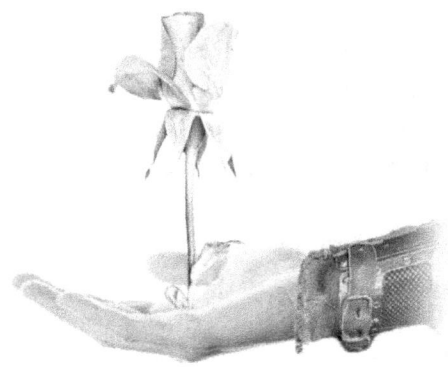

Shaz pulled his traveling cloak on over his blond hair and cinched the straps tightly around his slender but muscular frame. He made sure the honor blade was covered before he left the shadows of the trees. Serin and Riddick also covered their heads with their cloaks and Serin pulled her fine riding gloves on to cover her tattoos. Ladtwig and Turkill wrapped themselves in as much clothing as possible to make themselves appear bigger than they were and tried to walk as if they were three feet taller. Riddick searched the ground with his magic a few times listening for footstep vibrations in the earth's surface as they maneuvered through the grassy flatlands toward the settlement. Shaz and Riddick hurried to the backside of a long, worn stone building and Serin followed with the Minca.

"We need to stay hidden as much as possible," Shaz said.

"Aye," Riddick said.

Riddick stepped out from the shadows and scanned the surrounding buildings. The blacksmith building gave off a strong odor of smelted minerals as the burly dark-haired man slammed his heavy hammer against a dull nugget of steel. Riddick passed the bakery and found the aroma of freshly baked bread much more appealing than the black-smith and noted his stomach lurch with excitement. He hadn't had a hot meal in such a long time and found the temptation hard not to veer into the bakery.

Serin and the Minca stepped out from the shadows next and made their way passed the blacksmith and the bakery, however, Ladtwig stopped and sucked in a hefty lung full of the sweet bread from the bakery. Turkill bumped him and pushed him along much to his cha-grin. Serin smiled but also succumbed to the sting of hunger as she made her way toward the tavern. A prick of energy snapped at the back of her mind, and she turned toward the small alleyway which was be-tween the bakery and the tavern. A faint recollection sat at the back of her mind, but she couldn't quite figure it out. She scrutinized the dis-tance but came up empty.

Riddick gripped the cold iron handle and pulled open the heavy wooden door. The soft morning light left a glow on the first few feet of the tavern and instead of the usual ruckus which often accompanies places such as these, the only noise Riddick detected was the loud snor-ing of a patron, presumably, sleeping off last night's drinking. Riddick kept his head down as he maneuvered around several unorganized ta-bles and chairs and found a seat in the back. Serin pulled the door open for the Minca. Riddick started making a mental note of all the people both seated and standing, which wasn't many. He studied the bartender as Serin and the Minca found a booth near the middle. The bartender was a trim fellow of middle age with a tightly trimmed dark beard. The barkeep finished drying the tankard and hung it on a rack next to the bar but didn't take his eye off Serin.

"Do you think we can secure some breakfast?" Ladtwig asked.

"Of course, that's why we are here, you daft head," Turkill said.

"Don't call me that," Ladtwig said.

"Stop it, don't draw attention," Serin said.

Ladtwig slouched in the booth which he was already too short for. Serin searched the dingy tavern and found Riddick in the back cor-ner and turned to the bar. The man's eyes caught hers and he smiled.

She smiled politely in return and turned away catching Riddick sticking his finger in his throat and pretended to gag. Serin scowled but also snickered as if that were possible. The bartender moved out from around the bar and pushed in a few chairs as he made his way to her table. Shaz pulled the heavy wood door open and stepped through the opening and pulled the door shut behind him. He quickly scanned the room and found Riddick in the back corner and Serin and the Minca. He started toward her but stopped as the man approached her table.

"Well, what a pleasure, we don't often find the likes of a beautiful young lady in these parts," the barkeep said.

Turkill turned his head up at the man and stared. His usual harrumph expression turned into a 'how dare you', and '*I'm going to slice your throat*', in which the man paid no attention to, but Ladtwig covered his mouth to keep from laughing.

"Oh, well thank you, I guess," Serin said.

"What brings you to these parts?" the barkeep asked.

"We're just passing through," Serin said.

"Passing through, nothing is out this far to pass through," the man said.

Serin smiled and tilted her head enough to be able to push a fallen lock of hair behind her ear and the man stepped closer to the table. A flare of jealousy spiked and Shaz wanted to throw a ball of fire at the man, but he decided maybe this would be a good distraction, to scout out the surroundings, and keep from being discovered together. He sidestepped a table and moved to the other side of the room and sat down where he could spy both Riddick and Serin. Shaz caught a glimpse of Riddick sticking his tongue out in disgust. Shaz chuckled and relaxed as he knew even if Serin showed kindness to someone else, he had nothing to worry about.

"What do you have to eat, we're pretty hungry," Serin asked.

"Oh, yes of course, well, we have fresh seared mutton chops and eggs with bread and fresh berry spread, or pork strips and eggs with squeezed fruit juice," the man said.

"I'll take the pork strips," Serin said and turned to Ladtwig and Turkill.

The man turned and jumped at the two little men staring at him with scowls.

"I'll have the mutton," Turkill said,

"I'll have them both," Ladtwig said.

The barkeep studied them with an unusual glance until Serin put her hand on his arm.

"If it's not too much trouble, we would like your discretion on our whereabouts," Serin said.

The man turned to Serin, nodded and smiled back at her. Riddick was still making faces and Shaz sat with his arms folded across his chest. The barkeep went to the kitchen and a few minutes later came back out with three trays of food. A young woman around fifteen came out of the kitchen and wiped her hands with her apron and began to wipe down a few tables.

"Excuse me," Shaz said.

The girl turned in surprise.

"Oh, I'm sorry sir, I didn't notice you come in," the girl said.

"No problem, but I would like to order what you're serving this morning, and the man over there as well," Shaz said.

The girl peered around a hefty pole at Riddick who waved.

"Yes, of course, sir, I'll bring it right out," she said.

The girl hurried to the kitchen, and a few minutes later returned with food for both Shaz and Riddick. The hot meal was one of the most satisfying events in days and the whole party had a hard time not scarfing as fast as they could, even Serin found herself feeling the need to shove the hot food into her stomach. The barkeeper tended to his duties but kept watching Serin, who was trying not to pay him the kind of attention he was searching for. Serin finished the last bit of juice and set her glass down and rested her fork on the edge of the plate to signal she was finished with her meal.

The young girl started to take her dishes and Serin nodded. Turkill also agreed she could take his dishes, but Ladtwig was nowhere close to finished. The girl piled the plates on her arm and started back to the kitchen, but one slipped off and clattered to the floor. The bar-keeper barked ugly words at the girl and the man in the corner who was steadily snoring stirred and snorted then began snoring again. Serin slipped out of her seat and helped the girl pick up the dishes.

"Oh, no you don't, this girl needs to learn her lesson," the bar-tender said.

Serin rose and stared into the man's eyes, the hood of her cloak left a shadow over the top half of her face. He was several lengths taller than she was, but that never stopped her before. Shaz and Riddick shared a knowing glance at what was coming next, and they tried not to snicker.

"*I* will do as *I* please and no one, especially you, will tell me otherwise, is that clear?" Serin said.

Serin's tone was as sharp as a blade, her eyes locked on his, and she stood with calm assurance. Her magic penetrated the air surround-ing him, and he shivered from the tingle against his skin. The girl hurried to the kitchen and Serin continued to keep eye contact. The man wasn't sure what to do, he was both terrified and intensely attracted to her. Shaz sensed his energy shift and decided he didn't like the way this was playing out and pushed his plate off the table. The clang of the plate hitting the floor startled everyone and the barkeeper turned toward Shaz.

"Oiy, what's your problem?" the man barked.

Shaz acted as though the plate fell by accident and Serin sat back down. She realized she had started something she shouldn't have and now needed to find a way to smooth things over to stay hidden. The girl returned to Riddick and began loading his plate onto her arm. He held out a closed fist, and she studied him with confusion. He rolled his hand over, so his palm faced up and opened his hand. From the center grew a tiny green bud. The girl's eyes squinted on the little stem and it grew bigger as the stem grew taller. A bright pink blossom opened, and a beautiful flower stood in the center of his hand. The girl stepped back as the realization started to form in her mind, and she peered at him with fear in her eyes.

"No need to be afraid, go ahead, take it," Riddick said. The girl hesitated and Riddick nodded again. The girl picked the flower from his skin and Riddick closed his hand. "You can't guess what magical things are around the corner, but do me a favor and don't tell anyone," Riddick said.

The girl gazed at the flower a minute and back at Riddick, smiled and nodded. The snoring man stirred and sat up and rubbed his face. He blinked several times as he tried to focus from the drunken sleep. The stink of alcohol was strong, and Serin could tell he had been at the tavern for at least a few days.

"About time you woke up," the barkeeper said.

"What day is it?" the man asked.

"Wouldn't matter if I told you, you'll drink yourself into next week anyway," the barkeeper said.

The man rubbed his face and tried to scoot out of the bench but wobbled and fell back into the seat. Turkill shook his head and Serin frowned. Shaz studied the man but couldn't detect any magic or form of enchanted trinkets, however, a familiar air about him, he couldn't quite place, intrigued his mind. The barkeeper returned to the bar and mixed a concoction of a few vegetables and some strong spices and set it in front of the man.

"Here, drink this,"

"Is this that nasty garbage you keep trying to make me drink instead of booze?" the man asked.

"As much as I like how much you drink, you haven't paid me in days, so time you leave."

"Ah come on, one more?"

"No, now drink and get out."

The man grumbled and rubbed his hands over his face and scraggly beard. He gripped the thick handle and lifted the cup to his nose and sniffed. He pulled back and cringed, plugged his nose and gulped down the thick beverage.

"This stuff is incredibly nasty!" the man said.

He slammed his fist into his chest and coughed as the last of the mixture made its way into his belly.

"Good, I made this one extra strong, especially for you," the barkeeper said.

"Why I oughtta,"

"Oughtta, what? You can't even stand up, let alone hold a sword. Your nothing but a washed-up has been. You may have been the general of Ebassia, but your nothing now,"

"If it weren't for that young Queen and her new Grand Vizier,"

"Yeah, yeah, yeah, we all know the story,"

The man threw his hand at the barkeeper and tried to climb out of the booth but found the effort difficult to navigate his over-sized trench coat and slipped and slammed his head on the edge of the table.

"Ouch blasted all you bugger," the man cursed.

Blood dripped from the cut in his forehead, and he dabbed his wound and examined his fingers. He slammed his fist down and grabbed his coat and yanked the smelly garment out from under him and climbed out of the bench. Shaz couldn't believe the man could be so out of sorts and wondered what the big deal was back in Ebassia which made this man so distraught. Serin tried to examine the gash on his face from under her hood as he walked by.

"Barrick?" Serin asked.

She slipped out of her chair and the man turned around.

"No, I'm not Barrick, he's my brother, how do you know him? Who are you?"

The man's eyes shifted around as he tried to make them focus on Serin, but she could tell he thought she was moving about.

"Barrick and I met a while ago. Does he live around here?" Serin asked.

"Why of course he does," the man stammered.

The man tried to point in the direction of where Barrick's house was, but he was so wobbly he nearly fell. Serin used a tiny bit of her wind magic to help her muscle his bulky frame into a chair before he hit the ground and hoped the barkeeper hadn't noticed the sudden breeze inside the tavern.

"That's Bowen, Barrick's brother, I can't believe he's that drunk," the barkeeper said.

"It's not the drink, there's a wound on his head, where can I find Barrick?" Serin said.

"He's several lengths out of town to the west by south-west," the barkeeper said.

Shaz was now standing behind the barkeeper and observed the man from over his shoulder.

"Is everything alright?" Shaz asked.

"Oiy, this is none of your business," the barkeeper said.

"Is that right?" Shaz asked.

The barkeeper puffed out his chest and balled his fist. Shaz pushed passed him and put his hand on Serin's shoulder and leaned in close to her.

"I have to heal him, this is more than a cut on his forehead, I think something else is going on here," Serin said quietly.

"Alright, but do it as slowly and quietly as possible,"

The bartender huffed and cocked his elbow.

"Do *not* throw that punch sir, and fetch me some cold water," Serin said sternly.

The man studied her with a scrunched face, he couldn't figure out how she knew he was going to throw a punch when she was turned away from him. Shaz turned in time to find the man's fist cocked back and ready to strike. At first instinct, he analyzed how poorly the man's stance was and the elevation of his elbow, the hit would be meager at best. He needed to drop his elbow, twist his waist and use his hips to propel his hand through and imagine hitting on the other side of the target, so he would have maximum penetration, but the man was fixed on Shaz's nose and not the wall behind Shaz. Shaz smiled an obnoxious grin and shrugged.

"You heard the lady, she needs some cold water," Shaz said.

Shaz slipped one foot backward and readied his body to maneuver and duck away from the hit if the man decided to ignore Serin's warning. Serin turned around and put her hand on the man's arm.

"I think we got off on the wrong foot, what is your name?" Serin asked.

"Lew," Lew said.

"Well, Lew, help me help Bowen, his brother is a good friend of mine and I would be very unhappy if anything happened to him, in which I might return the favor," Serin said.

Shaz's eyes opened wide as did Lew's, both for different reasons. Shaz was intrigued she decided to shift tactics and Lew was hopeful. Lew studied Serin's eyes for a moment and gave in and went off to the kitchen.

"What was all that about, what did you do to him?" Shaz asked.

"What do you mean, what did I do to him, he's the one thinking what he's thinking. I haven't done anything," Serin said.

Shaz admired the little scrunch of annoyance in her brows and smiled.

"Hey, where is Ladtwig and Turkill?" Shaz asked.

Serin surveyed the surroundings and shrugged. Lew returned with a bowl of cold water and gave Shaz the stink eye as he set it down. Serin dipped her hands into the water and a surge of healing magic rippled across the surface. She snagged a napkin from the table, soaked the cloth, and pressed firmly on Bowen's head. Bowen mumbled but was unable to speak, his eyes still sat in the back of his skull and Serin waited as the magic worked slowly.

Lew stepped a little closer and tried to act as though he were interested in what she was doing. Shaz crossed his arms over his chest and glared back at Riddick who was beat red with laughter. Shaz scowled and shook his head at him which made him blurt out a hearty ga-fa. Serin pictured the magic seep into Bowen's body and search for the reason for his lack of conscientiousness but the fact Lew was standing so close to her frustrated the process.

"Lew, what did you put in that drink you gave him?" Serin asked.

"Umm, vegetable juice from the spiny rag weed, mint, burred mugwart, tinplat, and skunuts. This is my father's secret recipe to cure a hangover real quick," Lew said.

"Will you mix up another batch, I think he might need a little more incentive," Serin said.

"Yes, of course, but it will cost you," Lew said.

"Cost me what?" Serin asked.

She reached into her coin purse and grabbed several coins.

"Naw, not money," Lew said.

Serin rolled her eyes, and Shaz's heartfire skipped a beat and raced straight to hot.

"We can talk later, but right now I need the mixture," Serin said.

Lew nodded with a big grin and hurried back to the counter.

"This is getting ridiculous, just heal him and let's go," Shaz said.

Serin pulled her gloves off and put her fingers on the sides of his head. She searched for the cause and found a blood clot at the back of his head. She sent a steady surge of magic into his body and un-clogged the clot slowly so the sudden rush of blood back to his brain wouldn't overwhelm him. She dissipated the remaining alcohol from his body and healed the sores in his stomach from too much alcohol and not enough food. Bowen blinked several times and tried to sit up. Serin pulled her gloves back on and stepped away. Bowen examined the tavern as though he had no idea how he got there.

"What in the world happened? Who are you?" Bowen asked.

"I'm a friend of Barrick's, you said he was around here?" Serin said.

"You're a friend of Barrick's, now that is an intriguing matter. Barrick isn't the type to keep the company of a lady like you," Bowen said.

Shaz scowled, what did he mean by a 'lady like you'?

"Let me help you out and you can take me to him, I would really like to meet up with him and his wife again," Serin said.

"That might not be possible, she's been ill for weeks and might not even be around anymore," Bowen said.

"Then we really need to hurry," Serin said.

Serin grabbed his arm and pulled him out of the chair and hurried toward the door. The sunshine hit her in the eyes, and she squinted and shielded her face.

"Wait, your drink," Lew said as he rounded the bar.

4-Do I Need a Reason?

"Don't be stupid Garrison, I thought you said you would do anything for me," she said.

"This has nothing to do with whether I would do anything for you, and I never said I would Isot," Garrison said.

Her long skinny fingers flicked the air with a delicate ease, and she brushed him off like a fly. His teeth reflected the green hue of the potion brewing on the small table in the corner of the room. The sizable room spanned a distance with plenty of space for a large bed and night table, two lounges and a chair sat around a stone inlaid fireplace. Candles hung from sconces around the room while tall candle holders sat strategically placed to give the maximum light when needed.

"Oh, you didn't, my bad, I guess you don't love me then," Isot said.

Isot's tone was mischievous but her eyes narrowed with a furrowed brow. Her long deep-red colored fingertip touched the soft skin of his throat, and she slid them up toward his chin. He balked heavily, gripped her wrist and pulled her hand away. She twisted her wrist from his tight grip and rubbed it.

"You're toying with me again, now, aren't you? I told you we are not a *thing*," Garrison said.

"That's not what your...um, body says," Isot said.

Garrison sucked in a deep breath and tried to calm himself while adjusting his scarlet red robe and flattened his ruffled shirt.

"Don't flatter yourself," Garrison said.

"Then why are you here?" Isot asked.

Her tone was stone-cold, but her face hung relaxed with no expression.

Garrison glared at her and tried to figure out what she was trying to tell him. He reached for a book sitting on the edge of the table about to fall onto the floor.

"I need a favor," Garrison said.

"I suppose you are going to tell me about it," Isot said.

She turned her back to him and pulled a small dried herb from a black velvet pouch, crumpled the leaf in her hand and dropped the crumbs into the potion. The brew sizzled and foamed then dissipated back to a gentle boil.

"Yes, I think you would be quite interested in fact," he thumbed through the pages but didn't really care about the contents.

"Well, don't keep me in suspense, go on," Isot said.

She stirred the now purple liquid with a thin metal stirring stick.

"I need the Dodjen removed," Garrison said.

"Why the change of heart, I thought you liked them?" Isot said.

"You have your reason's I have mine," Garrison said.

Isot found the irritation in her voice hard to hide, and he was annoyed because Isot always made him spell everything out to her as though she had no brain of her own, which he figured was her way of deflecting. Isot stared into the back of his brain and tried to figure out what he was really up to.

"And what do you want me to do about it?" Isot snapped.

"Get rid of them," Garrison said.

He glared back into her eyes. Garrison had learned rotations ago after joining the Velshari the trick to keeping someone out of his mind was to stare directly back into their eyes and focus on what he saw in them. Plus, only think of random stuff, things of non-importance, and pretending to be something he's not. He had become so good, most members thought he was nothing but an idiot with half a brain. The woman stood seething with anger, her soft pale cheeks reddened, and her body grew stiff as she contemplated his presumptuous request. Garrison studied her passively, a small smile crept onto one corner of his mouth, while his eyes glinted with amusement.

"Kill them, I don't care, I have other things to worry about right now," Isot said.

"I was thinking more along the lines of the dungeons," Garrison said.

"Fine, send for Gitre," Isot said.

"Wonderful," Garrison said.

"Have her come to the castle as soon as she gets here," Isot said.

Garrison examined Isot, her long hair and high cheekbones delicately framed her deep eyes and her stern features had a sense of alluring beauty and his heart pumped a heavy thud into his ears and a tightness encompassed his chest.

"You heard me, go," Isot said.

"Yes, your grace," Garrison said.

He bowed and threw his long cloak behind him as he strode toward the door. He stopped momentarily and gripped the door handle harder than he needed to and threw open the door. The hallway was dark and musky, being in the basement levels of the castle had its perks of privacy, no one ever came down here, but this was certainly not the most enjoyable place to be. He covered his head with his hood and scoured the long hall. He had never been any further than this and never wanted to be, the lights went darker the deeper the corridors went, and he imagined the walls had eyes and were watching him. Garrison caught himself from time to time and wondered how many levels there were in this secret part of the castle.

Garrison had played both sides for so long, and he didn't dare risk being revealed. He found it hard enough pretending to obey the order of the Velshari while secretly gaining Intel for the Dodjen. A slight shudder crept up his spine, and he picked up his pace as he moved back up the hall and into the upper chambers of the lower levels of the castle.

The dimly lit hall came to an end where he would have to go left or right. He turned left and made another sharp left. The next hall was smaller and almost invisible because the passage was hidden by a tapestry which hung from the ceiling and draped onto the floor. He pulled back the tapestry and slipped passed and into the hallway, he whispered, and the passageway went dark and the tapestry hung still as though nothing had bothered it.

On the other side of the tapestry was a small table at the entrance of a tall wooden door. A slender wood-like candlestick sat in the center, Garrison waved his palm over the top. A small flicker of fire came to life on the wick and he held the flame under a cold iron handle secured to the door.

The handle heated up and twisted open. The latch released with a small thud and echoed in the corridor. Garrison opened the door and slipped inside.

****

Heavy thuds echoed as the pounding of the drum-like vibrations hit the outside edge of the rock walls. Darkness eroded the eager efforts of the fire lit sconces which were staggered around the room. A gripping stench of rancid ore wafted around the cavern as Isot made her way down the long corridor. The tapping of her slick soled shoes bounced off the cold stone and made a clicking in her ears. The dancing shimmer of the portal reflected a cast of eerie green and orange from the sconces. Her long red robe draped onto the floor and followed her long silky strides with a soft whooshing sound.

The tall woman stood in front of the misty surface, and she rubbed the pale skin of her first finger on the shiny metal of the medallion which hung around her neck. Particles of the portal rippled across the surface and faded in the center in a corkscrew effect as the energy opened into the Shadow Empire.

The Shadow Empire was riddled with pockets of seeping gasses that wafted into the atmosphere and left a contaminated residue in Isot's mouth. She stepped over the jagged rock and onto a ridged pathway. Her dark red dress draped delicately over her slender form and brushed the dirt dragging small pebbles behind her. The Shadow Empire was always at dusk and the sun never shone there, not that she was used to the sun anyway. She remembered the night her captivity began. The mages of Srinna Vossa were tasked with destroying the Binding of the Crypt scroll. Ebassia was selected because of the recommendation of one of the members who thought the castle would be the most obscure being the current king was disloyal to Queen Ambrosia of Srinna Vossa.

Isot was the one who held the scroll when they enacted the magic spell. What they didn't understand was, the scroll is indestructible. The power was so strong the blast killed the other mages and left her permanently affixed to the Ebassia Castle. There she remained. Over the hundreds of annual rotations, she learned she was unable to die but hadn't figured out why?

At first, the idea she wouldn't die was exhilarating, but when she realized everyone she might love, would die, the anger and bitterness sunk in. Things worsened when she learned she could never leave the castle either. The Shadow took hold of her heart, and she succumbed to the efforts of the Shadow. She turned a corner and found the access to the Shadow Temple and opened the latch. The cold iron door swung open slowly. A cascading chandelier draped from the ceiling to the floor and gave a soft green hue to the iron and stone walls. Glyphs etched into the walls drifted in and out of green and gray as she walked by. She pulled the heavy handle of the double doors on the far side of the reception hall.

A grand entertaining room opened with smaller but similar chandeliers that hung around the room. She had always been amazed at the beauty the Shadow world held. Even the evilest of evils had good taste. An elaborately carved iron and gem-encrusted throne sat at the far side of the room in front of enormous windows. Heavy fabric framed the windows in a manner which made the windows have a feel of them being alive. Isot started to cross the smooth floor but perceived the shadows in the corner of the room. Shadows of what used to be men and creatures, but it was the shadows who didn't have a form that made her stomach churn.

A deeper kind of soul penetration wreaked havoc on her sense of security. Isot stopped and turned to find a shadow, which slipped into the darkness, and she couldn't tell what kind of shadow had spawned. She quickened her pace and hurried to the throne and turned to one side. Isot started toward the long table up against a wall but was interrupted by the glass windows. She stopped and found the temple stood over the land of the dead. She understood this but this time for some reason the landscape stood out to her more.

"Isn't this beautiful?" A deep raspy voice asked.

The hair on the back of Isot's neck stood out, and she swallowed the lump in her throat.

"I'm surprised you're here," Isot said.

"I am everywhere," the Shadow said.

"Yes, of course, I only meant you surprised me," Isot said.

"What are you doing here?" the Shadow asked.

Isot tried to keep her stomach from lurching, she fully understood how much the Shadow wanted the scroll and what it was willing to do to secure it for itself. But she wasn't sure if the shadow was aware, she *was* the scroll. She, the castle and the scroll were now one entity. Many rotations passed before she learned the depth of what had happened. Instead of dissolving into nothingness, the scroll encompassed itself to the walls of the castle, but so did Isot.

"You are conflicted?" the Shadow asked with a hint of pleasure.

"You are about to receive another soul, but this one is mine," Isot said.

"I don't give souls," the Shadow said.

"I am asking," Isot said.

"Why does this soul mean so much to you?" the Shadow asked.

"Do I need a reason?" Isot asked.

The Shadow darkened and sifted from the blackness of the iron walls and formed its best impression of a man. The Shadow didn't have the remnant form of a being and so the edges wafted around with a force of being everywhere but nowhere.

"Yes, you must give me a reason, why I should preserve this soul and not devour him like the others," the Shadow said.

Isot swallowed hard.

"Because I love him," Isot said.

"We do not love, plus he loved another," the Shadow said.

"*You* do not love, I, however, am still human and *do* love," Isot said boldly.

"You are willing to pay his price?" the Shadow asked.

Isot nodded and closed her eyes. The Shadow crept closer and wrapped around her frame. Isot held her breath and the ice-cold darkness encompassed her frame. She shivered and the pain of the cold stabbed at her chest. She gasped as the pain hit the back of her head. Isot sucked in a labored breath and cried out with agony. The shadow swirled around her body several times until almost all her life force was taken without killing her. Isot's body crumpled to the floor and lay in a pile of red fabric. The Shadow drifted away and reformed into a partial human shape.

"I will give you this one soul, but you will never challenge me again," the Shadow growled.

Isot choked on her spit as her lungs regained the ability to inhale. She nodded weakly and gripped the soft cloth next to her face, her knuckles turned bright white under the pressure of the pain which wreaked havoc on every part of her being. Isot now understood the Shadow was getting more aggressive in his discipline. She feared how much pain she would have to endure since she's already lived multiple lifetimes. The shadow drifted into the blackness and Isot laid on the cold stone wishing she could die.

The minutes turned to hours but Isot still couldn't gain the strength to lift herself off the floor. Tears soaked the fabric under her face as she cried through the lasting pain. The dimly lit room faded, and the darkness set into her mind. The sting of the pain tingled her muscles, and she closed her eyes. She tried to think of only the pain in case the Shadow was still lurking. She had learned many rotations ago the Shadow had a way of knowing what you were thinking. As if he understood you better than you did yourself and what you would or wouldn't do.

Isot regretted ever getting caught up with the Shadow in the first place, but she was young and impetuous and wanted success more than her own freedom, but she didn't understand what that meant at the time. She drifted in and out of an unrestful sleep, which was enough for her body to regain enough strength to scoot her hands underneath her body and shoved. Her head wobbled, and she found it hard to focus on anything. Isot tried to maintain eye contact with the chandelier, which only made the matter worse. She found a spot in the center of the iron door at the other side of the room and breathed in slowly and steadily. Her sore body scooted to the throne and she pulled herself into the seat. She rested for a few moments and tried to stand. Her legs were wobbly and weak, but she managed to stay upright. She made her way across the floor only stumbling a few times until she reached the door.

She lifted the latch and the door opened with a puff. The bitterness sank into her senses and she gagged. She held her breath and went as quickly as she could down the path back to the portal. The portal wall thinned and faded away in time for her to cross the threshold. Her soft amber eyes were red and puffy, and she had a hard time adjusting to the lighting of the Ebassia Castle. She pulled on an overcoat hanging on a hook and wrapped the heavy wool around her shivering body. Her delicate rose lips were now pale pink. The Shadow Empire was usually much colder than Ebassia, but this time was more so. The drums began to fade from her consciences the further she traveled from the portal.

Isot rubbed her arms and tried to bring the blood back to the surface to warm her body. The warm yellow lights flickered on as she moved along the long corridor. Even though she was tired of being stuck in the castle, the welcoming sensation to be here and not in the Shadow Empire overcame her. She managed her way to the end of the hallway and put her hand on the lever of the wood door. The warmth was enticing on her cold hand, and she heaved the latch open.

The door slid across the smooth surface of the soft gray stone and closed effortlessly behind her. She breathed in heavily and sighed as the warmer air filled her lungs that were now getting their strength back. She had never had to give so much to the Shadow before. Isot smiled at the thought she had been able to save her prize. She hurried through the next set of doors and out from behind the tapestry which hung on the wall shielding the secret passageway from the Ebaasians. Her slick soled shoes whooshed against the floor as she still couldn't lift her legs completely. She stopped and fixed her dress and hair in the reflective glass hanging on the wall outside the King's chambers. The light under the doorway flickered and she hesitated. She put her ear against the wood, and all was quiet, so she lifted the latch.

The spacious chambers took forever for her to cross before she came to the king's bed. His weak and frail frame laid in the massive ornately carved bed which they spent so much time in before he became ill. Isot took his hand and sat on the edge of the soft mattress. The king blinked at her barely turning his head. She smiled at him and he tried to smile back.

"I secured your safe passage through the Shadow Empire. You will be safe," Isot whispered.

"Thank you, now I can be with my love, Alicia," the King managed.

Isot had learned he did not love her, and she only loved him for what he gave her.

"Your safe passage is not for you to return to her. You belong to me now, and will do my bidding, even in death," Isot said.

The king opened his eyes as wide as his failing form could. Fear raced across the dark gray and Isot's heart skipped a beat. Her energy soared to full again as though she had dined at a mighty feast. The king coughed and sputtered and Isot took a damp cloth and wiped the blood from the corner of his mouth. The door opened and Isot turned as the princess entered the room. Isot leaned into the king's ear.

"And now I will own her too," Isot said.

The king struggled to breathe through the mucus and blood in his throat.

"Father," the princess said.

The king's chest lifted once more, and his final breath escaped his lips. His dark gray eyes stared blankly at the ceiling and Isot closed his eyelids before the princess got to the bed. Isot moved and allowed the girl of eighteen to sit next to her father. The princess cried into his chest and Isot ran a gentle hand over her long brown hair.

"Take as long as you need, and when you're ready, I will help you make the arrangements for his burial and your coronation," Isot said softly.

The princess with puffy eyes nodded.

"Thank you Isot, you have been so good to our family, my father trusted you with everything,"

Isot smiled gently and caressed her hair one more time and left the room now filled with a new vigor.

5-Nowhere Close to Being a Queen

The candle flickered and Isot lifted the quill off the parchment. A cold breeze eased around the room and Isot turned around slowly. Her blank stare was vacant of life, but she somehow managed to search the room. She found nothing out of sorts and returned to her scripting. The symbols on the page she was transferring from were the last of the markings she had found from the walls of the castle. She gazed dangerously at the stacks and stacks of parchment notes she had gathered over the rotations. She needed a form of parchment that would stand the test of time. She learned that paper didn't last more than several rotations, so she turned to the skins of baby pigs.

The process was quite simple, and it didn't take long to tan and treat the hides, but it was the sewing them together that she had to learn how to do properly. The needles would rip the skins and cause them to pull apart, so she mended the seams with the stronger deer hides. She had to make sure not to waste her delicate pig skins as she remade the scroll, so she scripted the marks on regular parchment first. She organized them in as many ways that made sense based on her understanding of how the directions of the Binding of the Crypt spell might have originally been. A flicker of angst sat in the back of her mind with the fear she might have written it wrong, but she ignored it and kept the reassurance the Shadow gave her as she worked.

She dipped the quill into the ink jar and finished the last symbol. She returned the quill and blew on the ink and then held up the last of the scroll. A satisfying assurance emerged from her soul and her prominent cheek bones glowed a soft pink as her full-lipped mouth formed into a cruel line. She stood from her wood chair and poured a tall glass with a bubbly drink and waited for the foam to settle before she lifted the thin edge to her lips. She sipped the beverage with an appeased sigh. The coolness ran down her throat coating the dryness, and she absorbed the sensations thankfully. She set the glass on the long table next to her writers' desk and picked up a short stem of bright blue buds and picked one off the top. She ran the velvet peddles between her fingers and the bud pulled apart, and she dropped them into a black cauldron. The simmering liquid swallowed the peddles before they could sizzle, and the fluid shifted colors until it settled on the same shade of blue.

Isot took the metal stirring stick and moved the bubbles of the brew around. She pulled the cauldron off the small fire stand and set in on the stone floor. The black marks on the stone that the hot iron kettle had made over the rotations made it easy to make sure she put it in the correct place. It would take time for it to cool enough for her to be able to pour the ink into the small jars. The special ink she made was a unique combination of ingredients that created the longest lasting ink because it soaked into the pig skin without bleeding all over and making a mess of the writings.

She returned to the desk and touched the ink to make sure it was dry and then unrolled the scroll several lengths. She read through the marks and tapped on her chin as she came to a spot, she wasn't sure about. She dipped the quill into the ink and scratched a new mark and read through it again. She nodded with approval and then let the rest of the scroll drape onto the floor. She carefully picked up the top and unrolled the now permanent crease and started from the beginning. Her eyes crossed the page as she digested the words and her an eagerness emerged from her center.

She caught herself a few times muttering the incantation and quickly silenced her lips. If the incantation was spoken out loud it would evoke the power of the magic, and she wasn't ready yet. She still needed her sacrifice and the members of the Velshari present for the entire casting to be fulfilled. The sacrificial offering had to be of purity and offer a clean vessel for the magic to reside it while it sealed the doors of death. It had been her plan to recreate the Binding of the Crypt spell for herself and remove herself from the castle, but learned halfway through, that the incantation could work for anyone that was bonded to the recipient of the incantation. The Velshari already required a magic bond from its followers and this gave Isot the opportunity to grow a mighty army.

Hours later Isot rested the last part of the scroll she had finished that day down and sat on her padded lounge. Her mind was spinning with the complexity of the words and her heart thudded heavily in her chest. She was proud of herself for finally completing the scroll and the angst she had earlier was now changed to fluttering excitement. She hadn't been this excited since she was a child and almost laughed out loud. Her next task would be to find the right sacrifice and send the word to the Velshari to come to Ebassia. She rested her head on the soft padding and closed her eyes. Her stomach rumbled, and she debated if she had the strength to find something to eat or if she wanted to go to sleep

She decided on sleep and let her eyes shut. An image of the new Queen crossed her mind, and she sat up. Of course, the Queen, she would be a perfect sacrifice, and if she held a public coronation that would allow the Velshari to be able to assemble undetected.

****

The young princess sat on the soft padded stool in front of the mirror. Her bedchambers had tall delicately framed windows which let in the morning sunlight. Isot carefully pulled the brush through the princesses long warm-chestnut hair. The princess clasped her hands tightly in her lap as she watched the reflection in the mirror.

"You will be fine Oladesni. This has happened many times before," Isot said.

"I know, but not to me," Oladesni said.

"I will be right by your side the entire time," Isot said.

"Thank you, will you explain the process again,"

"All the Viziers will be sitting around the room. You will go in and stand on the rug in the center. You will face the head of the circle which is the largest chair on the back side of the room. When the Grand Vizier stands, he will motion for the rest to stand and place their votes. Upward raised hand is a yes, downward is a no. After the votes are counted, the Grand Vizier will declare you the new queen and you will then take your seat next to the Grand Vizier," Isot said.

"What if there are any negative votes?" Oladesni asked.

"There won't be, but if there are, the majority will overrule, and you will be queen anyway. Then you will have a chance to replace those who voted against you," Isot said.

"When will I do that?" Oladesni asked.

"Child, why do you think anyone will vote with a negative?" Isot asked.

Isot set the brush on the table and picked up a bright silver and jeweled necklace and wrapped it around the girl's neck securing the clasp at the back.

"I guess it's just a fear, I don't have any proof or reason anyone would," Oladesni said.

"If you get stuck on what to say or do, I will be right there to help prompt you." Isot sat on the bed next to the princess and smiled softly. "But, if you make me the Grand Vizier, I will be able to make those difficult decisions for you until you are older and have more experience, with you being only eighteen," Isot said.

The princess sighed and smiled.

"I would very much appreciate that," Oladesni said.

"Then I will help you know what do to make that happen," Isot said.

"Thank you Isot, that does make me feel much better," Oladesni said.

"Good, now let's finish getting you ready," Isot said.

Isot picked up the ceremonial dress and unlatched the fasteners at the back. Oladesni slipped her night-dress off and stepped into the soft pink silk dress. Isot fluffed the edges as she pulled the heavy gown up. Oladesni slid her arms into the sleeves and Isot refastened the hooks. Isot pulled the princesses' hair out of the gown and fixed it over the delicate lace. Oladesni picked up the lacy layers and put her shiny shoes on. The dress came to a length above the floor with the shoes, and she smoothed the layers out. Isot opened the door and the princess walked out of the room and down the corridor.

Oladesni was glad her dress was made of mostly lace because the castle was hot this time of year. Oladesni rounded the corner and the long train followed as it rippled in the breeze. The clicks the shoes made was muffled by the swooshing of the fabric but the only thing Oladesni heard was the beating of her racing heart. Isot carried herself with dignity and kept her chin level only making brief eye contact with the guards along the corridor. Oladesni passed the guards at the main hall and rounded the corner to the section of the castle where the political meetings were held.

A bulky guard gripped the handle and heaved the intricately carved door open. Oladesni hesitated at the doorway. She lowered her dress and sucked in a deep breath. She stepped into the room and the heat hit her in the face. Oladesni stifled the gasp she wanted to expel and found the carpet at the center of the room. She rolled her shoulders back and straightened her back. She held her chin level and made a quick assessment of how she was going to get to the carpet. There was nothing in the way, so she mimicked Isot's grace and poise the best she could as she made her way to the carpet. Oladesni felt a trickle of sweat drip down her back, and she prayed no one notice. She stopped in the center of the rug and turned to face the Grand Viziers chair.

The chairs were lifted on a platform as to be several lengths taller while sitting. Oladesni entertained a few notions as to why but couldn't settle on one which made the most sense. She managed a soft smile as the knots in her guts rippled through her body. The room was so quiet Oladesni was certain she could hear the mice behind the walls. The Grand Vizier stood and nodded to the princess who nodded in return. Oladesni kept her focus on the old man but snuck a peak at the Viziers sitting next to him. The weathered and faded expressions sat heavy on her heart, and she understood the toll it took on them to lead Ebassia. Isot stepped into the room and stayed in the back corner from the princess.

The guard closed the door and the Grand Vizier motioned for the rest of the Viziers to stand. The room was filled with the sounds of chairs scooting and fabric rustling. Oladesni's heart pounded in her chest, and she found her knees weaken. Isot cleared her throat and the princess turned to her. Isot pointed at her knees and the princess remembered what she had told her. Oladesni bent her knees slightly, so they wouldn't lock up and make her pass out. Isot smiled and nodded. The princess smiled and returned her focus to the Grand Vizier. His dark eyes were framed by dark circles of puffy skin Oladesni assumed to be from a lack of sleep. She hadn't had much sleep since her father passed either and was sure he could use a break.

The Grand Vizier raised his hand and the others signaled their vote. A middle-aged man with a parchment and quill came from the back of the room by the door and made a mark on the paper as he passed each Vizier. He finished the count and handed it to another man at the other side of the half-circle who checked each of the marks and then handed it to the Grand Vizier. The man sat the parchment on the table in front of him and the Vizier lowered his arm and read the parchment.

"The vote is unanimous," The Grand Vizier said. Oladesni tried not to sigh but the relief overcame her, and she sagged. Isot cleared her throat and Oladesni straightened. "On behalf of the Council of Viziers,

I declare you, Oladesni Okin, daughter of the late King Oliver Okin, Queen of Ebassia," the Grand Vizier said.

One of the men, who took the vote, carried the crown of Ebassia on a flat board draped in the city's colors of purple and green, and stopped in front of the Grand Vizier. The Grand Vizier took the crown and stepped down from the platform. He crossed the few lengths and stopped in front of the queen. She wasn't especially tall, and the Vizier didn't have to reach his short body very far to set the crown on her head. The crown was heavier than she expected but held her posture still. The Grand Vizier motioned for her to take the throne. Queen Oladesni carefully moved to the throne. She now understood why Isot had taught her to keep her head level, because if she didn't her crown would fall off.

Queen Oladesni found it a bit harder to pick up her dress and spin around, so she could sit in the throne. She managed to sit and not let the crown fall off and pleased with herself smiled. The Viziers returned to their seats and Isot nodded at Oladesni. The Queen wasn't sure what she was supposed to say and stared at Isot with a look of panic.

"If I may your grace, the Queen has asked me to address the council on her behalf," Isot said.

The Viziers all turned with surprise and found Isot in the center of the room.

"Is this so?" the Grand Vizier asked.

"It is," Queen Oladesni said.

"Very well, you may proceed," The Grand Vizier said.

"The Queen has an item of business to address and asked I speak for her as her training is still in process. The Queen," Isot turned to Oladesni and then back to the council, "is declaring that I Isot take control of the Grand Viziery," Isot said.

The room filled with gasps and hushed murmurings.

"There has never been a woman Grand Vizier before, that is not our custom," A Vizier from the side said.

"There has also not been a Queen to rule Ebassia for such a long time, no one really knows, but you have all voted in the affirmative. Why would having a woman Grand Vizier to a Queen. Perhaps we as women are not equal to men?" Isot said.

"That is not what we mean," the man said.

"What is it that you mean then?" Isot asked.

"Women have no place in the government," another Vizier said.

"Oh, so you mean, that you see us, your new Queen and I as inadequate?" Isot asked.

"I am sure you are plenty adequate; however, you would know nothing of how the government works," another man said.

"So, you're saying because we, as women, haven't been in government before, we are incapable of managing." Isot asked.

"You wouldn't be able to handle the strife of leadership," another said.

"And yet we as women bear children and rear them and teach them everything, but we wouldn't have the fortitude to deal with hard things?" Isot said.

Queen Oladesni admired the calmness Isot had. The glint in Isot's eye gave her the inkling she was enjoying the exchange.

"This is simply not done," the Grand Vizier said.

"I think you have all forgotten the Queen has the right to call her cabinet of leaders and just because it hasn't been done in your lifetimes, doesn't mean it can't be done or that it shouldn't be done," Isot said.

Isot turned to the Queen and held out her hand. The Grand Vizier turned to the Queen with a bead of sweat dripping down the side of his pudgy face.

"I so declare it, and anyone who should find the need, I will accept your full resignation by morning," the Queen said.

Isot smiled. She was a beautiful woman with delicate features and sparkling eyes. Her deep red lips were strong but sensuous, and she loved how the surrounding men would sneak extra glances in her direction. The noise in the room began to escalate and Oladesni wasn't sure what to do next.

"I will leave you to your decisions, but the Queen and I are needed to make arrangements for the late Kings burial," Isot said.

Isot held her hand out to the Queen, and she stepped off the throne. Oladesni moved with a new confidence toward the door with Isot right behind. The guard opened the door, and they left, the now even hotter, room quickly. They made their way back to the Queens bedchambers and Oladesni fell onto her bed.

"Are you alright?" Isot asked.

"Yes, but I am nowhere close to being a Queen,"

"Sit up," Isot said.

The Queen sat up and shifted herself on the bed.

"No one said you had to be the perfect Queen or even that you would be a good queen. You are young and have much to learn. Now that I'm the Grand Vizier I will help you make all those hard decisions and teach you what you need to know," Isot said.

Isot lifted the Queens hair out of her eye and smiled. The new queen smiled and nodded.

"Thank you, I don't know what I would do without you," Oladesni said.

"It's true, you do need me. Now as long as you do as I tell you, you will just fine," the Queen nodded. "Now we must make the arrangements to bury your father and then organize your coronation," Isot said.

"Coronation?" The Queen asked.

"Why yes dear, today's events were the official proceedings, but you must show the people in a grand ceremony you are dedicated to the throne," Isot said.

"But I don't want to go in front of everyone,"

"You must, and you must stop being so insecure. You will never lead a nation that way," Isot said.

Isot motioned for the Queen to stand, and she unlatched the fittings on the lace dress. Oladesni pulled her arms out of the sleeves and the dress fell to the floor. She stepped out and Isot handed her a day dress. Oladesni pulled on the soft polished cotton dress and Isot secured the back.

"Where do we need to go now?" Oladesni asked.

"We need to meet the arrangers to finalize the decorations and food for the services. I have already made the list of items to select from based on your father's wishes to me, but you must pick the ones you would like," Isot said.

Isot removed the jeweled necklace and placed it back in its box and pulled a less decorative one and placed it on the Queen.

"I liked the other one better,"

"Of course, you did, but you can't go around giving people a reason to want to steal your things, now can you?"

"No, I suppose not,"

"Come on then, we have things to do,"

6-It's Been Grim at Best

The settlement was more spacious with enough buildings to fill the space than they had expected and Serin found her nerves increasing with panic the longer they took to reach the outskirts where she could buff them. The village people were now mingling about the shops and some stood outside with their goods waiting for the next customer. Bowen was a tall lean man and now that he wasn't drunk and had his full vigor back, he kept a steady gate. Serin's smaller frame lent to her having to partially run to keep up, but she didn't complain.

"I'm not sure what this is all about, but you sure do make an impression on people," Bowen said.

"I'm not sure what you mean," Serin said.

"Your new friend, Lew, he thinks you two are going to be an item now," Bowen said.

"Ewww. He thinks a lot of things, but that one is not going to happen," Serin said.

"You're going to have to tell him," Bowen said.

"We won't be here long enough to worry about it," Serin said.

"We?" Bowen asked.

Bowen rounded the corner of the last building and Serin peeled off after him. Shaz and Riddick galloped up to them and stopped a few lengths away.

"Bowen, this is Shaz and Riddick," Serin said.

They nodded and Shaz held out the reins of Serin's horse to Bowen.

"We found the Minca, they will catch up to us with Jag later. They said they had some exploring to do. I think they are on an errand for the Chief," Shaz said.

Bowen took the reins and shoved his foot into the saddle.

"When did we acquire saddles?" Serin asked.

Riddick shrugged and Serin scowled. Bowen and Shaz held their hand out to her, and she took Shaz's. He pulled her up as she leaped onto the back of the horse. Bowen pulled his hand in and shifted in his seat.

"I don't think wind-walk would be a good idea right now," Shaz said.

"Then let's go," Serin said.

"Lead the way," Shaz said.

Bowen dug his heels into the animal and lurched forward. Shaz grabbed the reins and Serin held onto Shaz's waist as their horse took off after Bowen with Riddick right next to them. The sun beat down hard and the heat was uncomfortable at best. Serin panned the sky trying to find any sqwalls, but the sky was clear and the only thing the wind gave her was bits and pieces of ramblings like usual. A few times the same words surfaced and Serin tried to commit them to memory, so she could discuss them with Shaz later. He was excellent at solving puzzles and it was fun to guess what the wind was trying to say. She focused so much time on her healing magic her wind magic was in need of improvement.

"Not far now, just over the ridge," Bowen said.

A modest home rested against a gentle rolling hill and was surrounded by several animal corals and a few sheds. Bowen slowed his horse and veered off toward the stable. Shaz slowed his horse quickly, but he stopped in front of the main house. Serin jumped down and started toward the door. Shaz dismounted and snagged her hand.

"You need to be prepared for what you might see," Shaz said.

"I understand," Serin said.

Shaz nodded and Serin hurried toward the door. Riddick pulled up beside Shaz and took the reins for him, so he could follow Serin.

"Barrick," Serin called as she opened the door. "Barrick are you here?"

"Back here," Barrick said.

Serin hurried toward the back room not even paying attention to the disheveled house. The dishes were piled in the small sink and strung along the thick crude table. The floor hadn't been swept in forever and plies of clothes were strewn about.

"Barrick, what is going on?" Serin asked.

Barrick peered at her through dark puffy eyes.

"Serin? Is that you?" Barrick asked.

"Yes, and Shaz is here too," Serin said.

Barrick turned around and found Shaz standing in the doorway.

"But how, how did you find us? What's wrong?" Barrick asked.

"We met Bowen in town, he's got a story to tell," Shaz said.

"Doesn't he always," Barrick said.

"Barrick, tell me what is wrong with Helen,"

"I have no idea, no one does, not even the town medicine women. I tried to use your poultice, but we ran out, and I never learned how to make more, she's been in such pain and now she won't even wake up. She's breathing, but she won't wake up," Barrick's voice cracked.

"Let me take a look," Serin said.

"What can you do?" Barrick asked.

"Shaz, maybe you can take Barrick out to meet Riddick and catch him up on what's been going on," Serin said.

"No, I can't leave her," Barrick said.

"She's in the best hands on the planet, I promise," Shaz said.

Shaz nodded to Barrick and Barrick left the room. Serin slipped her gloves off and put her cool hands on Helen's chest. Serin pulled the magic within her and pushed the glowing particles into Helen's body. For several minutes she allowed the magic to do a full inspection of the intricate details of the human frame until she understood what Helen was suffering from. A broken heart. Helen had lost a baby and had decided she didn't want to live anymore. Even Serin couldn't heal this one, only Helen could.

She would need to decide to keep living, to accept her loss and choose to stay in the realm of the living. Serin closed her eyes and sucked in a deep breath. She calmed the pain in Helen's body, the pain which comes with heavy grief, the pain which comes with desperation, with fear and sorrow. Serin surrounded Helen's frame with several shades of blue energy rays that danced around her in constant movement creating a soothing warmth.

Helen's body began to relax from its former rigid state and Serin hoped she could entice Helen to open her eyes. Serin's magic encased Helen's frame, and she pulled a ball of water from the air. She dripped a few drops onto Helen's lips in hopes the liquid would trigger a response to drink. The drops leaked off Helen's cheek and Serin tried again.

"Helen, it's me Serin, I'm so glad I found you. You would not believe what's happened since we left you in Ebassia. You remember what you said to me, if I ever needed you, I could find you at your mothers in the grasslands, well I need you now," Serin said softly.

Helen's eyes twitched under her closed eyelids.

"I hoped you could hear me, I have so much to tell you, so much has changed," Serin said.

Helen's eyes twitched again.

"If you wake up, I'll tell you everything. You are nowhere close to finished. I have healing magic and I can detect another little heartbeat inside your womb," Serin said.

Serin found the baby's heartbeat and brought the echo into Helen's ears. Helen gasped but her eyes didn't open.

Realms of Edenocht

"You still have much to live for,"

Serin dripped another few drops on Helen's lips and Helen pulled them in with her tongue. Serin took a cloth from the side table and soaked the soft fibers with her water bubble. Helen wriggled as the cool cloth touched her forehead. Serin squeezed her hand and Helen squeezed back. Tears escaped Helen's closed eyes and fell onto the pillow. Helen's lips trembled, and she opened her mouth a few times.

"It hurts so bad," Helen whispered.

"Grief is one of the hardest things in the world," Serin said.

"I can't make it go away," Helen said.

"You don't make grief go away, you hold grief close and keep it safe, there's no shame in being sad, mad and hurt when you lose something so precious," Serin said.

"How do you know, you're only a child yourself," Helen said.

Serin laughed gently.

"I have witnessed much more grief than you can imagine, and maybe one day I'll tell you, but right now we need to focus on you being better. I will heal your body to ensure you don't lose this baby too," Serin said.

Helen blinked several times and found Serin smiling at her, but she couldn't make sense exactly of what was going on.

"You haven't aged a day," Helen said.

"Would it twig you out if I told you I was actually over three hundred cycles old," Serin said.

Helen sat up on her elbow.

"You're pulling my leg," Helen said.

Serin shook her head. Helen studied Serin's face and determined she couldn't figure out if she was telling the truth or not.

"Like I said, so much has happened since Shaz and I left you and Barrick," Serin said.

"Is he here?" Helen asked.

"He is, and his best mate Riddick, and we found Bowen in the pub and brought him too," Serin said.

Helen rolled her eyes.

"That drunk, wonderful, now we'll have a house full of non-sense," Helen said.

Serin chuckled.

"Are you hungry?" Serin asked.

"I think so," Helen said.

"I bet you are, let's tell Barrick you're much better and find you some food," Serin said.

"Barrick is a lousy cook, just saying," Helen said.

Helen pulled off the blanket and wriggled her toes.

"I guess Shaz's will cook tonight," Serin said.

"Shaz cooks?" Helen asked.

"He's actually quite good, but his methods are a bit different than usual," Serin said.

Serin helped Helen stand, but she didn't have the strength yet and Serin moved her to a soft padded chair. Serin went to the window and cracked the glass open to let in some fresh air and secured the drape over a small hook at the side and whistled into the breeze.

"That's Serin, let's go," Shaz said.

Shaz started toward the house with a quick step and Barrick blasted passed him. Riddick and Bowen hurried behind Shaz. Barrick skidded around the corner and barreled into the room. His eyes lit up, and he launched himself into Helen's arms. He kissed her all over her face and neck.

"You need to be gentle with her, she's had a long journey back," Serin said.

Barrick's confusion left his face in a twisted form but turned his attentions back to Helen. Nothing was making much sense to either of them but at this moment they didn't care. Serin left the room and pulled the door closed.

"So, what was wrong?" Shaz asked.

"A broken heart, she lost a child and found the grief too much to bear," Serin said.

"Can you heal a broken heart?" Riddick asked.

"No, a person needs to choose to stay in the realm of the living, I only healed her body from the pain which was caused and gave her a reason to want to live," Serin said.

"Which was what?" Bowen asked.

"While examining her, I found she is with child again, so I told her and allowed her to hear the heartbeat. But she hasn't eaten in days and needs food quickly," Serin said.

"The last several moons have been grim at best, sadly we have nothing," Bowen said.

"How so?" Shaz asked.

"Ever since the King died and his young daughter appointed a scum to be the new Grand Vizier, taxes have gone up, she kicked me out of my position as the general and new Prime Viziers are being put in place all over Ebassia. Laws are changing and the wealthy are getting more and more power over the poor. We've been hit the hardest here, but settlements all over are suffering," Bowen said.

Shaz could sense Serin's blood start to boil with the news and nudged Riddick.

"Riddick and I will dig something up, we'll hurry," Shaz said.

They hurried from the house and passed the stable.

"What are we going to do?" Riddick asked.

"You're going to grow some vegetables and I'm going to find something to hunt," Shaz said.

"Aye,"

Riddick shoved his hands into the soft dirt and told the earth to produce several different kinds of plants and vegetables. Shaz blurred his eyes until a different kind of vision came into view. Echoes and faint markings of animal burrows illuminated under the surface of his vision, and he found three den holes nearby. He crouched closely to the ground and moved effortlessly through the tall grasses. Several lengths from the house Shaz pulled his knife which was sheathed in the small of his back and cut his hand.

He squeezed several drops of blood onto a long rag weed stem and smeared it around the leaves. He tipped toed to one of the animals' holes and waved the blood tainted weed around and dragged it on the ground. Shaz left the weed in the grass and hoped to the back side of the raised earth of the hole and lowered to the ground. He pulled his bow and a few arrows and set them on the ground and smacked the top of the den and waited. A few minutes later the small four-legged animal began sniffing the trail.

Shaz steadied his breath and slipped an arrow into the string, gripped tightly and pulled back. The animal sniffed and scratched at the ground and searched around but when there was no source to the blood it started back to the den. Shaz let the arrow loose and it whipped through the air silently penetrating the animal's dark gray fur and sank deep. It fell backward from the momentum of the arrow and flopped around until its body fell lifeless. Shaz waited another few minutes until the next animal sniffed the air. Shaz let another arrow sizzle, and after the animal was dead, grabbed them both and headed back to the house. Shaz found Riddick combing through the dirt searching for the bulbous roots he had grown with the two animals one in each hand.

"How is everything?" Shaz asked.

"Not sure, Serin's been in the house the whole time, and Bowen in the stables. You've been productive," Riddick said.

Shaz nodded and they returned to the house. Serin had decided to take this chance to enhance her wind magic and practiced making the air pick up items and put them in their proper places. She had cleaned most of the living area and was now in the kitchen when Shaz and Riddick returned. Shaz ducked as a pitcher flew over his head and landed on the shelf behind him and several small bowls settled on the shelf above the table.

"Are you making things move with your wind?" Shaz asked.

Serin nodded and whooshed a plate passed him and onto the shelf next to the bowls. Barrick and Helen were still in the bedroom and Shaz threw a burst of fire onto the coals in the fireplace. The bedroom door opened, and Barrick carried Helen out of the room. He set her on a small sofa and placed a blanket over her legs.

"I'm not sure what to say, I owe you the world," Barrick said.

"You don't owe us anything, this is what friends do," Serin said.

"Barrick was telling me a little about what was going on," Helen said.

"Do you think the Velshari has something to do with the new Grand Vizier?" Barrick asked.

Bowen cocked his head and stared at Barrick.

"Certainly, wouldn't surprise me, and if they're Velshari things are going to be a great deal worse, unless we do something about it," Shaz said.

"We need to talk to Inelius first for more information or from your castle library before we go storming the most powerful city in Ebassia," Serin said.

"Aye and add that to our 'to do' list," Riddick said.

Shaz ran his hands through his hair and sighed.

"Things are already out of control. How are we going to manage all this?" Shaz asked.

"Sounds like you guys need bigger forces," Bowen said.

"And that's where you come in? You aren't the general anymore, remember," Barrick said.

"True, but I'm sure my men are loyal to me and if I had a way to take out the Grand Vizier and make contact with the young Queen, I'm positive I can secure my position with her, then you would have the whole of Ebassia as an ally which is not a minor thing," Bowen said.

"I can head back to Turob and check in there, plus I think I found the staff's hiding place. I will check and make sure, secure the staff then I can meet up with you again," Riddick said.

"He can use the portals at the castle to travel through," Serin said.

"No, I think I will need his help in Ebassia, the staff can wait for now," Shaz said.

"And then what are we going to do?" Turkill asked.

Helen jumped and Barrick and Bowen turned with a start.

"About time you made you way out here, is your errand complete?" Shaz asked.

Turkill nodded and stepped out of the way as Ladtwig pushed his way into the house.

"Are we going to stand here and stare at this food, or cook it?" Ladtwig asked.

"These are our friends the Minca, Turkill and Ladtwig," Serin said.

"Ah, the ones you were telling us about earlier," Barrick said.

"I hope you are feeling better, Serin has a *magic* touch you know," Ladtwig said.

Helen smiled and nodded. Shaz took the animals outside and prepared them while Serin and Riddick worked on the other food. Ladtwig climbed up next to Helen and Barrick and began recounting the events of the last few moons in their realm. Helen smiled in amazement as the little man used every kind of emotion and facial expression imaginable. Shaz returned and set the meat into a pan and placed it on the stove. He rubbed his hands together and pulled the forces of combustion from the universe. The surroundings around the meat heated up with a warm glow and the meat began to change colors as the heat started to cook it.

"What are you doing?" Barrick asked.

"I'm cooking," Shaz said.

Helen remembered what Serin had said about his unusual methods.

"How are you doing that?" Helen asked.

"With heat," Shaz said a little sarcastically.

"In fact, where did all this food come from, we haven't had crops is moons," Barrick said.

"I grew them," Riddick said and flashed his toothy grin.

"Alright, what is going on, my head is spinning, I don't understand any of this," Barrick said.

"We'll explain everything while we eat," Serin said.

Realms of Edenocht

7-Let's Call This Horse 'Lew'

The evening passed with warm food and good company, but as the night pressed on, Shaz grew uneasy with the growing darkness.

"Serin can I talk to you?" Shaz asked.

"Is everything alright?" Barrick asked.

"Yes, of course, I need to talk to Serin for a bit," Shaz said.

Shaz stood and moved toward the door and Serin followed. He closed the door behind them and took her hand.

"Shaz, what's wrong?" Serin asked.

"I'm not sure, I have a lot of energy brewing inside, and I have no idea why,"

Serin touched his chest and searched with her magic for signs of unrest.

"I don't sense anything except your shadow magic is rising higher than usual. I thought when I am close when you can push the discomfort away," Serin said.

"True, but the negativity here is more intense. I'm having a hard time sorting through everything," Shaz said.

An ear-piercing screech ripped through the sky.

"Sqwalls," Shaz said.

"I *was* right, they did track us here. Blasted all!" Serin said.

"Fetch Riddick," Shaz said.

Serin hurried inside and called to Riddick. Riddick hurried from the house and Bowen followed. Turkill and Ladtwig grabbed their darts and each hurried to a window.

"What's wrong?" Bowen asked.

"You wanted to find out what was going on, well you're about to find out more than you want to," Shaz said.

Bowen's brows scrunched and Shaz lit his hand on fire.

"Oiy," Bowen yelped as he jumped back.

Shaz threw a fireball into the sky and sent several more. The night lit up with the bursts of flame and Bowen stood frozen in place. Riddick pulled his ax and Serin stayed several lengths away. Shaz pulled the honor blade from his side and waited.

"How many?" Riddick asked.

"How many what?" Bowen asked.

The fierce blackbird swooped from the darkness and lunged with a jagged beak. Shaz ducked and parried and threw a side strike but caught the creature's tail feathers. The bird veered up into the night sky and disappeared into the darkness.

"How are we going to fight with this thing being able to fly?" Riddick asked.

"Serin, you need to ground the sqwall, make a wind funnel or something," Shaz called.

Serin threw her arms out and over her head and gripped the air. She twisted the surrounding energy, and the wind obeyed. Heavy gusts shredded the tops of the tall grasses and ragweeds as the force barreled in from every direction. Bowen shielded his eyes from the sudden bar-rage and shifted his feet to keep from falling over. Screeches from the distance echoed as several sqwalls were sucked into the vortex and propelled toward the ground.

"Keep them grounded," Shaz called.

Shaz and Riddick hurried toward the first mangy black bird-like-creature they saw hit the ground and Bowen followed. Serin lifted the vortex and left it hovering over them and moved closer to Shaz and the others. The bird hopped up and jumped back into the sky, but the wind pushed the body back to the ground. After several attempts, the creature screeched in frustration. The creature spun around and with a loud crack transformed into the human-like figure. Shaz, Riddick, and Bowen flew backward from the force of the blast. Shaz rolled head over heels and landed back on his feet and Riddick flipped his legs over his head and came to a standing position, unprepared, Bowen went sprawling backward and landed square on his tookus with a thud. The creature's half-human-like nose snarled and gagged as it sucked in the air and side hopped a few lengths backward.

"So, you think you could escape us?" the creature gurgled.

"Yeah, how did you find us?" Shaz asked.

"We couldn't find you until you used your magic, we are genetically imprinted to track your magic," the sqwall said.

"Imprinted to track my magic?" Shaz asked.

Shaz tried to piece all the pieces together but couldn't figure out how Gavin Rhill had done it, nor how the sqwall returned the information to Gavin Rhill. Riddick made the grass grow around the creatures three-toed bird-feet and the sqwall squirmed. Riddick touched the ground and searched for the vibrations of the other creatures.

"There are five more," Riddick said.

"For now, but a signal has been sent and now we all can find you," the sqwall said.

"How comforting," Shaz said.

"Serin's not going to like that," Riddick said.

"I heard that," Serin said.

Riddick made the grasses climb up each of the creatures and grow tightly around their bodies and kept them from transforming. Bowen picked himself up and hurried to Shaz and Riddick.

"I'm done, swallow them all, let's go," Shaz said.

Riddick stomped his foot and the earth opened and the creatures fell into the blackness and the ground grew over them burring them alive. Bowen blinked and rubbed his eyes.

"I'm not sure I want to see much more," Bowen said.

"Sorry man, you're stuck with us now," Bowen's pale face searched Riddick's, and he swallowed hard. Riddick laughed and slapped him on the back. "Don't worry, we like you," Bowen smiled grimly and put his sword away. "Come on," Riddick said.

They hurried to Serin and returned to the house.

"Everything alright?" Barrick asked.

"No, not really, I'm afraid we've made things worse. *I've* made things worse," Shaz said.

"How so?" Barrick asked.

"The sqwall told me they are imprinted to my magic," Shaz said.

"That's how they track you, but they don't detect us?" Serin asked.

"I don't think so, it didn't even notice Riddick, it was if he couldn't tell he existed," Shaz said.

"Interesting," Serin said.

"But they've alerted the others and will be on our trail soon," Shaz said.

"We need to lead them away from the settlement," Serin said.

"If it didn't care about me, maybe it won't attack others," Riddick said.

"They still need to eat," Turkill said.

"True," Riddick said.

"I agree with Serin," Shaz said.

"What I'm curious about, is how are they *imprinted* to your magic?" Riddick asked.

"Me too," Serin said.

"Me too," Turkill said.

The door opened and Jagwynn crept through the door. Bowen pulled his sword and crossed the room in front of everyone.

"This is Jagwynn, she's with us," Shaz said.

Bowen twisted and stared at Shaz.

"This enormous jungle cat is with you!" Bowen said. "What else aren't you telling me? You are the craziest group I've ever met."

Turkill chuckled at Bowen's even paler face, he was amazed the fair-skinned man could become any paler than he already was.

"The reason the sqwalls were imprinted to your magic Shaz, is because when Gavin Rhill murdered your parents, he tried to take their magic, but he was only able to secure enough to imprint one type of creature," Jagwynn said.

"How awful," Helen said from the doorway.

"Is there a possibility to un-imprint?" Serin asked.

"Not that I'm aware of, however, Mathieu's been working on something for quite some time and I'm unaware if he's figured out anything yet," Jagwynn said. Jagwynn nuzzled Serin as she passed and stopped in front of Helen. "Don't be afraid child, the Sun Goddess has a wonderful plan for you, you will name your son Garret, and he will be a very valuable asset to her when he is grown."

Helen squeaked and put her hand over her mouth and Barrick grinned from ear to ear.

"Grandfather? Where is he?" Shaz asked.

"He is on an errand for the council, but you will see him soon," Jagwynn said.

"What are we going to do about the sqwalls and the settlement?" Serin asked.

"Come, I've gathered some friends to help," Jagwynn said.

"Friends?" Shaz asked.

"Oh, I got to see this," Turkill said.

He hopped off the sofa with Ladtwig right behind him.

"You too, Helen and Barrick, for you are who they will report to and answer to," Jagwynn said.

Jagwynn caressed the floor softly as she walked back out of the house. Shaz and the others followed her passed the porch and stopped at the edge of the dirt path. Several bright green eyes emerged from the darkness as a pack of enormous wolves came into the light from the windows of the house.

"Oiy," Barrick yelped.

Bowen reached for his sword but stopped himself and stepped back.

"This is Bolgan, he and his pack will keep watch of the settlement from now on, they will also send for instruction for all Plains Ukari to protect the plains from the sqwalls," Jagwynn said.

Bolgan lowered his head and bent one knee.

"I've never seen these creatures before and I've lived here all my life," Barrick said.

"They too have lived here for centuries, but they are not usually interested in human troubles, so they keep their distances. They are very good at being invisible," Jagwynn said.

"Is this the war wizard you speak of?" Shaz stepped toward Bolgan and nodded. "I have a special request of you," Bolgan said his voice deep and raspy.

"What is it?" Shaz asked.

"An ancient amulet was taken from my kind centuries ago and believed to have been taken to the city of Ebassia, I want it back," Bolgan said.

"What does this amulet do?" Shaz asked.

"That is a private matter," Bolgan said.

"I can sense your hesitation, however, if I am going to unleash an amulet capable of destroying the world, I need to know," Shaz said.

"No, nothing like that, the Sistine Moon is the passageway for our kind to speak with the moons. Since it was taken, we can't howl at the moon's and seek their guidance," Bolgan said.

"How dreadful," Helen said.

"I will do what I can, how do I recognize this amulet, where would I find it?" Shaz asked.

"The amulet bears the mark of a quarter moon, an Ukari and the symbols for both, it was taken by the mage Argus to Ebassia where it was given to his future bride, who killed him before they were wedded. The rumor is, she still lives in the castle of Ebassia and summons dark magic from the secret rooms of an ancient temple," Bolgan said.

"I've never heard of such a place, but until now I wouldn't have guessed any of this," Bowen said.

"We'll find it," Shaz said.

"We thank you, now as for your bird friends, we have detected several moving in if you are going to travel, now would be the time," Bolgan said.

"Thank you," Serin said.

"Your welcome, daughter of the light. As for you two, we will return each night after nightfall to give our report," Bolgan said.

Barrick and Helen nodded and Bolgan growled at his pack leaders and darted into the darkness.

"I can't tell if I am more terrified of them or in awe of them," Helen said.

Serin helped Helen back into the house and found a jug and filled it with water. She dipped her hands and released her magic into the water. To Helen's amazement, the blue magic swirled around the jug and Serin's tattoos glowed their gentle silver.

"Now, I want you to drink one cup of this water every day, oh, and here," Serin pulled another jar of Mrs. Bailey's pain relief from her satchel.

Helen hugged her and Serin hugged her back.

"What do you think of Bolgan?" Helen asked.

"I think he's going to become a mighty and devoted friend to you and Barrick and your little one. Keep the Ukari as close as you can," Serin said.

"You think so, alright, I will," Helen said.

"We'll be making a stop at my castle, and then we will head to Ebassia and stir up some trouble. I assume you're coming," Shaz asked.

"I most certainly am," Bowen said.

"We'll need another horse," Shaz said.

"I know where we can find one," Riddick said.

Serin noted the sly grin on his lips and rolled her eyes.

"I can't believe you," Serin said.

"You'll need to ride with Shaz till we reach town, but I don't think either of you will mind that," Riddick said.

Barrick gripped Shaz in a tight embrace and hugged Serin.

"I can't repay you, but you have my total allegiance if it's worth anything," Barrick said.

"It means a lot to us, thank you," Serin said.

"Bowen, another thing you need to be made aware about us," Shaz said.

Bowen's brows raised. Serin buffed Riddick's horse and Jagwynn who had the Minca already on her back and turned to Bowen.

"Are you ready?" Serin asked.

"I'm not sure for what, but sure why not?" Bowen said.

"Magic speed. As soon as she casts her magic, your horse will be a few inches off the ground and move at least three times the speed, so you'll need to grip tightly and hold on," Riddick said.

Serin cast her magic spell and sent the wind to envelop Bowen and his horse. Bowen gripped the reins tightly and wobbled as the steed lifted off the ground.

"I was thinking, can you make the wind constantly move overhead, keep us shielded from the sqwalls?" Shaz asked.

"I'll try, but if they track your magic, it won't do much good," Serin said.

"Alright, I won't use magic," Shaz said.

Serin buffed Shaz's horse and boosted herself onto the back behind him. Riddick kicked the sides of his horse and it leaped into a run. Bowen's horse lunged after Riddick and Bowen grabbed the horn of the saddle before he fell off. He huddled close to the horse's neck and tightened his grip. Bowen's horse was already used to the wind-walk and settled into a fast gate. Shaz and Serin took off and Jag and the Minca rode next to them. They traveled quickly and soon they reached the settlement and Riddick gave Serin his horse and went in on foot. Several minutes later he galloped toward them on a chestnut brown.

"I'm not going to ask where you got this horse," Serin said as she climbed into the saddle and buffed the chestnut.

"Let's call this horse, Lew," Riddick said.

Serin laughed and kicked her horse and raced into the night.

8-It's Good To Be Home

Three long days passed since they left Barrick's and the sun was hot and beat down on the crew as they raced over the grassland and into the rolling hills surrounding Shaz's castle. They were traveling so fast the whooshing wind made for hearing anyone near impossible, so most of the time they traveled with their own thoughts. Serin spent much of the time trying to listen to the winds words but nothing was making sense. Shaz tried to reach deep into his awareness and come up with a way to throw off the sqwalls tracking ability, but he needed to understand what they were capable of and how.

He tried to focus on the shadow magic enough to find the secrets Gavin Rhill might use but nothing came, except the man dressed in black from his dream and the Velshari temple. Riddick spent his quiet time thinking about Turob and the Kar-ka-dannon. He was growing uneasy knowing he now had a magical connection to the Kar-ka-dannon, and Crolos was still out there and then the less-than-useful Chairman who could cause a good ruckus to sort out. Bowen went through every scenario he could think of as to how he was going to remove the Grand Vizier and convince the young Queen she needed him instead. The Minca used their time to ponder the last several moons and the new tasks they were now in charge of.

Shaz examined the direction the sun was heading and adjusted his course. Light fluffy clouds began to spot the blue sky, and some blocked the sun. The shade was a welcome gesture and Serin searched for Jagwynn and the Minca. She found them a few lengths behind Bowen who was now slouching in his saddle. Serin wondered if he was sleep riding and wished that she could sleep while riding.

The wind magic began to wear off and Shaz maneuvered his horse toward a small ravine. Shaz slowed his horse to a moderate gallop as the terrain steepened. The tall grasses became spars and began to blend into the shorter grasses. Trees emerged and the sun cast shadows between them. The hill steepened and Shaz slowed his horse even more. The others followed in a single file line as the ravine narrowed and carefully guided their horses over the now rocky edges. Jagwynn padded carefully over many of the rocks and Ladtwig had to grip tightly onto Turkill, so he wouldn't fall off, which lent to Turkill's extra grumpy demeanor.

"Hey, the castle!" Serin said.

"Aye," Riddick said.

"Not much to look at," Bowen said.

"What do you mean?" Serin asked.

"Well, the whole structure is run down, I thought you said your castle was a full functioning structure," Bowen said.

"It's in great shape," Ladtwig said.

"I'm sure the inside will be better," Riddick said.

"Ah, well, the castle *is* under disguise," Shaz said.

"The castle has a disguise?" Riddick asked.

"Yep, appears old and run down so no one will want to try to take it," Shaz said.

"A little disturbing, but quite ingenious at the same time," Bowen said.

Shaz chuckled.

"We're not far now," Shaz said.

"About time," Turkill grunted.

"I sure hope the Whispmother has a huge feast waiting," Ladtwig said.

"The who?" Riddick asked.

"You'll find out," Shaz said.

The rest of the ride went quickly and soon they were trotting through the once invisible door and into the courtyard. Riddick and Bowen were is awe as the dilapidated structure fizzled away and the fresh bright stone came to life. The dingy clouds which hung over the building faded, and sun left a sparkling touch on the specs in the white stones. Shaz maneuvered the crew toward the side gate and into the stables.

"Shaz my boy, so good to have you here again," Inelius said.

"Inelius, how are you? It's good to be home," Shaz said.

Shaz climbed off the horse and embraced Inelius's old frame gently.

"Serin my dear and the Minca too, and you brought friends," Inelius said.

Riddick, Serin, and Bowen all dismounted and Serin hugged Inelius.

"This is Riddick, I think you've met him but from when he was young," Shaz said.

"Ah yes, I should have guessed, with that red hair of yours you're quite like your mother," Inelius said. Riddick gripped his hand and squeezed. "And your grip is like your father's,"

"And this is Bowen. He's the brother to Barrick who helped us in Ebassia," Shaz said.

"Nice to meet you," Bowen said.

"I bet you're famished. The Whispmother has prepared food, why don't we go inside," Inelius said.

"Oh yes," Ladtwig said and ran inside.

Deep blue carpet met them at the bottom of the stairs and cascaded up crystal white stone. The bright crystal chandeliers lit up as they walked in sending a burst of sparkling glitter around the room. A fresh scent of flowers wafted around the grand lobby.

"Well this place certainly isn't run down," Riddick said.

"Pretty clever, this spell could come in handy in so many strategies," Bowen said.

"Aye, but what kind of magic would be needed to do this for an entire village, or city?" Riddick asked.

"Far more than I've ever seen," Inelius said.

Inelius led them to the dining hall slowly as his old frame showed a sufficient amount of tiredness. Ladtwig and Turkill had already piled plates as high as they could and were sitting at the end of a long banquet table. Shaz and Serin veered to one side and Riddick and Bowen the other. The hot fresh food pelted their senses and it was hard not to shove every bit of food into their mouths.

"Master Shaz, you have returned," the Whispmother sang.

Her tiny frame, draped in her delicate feathery yellow dress, drifted from a high ledge of a shelf at the corner of the room.

"So good to see you again, how have things been?" Shaz asked.

"Mostly quiet, however, the Jaduuk found your sent several times and have returned quite regularly," The Whispmother said.

"Have they breached any defenses?" Shaz asked.

"No, but I fear now with your return they will bring more forces and at some point, they may," the Whispmother said.

"Well, we are going to need to fix that. Riddick, what do you suppose we do?" Shaz asked.

"Eat, then talk," Riddick said.

Riddick stared at the table of food and his stomach rumbled.

"Yes, of course, please, be my guests. I'll be back in a minute, I want to check on a few things," Shaz said.

Shaz grabbed a handful of nuts and left the room. He crossed the expansive entrance hall and into the dim corridor hiding behind the grand staircase. He rounded a few corners and came to a set of stairs leading to the earth portal below the main castle floors. The familiar scent of mint and musk met his nostrils, and he sucked in a deep breath. He hurried down the wooden stairs and rounded the corner into the stone cavern. He wasn't sure if he would find anything useful from the earth portal, but he needed to find out more about the mysterious figure and anything else which would tell him what the next steps would be. With the dim light from the staircase, Shaz found the face in the naturally chiseled surface which now sat dormant. Shaz closed his eyes and pulled his magic essence into his hands.

"May I?" Shaz asked the portal.

He swirled the energy into a ball and released it and sent it toward the wall. The colorful sphere wriggled and swayed as it drifted to the earth portal and fused into the rock. A strong breeze surged around the eroded rock cavern and blew his blond hair around. The eyes blinked and opened.

"Shazmpt, I'm glad to have you here again, what can I help you with?" the portal asked with a deep voice.

"I need information on a certain figure that plagues my mind," Shaz said.

"Ah, I do not carry such information, however, we earth portals are all connected, I must search through the eons of records to find your answer."

"You can talk to the other earth portals?" Shaz asked.

"Yes, we are all connected, but you must show me to whom you are requesting. Place your palms on the platform, so I may assist you," the earth portal said.

Shaz stepped closer to the wall and two small platforms on either side of the face lit up. Shaz put his hands on the illuminated surface and pictured the man in black. The portal absorbed his thoughts and the eyes closed. Images and faces whipped past Shaz's eyes as though he were scanning a book as fast as the wind. Shaz's stomach tumbled around and made his head sway with dizziness. His hands were stuck to the stone, and he breathed heavily. The portal's information was staggering and Shaz began to feel a stifling weight pushing on him from above. He dug his boots into the stone floor and focused on the strength in his legs to hold himself up. Sweat formed at his hairline and dripped down his back as the coolness in the cavern transformed into a stifling heat. Shaz scrunched his eyes tight as he tried not to let the pressure continue to fall on his body. A cool breeze circled the room and the heat dissipated. The images slowed and the weight lifted. Shaz opened his eyes and pulled his hands from the platform. He sucked in a deep breath and wiped his brow.

"I have found your information," the earth portal said.

"Am I going to like it?" Shaz asked.

"That is not a question I can answer,"

"Never mind, what did you find?"

"The answer to your inquiry is, Alisdair, the black wyvern in his human essence. We have little information about him. However, the rumor is, if the black wyvern comes to you, he's chosen you."

"What's he chosen me for?" Shaz asked.

"He's the only one with that knowledge,"

"Where is he, in Wyvern from?" Shaz asked.

"He dwells in the realm of the wyverns at the peak of Wyvern Summit."

"Where is the wyvern realm and how do I get there?"

"One can only travel by wyvern to the wyvern realm."

"Well, I guess he'll need to come to me since I don't own a wyvern," Shaz said.

A sudden shift in energy echoed in the room and Shaz sensed Serin behind the wall.

"Wyverns have been kept beneath Ebassia since the beginning of the Sixth Dispensation," the portal said.

"Under Ebassia?"

"Caution to you Shaz," Shaz peered at the face, but the lips were not moving as they had before, "future events will meet you with dishonesty and treachery."

Serin touched his arm and he turned around.

"Are you alright?" Serin asked.

"Yes, why?"

"I discerned your pain, but I couldn't find you,"

"I'm sorry I didn't expect this to cause pain, I didn't mean to worry you," Shaz said.

"What is this place?" Serin asked.

"The earth portal," Shaz surveyed the cave, "How long have you been standing here?" Shaz asked.

Serin nodded and remembered when he told her about his first meeting here.

"Long enough to hear about the black wyvern," Serin said.

"Ah," Shaz said. His stomach grumbled and he rubbed his midsection. "Let's go, we can talk more later," Shaz said.

Shaz grabbed her hand, and they walked back up the stairs. He escorted her across the foyer and back into the dining hall.

"Are you alright mate, Serin said you were in pain," Riddick asked.

"Yes, thanks, I was speaking to an earth portal and I expended more of my magic than I thought, but I'm alright," Shaz said.

Shaz pulled the chair out and let Serin slide in and then pulled out his chair. He piled some vegetables and roasted meat onto his plate. The food was still hot and Shaz was thankful for the Wispmother's magic. Serin studied him with tight lips and tried to shove the knot in her stomach down. She didn't know why, but something about what Shaz *wasn't* telling her made her uneasy. She took a slice of bread and slathered it with soft butter.

"Where would one go to, umm," Riddick started.

"Oh yes, through those doors," Shaz said and pointed to the other side of the room. Riddick excused himself and with a few long strides was out of the dining hall. "Whispmother, will you show Bowen to a room?" Shaz asked.

A tiny soldier drifted from the ledge and hovered in front of Bowen. Her tiny frame secured a full set of armor, and she held a staff twice her size, which was no bigger than a man's thumb. Her long brown hair flowed behind her as she drifted toward the door.

"A tiny soldier," Bowen said.

Bowen's eyes popped, and he rubbed the back of his neck. The soldier turned around and glared at him sharply.

"I don't think they like to be called tiny," Serin said.

"Oh, my apologies, but this is unreal," Bowen said.

He scooted his chair out and followed the little soldier out of the dining hall.

"Something isn't right Shaz," Serin said.

"Like what?" Shaz asked.

"I can't tell yet, but I can sense a different atmosphere to the castle this time," Serin said.

"Yeah, same here," Shaz said.

"What is it?" Serin asked.

"I'm not sure, I'm exhausted, tomorrow we can go to the library," Shaz said.

"Alright," Serin said.

Serin finished her meal and dabbed her lips and sat back in her chair. She closed her eyes and focused on the warmth of the late afternoon sun as the bright rays sunbathed her skin. Shaz smiled as he gazed at her beautiful face. He loved her soft silvery lilac tattoo at one temple, her soft creamy skin and delicate lips.

"Why are you staring at me? Do I have something on my face, it better not be another orange boil," Serin said.

"No, no orange boil," Shaz said. The rush of blood settled in her cheeks as she blushed. "You're beautiful, and I don't have the chance often enough to simply see you," Shaz said.

Serin rose, reached across the table and put her hand on his forehead.

"Well you don't have a fever, so you must be delirious. Maybe several hours of sleep will help," Serin said.

Shaz chuckled,

"I am delirious, deliriously in love with you," Shaz said.

"Did you know you have a fully stocked armory?!" Riddick asked. Shaz and Serin jumped and Riddick stopped. "Did I interrupt something?"

"No, we were just finishing," Shaz said. Shaz scooted out his chair and turned to Riddick, "Quite impressive aye? I'm turning in for the night. The Whispmother will show you to a room when you're ready, and we'll meet up tomorrow to figure out what we're doing next," Shaz said.

"Aye, I'm going to check things out if you don't mind," Riddick said.

"Nope, not at all, help yourself," Shaz said.

9-Did We Finish Them All?

Shaz scooted in his chair and held his hand out to Serin. She took his hand and his warm grip caressed her senses. They left the room and made their way up the staircase.

"I wish we could stay here forever," Shaz said.

Serin stopped at the front of the long hallway to the sleeping quarters.

"Shaz I love all your attention and I feel the same way, but this is not like you to be this vocal and I'm not sure what to think," Serin said.

"I can't help but be more and more attracted to you since we arrived at the castle. Not saying I didn't before, it's just, maybe the level of safety here allows me to be at peace instead of having to always be on my guard, which lets me enjoy my love for you."

Serin searched his eyes, she had noted his heartfire was more even and relaxed. She gazed into his blue eyes and understood him, this wasn't new, but now it was on a deeper and stronger level than before. She reached onto her tiptoes and kissed him. Shaz wrapped his arms around her and kissed her back. His energy was usually an organized chaos but now he was streamlined and focused.

"I am in love with you," Serin said.

"Things will only worsen, and a time will come when our love *will* be tested far beyond anything we can imagine. I fear there is no way around the shadow in this, so understand, *nothing*, I mean *nothing* will ever make me turn from you, I will die first," Shaz said.

"Don't say things like that," Serin said.

"I have to, I need you to understand. It *will* happen, the shadow will force our hand at some point, that's what it does. The others succumbed to the temptations. I've witnessed it. They didn't start out bad, but they were weak-minded and were able to be persuaded by something or someone. I have thought a lot about it, and the only thing the shadow can use against me, is you," Shaz said.

Serin's brows scrunched deep, and she bit her lip. Shaz took a deep breath, pulled her close, closed his eyes and held her.

"Master Shaz, do you have a moment?" the Whispmother sang.

The tiny woman floated near his head, and he opened his eyes.

"What is it?" Shaz asked with a sigh.

"Jaduuk are coming toward the castle. What do you want to do?" the Whispmother asked.

"Can you tell how many?" Shaz asked.

"Several packs," the Whispmother said.

"How far away?" Shaz asked.

"Only a few hours."

"Inform Riddick and Bowen, we'll take some horses and try, and cut them off before they reach the castle territory," Shaz said.

The Whispmother nodded and floated away quickly. Serin squeezed Shaz. His eyes closed and Serin was aware of the tiredness in his energy.

"I'll come too," Serin said.

"I think we'll be fine, especially if we catch them off guard. You stay here and rest," Shaz said.

"Are you sure?" Serin asked.

"Aye, we'll be alright, we won't be too long, plus I want to make some additions to the defenses and with Riddick's help it shouldn't be too hard," Shaz said.

Shaz closed his eyes and rested his chin on her head. His grip was amazingly strong and Serin didn't want to move.

"Well, you're going to have to let go of me at some point," Serin said.

"Never," Shaz said.

"There you go again, being all sappy," Serin said.

"Not sappy, happy, remember?" Shaz said.

He released his grip, and she pulled away and smiled at him. He kissed her then headed toward the stairs. Riddick and Bowen were waiting at the bottom of the stairs as he descended.

"What are your plans?" Riddick asked.

"Kill some Jaduuk," Shaz said.

"Easy enough," Riddick said.

"I hope so," Shaz said.

"Well, you wanted to find out what a Jaduuk was, now's your chance," Riddick said.

Bowen nodded but gulped slightly. Riddick smiled and slapped him on the back.

"It's never a good thing to be slapped on the back before you're about to do something that involves weapons," Bowen said.

Shaz and Riddick laughed. The three men stopped at the armory and grabbed a few weapons of choice and went to the stable. The horses nickered as they saddled them up. Shaz shoved his boot into the stirrup and hoisted himself onto the horse. Serin moved from the shadow and raised her arms over her head. She sent her air magic toward each horse and Shaz and the others kicked into their sides. The horses jumped into a fast run and Shaz led them down the long lane until they disappeared behind a rolling hill.

Shaz had no real idea where he was going for sure. He was a child when he lived here, but he would have been quite small, and he had no actual memories of the castle or the surroundings, but a familiarity of the hills gave a certain peace to his being. Riddick and Bowen kept a quick pace following behind one another. Riddick made mental notes of the hills and several times peered into the sky to determine where the sun was, so he could tell which direction he was heading. Riddick was the one who always made extra care to be as thorough as possible. The wind whipped through the valleys with determination and Bowen found the task to keep up with Shaz and Riddick harder than before. Shaz slowed his horse to a trot and Riddick and Bowen caught up to him.

"Where are the Jaduuk?" Riddick asked.

"I'm not sure, the Whispmother indicated they were toward the South-southwest," Shaz said.

"So, that way," Riddick said.

"Aye, I want to inspect the surroundings and gain a feel for the landscape here and figure out a way to keep the defenses strong as far away from the castle as possible," Shaz said.

"What defenses?" Bowen asked.

"Aye, that's what I mean," Shaz said.

They trotted along the forest edge and studied the landscape for several long lengths and made note of the trees, rivers, peaks, valleys and anything they could use. Serin's air spell wore off and the horses slowed to their normal pace. Riddick climbed off Lew and walked him into the forest several lengths. The trees were tall and skinny without many leaves and there were few bushes or briers. Riddick leaned against a tree and was surprised to receive a tickling sensation in his skin. He gripped a tree trunk and cleared his mind. The trees came to life in his mind, and he understood they were a different kind of tree.

Their spirits had advanced more than others and had a kind of intelligence. He understood their root system was where they were mobile and could move around. Riddick made note of the uniqueness of the trees and after a few minutes he grabbed the reins and left and caught up to Shaz and Bowen.

"I think we will be able to use the trees as a barrier," Riddick said.

"How?" Bowen asked.

Shaz raised his eyebrow in anticipation, Riddick's quite a jokester and he wasn't quite sure if he was playing this time.

"I think I'm going to tell the trees to eat them," Riddick said.

Bowen stared at Riddick and turned to Shaz to note his reaction. Shaz shook his head while rubbing his now tightly trimmed blonde beard.

"That might work," Shaz said.

"You have to be joking," Bowen said.

Shaz and Riddick turned to Bowen with a 'what' expression. Bowen cleared his throat and rubbed his face.

"I know this is all new to you, but you have seen magic used before," Shaz said.

"Yeah to make horses run faster," Bowen said.

"Well, it might not work so let's keep thinking of other things," Riddick said.

"Hey, what about those spikes you made last time. Can you make more? We can use them to make barriers along the river and hill sections," Shaz asked.

"Great idea. I'm on it. Bowen, you can help me. We need to gather as many small sticks as we can," Riddick said.

Bowen shook his head but agreed and followed Riddick into the trees. Shaz studied the horizon and made note of all the areas the spikes would be useful. Riddick and Bowen returned with arms full of medium-sized branches. Riddick made a pile and waved to Shaz. Shaz trotted over to them and climbed down.

"So, how do you want to do this?" Shaz asked.

Riddick grabbed a stick and wriggled his fingers. A cracking and popping sound ripped from the twig as it soared into an extensively sized spike. Riddick had to hold tightly with both hands so the beam wouldn't topple him over.

"Oiy!" Bowen yelled.

Shaz and Riddick laughed.

"Alright, but we don't have any shovels, how are you going to put this monstrosity in the ground?" Bowen asked.

Riddick leaned the heavy spike onto his shoulder and heaved it up. He carried it a few steps then rested it on the ground. He stomped on the ground with one foot and a hole opened. Riddick heaved the beam into the hole and estimated how much of an angle would be needed to get the best defense and stomped again. The displaced dirt wrapped around the pole and tightened against it. Riddick let go of the pole and stood back.

"Like that," Riddick said.

Riddick brushed his hand on his trousers and smiled. His dashing smile and deep brown eyes reflected the setting sun.

"I don't know what to say, except, that is amazing," Bowen said.

"We need to hurry, though, we are going to lose sunlight and I don't really want to be out here all night," Shaz said.

"Bowen, you hand me the sticks and I'll make the holes," Riddick said.

Bowen still had his pile in his arms, so he followed Riddick as he made several more holes and pikes. Shaz explained to Riddick where he thought the spikes would best be suited and left, he and Bowen to keep working, with instructions to meet up with him on the South-southwest side of the forest. Shaz hurried to where the Whispmother had indicated sensing the Jaduuk. The sun was setting, and a cool breeze came in and chilled his skin. He studied the distance and paid attention to the smells and sounds as he rode. A rancid odor wafted into his brain, and he pulled back on the reins. The horse slowed to a trot and then a slow walk. Shaz was well familiar with this smell and was certain Jaduuk were near.

With nowhere for him to hide and not knowing for certain how far away they were or how many, Shaz climbed off the horse and slapped it on the behind. The horse leaped into a run back toward Riddick and Bowen and Shaz crouched close to the ground. He closed his eyes and searched with his night vision. A faint image surfaced several lengths away. One Jaduuk stood on its hind legs and Shaz guessed this was a sentry. He continued to move across the hillside until a few more images appeared. Shaz counted the heat signatures and found more than thirty Jaduuk milling about or sleeping.

"Sssppp," Riddick said.

Shaz turned around and found Riddick and Bowen.

"You alright mate?" Riddick asked.

Shaz nodded and remembered he sent his horse back. The horse returning with an empty saddle had alarmed Riddick, but he was glad he had come.

"I count at least thirty, maybe more," Shaz said.

"Not too bad, ten for each of us," Riddick said.

"Aye, they are about twenty lengths that way, with a few patrols. We need to take them out first, then we can sneak up on the rest of the pack," Shaz said.

Riddick nodded and followed Shaz to a nearby boulder. Riddick put his hand on the ground and allowed the earth's magic into his body giving him a picture of where the beasts were. They hurried from the boulder to another group of rocks and another as they made their way toward the hill the patrol was on. Shaz reached for his bow but Riddick grabbed his arm. Riddick rose and stomped on the earth. The ground fell out from under the Jaduuk and the beast fell into the darkness. The earth closed over before it had a chance to yelp.

"Impressive, I'll just let you take them all," Shaz said pointing to each of the sentries.

Riddick hurried to the next Jaduuk and repeated the process. He waved to Shaz and Bowen who ran to meet up with him. They scurried down a steep hill and started to climb the next side. Shaz signaled for them to crawl on their belly's the last few lengths until they could peek over the hill. The Jaduuk were camped in a small valley at the bottom of a group of trees.

"Oiy vay, what are those?" Bowen asked.

"Those are Jaduuk," Shaz said.

"I figured, but *what* are they?" Bowen asked.

"Annoying," Riddick said.

"Part-wolf-part-" Shaz started, "actually I'm not sure exactly."

Bowen studied the creatures and panicked at their long fangs which went up toward their eyes and the long ears had tufts of hair-like fur at the tips. Their muscular bodies were covered in a tough blue-ish hide and was spotted with ragged tufts of black or gray fur. Sharp claws sat at the edges of a hoof and their long-wrinkled snouts stuck out from their bulky heads. He swallowed the bile now ripping through his esophagus.

"How do you kill them?" Bowen asked.

"They are hard to kill, but if you can go for their throat, which is the weakest part. Their skin is very tough, so you have to hit hard and pull to slice," Shaz said.

Bowen nodded. Shaz pulled the Honor Blade from its sheath. A clear ring sounded in their ears and Riddick pulled his battle-ax from his back. Shaz rose to full height and ran toward the first Jaduuk which was lying curled up in a ball. Riddick and Bowen followed each taking a direct route to the nearest beast. The Jaduuk's ears twitched in time to find the blade race across its neck. The male tried to sound an alert but was muffled by the gurgling of blood spurting from its main artery. Shaz pulled the blade back down and stabbed the back and sliced through the spine. The creatures overly proportioned head hit the ground with a thud. Riddick rolled the ax in his hand a few times as he approached the Jaduuk he had targeted and gripped the handle as the momentum was at peak position. He gripped the ax tightly and sent the butt encased in a sharp spike careening into the side of the beast's massive head. The Jaduuk yelped and started to rear backward but was unable to make sense of the pain now consuming its being.

Riddick yanked the spike out and slammed the ax's blade into its muscular chest. The Jaduuk smacked into a tree and fell to the ground. Bowen tipped toed as close as he could and dashed toward his target. The smaller Jaduuk's eyes flickered only a moment before Bowen's blade crossed its neck. The beast's oily blood spurted Bowen's face and tunic, and he gagged from the putrid odor. He wiped the nasty greasy fluid from his eyes and ducked the oncoming clawed fist. He parried to the side and spat onto the ground before thrusting his blade into the Jaduuk's fading frame.

Shaz took out three more and Riddick two but Riddick wasn't quite fast enough to catch the next one before an ear cracking howl ripped through the night. Jaduuk launched to alert and Riddick leaped out of the way of an extra beefy male Jaduuk's sharp teeth. Riddick rolled into a somersault and came to his feet and spun around. The Jaduuk sliced a jagged battle-ax through the air and took a full step toward Riddick. Riddick swung his ax but the Jaduuk blocked with its ax and yanked. Riddick let the ax roll through his wrist and grabbed the handle before the Jaduuk ripped it from his hand.

Shaz opened his palm and let the heat of the fire element come to life. He threw a fireball at the Jaduuk and back stepped. The fire hit the Jaduuk and wrapped around its body like a blanket. The creature bellowed a howl-like-yelp as the heat consumed the gnarly flesh. Bowen ducked and rolled out from under the attack of an oncoming beast. He came to his feet quickly and with both hands pulled his long blade through the beast's neck. The thick skin and bone were harder than he had expected, and the blade didn't sink as deep as needed. He let the momentum of the swing carry the blade back up and stepped closer. The Jaduuk swung around and roared in Bowen's face.

A deep chill ran through his body, and he almost froze. Bowen swung his hips hard and came full circle in time to send his blade through the neck again. This time the blade sliced the beasts flesh deep enough and it fell to the ground right in front of him. He sucked in a deep breath but wasn't able to control the reflex of his stomach, and he lurched forward and expelled all of his stomach contents. He wiped his mouth and breathed heavily.

Each time Shaz called the fire element, the fire made a pop and crackle sound in his palm. The fire surged across the distance with growing intensity as the air fed the inferno. Shaz's next target couldn't duck in time to evade the fierce fireball and was engulfed instantly. The heat was intense and Shaz liked the power of the fire element. He rolled around another beast and slashed the back of the hind legs slicing the tendon rendering it unable to move. The beast fell with a thud and Shaz stabbed his blade through its spine. The reflexes of the creature left the lifeless body writhing for several minutes.

Riddick stomped and several holes opened and swallowed some Jaduuk. Yelps and howls echoed through the darkening sky and Shaz wondered if they were signaling for help. Bowen made his mark on the last Jaduuk and ran around several trees for a better advantage. The Jaduuk snarled and sniffed the air. The Jaduuk lunged at Bowen taking him by surprise. The ragged clawed hoof of the Jaduuk hit him square in the chest and sent him flying several lengths. Blood seeped through his tunic and leather jerkin as the tips of the claws ripped through his skin. Bowen coughed and sputtered as he tried to bring air back in his lungs enough to even cry with pain. Shaz ran at full speed and sliced the beast through the belly releasing the animal's insides. Rancid blood sprayed Shaz in the face and the beast fell.

"Are you alright mate?" Riddick asked.

Bowen struggled to breathe, and his eyes were filled with tears. Shaz remembered what Serin did when she had this happened to her and focused on what he remembered and reached for Serin's calming energy. A blue light illuminated his skin and sank into Bowen. Bowen's breathing leveled out, and he sucked in a deep breath and sighed. The gashes eased and the blood stopped.

"What was that?" Bowen asked.

"A little bit of healing magic, but I'm not near as good as Serin," Shaz said.

"Did we finish them all?" Bowen asked.

"For now, but I don't think we're near done with these things," Shaz said.

"How many?" Bowen asked.

"With how many were in the Minca realm you would think we killed them all," Riddick said.

"I don't think even that was the half of it," Shaz said.

"Well, you're a killjoy," Riddick said.

Shaz chuckled.

"Come on let's get out of here," Shaz said.

"What about your magic, you used fire, are we going to attract sqwall to the castle?" Riddick asked.

"Blasted all," Shaz cursed.

Riddick helped Bowen stand, and they hurried back toward the horses. They found the horses milling in a nearby valley.

"You head back to the castle, I'm going to try to throw off the sqwall's senses," Shaz said.

"Alright, but be careful and don't take long," Riddick said.

Shaz nodded and turned his horse away from the castle.

10-Take Several of Your Best Soldiers

Oladesni rolled over and pulled the heavily weaved covers over her head. She kept her eyes shut but her mind was nowhere close to resting. It had only been three days since she became queen and five since her father died, and time wasn't going fast enough. A new sense of dread continued to sit at the bottom of her stomach, and she found it hard to eat anything. Isot's gentle coercion was comforting, however, she feared at some point she was going to have to accept things were never going to be the same.

Every thought of the enormous city she was now queen of raced around her head and her guts felt as if they were twisted into knots. She was certain Isot would help her, but she couldn't pass off her responsibilities forever. Even though her mind was racing around everything, one thought her father had said to her when she was young right after her mother passed kept running across, *There will be some who will try to deceive you and take your birthright, you must be wise and only trust yourself.* Oladesni couldn't stop the gnawing thought Isot wasn't who she said she was, but she had no reason to believe it or prove it, and she made her the Grand Vizier.

Oladesni pulled the covers off and sat up, the dimness of the castle left a bitter taste in her mouth. The death of her father and becoming queen had taken a toll on her emotions. She wrapped a heavy wool robe around her and put on her slippers. The windows on the east side of the room let in the early morning's darkened sky. Oladesni shivered and pulled the latch open. The hallway was darker and Oladesni hurried to the staircase and started down, but heard voices echo through the rounded staircase and carefully made her way to the last corner before the bottom floor. One of the voices she recognized as Isot's but the other female voice she had not heard before. Oladesni huddled against the cold stone wall and listened.

"How many recruits do we have now," Isot asked.

"Our numbers are growing, but we're still a long way from the desired numbers," the woman said.

"Announce for all members to come to the Ebassia," Isot said.

The woman's brows rose, and she licked her dark pink lips.

"You have figured out the scroll?" the woman asked.

"I *need* the medallion," Isot said.

"I am working as fast as I can," the woman said.

"Gitre, you do understand how pressing this is?" Isot asked.

"Of course, I do, don't try your stupid condescending comments and tone on me, I don't play that way. You do understand how much I am able to do and you're not," Gitre said.

"Fine, but if you can't find one soon, I'm going to have to extend the offer to anyone who can," Isot said.

"And what good would that do, send a bunch of fools on a wild goose chase? You've been locked in this castle for over two centuries, I think you can wait a few more rotations if needed," Gitre said.

Oladesni peeked around the corner and found Isot breathe in a deep breath and slide her long red fingernail down Gitre's throat. Oladesni held her breath and wanted to shrink back up the stairs, but she couldn't take her eyes off the two women.

"I think it's about time you up your game. Bring the council to their knees, lock them in the dungeons or kill them, I don't care, just get me a medallion," Isot said.

Gitre grabbed her wrist and yanked Isot's hand away from her face but kept a tight grip.

"I will do as I do, and you will thank me later," Gitre said.

Gitre shoved her hand away and gave Isot a hostile glare.

Isot smiled, she loved the energy she received when others were angry. It gave her a sense of control, power, and it was *fun*.

"I have a special something for you," Isot said.

Isot pulled a small glass jar out of her cloak pocket and held it out to Gitre who gauged her with angry caution.

"What is it?" Gitre asked.

"This is the Tonic of Illusions, but with a twist," Isot said.

"What do you want me to do with that, hold a fireside sing-along?" Gitre asked.

"You could, but I have laced it with a little something special. This is a special mixture, with sweet black coridalis. This will give your abilities a boost for a couple hours. Instead of your less than spectacular antics, you will find you will be stronger, faster, and draw more energy from your elements," Isot said.

Gitre's narrow-eyed alertness sank into Isot's soul and heat rippled through Isot's frame.

"How much does one use for this, added strength?" Gitre asked.

Gitre's jet-black hair flowed from a center part which framed a quiet oval face, dark, and delicate. Her eyes, however, were murderous under finely arched brows. Gitre snapped the jar from Isot.

"The bottle contains enough for you to take several of your best soldiers to get the job done," Isot said.

Gitre palmed the jar and spun on her toes. Her long polished-jade-green dress rippled in the wake as she barreled down the hallway. Her short strides and hard-soled shoes clicked against the polished stone which left a rawness in the air. Gitre cinched the laces around her chest and bosom and secured her outer dark gray over-cloak and left the castle. Oladesni waited until Isot rounded the corner of the passageway on the other side and slipped around the corner. Oladesni wasn't sure what to do or think, but now she was certain there was something else about Isot and this time she was right.

Oladesni found herself in the kitchen with the smell of the sweet bread the baker made every morning, and she sat in a chair. The older woman came from one of the back rooms which stored the jars and baskets of food supplies.

"Oh, Your Highness, I didn't hear you come in," the baker said.

"I'm sorry," Oladesni said.

"Is there anything I can get for you?" the woman asked.

"I would love some of your sweet bread and milk please," Oladesni said.

"Of course, let me put these down and I'll get right to it,"

"Thank you," Oladesni said.

Oladesni studied the woman as she shoved a few packages of dried meats into a drawer and dump a sack of sweetener into a jug. The baker lifted a panel and pulled out a loaf of sweet bread and rested the lid back in its cradle. She pulled a bowl down from a cupboard and ripped the bread into several bite -sized pieces and put them in the bowl. The milk was held in carafes inside a cooler, and she pulled the glass jar and popped the top off. She poured the milk and took out a spoon from the drawer and set it in front of the queen. Oladesni stared at the soaking bread and moved a few pieces with her spoon.

"Are you alright, Highness?" the woman asked.

Oladesni looked into the woman's soft brown eyes. Her gently grayed hair was pulled up and tucked under her cap. The soft glow of the warm kitchen rested on her slightly wrinkled features, and she reminded her of her mother.

"Yes, no, I don't know," Oladesni admitted.

"I understand very well, you certainly have been through a sufficient amount of turmoil in the last few weeks," the woman said.

"And I fear it will only get worse," Oladesni said.

"How do you suppose?" the woman asked.

"Can I ask you a question?" Oladesni asked.

"Yes, of course, Your Highness,"

Oladesni went to the door of the main entrance to the kitchen and checked each hallway. She turned around to find the gently aged woman's confusion.

"What would you do, if there was someone you knew who wasn't who they said they were, and after you did something that you shouldn't have, how do you reverse it without that person finding out or at least, getting mad," Oladesni asked.

"You mean Isot?" the woman asked.

Oladesni nodded and returned to her seat.

"How did you know?" Oladesni asked.

"I have worked for this castle since I was a child. I started out at tending the laundry and cleaning and eventually made my way here to the kitchen and I have known Isot the entire time. She is most certainly not a person to trust, but she isn't someone you want to cross either," the baker said.

"Then what should I do?" Oladesni asked.

"Since I don't know what you did, I suppose the only answer would be to find your loophole," the woman said.

"What is a loophole?" Oladesni asked.

"It's the secret rule or law that makes the rule or law no longer the rule or law," the woman said.

Oladesni stared at the woman, who chuckled.

"There's a book in the library that explains it, maybe you should spend some time there,"

"Thank you, I will," Oladesni said.

Oladesni shoved several bites of the now very soggy bread into her mouth and left the kitchen. She hurried to her room to dress and grabbed her satchel she used to carry to her social and political lessons her father made her take. She wondered if her old instructor would be able to help, and she slung the bag over her shoulder. The hallways had brightened some with the rising of the sun and Oladesni soaked in the brisk morning air as she made her way to the outer ring of the castle.

"My lady, what are you doing here so early," the doorman asked.

"I need an escort to the library please," Oladesni asked.

"What for?" the doorman asked.

"I think you have forgotten I don't answer those questions any-more, and you will address me as 'Your Highness'," Oladesni said.

"I beg your pardon, Your Highness, you've grown so fast, I fear I still see you as a child, that will never happen again," the doorman said.

Oladesni caught his eye and knew his gently aged mind didn't mean any harm. She smiled and touched his arm to assure him she wasn't angry. He had been a good friend to her, and she loved to tease him when she was young and then torment would be the correct term as a teenager's sassiness would deserve. He smiled back which creased his wrinkles around his eyes and softened his gaze. The man beckoned a soldier nearby and instructed him to assemble the escort and a few minutes later four soldiers arrived to take Oladesni to the kingdom li-brary. The doorman pulled the lever that unlatched the gate to the side entrance of the castle and the first two soldiers passed through the door and made a quick scan of the surroundings and waved to the other two and Oladesni walked into the fresh morning light. She turned her head toward the sun and smiled as it bathed her pale skin.

"Isn't it a lovely morning?" Oladesni asked.

The soldiers nodded and kept a comfortably quick pace. Oladesni stopped in the middle of the skybridge and looked out over the stone bridge banister. The city was beautiful with all of its buildings and shops and houses arranged in its labyrinth of mazes. The forest to the side of the city was magnificent and seemed to stretch forever as did the ocean on the other side. The colors that danced off the ocean from the rising sun sank into her heart. She had never been allowed to go into the city, or worse to the outer edges and had never seen the forest or the ocean for herself. She knew she had to change that some-day. One of the soldiers stepped closer to her and peered over the bridge and around the area while another searched the other side.

"We mustn't linger long Your Highness," a soldier said.

Oladesni nodded and they proceeded across the bridge and into the tall building on the other side. The castle itself was in the style of rotations past and some of the kingdom buildings, but the library was one of a more modern design and had a feeling of advancement Oladesni liked. Two of the soldiers went first and informed the library attendant that the Queen was present and cleared the area from any members of the kingdoms governing bodies. There were the committee of Viziers, Prime Viziers and the Grand Vizier which organized the process of law-making for the kingdom and many spent hours in the library preparing speeches and campaigns to change or secure certain laws. It was the subject she hated most, but her father insisted on her dutifully participating. Now she wished she had paid closer attention.

"Your Majesty? Where would you like to go?" the attendant asked.

Oladesni cleared her thoughts.

"I would like to search for a book that contains loopholes," Oladesni said.

The attendant's brows raised, and he cleared his throat.

"There are several books that contain loopholes, what law or rule would your loophole pertain to?" the attendant asked.

Oladesni pulled out a paper and with her finger over her lips, handed it to the man and he read the scribbles.

"Follow me," the man said.

The dark-haired man tucked the note into his tightly buttoned vest and straightened his jacket as he maneuvered the sitting area in the lobby of the building. He guided them up the stairs to the third floor and rounded a pillar that held the balcony before descending the row of shelves. He slowed his pace and hovered over a couple of largely bound books. He stopped on one in the center and heaved the sizable thing off the shelf. He carried the book to a nearby table and one of the soldiers pulled the chair for the queen and sat her in front of the book. The attendant opened to the back and skimmed the reference and flipped to the corresponding pages.

"I think this is what you are looking for Your Majesty," the attendant half-asked-half-stated.

Oladesni skimmed the headings and nodded.

"I think this will be helpful, thank you," Oladesni said.

The attendant bowed and returned to the lower level. The soldiers took strategic places on the balcony and behind the queen and Oladesni started to read the book. She pulled out her quill and ink jar and scribbled notes on a clean sheet of parchment as she studied.

11-You Won't Get Away with This

Merrick stood on the deck of the Daybreak. The Daybreak was a barkentine with two masts, the smaller mast had a ketch and was aided by three layers of sales similar to the Mirabella. Bright lights from the city burst over the buildings which danced on the ripples of the ocean against the shore. Merrick could live inside the city, but he felt more at home on the ship. He didn't take her out to sea anymore since he had left Turob and returned to Ebassia, and since his council duties had changed. He wondered at the moonbeams as they danced off the uneven surface of the ocean and breathed in the cool salty air.

Merrick missed Shaz more than he had ever thought he would and struggled with the unfamiliar feelings his absence left. He was Shaz's foster father and at first, it was a responsibility, but after his wife Elin was killed, Merrick took her desire and love of the boy to heart. The hole deepened as he remembered all the times they laughed and played. The first time he helped Shaz take his first hunt, his first hand-to-hand win, his first dance with a girl, who Shaz was not thrilled about at all. Merrick chuckled at the memory and sipped his lager. He estimated the time and returned to the upper cabin.

Merrick gripped the fire poker and moved the log in the fireplace at the far end of the main cabin. The flames bit into the fresh fuel and perked up. Merrick replaced the poker and relaxed into his oversized leather chair. He took a full gulp of his drink and sat the heavy metal cup on the side table. Merrick closed his eyes, but an unfamiliar creak perked his ear. He sat up and listened carefully. Merrick rose from his chair quickly and quietly made his way to the other side of the cabin to where his sword was hung on the wall. He gripped the hilt and lifted it out of the cradle. He eased his hand into the familiar form of the hilt and a comfort sank into his chest.

Merrick unlatched the hook on the door and peeked out and listened. He could tell it was soft boots of a male on the deck of his ship. He opened the door enough for him to pass and with two long strides made it to the end of the passageway. The sounds came from the port side, so he veered to starboard and snugged up against the wooden bulkhead. Merrick held his breath as he saw through the small porthole window, two sets of soft leather boots pass overhead. He recognized them as Garrison and Patriza and lowered his sword.

Merrick came out from around the corner. Garrison jumped out of his skin and cursed.

"Blasted, Merrick you scared me," Garrison said.

"Good, what are you doing here so late. I thought we agreed we would meet in the morning," Merrick said.

Merrick's deep voice shattered the quite of the night.

"We did, but there is something going on," Garrison said.

"What?" Merrick asked.

"We were supposed to check in with Mathieu, but he's not at the building or at home," Patriza said.

"Humm, doesn't seem like him, have you checked the headquarters?" Merrick asked.

"Yes, and the diner, but we can't find him," Patriza said.

"Maybe he's gone on one of his expeditions," Merrick said.

Merrick was certain Mathieu wouldn't go anywhere without at least indicating the possibility first and a sick feeling set into Merrick's stomach.

"I suppose, but don't you think it is a little odd to leave the night before he was supposed to meet with the new queen?" Patriza asked.

"Aye," Merrick noticed Garrison didn't seem as concerned and wondered what he was up to. "I'm sure he'll turn up by morning," Merrick said.

"I hope you're right," Patriza said.

Garrison turned around and started toward the ladder and Patriza moved in behind him. Merrick studied them as they began to descend the steps, but something didn't add up. Merrick searched his mind for anything he could to settle the debate in his forward-thinking. The idea Mathieu wasn't where he usually was, was unsettling, and he was positive he didn't have any plans to travel. Garrison wasn't concerned and Patriza was more worried than usual. Patriza was the current leader of the Temples and usually a very calm and collected woman. Her long slender frame was strong but nimble, and she had seen and experienced a substantial amount, as they all had over the rotations, so it didn't seem like her to be as frazzled.

A heavy sensation started to weigh in his chest and made him feel a bit weary. He opened his chest and allowed a firm breath of air to fill their entirety. He followed them to the lifeline rails and watched Garrison scale the ladder to the lower deck and then Patriza. Garrison hesitated and turned his head toward the end of the pier. Merrick followed his direction and saw a tiny movement in the dark. The pit deepened as did the heavy buzz.

"What are you doing Garrison?" Merrick asked.

"Something I should have done a long time ago," Garrison said.

"And what is that?" Merrick asked.

"Getting you out of the way," Garrison said.

"The way of what?" Patriza asked.

"You now serve the Shadow," Merrick said.

"I have my own agenda," Garrison said.

Merrick understood at this point Garrison had chosen a path he wouldn't come back from. Garrison scaled the last few ladder steps and landed on the dock. He then shoved the dock step leaving too big of a distance for Patriza to step down. Patriza hadn't noticed and continued down the ladder. Merrick leaped over the rail and onto the main deck and ran toward Patriza who was now almost to the end of the ladder. He reached her hand a second before she slipped off the steps.

"Merrick?" Patriza asked.

Patriza turned to find Merrick's thick fingers digging into her skin. The sudden discomfort sank into her awareness, and she looked down.

"Shhh, come back up quickly," Merrick said.

Patriza looked behind her and couldn't see Garrison.

"Where is Garrison?" Patriza asked.

"I think he has betrayed us, and I don't think we are alone," Merrick said.

Patriza climbed back up the ladder and onto the deck. Merrick took a quick inventory of the dock and pulled the mooring line from the thick iron head and tossed the line onto the pier. Merrick started toward the bridge but halfway across the deck, the thick weight in his chest deepened. He sank to his knees, and he struggled to reach the bulwark pole. He gripped a pile of rope wrapped around a peg and heaved himself up. A bead of sweat dripped off his thick brows, and he squinted as the salty droplet stung his eye. Patriza stopped and lifted his arm over her shoulder and helped him stand. She helped him to the bridge, but he was becoming so weak he could hardly grip the wheel on the helm.

"What is happening?" Patriza asked.

"I don't know," Merrick said.

A soft thud echoed over the wooden deck.

"This isn't good," Patriza said.

"Who is it?" Merrick asked.

"It's the Velshari," Patriza said.

"That lowlife scum Garrison, I knew I never liked him for a reason," Merrick said.

"So, it would seem," Patriza said.

"Well, now, look what we have here," Gitre said.

She held her arms out and gestured around the ship.

"What do you want?" Patriza asked.

Patriza's usually calm and resonant voice was pitched high and shook with anger.

"Why, I have come for the great Ranger, and you of course," Gitre said.

"Why?" Patriza asked.

It wasn't like she didn't know, but she was trying to gauge the woman and whether they had a chance to escape.

"Well, you see, Isot has figured out the scroll, and she needs you out of the way before the coronation of the queen when she plans on enacting the powers of the scroll," Gitre said.

Merrick slumped onto the rail and slid down onto his rump. He didn't believe she had figured out the scroll but without being able to find out on his own he had no way to disprove her and a fear he had never felt ripped through his mind. Gitre waved to her men, and they moved up behind her.

"What have you done to Merrick?" Patriza demanded.

"I have sucked out all of his stamina," Gitre said.

"How?" Patriza asked.

"My mages have been given the earth elements adaption of absorption of energy," Gitre said.

Gitre motioned for her men to bind them. The men pulled the shadow bonds from their cloaks and one man bound Patriza while two men bound Merrick. Patriza pulled against the cords as the pain they left merged into her blood.

"You won't get away with this," Patriza said.

"Oh dear, the thing is, I just did," Gitre said.

Merrick shook his head at Patriza who bit her lip.

"Shield your mind and secure your inner self," Merrick said.

Patriza exhaled a slow breath and tried to find a peace within herself but found it quite difficult with the pain of the shadow bonds eating her skin. Merrick flung his long chestnut brown hair from his face and absorbed as many details as he could. Everything from the sizes and shapes of the people to the sounds and smells. He wanted to make sure he remembered which ones were a part of this so when he made his revenge, he would know who to seek after. Cold anger ate at his heart, and he allowed it to grow. The men heaved the large stature of a man with all their might and buckled under his highly defined muscular frame.

"Where are you taking us?' Patriza asked.

"To the dungeons of course," Gitre said.

An uncontrollable twitch crossed Patriza's lip and Gitre enjoyed a fierce and malevolent grin.

****

Mathieu sat in a soft padded chair at the end of the long table. His long silver beard rested on his thinning frame and his frail hand gripped his long gold entwined staff. He found himself gazing into the high ceilings and admiring the intricate details. He had sat in this chair so many times before he couldn't count, but this time for some reason he had a different appreciation. Maybe it was his time was coming to an end, and he understood that he would never see it again. His twin brother Inelius, and he had been able to take advantage of the synergy magic, which was given them by Shaz's mother and father, but now that Shaz had taken on his role of War Wizard, and he no longer needed their protection. Mathieu's job was to teach Shaz about his role as the only war wizard in the world and how he would someday have to battle Gavin Rhill and the Shadow. When Shaz was old enough to begin learning his powers, a string of attacks from the Sqwalls began, one of which took Elin, Merrick's wife, and Shaz's foster mother.

Grandfather then realized Shaz must not use his powers, and he was forced to move into their home, so he could keep Shaz's powers undetectable to the shadow. Mathieu traveled to every temple and library he could to figure out a way to keep the Sqwall from finding him, but each time he thought he had found the answer, the sqwall would show up again.

Mathieu changed his protection spell several times and eventually accepted he wouldn't be able to teach him his magic, so, he resorted to telling him as many stories from the past, and all the realms that he knew. He taught him in every kind of greeting and every language he knew. Merrick taught him to fight and hunt and use his mind in every way possible with the hope he would be able to gain control of his magic quickly when the time came.

"Mathieu, we are finished for the night, do you want us to walk you home?" Valida asked.

'Oh, no thank you dear, I'll be fine," Mathieu said.

"Are you sure, it's no trouble," Valida said.

Mathieu turned his attention to the gently aged woman. Her soft wavy amber brown hair rested at her shoulders and her warm amber eyes decorated her sensuous but direct and challenging features.

"I'm sure, you and Ceros go on, I have a bit of reading I want to finish," Mathieu said.

"Alright then, see you tomorrow," Valida said.

She secured her side satchel over her chest and left the room. Valida and Ceros pulled the long cold steel handles of the tall doors of the building. This particular building had been used by the original council before the E.O.R. and an ancient magic shielded their floors from everyone else making it a highly secret place.

The night was cool, and a soft breeze whispered through the trees. The inner buildings were very tall and glazed with a shine that even reflected the moon's rays at night giving off a level of light that was unnatural. Valida followed Ceros across the courtyard toward the ally that would take them to the lower district where the housing units were. Ceros stepped off the last stone step and he stopped. He held out his arm and stopped Valida from taking the last step.

"What is it?" Valida asked.

A bright flash ripped across the pathway and hit Valida in the chest. The sound of the blast caught up a second later and blasted her eardrums. Ceros gripped his sword but wasn't fast enough to block the bolt of moonlight ray from sinking into his core. Valida screamed as the bolt of unrelenting pain hit her core, and she crumpled to the ground. Ceros' instant inhale slammed to stop in his throat as the pain shot icy hot flames into his brain. His majestic frame slowly fell to the ground.

A fiery dread encompassed Ceros as he fought to make his body move. His limbs sat unresponsive and as heavy as a lead brick. Tears flowed from Valida's oval eyes, she barely managed to let out a moan under her tightened jaw.

A small woman followed by eight other men and women emerged. Ceros raced through his mind to find an explanation on how they could have hidden from them but came up empty. Valida whimpered and tried to make her head move to focus on the people.

"Bind them quickly before the spell starts to wear off," Gitre said. A bulky dark-skinned man pulled out two sets of heavy cords from the inside pocket of his red robe and handed one set to the shorter bulky man next to him. They crossed the last few lengths and picked up the council's bodies. Ceros fought profusely but to his horror, his body still didn't respond to his commands. Gitre glared with a sickening sparkle in her dark slanted eyes.

"I thought this was going to be a lot harder, you have disappointed me," Gitre said. The men tied the cords tightly around their wrists behind their backs and folded their bodies into a front kneeling position and tied their ankles together. The biting of the shadow magic etched at their skin and a new sense of pain hit their minds.

"Maybe the old man will be more of a challenge," Gitre said.

A flicker of panic raced across Valida's face and Gitre clasped her hands together. "You two take them to the dungeons," Gitre said.

She motioned to the two who had tied them up and waved them to hurry. The men heaved Valida and Ceros' paralyzed bodies over their shoulders and hurried toward the castle dungeons.

"Now we wait for the old man," Gitre said.

The Velshari moved back into the shadows and disappeared. Mathieu set the book on the shelf and wrapped his cloak around his body. He rubbed the crystal at the top of his staff and allowed its energy to ease into his frame. The staff held a crystal that was unique to Denasia, the realm of the wyverns and their human keepers. The crystal was the essence of his once devoted wyvern whom he missed terribly, but there was still one more thing he needed to do and wasn't willing to enter his final rest until he completed it.

Mathieu slid his hand along the door and several clicks and pops of latches sounded. The door popped ajar, and he took the handle and pulled the large innately carved door open. He opened it enough to slip out and closed it sliding his hand over the door again and listened for all the clicks and pops of the latches locking. Mathieu took a few steps down the small corridor until he came to the full-sized tapestry which hid the hallway. He pulled the heavily weaved fabric and slipped through. The tapestry slapped snug to the wall and left no ripples of movement to show it had been adjusted. He began his slow descent to the ground level and made his way across the dimly lit lobby.

He yanked the heavy wooden object and stepped over the threshold and made it to the first set of steps. A buzzing energy touched his skin and vibrated is awareness. He stopped and searched the courtyard but didn't see anything. He gripped his staff and tightened his vision. As Denasian, Mathieu had heightened senses like Shaz, and he also was an elemental of lightning. Mathieu pulled the energy into his palm and readied his attack. The crackling of the lightning element tickled his skin, it had been such a long time since he had needed it, and he was reminded of its power. His old frame quickly became vibrant and steady, and he gripped the staff tightly.

Mathieu scoured the shadows of each underhang and eaves of the surrounding buildings until he spotted one of the Velshari. He shoved his hand out as fast as the lightning itself and sent the sizzling flash of energy through the darkening sky. A yelp echoed around the buildings and the body of the Velshari fell from the wall he was standing against.

Mathieu shot a second bolt at another Velshari and his body crumpled to the ground. A rapid burst of moonbeams careened toward him, but Mathieu deflected them with his staff, and they surged into the sky and fizzled out. With a renewed vigor Mathieu took a few steps toward the edge of the courtyard only to be met with another surge of light beams. Mathieu recognized them as the unrelenting pain of the mooncasters and steadied his mind. Now his suspicions were acknowledged. The council had been busy trying to identify the magics the Velshari was trying to create.

Gitre stepped out of the shadows. Her hood covered her face, but Mathieu could see her features under the darkened shadows. He didn't recognize her but the unnatural shine in her eye made him suspicious even more. Gitre held out her hands and another discharge of moonbeam ray shot across the landing. Mathieu crossed his staff in front of his body and the crystal absorbed the magic. A flash of nervousness crossed her emotionless face, and she signaled another attack. A barrage of energized elements ripped through the air creating a divide between the particles.

Mathieu readied himself for the attack and his inner shield encased his outer frame. The energy bolts crackled against the shield and Mathieu stumbled backward. He sucked in a heavy breath and pushed against the forces. He barely pulled in another breath when another surge pummeled his shield. Gitre signaled for her cronies to move up, and they took several steps closer to Mathieu. Mathieu called his lightning forces and aimed at Gitre. The surge crossed the air with such speed a normal person wouldn't have even seen where it came from. Gitre through her arms up and the lightning deflected. Mathieu's glare turned to a perplexed squint.

Another blast of energy hit him, and he felt his own energy fade. Gitre moved closer and closer and Mathieu soon realized he was surrounded, and his powers were diminishing. He made a mental shield and focused on securing his knowledge. If he was going to be taken, he wasn't going to give up any of his life's knowledge and especially anything about Shaz. The Velshari's attacks continued at a constant rate and Mathieu sagged as his shield dissipated. He prepared his mind for the pain of the unrelenting and sucked in a deep breath. The beam of light hit him square in the chest, and he fell to his knees.

Mathieu had experienced this pain before and understood how to diminish its effects, however, it still made his body unresponsive to his commands.

Gitre signaled to bind him with the cords and three men hurried up the last set of steps and wrapped the cords around Mathieu's wrists and ankles. Gitre picked up the staff and examined it carefully.

"What does this do?" Gitre asked. Mathieu glared at her small frame and spat at her. She clicked her tongue and shook her head with shame. "Now, now, don't be mad, I only defeated you because you're an old and dying man. If you were young, I bet you would have wiped the floor with our blood. In fact, I can't believe you are still alive. How are you still alive?" Mathieu steadied his gaze and found the woman's mind was drained and empty of any humanity. A pit in his stomach choked the breath in his throat. "No matter, Isot has fixed the scroll and in a few days the Velshari will all be immortal, a feat *you* were unable to accomplish," Gitre said.

Mathieu's pale skin turned ashen and Gitre soaked in the dread which emanated from his frame. Mathieu's heart sank when a figure standing in the shadow stepped into the dim light enough for him to recognize it as Garrison. A flurry of questions ripped through his mind as to why Garrison would be working for the Velshari, and then he remembered catching him going through the books in the room they kept highly classified material in. Mathieu then understood, Garrison was after the mythical portal of the Tooatha De Dannon. Gitre's thick boots against the rough stone brought Mathieu back to what was happening.

"You don't know what you have done. You won't be the kind of immortal you think you will be," Mathieu said.

"So, you can speak even with the unrelenting pain spell," Gitre stated.

Mathieu calmed his mind and his emotions and allowed the pain to race through his body. The secret to defeating pain was to not fight it as pain fed on the fight of emotions within a person. Gitre smiled, a veiled amusement crossed her face. Gitre signaled to the man to take Mathieu, who found the man's dark snappy eyes under his sun-stricken face interestingly alarming. The eerie stare from under the red robe sank into Mathieu's chest.

12-How Did Things Go?

Shaz plopped onto his bed with how tired he was, sleeping for a week wasn't unthinkable. The warmth of the water in the washroom exaggerated the fatigue he was under, and he nearly fell asleep while washing the grime of the Jaduuk from his sore body. He knew he wouldn't get as much sleep as he wanted as he had hoped to have turned in early. He closed the heavy drapes shutting the impending sun from his room. He pulled the covers and slipped into the soft silk sheets. His eyes closed quickly, and he found a deep sleep almost instantly. Serin stirred and woke to the sun hitting her in the face. She squinted and turned over. She closed her eyes tight but remembered Shaz and the others hadn't come back. Serin threw off the covers and her bare feet hit the cool stone. She reached for her tunic and leggings, but they were gone. Instead, she found a pink silk overdress. Serin wrapped the delicately embossed gown around her cotton nightdress and secured the broach under her breasts.

She moved to the dresser and in the mirror, found her hair messed up from the night's sleep which caused her to frown. Serin took the brush the Minca had made her and cleaned the tangles. Serin twisted her hair back into her wavy locks and hurried from the room. The castle was quiet, and the new days' sun shone in the skylights leaving dancing particles in the air. She hesitated momentarily to wonder if she should knock first but remember he could sense her anyway, so she gripped the latch and twisted until the door opened. Serin peeked around the door and found Shaz laying on his bed. The sheets draped over his bare muscular frame and his breathing deep. Her heart sank as she noted all the scars on his skin from each time he had been injured over the last rotation. She was good at healing but still couldn't make the scars disappear, and she was saddened he had to endure so much, and for what. A cause he didn't want to be a part of. She twisted the latch and closed the door quietly.

"Miss Serin, I was instructed to ask you to inspect Bowen's injuries as soon as you woke," the Whispmother sang.

"Oh dear, is he alright, you should have woken me immediately," Serin said.

"Bowen refused to wake you so Master Shaz asked me to have you examine him first thing,"

"Alright take me to him," Serin said.

Serin followed the Whispmother down the corridor to the last bedroom and quietly knocked on the door.

"Bowen, it's Serin,"

"Come in," Bowen said.

Serin pulled the latch and opened the door. She crossed the moderate room over the white fur rug and came to the bed where Bowen was laying on his side.

"The Whispmother told me you needed me,"

"I would move, but I don't think I can," Bowen said.

"You don't have to, I can already tell you are in pain, what happened?"

"I got hit by a Jaduuk."

"That would do something, I'm going to scan for injuries," Serin said.

"I think I broke a rib, maybe a few," Bowen said.

Serin touched his head and closed her eyes. She sent her soft blue magic into his body and waited for the report.

"Yes, you have three broken ribs, one has punctured your lung and you have internal bleeding, plus these wounds are becoming infected,"

"Is that all," Bowen said.

Serin understood his need to make a joke, most men did when they felt weak.

"It won't take long, and you'll be as good as new, but I need you to lay flat on your back. I'll try to be as quick as possible,"

Serin boosted his body with a heavy dose of her pain-relieving magic, and Bowen relaxed with the relief. With a flick of her hand, the wind lifted his heavy frame, and she rolled him over. She held her hands over his ribs and wriggled her fingers. Bowen studied her face as she thought deeply about what she needed to do to fix the torn vessels and punctured lungs. He found a stirring of attraction for her and was angry with himself. There was no doubt she and Shaz were devoted to one another, and he was foolish to think otherwise.

Serin slowed her fingers and ran her hands over the broken ribs like she was smoothing out a blanket. Bowen flinched as his body jerked as the bones popped back into place.

"You're all better now," Serin said.

"I can't begin to tell you how remarkable that is," Bowen said.

Serin smiled and pulled the covers up.

"Now that you are mended and pain-free, you should rest, so your mind has a chance to process everything," Serin said.

Serin turned to leave but Bowen grabbed her hand.

"Thank you," Bowen said.

Serin nodded but sensed a romantic awareness stir within him. She wasn't sure what to do, she could tell he had a great deal of respect for Shaz, and he would never do anything to mess it up, but he couldn't deny the new love in his heart.

"Your welcome," she patted his hand and pulled away. "Now rest," Serin said.

She closed the door behind her and moved back down the corridor until she came to Shaz's room. She had no idea when he had returned and wanted to let him sleep as long as he need to, but she wanted to make sure he wasn't injured either. She hesitated at the door while debating whether she should or not.

"Serin?" Shaz asked.

Serin opened the door and peeked in. She crossed the room and sat on the edge of the bed.

"I wasn't sure if I should bother you or not. Did I wake you?"

"Yes, and no, I can always sense you close by, and wanted to see how you were," Shaz said with his eyes still shut.

"How am I ever going to surprise you," Serin asked.

"I guess you're not," Shaz said.

"What a bummer," Serin said.

"How did you sleep?" Shaz asked.

Serin pulled a lock of his blonde hair from his face and tucked it behind his ear.

"Fine, how are you? How did things go?" Serin asked.

"About as good as usual," Shaz said.

"So, you blew something up?" Serin asked.

"Well, I guess not that good, I only caught things on fire," Shaz said.

Serin chuckled.

"So, *almost* as good as usual," Serin said, Shaz chuckled. "How is Riddick?"

"He's fine, did you tend to Bowen?" Shaz asked.

"He's going to be fine, three broken ribs and a punctured lung, no biggy," Serin said.

"Say's you, I couldn't help him like you do," Shaz said.

"So, next time, we all go," Serin said.

"I'm sorry, I guess I didn't think it was going to be a big deal."

"For us, but Bowen has never fought a Jaduuk, he could have been killed," Serin said.

"You're right, I didn't think of that," Shaz sat up and wrapped his arms around her. "I have no idea what I'm doing, and everyone keeps expecting me to," Shaz said.

"That's true, I just hope we're still friends by the end of this," Serin said.

Shaz pulled away, "Why would you think that?" Shaz asked.

"Well, hard things bring out the best and *worst* in people, that's all," Serin said.

"Why, who did what?" Shaz asked.

"Oh, nothing really, Bowen has become a little more interested in me because of my magic abilities, he's still very loyal to you, but I don't think he understands the *magic* gives him the euphoria and not real attraction," Serin said.

"So, that's how you did it, you euphoria-ized me," Shaz said with a grin.

Serin slugged his stomach and he laughed.

"Euphoria-ized is not a word, plus don't you have some planning, plotting, organizing, or some kind of maniacal plan to create?" Serin asked.

Serin pushed him away but not before he snuck a kiss.

"Go back to sleep," Serin said.

She tucked him in and pulled the door closed behind her.

13-You Locked It, So I Opened It

Serin stopped this side of the hall and listened to the voices coming from the landing near the front door.

"She's closer than you think, we are running out of time, we need to know what Shaz knows, can he do it or not?" a man said.

"I'm not at liberty to say," Inelius said.

"If he has the ability, the you must make him do it," the man said, his frustration growing.

"I can't make him do anything," Inelius said.

"Then let me," the man said.

"I think, you don't know who you are talking about," Inelius said.

"We aren't going to be patient for much longer," the man said.

The annoyingly high pitch for a man's voice sounded alarm bells in Serin's head.

"You will have to wait as long as it takes," Inelius said.

"See here old man, the Council won't wait much longer, there is no more time. Do you understand? You either tell him or we will. And if we do, things won't be pleasant," the man said, his voice raised.

"I *know* all the council and I don't think you are here on official council business. What do you think *you* are going to do to the most powerful being on the planet, spank him and make him do your bidding? You are fooling yourself, Shaz has more power in his little finger than all of you combined, and he will do things as he chooses. If you think for one minute you are going to manipulate Shaz into doing your bidding, you have another thing coming," Inelius said.

"And what do you think will happen if Isot figures out the scroll? Do you think the Shadow is going to wait until he *feels up to it?* You better do something and do it now," the man snarled.

The heavy wooden door slammed shut. Serin waited a minute before peeking around the pillar she was hiding behind. Inelius slouched and hobbled over to the round receiving table and caught himself before falling over. Serin hurried down the stairs, her sparkling overdress rippled in the wind as she descended the stairs.

"Inelius, are you alright?" Serin asked.

"Oh, Serin dear, I'm fine, just a bit out of breath this morning," Inelius said.

Serin glowered him square in the face,

"You do understand I know better," Serin said.

Inelius gazed into her eyes and smiled gently.

"You are so much like your mother, Shaz is lucky to have you,"

"So, who was that and are you going to tell me what that was about, or do I have to read your mind," Serin said.

Inelius's brows raised, and he studied her wondering if she could really read minds.

"Oh, alright dear, but first let's go to the Senate room, I need to show you a few things anyway," Inelius said.

He took her arm, and she wrapped hers around his and walked with him down the hall with all the pictures until they reached the round room with the desks placed in a circular pattern. He made his way to the only bookshelf and pulled a leather-bound book the size of his arms outstretched from the center. She took the book from him and was surprised the book wasn't heavy. He motioned to the nearest desk, and she pulled the chair out for him.

"My dear, I am afraid I am supposed to pull the chair out for you, but it would appear maybe my time here isn't going to last much longer," Inelius said.

"Nonsense, you're going to last another hundred rotations at least," Serin said.

"Oh my, I hope not, I dread to think how my body will ache in another hundred rotations," Inelius said. Serin smiled and found he had, in fact, become a bit older in the time they were away. She rested her hand on his arm and sent a soothing coolness to his hip bones, and he smiled. "Now, since you are so persuasive," he opened the book's cover, but this wasn't a book at all. It was a box disguised as a book. Inelius pulled out a torn piece of parchment and handed the delicate page to Serin.

"What is this?" Serin asked.

"This is one of the pages of the Binding of the Crypt scroll. This is but only a part. It was more like a book and not a scroll, however, the rest of the pages lie in the castle at Ebassia. The council didn't know that when they tried to destroy the scroll it backfired because it wasn't complete. I stole this page and the rest of the scroll was infused into the castle of Ebassia."

"You were part of the Council?" Serin asked.

"Not exactly, I was a scribe for the Council and one of your mother's dear friends. She instructed me to take it because she has the same intuitional powers you do, and she understood Gavin Rhill's true intentions were to get the scroll."

"Gavin Rhill was on the Council!" Serin asked.

"Ambrosia was always privy to Gavin's true intentions, and the safest place for your greatest enemy is right where you can keep an eye on them," Inelius said.

"I suppose that makes sense," Serin said.

"She was aware he was going to use the comet to destroy Srinna Vossa where the scroll had been being kept, so when Gavin left, she instructed the council to take the scroll and separate it into as many pieces as possible. The current king of Ebassia offered the castle with the intent he would resurrect the scroll one day for his own purposes. Queen Ambrosia also understood this, so she told me to take this piece from the scroll. I have had it ever since."

"Is this what that man was here for?" Serin asked.

"Not exactly, some believe the original council left a code that will help return the scroll to its original form and think that Shaz might be able to do it. They are desperate to figure it out before Isot does."

"Who is Isot?" Serin asked.

"She was one of the original council members. When the mages tried to secure the scroll in the castle, they didn't know I had a missing page, so the magic took Isot instead. She has been trapped and is part of the castle," Inelius said.

"Are you sure?" Serin asked.

"Yes, and I believe she has succumbed to the temptations of the Shadow," Inelius said.

"Is she dangerous?"

"Yes quite, she has been manipulating the Kingdom for so long, it would be impossible to restore Ebassia with her still there. But Isot can't be killed as long as the scroll is infused into the castle. The scroll must be removed first, and then she can be destroyed," Inelius said.

"The Ukari are correct then," Serin said.

"You have met the Ukari?" Inelius asked.

"Yes, at Barrick's."

"It is even more dire Shaz get to the council and use their help to remove the scroll from the castle and re-form the book and then destroy it," Inelius said.

"But why destroy everything, some say destroying is the best and others say not to," Serin asked.

Inelius's interest peeked.

"You bring up a valid point. One would need to be good enough so no harm would come to them by combining the forces. I think fear drives others to want to destroy them, the fear is, no one will have enough good in them to harness the evil the artifacts bring," Inelius said.

"What do you mean evil they bring?" Serin asked.

"A delicate balance of good and evil is required so to be equal in forces. The Sev-Rin-Ac-Lavah offers both an enormous amount of good *and* evil. One would have to have both, shadow magic and magic of light to harness all the power. This is the thing Gavin Rhill doesn't understand, if he or anyone for that matter, were to try they would only bring chaos and wickedness to the life on this planet."

"But Shaz has enough, light magic and shadow magic," Serin half-asked-half-stated.

"I am not sure, I have never been asked that, however, I doubt anyone will let him try. Fear is too much of a driving force, that or greed."

"Alright, then why have some offered he could join them rather than destroy them?" Serin asked.

"Perhaps they are more hopeful," Inelius said. Serin stared at the page and found the images and symbols to be perplexing. "This belongs to you now, your mother would have wanted you to have it, but you must never give it to anyone, not even Shaz, until you have the rest of the scroll."

"But I thought you said-"

"That way the shadow can't sneak the articles from him," Inelius said,

"How would he?"

"He would use you against him, of course,"

"Shaz said something like that too," Serin said.

"That is what the shadow does, it will stop at nothing to convince Shaz to give him what he wants, which is also why some in the council are so against your being synergized to him. They fear that will give the shadow more leverage against Shaz. It is already a serious task he is to complete without having you to cause a distraction. In fact, others suggest you will have to be the final offering."

"The what?!" Serin asked.

Inelius closed his eyes and rested his head against the tall chair. Serin watched him for a few minutes and wondered if he had fallen asleep.

"Oh dear, did I fall asleep? I'm sorry I do that every now and again," Inelius said.

"You were talking about the final offering," Serin said.

"Oh yes,"

Inelius pointed to a book on the shelf and motioned for her to retrieve it. Serin pointed to a few until he nodded, and she pulled out the book and wiped off the dust. Inelius indicated which page to turn to and Serin returned to her chair and read the proceedings of the destruction of the Sev-Rin-Ac-Lavah. She rested the book in her lap and closed her eyes.

"All this said was a sacrifice of ultimate desire would be required, nothing says another being is required," Serin said.

"This is true, but what else would be the ultimate sacrifice?" Inelius asked.

Serin closed the book and returned it to the shelf.

"Why isn't this book in the library?" Serin asked.

"These are the books which are the most important, they have information regarding everything we understand about the Sev-Rin-Ac-Lavah."

"What did that man mean when he asked what Shaz knows?" Serin asked.

"He wanted information whether Shaz has been taught the ancient language and if can he interpret the scroll."

"They don't know if he can read the ancient language?" Serin asked.

"No, we are not sure much of what Shaz can or can't do. Mathieu hid him and his powers quite well and not just from Gavin. He hid him from anyone he deemed, which included most of the council.

There haven't been war wizards in this world since before any of our time. Besides, just because one is a war wizard doesn't mean they have access to all the powers. One of the traits a war wizard could have is the adaption of power. If they need a certain ability it will come, but they won't always have access to it again. At least that's what we have been told. Which is also why many in the Council are so determined to test Shaz, to find out what he can and can't do. But there is one among them, maybe more, who's loyalties have been in question before, and Shaz must be careful. As Mathieu would say, *Don't show all your cards in the first hand,*" Inelius said.

"How many are on the council? Serin asked.

"There used to be many, however, we have lost contact with several when the realms were cut off, now there are but a few,"

"Are the few left still at odds about Shaz?"

"Most are on the same side,"

"You say most, which means there are some that aren't. I suppose this explains why they wanted Mrs. Bailey to send him to them. Shaz needs to be told about this," Serin said.

"Yes, he does, but not before the time is right. We mustn't give the shadow the chance to steal it from his mind or use you against him. You may tell him about the council but please keep the scroll secret for now," Inelius said.

Serin could understand the need Inelius had to keep this from him and would have to think about how to handle it, at least the part of the scroll. She knew Shaz would be upset, but she was willing to if it meant keeping the shadow from his mind.

"What do you think he should do? Should he go and if he does should he show them everything he can do?" Serin asked.

"I do think so, but he shouldn't show them everything. Mathieu was firm on keeping his talents hidden, and not understanding everything he does, I mimic his sentiments. He had his reason he kept him so hidden,"

"Then why go at all?" Serin asked.

"To keep the forces in motion, the council still needs to do quite a bit and Shaz will need their help when the time comes. There is still much he doesn't know about his past or his future, and they can give him answers," Inelius said.

Inelius rested his head again and Serin patted his arm. His old skin was soft but cool, and she sensed his time was coming to an end here. She sensed the pain of an old frame and sent a soothing dose of magic into his body. He smiled gently with the relief and Serin stood and started to the door. Shaz walked into the room and Serin put her finger on her lips to tell Shaz not to speak. She took Shaz's arm and walked out of the room with him.

"What's going on?" Shaz asked.

"Inelius and I were talking, and he fell asleep," Serin said.

"I *can* tell when you're not telling the whole truth," Shaz said. Serin's brows rose and she studied him. He stopped and crossed his arms over his chest. "But you usually tell me the truth when I ask," Shaz said.

Serin gazed into his eyes and found they had a bit of disappointment, almost anger in them.

"You're right, I'm not telling you the whole truth *yet*, but this isn't what you think," Serin said.

The scowl on Shaz's face deepened and Serin was certain he was about to light something on fire. Shaz started down the hall at a quick pace. Serin hurried to catch up but her shorter legs couldn't keep up. He scaled the stairs and slammed the door to his room. Riddick and the Minca came out of their rooms and peered down the hall in time to find Serin coming at a quick pace. She gripped the handle, but the door was locked. She pounded on the door and stood back and squeezed her hand tightly. The anger in her frame ripped from her body and Serin's calm demeanor shifted to chaotic energy. Riddick and the Minca stood with total amazement. She took a step back and with her full body, she threw her wind against the door. The door shot off the hinges and the lock ripped the frame as shards of wood splinters flew every which way.

Riddick snickered but decided to go back in his room and closed the door and the Minca quickly scurried back into their room and closed their door. Shaz jumped and spun around in time to block several shards from pummeling his head as Serin crossed the thresh hold of his room. The shock on his face almost made Serin laugh, but she kept her lips tightly bent into her own scowl. She folded her arms across her chest and glared at him. Shaz stared at her. He was shocked, impressed, scared, and even more attracted to her.

"Now, would you like to hear the rest of what I have to say or are you going to behave like an idiot?" Serin said. Shaz couldn't help himself and smiled at her intense beauty. Serin was impressed with her locked door opening skills and was finding a bit of pleasure in Shaz's reaction to her, but her body was breathing heavily with frustration.

"Serin," Shaz started.

"You have no right to act this way with me, you didn't let me finish and you most *certainly* better think carefully about what you are about to say," Serin said.

Shaz stepped over the broken door and crossed the room. He pulled her into his arms and gave her a tight squeeze. Serin listened to his heartbeat and couldn't help smiling at his new mixture of emotions.

"You're right, I'm sorry," Shaz said.

Serin wasn't sure what to do, he could already sense her emotions and probably hear her thoughts. Which meant he already knew about the scroll, so she guessed it wouldn't do any good to keep it from him. She couldn't hug him back because her arms were stuck in *his* hug, and she couldn't yell at him either. She decided that was his plan and scowled harder. Shaz chuckled.

"I don't understand you, you're such a derp," Serin managed. Shaz pulled away enough to kiss her. She let him for a brief minute then pushed away. "Schmoozing me isn't going to get you out of this one. What is your problem?" Serin said.

"You're so beautiful when you rip my door to shreds with your wind magic," Shaz said.

"You're deflecting," Serin said.

"No, I'm not answering you yet," Shaz said.

"You are aware I can read you," Serin said.

"If you're so keenly aware, why would you doubt I would keep you safe and that I couldn't handle knowing about the scroll?" Shaz asked.

"I trust that those *are* your intentions, and you believe you would die first. It's the Shadow I don't know about, what is *it* willing to do to you in order for you to give in to it. Maybe I can't handle that, wondering when I'm going to have to watch you die. What if I can't let you do it, what if,"

"Don't go down that road Serin, all the what if's," Shaz said.

"Well, what am I supposed to do?" Serin asked.

"I didn't think about that," Shaz said.

"I'm not trying to make things harder for you, in fact I'm trying to keep *you* safe *and* alive, because believe it or not, I like having you around," Serin said.

Serin found the truth of her words hit her deep in the chest and she stifled the lump forming in her throat. Shaz squeezed her tighter as he internalized her turmoil. He took a deep breath and tried to calm his frustration. He hadn't realized how much of his chaos Serin had to carry and his insecurities flowed to the surface.

"So, what can you tell me about what Inelius told you?" Shaz asked.

"There are several members of the Council that believe, or rather fear, the shadow *can* have a substantial amount of control over you."

"That's comforting. So, I guess no one has any faith in me," Shaz said.

"That's not it, those of us that know you have faith in you. That doesn't take away the fear though. They're clueless as to any of your abilities, and I bet they are totally afraid of your shadow magic. They have no reason to trust you yet, which scares them. I don't know why your Grandfather hid you from them. He must not trust them all, or there is way more at play than we are aware of. Either way, they want to test your abilities for themselves. Which is why the council told Mrs. Bailey to send you, and they want to know if you can read the ancient language, at least that's what the man at the door wanted," Serin said.

"Here at the castle? At my door?" Shaz asked.

Serin pulled away and looked into his eyes. She was surprised that he had a look of worry, almost panic, a sense of being violated.

"Inelius didn't let him in but he was very angry. They believe there was a code of some kind that tells how to reorganize the scroll and want to know if you can read it, I'm sure Inelius can tell you more about it, when he wakes up of course," Serin said.

Shaz nodded and noted the shattered door all around him.

"You made a pretty big mess of my door," Shaz said.

"You locked it, so I opened it," Serin said.

"You can be kind of scary at times," Shaz said.

"You can be kind of difficult at times," Serin said.

"You can both be quite annoying sometimes," Riddick said.

Shaz and Serin turned to find Riddick and the Minca standing in the missing doorway.

"Are you two done doing, whatever you're doing?" Turkill asked.

"Yes, I suppose we are," Shaz said.

"So, who's going to clean this up?" Serin asked.

"I guess I am," the Whispmother sang.

The Whispmother and a group of her soldiers floated down from a ledge at the upper section of the wall near the door.

"Who else are we missing?" Shaz asked. Bowen peeked around the corner over Ladtwig's head and Jagwynn peeked around the other corner of the doorway and Inelius stood at the back of the group. "I guess everyone's account for," Shaz said.

Everyone laughed.

14-I Can Use the Portal and Be Back in No Time

Shaz stood in the center of the portal room. The tall window-like frames circled the round room and Shaz studied the glyphs and pictures in the domed ceiling. He tried to study the languages, three in total, for a better understanding of everything he hadn't learned yet, which was daunting at best. The room reminded him of the Mountain Temple and his new temple, the place where they had defeated Semias. He hadn't named the temple yet but didn't want to have there be any knowledge of what happened, so he sealed the entrances. Shaz didn't think he would understand everything because there was so much information. He did figure out what the symbols for each portal were and where they led to, but he was only aware of three of the places.

Azrack's world, which was called Olorim Realm, meaning the Edge Dominion. The Minca realm was called Eoddetha, being translated as The Miniature Realm. His homeland of Turob was Atamar, or The Island Nations, and the realm of Ebassia was called, Ebassia and was translated to The Trial Territories. He, Serin and the Minca had already learned about the Trial Territories when they were trying to reach the Bairr Tiornecht Mountains in Eoddetha. The whole time was a very unpleasant experience traveling through the desert and being hunted by the Jaduuk. That's when they figured out what the Jaduuk were. He had no interest in finding out what the rest of the trials were but had a sick gnawing in his stomach said he would anyway. He wondered things like, which of the realms would have the giants, and which would have the wyverns.

Hidden in the very center of the castle under the main level left the portal room warm and Shaz wiped the sweat from his forehead. A glint of a shimmer rippled off the black surface of one of the portals. Shaz had been in the portal room for quite a while and this was the fifteenth time the same portal had shimmered. The last time he was in this room, and he had been drawn to a portal shimmering, he and Serin were sucked into and propelled into the realm of Olorim.

The active portal had the name of Yinavion, or The Forged Lands. When Shaz spied the first movements, he checked in the Book of Time Inelius had brought and found this realm was inhabited by the Forrne species. According to the book the Forrne were larger than the average man and resembled deer-like human. Except they were a highly-trained warrior with very little sense of humor and an enormous sense of duty. Shaz couldn't help his curiosity and was drawn to the magic, but he had learned the hard way there was no predicting who was on the other side. In addition, he learned the portal on the other side wasn't always, if ever, readily available to return the same way. He had learned through studying the symbols and books when the disruption of the realms by Queen Ambrosia, Serin's mother, created a shift in the placement of the original portals, so he had no guarantee he would be able to return the same way he entered.

Helios had been able to reaffirm the location of the original portal after Shaz and Serin closed the rift. He wanted to go and check on how the gryphton's were and even though their time shift was so much faster than Ebassia's, and he would only be gone a few short lengths, he needed to stay focused on what was currently at hand. Reminiscing about Azrack and the others reminded him of the orb which hung from a chain around his neck. He never did find out what was so special about this orb that Gavin Rhill caused so much grief with Azrack and his kind for. The gold encased locket had been around his neck ever since he rescued Serin from the witch and received it from the Gryphtons. A tinge of anger surged as he remembered how helpless he was when he was bound in the darkness listening to Serin's screams of pain.

"Don't be upset with yourself, we both learned a lot from those experiences," Serin said touching his arm.

"I can't help it. No matter what I do there is always something I can't control," Shaz said.

"You're not supposed to control everything," Serin said.

"I understand that but that's not how I feel," Shaz said.

"I understand that too," Serin said.

"You might have died, and that was my fault. It started right here in this room," Shaz said.

"No, this started long before we were born, but yes you did touch the portal which sent us there. Is this what you have spent hours in here doing?" Serin asked.

"Not the entire time, but yes, I need to understand how these portals work, so we can secure them *and* use them," Shaz said.

"What does the book tell you?" Serin asked.

"A lot, but I still don't understand everything," Shaz said.

"You still have the orb? Have you learned anything about it yet?" Serin asked.

Shaz shook his head, "I've been trying to find the correct book or scroll or something but so far I haven't found anything," Shaz said.

"I guess the universe doesn't need us to know yet," Serin said.

"There you go again, being all positive and all," Shaz said. Serin smiled and walked across the room to the book and started scanning the symbols, most of which she was able to read. "Is the portal still active?" Serin asked.

"Ummhumm," Shaz said.

"What do you think is going on?" Serin asked.

"I have no idea, but I hope they'll be on our side."

He let go of the orb and shoved his hands in his pockets. His eyes followed a string of glyphs which rounded the circular ceiling and ended at a group of constellations.

"What does it say?" Serin asked.

"It talks about the divinity of the stars and alignments of the planets and their moons." He pointed to a section and said, "this is where we're told about the Comet of Sariandi and how the pull against the planet makes the magic of the Teorran Belt stronger."

"My mother used the comet's power to sink Srinna Vossa."

"And it's supposed to be coming again," Shaz said.

He indicated the figures and pointed to a section on the wall with the time and calendars.

"How long?"

"Within twelve moon cycles. If this calendar applies to this realm, that is," Shaz said.

"So, we have that long to find the Sev-Rin-Ac-Lavah and return the realms to their proper state," Serin said.

"Why do you say that?" Shaz asked.

"Because, if that is what my mother needed to sink the city of Srinna Vossa that is what we will need to bring it back," Serin said.

She closed the cover of the book and found Shaz staring at her. He ran his hands through his smooth wavy hair and sighed.

"There's no way," Shaz said.

"Riddick said he knows where the staff is, and you have the sword already, so all we need to do is find the scroll and cauldron. The scroll won't be hard because it's in the castle at Ebassia, so that leaves figuring out where the cauldron is," Serin said.

"Who told you this?!" Shaz asked.

He crossed the room and stood directly in front of Serin.

"I'm sorry I didn't tell you. I was focused on the other secrets I'm keeping from you, oh wait that was it, Blast!" Serin said.

"What else did Inelius tell you that you don't think I can handle?" Shaz asked.

The pain of hurt in his voice hit her heart and Serin hung her head.

"Inelius told me, when my mother sent the mages of her council to destroy the scroll, she feared they wouldn't follow through, so she had Inelius take a section to hide. So, if Gavin Rhill found it they wouldn't be able to enact the incantation because it wouldn't be complete. Inelius has hidden it here in the castle, and he showed me. But Shaz, the shadow could gain this information from you and use it against you. At least they think so," Serin said.

Shaz lifted her chin, his soft eyes were gentle and calm.

"What do you think?" Shaz asked.

"I think you are amazing, and you are only at the beginning of your powers. This is not what I think you can or can't do, I'm uncertain what the Shadow can or can't do. I wake several times a night, every time you have a nightmare. I sense your beating heart and how much chaos is in you, and I'm helpless," Serin said.

"I didn't know they affected you too," Shaz said.

Serin nodded and bit her lip. Shaz ran his hands through his hair and paced the room. The portal shimmered, and he stopped in front of the thick carved stone frame.

"What are you thinking?" Serin asked.

"Don't tell me where the missing scroll is, at least not yet, but you will need to trust me when I do ask for it," Shaz said. Serin nodded, she wrung her hands together, and she shifted from one foot to the other. "We need to focus on retrieving the rest of the scroll from the castle, and help Bowen reach the Queen. I'm betting this is the only way into the castle," Shaz said.

"Inelius also told me about Isot, the woman said to be living in the lower chambers of the castle. She was infused into the castle when the council infused the scroll there, and she has been manipulating the kingdom since. Inelius said she has succumbed to the Shadow," Serin said.

"So, we need to get to Ebassia castle, infiltrate it, take out Isot, remove the scroll and re-enchant it back to the book, find the amulet and free the Ukari, restore Bowen to the Guard and convince the Queen she wants to be on our side, and keep the Shadow from finding out what we are doing. Did I miss anything?" Shaz said.

"I feel awful about all of this, this isn't what I wanted at all," Serin said,

"No, but you're right, the shadow does torment my dreams and I can't take that risk," Shaz said.

"Maybe Nitida and Amirra could help," Serin said.

"How?" Shaz asked.

"Maybe they can enchant a dream spell with Runemagic for you or something," Serin said.

"That would be nice," Shaz said.

Serin could tell he was getting tired of waking so often. She was too, and the shadow has ramped up its efforts in the last little while.

"I can use the portal and be back in no time if you like?" Serin said.

"Alright, but don't take long, a few days here is only a few hours to them, and I get nervous when your gone," Shaz said.

"I'll go right now," Serin said.

Shaz nodded and opened the book to the page of instructions on how to access Nitida's Mountain Temple through the temple portal, a separate portal reserved for the temples only. He scanned the writings and took her hand and walked her to the intricately carved frame. He spoke the incantation and directed the energy to the Mountain Temple and watched as the black shimmering wall drifted and swayed through the colors and settled on an autumn orange.

Serin stepped toward the opening but Shaz pulled her into him. She reached up and kissed his warm lips. He pulled her in tight and kissed her back. Serin pulled away.

"I'll hurry, but what if they take a long time to enchant the spell, you know how runes work?" Serin asked.

"Send me a message," Shaz said.

Serin nodded and started through the gate.

"Wait, you might need this to return through the portal," Shaz said.

Shaz handed her the medallion from his buckle and wrapped her hand around it. She squeezed his hand tight then slipped into the mist of energy and disappeared.

Shaz sighed heavily and tried to hold back the knot forming in his throat. He didn't expect ever saying 'goodbye' or even 'see you soon' and it was harder than he had thought. He was a war wizard for crying out loud, and most definitely shouldn't be crying, but he loved her and was certain the shadow knew it too.

"You alright mate?" Riddick asked.

Shaz cleared his throat and coughed and turned around. Riddick was standing in the doorway with concern on his face.

"I'm fine," Shaz said.

"Don't worry she'll be alright and so will you," Riddick said.

"Is it that obvious?" Shaz asked.

"Oiy mate, are you serious? You are the worst lovesick pup I have ever seen!" Riddick said.

"No, I'm not," Shaz said.

"Yes, my friend you are, but I won't hold it against you. If I had a woman like her, I might be as bad as you," Riddick said.

"You're not going to let this go, are you?" Shaz asked.

"Nope!" Riddick said.

Shaz rubbed his face and Riddick laughed.

"Come on, let's find something to distract you," Riddick said.

Shaz left the room behind Riddick and closed the door.

****

Serin stepped into the energy and noticed a prickling against her skin. The magic was uncomfortable but wasn't painful. The specks of orange energy dance around her and began to fade as she continued to walk toward the dark opening on the other side of the time barrier. The closer she got to the end of the portal she found the white stone of the Mountain Temple brighten just as Shaz had described and hoped she wouldn't run into a closed portal. She reached the end and checked if she was able to breach the tunnel. Her hand slipped through, and she moved the rest of the way out of the portal.

The white stone shone in the dancing lights that surrounded the room and ceiling. It was like the room she had come from. She studied the room and found two other frames and a few desks. The light flickered, and she moved away from the dancing particles.

"Someone has accessed the portal," Amirra said.

"Who is it?" Nitida asked.

Amirra shrugged.

"I'm afraid to go in there," Amirra said.

Nitida straightened her dress and touched several of the rune rings on her fingers and opened the door. Serin smiled as the little woman pushed the heavy door open.

"Serin!" Amirra screeched.

Amirra ran around the doorway and nearly knocked Nitida over as she raced across the room. Serin embraced her in a tight hug and laughed at her enthusiasm.

"Amirra, how are you doing?" Serin asked.

"I'm wonderful, I'm so excited to see you," the expression of joy quickly turned to panic, "why are you here, what's wrong. I mean I'm glad you are here, and I would hope you would want to come for a visit, but I know you and Shaz too well for that," Amirra said.

"Oh, nothing really, but I do need your help," Serin said.

"What's the matter dear," Nitida asked.

"Well, Shaz,-"

"He's not hurt or lost or-" Amirra started.

"Oh, no, nothing like that, dreams, or rather nightmares are getting quite bad," Serin said.

"Humm, the shadow?" Nitida asked.

Serin nodded.

"Come, let's see what we can do," Nitida said.

Amirra grabbed her hand and hugged her with the other as she led her out of the room after the old woman.

"I can't wait to show you my room and everything I have learned. It has been such an amazing time. How is Riddick? Does he ask about me? Of course, he doesn't, why would he? How are the Minca? What have you been doing? You have to tell me everything!" Amirra said.

Serin laughed and tried to answer but Amirra dragged her into her room and started to show her all of her new things. Nitida smiled and indicated to Serin when Amirra finally took a breath they could meet her in the temple. Serin was pleased at Amirra's enthusiasm, and she had adjusted well to her new role as RuneCaster apprentice. Serin explained what she could to Amirra through her excitement and in between Amirra's enthusiasm.

"Riddick does think about you, but he won't admit it to anyone," Serin said.

Amirra was about to explain the intricate details of the jewelry box she had rune enchanted but shut her mouth quickly. A series of thoughts ran across her face and Serin smiled.

"How, if he doesn't say anything?" Amirra asked.

"Intuition is one of my skills, I can tell a person's true intentions, which often includes bits and pieces of the thoughts they have that led them to their desires, Serin said.

"Oh, so you can read his mind?" Amirra asked.

"No, not exactly, more like impressions, but he does like you a lot and hopes to be with you again soon," Serin said.

Amirra blushed and for the first time since Serin arrived didn't have anything to say.

"You've been happy here and learning a lot?" Serin said.

Amirra smiled, "I have, but I miss being with you and the others and being outside, Nitida says I'm not safe yet to leave the Temple,"

"Why?" Serin asked.

"She said she can sense the Velshari trying to find me, and she wants me to be stronger first. Maybe she's right," Amirra said.

"Hopefully soon, maybe if Nitida gives permission you can come back with me for a few days. It's only a few hours here, but in Ebassia it would be three days," Serin said.

"Oh, that would be wonderful!" Amirra said.

"Come on, let's go check if Nitida has an answer yet," Serin said.

Amirra gripped Serin's hand and pulled her through the door and down several passageways until they found Nitida at the center altar in the temple. Serin gasped as her eyes took in the majestic waterfall at the edge of the spacious cave. The delicate fauna decorated the cave walls and gave a soft green glow to the gray stone. Amirra smiled and led her over the pathway to the gazebo in the center where the altar sat. Nitida pulled the runestones from the velvet pouch and moved them around in her palm and dropped them on to the altar. The hand-carved stones toppled over the other and settled into place. Amirra studied the symbols and peered at Nitida.

"Is that what I think it is?" Amirra asked.

"What do you think it is?" Nitida asked.

"An Empyral casting," Amirra said.

"Yes, that is correct," Nitida said.

"What is an Empyral casting?" Serin asked.

"All nine stones are upright, and none are inverted, but these two are touching and no others. This is only the rarest and most intricate casting possible," Amirra said.

"Oh, what does it say?" Serin said.

"I don't even understand, I am going to have to study this myself," Nitida said.

"How long will it take, I can't be long," Serin said.

"This will take some time, but to enchant Shaz a dream protection charm won't take long, and we will find you when we understand more about this casting," Nitida said.

She and Amirra followed the little woman back over the pathway over the bridge and stream which flowed around the altar from the waterfall.

"Are you in a hurry dear," Nitida asked.

"Well, yes, kind of, Shaz doesn't want me to be gone for too long, and we do need to head out to the castle at Ebassia," Serin said.

"Does Shaz have more angst with you lately?" Nitida asked.

"How do you mean?" Serin asked.

"I'm sensing the feeling he has been a bit moodier and perhaps fearful of your being out of his presence?" Nitida asked.

Serin nodded.

"Should I be worried?" Serin asked.

"No, I don't think so," Nitida said.

"What is it then?" Serin asked.

"Love," Nitida said, "and a lack of sleep, let's focus on that charm for you," Nitida said.

Serin blushed and Amirra smiled.

"Oh, would you be alright if Amirra came back with me for a few days, until we leave for Ebassia?" Serin asked.

Amirra slouched with trepidation. Nitida studied them and nodded. Amirra jumped and clapped her hands surprising both Serin and Nitida.

"Oh, I'm sorry," Amirra said.

"But first you must help me with this, what charm do you want to use Serin?" Nitida asked.

Serin thought about a necklace, but he was already wearing two.

"How about a ring?" Serin asked.

Nitida nodded and after entering a room at the end of the long corridor she rummaged through a wooden box about as tall as she was and had several small drawers from top to bottom.

"Ah, how about this one?" Nitida asked.

She handed the shiny silver ring to Serin who inspected the tiny details. The engravings resembled the swirly lines and marks of her tattoos mixed with the sharp-pointed marks of the ancient language.

"What does it say?" Serin asked.

She handed the ring to Amirra who examined the writing and handed it back with a shrug.

"The words of a poem between lovers," Nitida said.

Serin's thin brow raised, but she could tell she wasn't going to fill her in on the details.

"This will be perfect, let's hope it fits," Serin said.

"I will add that to the casting, so no matter what finger he chooses it will fit," Nitida said.

"How will you do that?" Amirra asked.

Nitida pulled a book from the shelf behind her and skimmed the pages until she reached the one she wanted. She handed the book to Amirra who scanned the glyphs and symbols.

"Oh, very cleaver," Amirra said.

Nitida held out her hand and Serin placed the ring in her wrinkled but soft skin. Amirra gripped Nitida's hand smothering the ring between hers and Nitida's and gripped the other. Nitida started to say the words of the enchantment and Serin stepped back. Amirra joined in when Nitida had finished the whole spell once. Their voices blended together with a delicate balance of high and low pitches as they repeated the words. The sounds grew louder and softer as they chanted. Serin's amazement grew as she began to understand the power of the words. She didn't understand everything they were saying, but she was grateful for their help.

A pale-yellow glow emerged from their joined hands and the ring's temperature began to increase. Amirra winced slightly as the ring heated up but Nitida didn't notice. Several lengths of time passed and their tune like chant died off. The yellow hue fell off their skin, and they opened their eyes. Amirra took the ring and inspected the new details. She pointed to several new symbols now engraved into the ring replacing some old symbols and intertwined with the old ones to form new ones.

"Now what does it say?" Serin asked.

"It says, Softly *sleep my darling rest your mind, your heart, and eyes. Know as you sleep you are protected from the shadow as I will never leave your side. Dream my dearest pleasant dreams, of the way your life you wish to be, in your dreams my darling always find a place for me for I am light. Sleep my darling, and as you do, you will find, that even in your dreams at night, you'll have the peace which our love brings. For you are the truest pleasure of life to me, so while you quietly rest, know by your side I will always be.*" Nitida said.

"It says all that?" Serin asked.

Nitida smiled as she witnessed the red under Serin's cheeks deepen and nodded.

Serin took the ring and placed it on her middle finger for safe-keeping. The metal was still warm, and she sighed as the peaceful effect encompassed her frame.

"Thank you," Serin said.

"I'll fetch my things," Amirra said excitedly.

Serin followed her out of the room and through the corridors. She stopped at the arched windows which showed the night sky and soaked in the beauty of the stars and planets. Shaz had explained to her how the temple mimics the outside so living inside a mountain wouldn't make a person crazy but now witnessing for herself she found it marvelous. She wondered if they ever saw the daylight in the temple as it also was night when Shaz was there. She hadn't realized Amirra had gone on ahead until she returned with a stuffed satchel and her new cloak.

"Purple suits you far better than red," Serin said.

"I think so too, thank you," Amirra said.

"You ready?" Serin asked.

"I sure am, but what am I going to say to Riddick?" Amirra asked.

Amirra's heart began to race and skipped a beat.

"Start with hello?" Nitida said.

The girls laughed, and they made their way to the portal room.

"I didn't learn of this room until the lights started shinning from under the door and the chimes went off," Amirra said.

"Chimes?" Serin asked.

"Uh huh, and they were loud too," Amirra said,

"They're our signal someone is passing through the portal. But they can't open it from the other side, unless they have the access keys," Nitida said.

"Very clever, I will have to share this with Shaz," Serin said.

Serin walked up to the portal and the orange glow illuminated. Amirra gasped but her eyes were huge with excitement. Serin took her hand and walked into the shifting energy.

15-You Think It's Only for the Prisoners

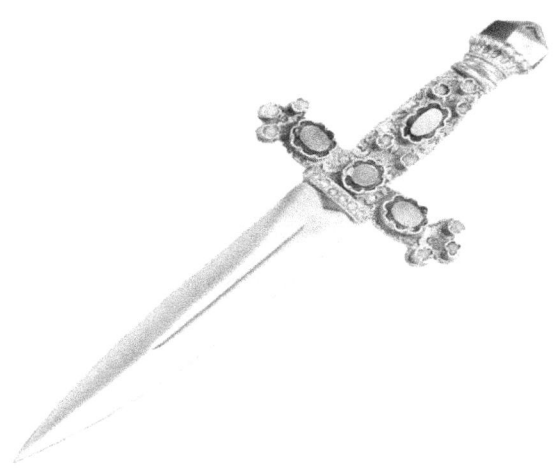

Merrick's head spun and his stomach churned with an uneasy feeling he hadn't had since he was a child, and he couldn't open his eyes or move his body. The darkness wasn't from the night sky but from the magic that was shrouding his eyes and Merrick struggled to make sense of what was happening. His skin tingled as a cold wind caressed his bare chest and his shoulders ached from his hands being secured behind his back. He tried to speak but his mouth was so dry that he couldn't make any noise. He stilled the panic starting to rise in his chest and focused on listening to everything around him.

Merrick could tell he was inside a stone-walled building near an exit because he could hear horses in the distance and the cold wind meant he was still outside or at least uncovered. He figured he was in a courtyard near a large building, the castle perhaps. He studied the sounds and picked out a set of footsteps that were coming toward him at a quick pace. A strong odor of herbs and minerals stung his nose, and he immediately knew who it was. Anger billowed into his core but the magic he was under didn't allow for his body to move.

"Tell the Interrogator that I must know where the wizards keep is before he kills them, that is an order," Garrison said.

"Yes Sir," the guard said.

Merrick's shock mounted in his heart, and he reexamined the last several moons of Garrison's actions. He chided himself for not seeing it sooner and wanted to rip the bands off and tear his limbs to shreds, but the bonds that wrapped around his whole body were enchanted with a powerful magic Merrick hadn't encountered. He started to move, and he could tell he was on a cart being pulled by several men. The movement was bumpy, and he figured he was moving over rough cobblestone. A stifling weight sat on his chest, and he found it harder to breathe the further they traveled. A darkness settled on his mind, and he could no longer hear or feel anything.

The small flickering flame danced eagerly in the lantern on the wall across from the cold iron gate sending barely enough light to leave shadows on his face. Merrick lifted his head as the throbbing gripped the back of his skull and forced his eyes to blink. The soft squishy tissue around his eyes didn't allow him to close them completely, and he licked his dry and parched lips. The metallic sting of blood painted a picture in his mind and his heart sank. Merrick shifted his weight but was unable to move more than a few tiny lengths. His mind wrapped around the pain throughout his body, and he identified the shackles at his wrists and ankles and the leather strapping around his waist and chest.

He shoved back the thick pit in his stomach that had risen to his throat and pulled in a slow and steady breath. His lungs stung with the putrid air and he gagged. He wasn't sure exactly where he was, but he had a good idea and perhaps the others wouldn't be far. He eased his eyes shut and opened his mind to the reach out to see if he could find Mathieu. Merrick didn't have mind conference, but Mathieu did, and if he were close enough, he would be trying to find him. A wave a relief flooded his frame as Mathieu's voice caressed his internal ears.

'Are you alright?' Mathieu asked.

'Aye, but beaten badly and chained, you?' Merrick said.

'Yes, me too, did you tell them anything?' Mathieu asked.

'I have no idea, this is the first time that I have been conscious since the attack, I might have,' Merrick admitted.

Merrick felt the tingle of Mathieu's magic climb through his memories, and he breathed slowly.

'No, you didn't,' Mathieu said.

'The ladies, are they here?' Merrick asked.

'I have only sensed Patriza, but she is in bad shape, I fear Valida is no longer with us,' Mathieu said.

'How did they overpower us?' Merrick asked.

'Magic,' Mathieu said.

'I didn't think they had magic,' Merrick said.

'I am not positive, but I think they have found an ancient ritual which forces the elemental powers to be infused by blood into their victims,' Mathieu said.

'I wonder how many corpses' they need for those rituals,' Merrick said.

'Where are you, what can you see?' Mathieu asked.

Merrick slowly opened his eyes and the sting of hot air hit his pupils, and he shut them. Tears ran around his eyelids and escaped the corner when he opened them again. He blinked carefully a few times and focused on as much detail as possible.

'Not much, it's quite dark and there's only one small lantern on the wall across from my cell. I can make out a blanket on the ground underneath me and an empty pail near the door. The walls are carved stone and it stinks like the dead,' Merrick said.

'We are near to each other then,' Mathieu said.

'There's heavy breathing and soft whimpers,' Merrick said.

'Patriza and the guard,' Mathieu said.

'What did they do to her?' Merrick asked.

'What do they usually do to women,' Mathieu said.

Merrick's blood began to heat up and his fists tightened against the shackles.

'*I'm gonna kill them,*' Merrick said.

'*Before you do, let's get out of these shackles,*' Mathieu said.

'*Aye,*' Merrick said.

'*What is your plan,*' Mathieu asked.

'*Rip them to shreds,*' Merrick said.

'*I don't think it will be that easy, they overpowered us once, I don't think they are going to drop their guard,*' Mathieu said.

'*Maybe not the Velshari, but these boneheads are simple guards, they don't have any magic,*' Merrick said.

'*If we are in the dungeons then we aren't getting out anyway,*' Mathieu said.

'*Someone is coming, prepare your mind,*' Merrick said.

The soft tink of slick pointed boots against the stone floor grew as they rounded a corner and moved toward them.

"Wake up you derp," a soft raspy voice said. The small-framed man kicked the guard's chair and the guard jumped to alertness. "You're a waste of flesh," the man said.

"What do you expect, it's nighttime and there is no way anyone is getting out of here anyway, so what's eaten you?" the deep voice of the guard barked.

"Spshhh," the man said.

The man waved his hand at the guard and turned on his heel. Merrick dropped his head and pretended to be asleep. The man motioned to the guard to unlock the gate and the heavy key slid into the lock and the latch opened with a thud. A guard pulled the lock off the iron gates and heaved the door open and stepped out of the way. The man studied the cell and then stepped inside. Merrick cleared his mind and locked it with the mind trick Mathieu had taught he and Shaz. Merrick focused his thoughts on his favorite place as a child and the current surroundings.

The man stopped in front of Merrick and lifted his chin. Merrick slowly opened one eye to find a pinched faced man standing in front of him. Merrick made a quick scan of the man and noted his features. He knew it would take a half-second to snap the man in half, killing him instantly but would only happen if he was unshackled.

"So, you are busy planning your escape," the man said.

The soft raspy nature of his voice irritated Merrick's core, and he shivered.

"No, just how easy it would be to snap you in half like a twig," Merrick said.

The man took a step back but smiled.

"Ah, the mighty Merrick, son of the Rangers of Hammerstead, you probably could and without even raising your heart rate, but you see, you are shackled, and I am not," the man said.

"That won't be the case for too much longer," Merrick said.

"Oh, you Rangers are all alike, so tough, so fierce, so indestructible, but others aren't so lucky," the man said.

The short man turned to the guard and waved for him to open another cell. The guard smiled a partially toothy grin and shoved the key into another lock and unlatched it. He slung the gate open and Merrick internalized Patriza's cries. He gritted his teeth and tightened his fists.

"Take her to the interrogation room," the man said.

"My pleasure," the guard said.

"No, no, please, I can't take anymore," Patriza cried.

"I might not be able to torture you with pain and suffering, but I can make you watch me torture her," the man said.

The man turned on his heel and followed the guard as he dragged Patriza from the cell. He stopped at the edge of the wall.

"I can make this all stop if you tell me what I want to know," the man said.

"Which is what?" Merrick asked.

"Where the War Wizard is of course," the man said.

Merrick looked away.

"Suit yourself, but be sure of this, from now on anything that happens to her, is your fault," the man said.

Merrick lowered his head and listened to Patriza's cries as they shoved her down the hall.

"Mathieu are you here?" Merrick asked.

"I am here," Mathieu said.

The wall on the other side of the hallway had small openings in the top and Merrick and Mathieu could hear the scuffling of the guard shoving Patriza into the interrogation room. Merrick tried to close out the screams from his mind as the man did, who knows what to her. His chest heaved with red-hot anger and his blood boiled under his skin. Merrick yanked the chain with one arm, but they didn't budge even the tiniest length. He yanked again and again until his skin was raw and bleeding.

"Merrick there is no way we are getting out of here anytime soon. This heathen feeds off the pain of others, he's not going to stop," Mathieu said.

Merrick yanked one more time so hard the throbbing in his head nearly knocked the breath from his lungs. He panted and coughed and rested his eyes. Several hours past and the guard returned Patriza to her cell. Merrick stirred and peeked out from under the bruised flesh covering part of his eye. He scoped out the guard's build, his gate in which he stood and walked, his mannerisms in holding the keys, cinching his belt, and how he slumped onto the chair. He could tell the man was several pounds overweight, was right-hand dominant, used to be a fighter but hasn't been in a hand-to-hand combat in a very long time. Patriza's soft sobs echoed in his head, and he wanted so badly to rip the man to shreds.

"So, you think you're a man, do you?" Merrick asked.

"Shut it," the guard said.

"You can show a woman such a good time, can't you?" Merrick said.

"I said SHUT IT," the guard said.

"What, you couldn't make it in the ring, so you got shipped off here, wow you're such a stallion you are," Merrick said.

The guard launched himself off his chair and slammed a long hefty shin stick against the iron gate. The clang rang around the corridor and Merrick now understood how large the area was and there were two exits, one on the side they had used earlier and one behind the cells.

"You think you're such a tough guy, a Ranger, well *Ranger*, who is in there and who is out here," the guard said.

"We both are, you're not free, you're stuck in this blasted place just as I am, the only difference is when the time is right, I will be the one to get out of here and you'll die here," Merrick said.

The guard laughed but then faded off. Merrick had nailed it. The guard hadn't realized his situation and was now contemplating his ultimate future.

"Stinks doesn't it, they tell you how glorious serving the kingdom will be and how much they need your expertise, but then they shove you into the dungeons, not even the guards can get out of. You think this is only for the prisoners, but you're a prisoner yourself," Merrick said.

"I said, SHUT IT," the guard growled.

The guard burst into Merrick's cell and slammed his clenched fist into Merrick's jaw. Merrick braced for the hit, but the jarring pain ripped through his being and blood splattered from his broken skin. The guard laughed and slammed his shin stick against the gate as he left the cell and stomped down the second corridor. Merrick counted the seconds it took for the man to reach the next door or hallway and made a mental image of what he interpreted. The man slammed a door which sounded solid but not iron and Merrick guessed it to be made of wood. He listened for another few minutes, but all went silent and all there was, was the pounding of the blood pulsing through his head.

"Patriza dear, are you alright," Mathieu asked.

Merrick heard her soft sniffle.

"I'm going to crack them over my knee as soon as I have a chance Patriza, that I promise," Merrick said.

Patriza sniffled again.

"I know you don't want to, but Patriza, I need you to tell me what they are asking you," Mathieu said.

Several lengths passed and Merrick listened to her breathing even out.

Her voice cracked a few times, and she stifled the tears now about to flood out again. Her skin was so dry and cracked from no food or water she was surprised her eyes still made tears. Patriza's stomach ached from the hunger and her throat was so dry she could hardly speak.

"The Interrogator is very determined to find out where Shaz is, and the wizards keep," Patriza managed slowly.

"The Interrogator, so he's the mysterious and infamous Interrogator," Mathieu said.

"I wonder why he is so determined to find Shaz," Merrick said.

"He said, he had a debt to settle with him. Apparently, Shaz rescued a girl and escaped the dungeons, and if it ever got out the Interrogator would lose his perfect record," Patriza said.

"Escaped the dungeons?" Mathieu half-asked-half-stated.

"How?" Merrick asked.

"I don't know," Patriza said.

"His shadow magic," Mathieu said.

"That would make sense," Merrick said.

"I guess it would come in handy about now," Patriza said.

"What's that?" Merrick asked.

"Shadow magic," Patriza said.

"Why does he want to know about the wizard's keep?" Mathieu asked.

"Garrison, he was the one that made this all happen," Merrick said.

"Garrison? Why?" Mathieu asked.

"He's after the mythical portal of the Tooatha De Dannon," Merrick said.

"Only a war wizard can open the keep," Mathieu said.

"That would be good motivation to find Shaz then, wouldn't it? Does Garrison even know the portal is in there, or what *is* in there?" Merrick asked.

"No one does, it hasn't been accessed in hundreds of rotations, and there is no literature on it either, trust me, I have searched," Mathieu said.

"Is that what you spend all your time doing?" Merrick asked.

"Partially,"

"Why?" Merrick asked.

"It was something Queen Ambrosia wanted before the end of the realms," Mathieu said.

"For what?" Merrick asked.

"She never said, but that is why I have continued to search, maybe if I found out I could know what she wanted it for," Mathieu said.

"So, what does Garrison want with the portal?" Merrick asked.

"The only thing Ambrosia said was that Gavin Rhill was searching for it," Mathieu said.

****

Isot waited until the soldiers finished their nightly sweep of the castle's corridors and pulled on her night robe. Isot peeked through her door and watched the nightman blow out the last lantern at the end of the corridor and waited for his footsteps to fade away. She slipped through the door and closed it quietly and made her way down the dark hallway. She had traveled this passageway in the dark so many times she could almost see where she was going. The hall ended, and she turned left which took her to another hallway no one ever used. The hall dead-ended with a large tapestry that hung from the very top to the bottom and held snug against the wall. Isot picked at a torn fiber at one edge and the tapestry eased off the wall and flowed gently with a small ripple that came from the top.

Isot pulled the side of the drapery and felt for the latch that was hidden behind it. She found the cold iron and gripped it tightly and with a heavy twist, the door that looked like the wall popped open. A gasp of musky stale air emanated the hall and Isot pushed the door open. She closed the door behind her and listened for the sound the tapestry made as it sucked back onto the wall. Isot reached for a sconce on the wall just above her head and found the flick stick. She struck it on the stone wall and a spark leaped from the strike illuminating the oil-soaked torch sitting next to it. She took the torch off the wall and struck the flick stick again and the torch caught on fire. The flame was warm as it bathed her face, and she warmed her cold fingers over the flame for a moment and started down the hallway.

The old passageway didn't have a stone floor like the rest of the castle did and instead was soft dirt mingled with old debris Isot assumed was from the remains of an ancient attack of some kind. The old and very dry skeleton halfway down was the solid indicator of the truth, and she often found herself imagining all the scenarios as to its demise. Isot rounded a corner which always made her stomach turn because the floor shifted and started to descend in a steep enough decline that Isot had to focus on standing back to steady herself. The decline wasn't too long before it leveled out again and Isot gripped the torch. She pulled her night robe tightly around her neck as the coldness of the underground passageway seeped into her bones. It was the only thing she didn't like about having her secret lair not inside the castle, well, not inside the known part of the castle.

She passed a few hallways she had already explored which led to nowhere and reached her door. She tapped on the knob three times and whispered her passphrase and the latch lifted. She twisted the knob and entered her sizable lair. The light of the torch illuminated the lantern on the wall closest to the door, and she opened the flap and lit the wick inside and proceed around the room. She crossed the room and lit the log in the fireplace and set the torch in the cradle near the door.

Isot pulled out a small tightly rolled parchment and unrolled it and secured to the stand. Isot ran her finger over the text and muttered the instructions to herself. She took a pitcher of water from the mantle on the fireplace and filled the cauldron that was hanging over the fire and returned the pitcher. She picked a stem of a dried herb and crushed it into her hand and sprinkled it over the water. Isot moved to a medium-sized wood box with gold and brass fittings on the corners and edges and opened a thin drawer from under the surface and pulled out a short fat iron key. Isot slid the key into the lock and twisted. The lid of the box cracked open and Isot lifted it carefully. The lid was hinged to the back of the box, and she secured the metal stand that held it open.

Isot reached inside the box and pulled out a silver dagger. The hilt and blade were crafted as one whole piece, but the hilt and pommel were heavily encrusted with gems and jewels which glinted and reflected the light. She moved the blade in her hands a few times and remembered the first time she ever saw the dagger. She was a new junior officer of the Council and was given to her as a welcome gift from her mentor and first love, Reinholt. The fond memory of his beautiful face shifted to anger and loathing because when she had reached her next advancement and it was not considered inappropriate to seek his company, he turned her down for another woman.

She gripped the hilt and felt the justification that she had chosen the blade as her ritual blade and it was now going to be used to take back what she had lost and more. Isot set the blade on the table and pulled a ruby necklace out and rubbed her thumb on the smooth surface. She set it next to the blade and pulled out a black candle and two small silver dishes. She sat a glass jar of pure salt next to the blade and removed a cloth wrapped in string and pulled the string to loosen the knot. The flap opened to reveal an intricately carved statue and she removed a black velvet cloth from the box. She placed it next to the knife and scooted the box to the back edge of the table.

Isot checked the water to see how warm it was and unhooked her night robe. It fell to the floor, and she unlaced her silk night-dress and let it fall to the floor. Her body shivered as the heat left her, and she dipped a cloth into the water and began to wash. She spoke the cleansing ritual into the silence and the disruption almost startled her. She dipped the cloth several times and when she was finished, she pulled up the silk night-dress and laced it back up and pulled on her robe. The warmth wrapped her skin and she relaxed.

Isot returned to the table and took the black candle and held the wick over the torch. The flame took hold, and she returned it to the table but set it on one of the dishes. She arranged the black cloth on the table and the other implements in a pattern around it. She closed her eyes and sucked in a deep breath. She visualized herself making contact with the energy of the magic around her. The darkness started to fuse into her body and her eyes glazed over. Her words continued but she spoke without emotion or inflection. She imagined the black energy transition to green and become a fluid motion which wrapped around her frame. The force lifted her slightly gray hair and rustled it as it moved around.

The shifting energy tendrils sank into her being and started to grow into the ground from her feet and sink deep into the earth's core. The force the shadows gave her rooted her body to the ground, and she couldn't move. She watched on the backs of her eyelids the magic climb her legs and around her torso and wrap around her bust and neck. She gasped when the coldness the magic gave closed in on her neck and her adrenaline surged. Isot opened her eyes and picked up the dagger and ran it through the flame of the candle. The steel warmed a little and she rested it back on the black velvet. She repeated the process for the statue and the ruby and secured the ruby onto her neck.

Isot picked up the jar of salt and poured a small pile onto the second dish and then picked up a pinch and drizzled it over the flame. The flame flickered and sizzled as it consumed the gritty substance letting off tiny sparks of combustion.

Isot poured the rest of the salt into a circle around the dagger and statue and picked up the dagger. She arranged the salt into a pattern so that it touched everything on the cloth and gripped the blade in her hand. She opened her palm and drug the sharpness across her skin and grimaced. She cleaned the blood from the blade by running it through the flame and then set it down. Isot pinched some salt and sprinkled it on the open skin. Isot hissed at the sting it made and squeezed her hand tightly.

The black magic surged from around her body and consumed the salty blood and formed a scab-like scar. The black line sank into her skin and turned a bright red and then a soft pink. Isot sighed and blew out the candle.

16-Your Welcome, Now Scoot Over

The room was dark when Serin and Amirra stepped through the other side of the portal. Serin had no idea what time of day or night she would return and if Shaz would be waiting or not, so she wasn't surprised when he wasn't there. Serin took Amirra's hand and took a few steps into the room and the lights lit to a dim shine.

"Looks like nighttime here, are you even tired?" Serin turned to the brightest eyes ever, "I'll take that as a no, are you hungry?" Serin asked.

Amirra nodded, so they decided they would go to the kitchen to find something to eat. The lights in the castle lit as they walked from the portal room and down the passageway and through the front entrance. Amirra took in as many details as possible, but she couldn't hide the excitement on her lips. The kitchen had a long-polished stone counter in the center with cupboards and shelves on both sides that lined the entire length. Serin pulled open a large ice chest in the middle and took out a glass carafe of milk and some cheese and meat.

"Miss Serin, you have returned," sang the Whispmother.

"Yes, and this is Amirra the Runecaster," Serin said.

"Ah, yes, you resemble your mother's delicate features, but she wasn't a Runecaster, she was a Wyvern rider," the Whispmother sang.

Amirra admired her little frame, big eyes, and feather-like dress as she floated above her head. The smile on Amirra's face said it all.

"Is Shaz asleep?" Serin asked.

"Yes," the Whispmother said.

"How much time has passed here?" Serin asked.

"Going on the fourth night," the Whispmother said.

"I was hoping not to be gone that long," Serin said.

"Go to him, he hasn't done well without you, I fear the shadow has begun to poison his heart. I will show Amirra to a room and help her settle in," the Whispmother said.

Serin frowned, she didn't want to cause him so much angst. She nodded and hurried out of the kitchen. She took two steps at a time and nearly ran down the hall to his room. Serin found the door had been repaired and reached for the latch. The door clicked open, and she pushed it out of the way. Shaz's breathing was deep but labored. She hurried to the side of the bed and touched his shoulder.

"Shaz, I'm back," Serin said.

She expected him to sense her presence, but he didn't stir. He'd been like this before, and she was sure he was in the middle of a dream-like interaction with someone. Serin touched the sides of his face and closed her eyes. She imagined her body moving through her magic and into his mind. His magic was swirling around like a storm, and she had a hard time getting her bearings to detect if she was going to be able to access his mind again. She gripped harder and focused on finding him. She stumbled around the wind-like magic for a few minutes until his body came into view, and she picked up her pace. Shaz was still with his hands at his side, his head drooped, and he was suspended in air. At first, the thick cords wrapped around his body were undetectable.

A jarring pain of realization hit her mind, and she screamed. The cords came into view and tightened making his body begin to crumple. Serin ran to his body and tried to loosen the cords, but they were so tight she couldn't budge them. She was barely tall enough to reach the cords in the first place and panic surged through her body. She gripped the air element and thrust all her strength at the cords, but they didn't budge. Serin pulled water from the air and soaked them and blasted them with the wind again. The frozen water only shattered away from the cords.

Tears ran down her cheeks, and she found a cold darkness sink into her chest. She raised herself with the air, so she was face to face with Shaz.

"I need you to fight, the shadow is trying to bind you, but it can't have you. You are mine. Shaz wake up, I need you to wake up," Shaz didn't respond and Serin wiped her tears. She kissed him and his lips were cold. She pulled away and tried to loosen the cords once more. The cords tightened again, and Serin heard the last bit of air escape Shaz's lungs.

"You can't have him!" she screamed.

The darkness was getting so thick she could barely make him out even though she was right in front of him. Her mind surged through every possibility she could think of until a certain understanding sat in front of her mind. *Of course, I am the light,* she thought.

Serin wrapped her arms around Shaz's lifeless body and thought of the brightness of the sun surge from her body. The white light started out small but the more she thought about the sun and the light she loved, the brighter her new magic grew. The cords started to wrinkle but still wouldn't let go. She gripped the cords and focused her light down her arms and into her hands. The cords shriveled up and fell from his body. Serin hurried and breathed her magic into his lungs and filled them with her healing power. Shaz gasped and sucked in the air and coughed as his lungs sprung to life. Serin checked all his vitals with her magic. Shaz blinked several times and when he was able to focus, he found Serin's beautiful green eyes staring intently at him.

"Are you really here?" Shaz asked.

She kissed his lips and all over his face and neck, and she gripped him into an embrace. His cold skin made her shiver, Shaz held her in return and sank into her neck.

"Shaz you need to wake up now," Serin said.

She pulled away from his dream state and waited for him to return from the dream world. Shaz blinked again and found a teary-eyed Serin smiling at him. He sat up and gripped her tightly.

"You're back," Shaz said.

"I am, why didn't you tell me about this?" Serin asked and wiped her eyes, "The shadow nearly took you from me."

"I didn't think it was too bad, I guess this is something I have been dealing with for so long, I didn't know," Shaz said.

"Here, I have something for you," she pulled the ring from her finger and slipped it onto his.

"What's this?" Shaz asked.

"An enchanted ring to help you sleep, and it appears none too soon either," Serin said.

"Thank you," Shaz said.

"Your welcome, now scoot over," Serin said.

Shaz scooted over and Serin climbed under his covers and laid her head on his chest and wrapped her arm around him. Shaz wrapped his arms around her and sank into the soft padding of the bed. Serin listened to his steady heartbeat and scanned his blood pressure and checked for signs of disruption in his lungs.

"Are you doing magic?" Shaz asked.

"Yes, you should know that," Serin said.

"Is that why you climbed in my bed, to keep checking on me?" Shaz asked.

"Yes, now shush, I'm counting your heartbeats," Serin said.

"I'm fine, you're going to make yourself crazy, why don't you tell me how things went with Nitida," Shaz said.

Serin found Shaz laying with his eyes shut but sported a mischievous grin.

"You scared me, more than I can bear," Serin said.

"I am sorry, I'm not even sure what happened exactly?" Shaz said.

"You were dangling from the shadows cords, *lifeless*," Serin said.

Shaz sensed her real turmoil over it.

"Ah, I'm sorry," Shaz said.

"You say that as though you know what I'm talking about," Serin said.

"Yeah, I have that dream most nights," Shaz said.

Serin sat up and stared at him.

"I don't think this is a dream Shaz," Serin said.

"How so?" Shaz asked.

"I had to use real magic to release those bonds from off you and breathe magic into your lungs. You weren't breathing and I couldn't find a heartbeat," Serin said.

"It does seem pretty real," Shaz said.

"I wish you would have told me sooner. we're both so worried about protecting the other we aren't doing a very good job protecting each other," Serin said.

Shaz chuckled.

"Yeah I guess you're right,"

Serin laid her head on his chest and yawned, she closed her eyes and found herself counting his heartbeats again, but this time the endless counting made her drowsy, and she slipped off to sleep.

A flash of lightning illuminated the bedchambers and Serin stirred. Thunder rumbled across the horizon and rattled the glass in the windows. Serin woke to find she was still laying on Shaz's chest. His heartbeat was strong, and his body was now quite warm, warmer than usual. She did a quick scan of his heartfire and found it was burning at a higher rate than usual. She realized that with his heat and hers and the covers she was roasting. Serin tried to lift herself off him as quietly as possible and pulled the covers away to be able to climb off the bed.

"Where are you going?" Shaz asked.

"I can't stay here all night," Serin said.

"Yes, you can, I won't tell," Shaz said.

"Why aren't you asleep?" Serin asked.

"I can't sleep, I'm not sure why," Shaz said.

"But you have the ring now," Serin said.

"Yeah?" Shaz asked.

"You're not in pain, but you're heartfire is burning hot, have you tried the water soothing?" Serin asked.

"Yes, nothing works. Maybe I'm just thinking about too much, so I figured I would work on the plans for when we reach Ebassia, but I didn't want to wake you," Shaz said.

"Well, I need a drink and to check on Amirra, plus this storm won't let me sleep either," Serin said.

Shaz sat up, "Amirra is here? Why can't you sleep through the storm?" Shaz asked.

"She came back with me, but she can only stay for a few days until we are ready to leave for Ebassia. The energy from the moving water and wind keeps me up," Serin said.

"That stinks, but Riddick will be very happy," Shaz said.

"Oh, why is that?" Serin asked.

"Don't tell me you can't tell he misses her too," Shaz said.

"No, I can tell, I just thought maybe I would find some juicy tidbits to gnaw on," Serin said.

"Serin, you sound like Riddick," Shaz said.

Serin laughed and climbed off the tall bed. Shaz followed, and they made their way down the hall where they supposed the Whispmother would have put Amirra and Serin cracked the door open. Serin shook her head and closed the door, and they checked the next room, then the next as they went down the hall.

"Shhh, do you hear that?" Shaz asked.

"Really?" Serin said.

"It was a rhetorical question, it's coming from downstairs, come on," Shaz said.

They hurried down the cascading staircase and rounded the corner to find Riddick, Amirra and the Minca sitting at the table. Amirra was laughing so hard her pale freckled face was bright red and Riddick quickly pulled tiny sticks from his lips and coughed to clear his throat. Ladtwig scurried off the table while gathering his oversized clothes and Turkill tried to wipe the smile off his face and return to his usual hurmpf demeanor.

"What is going on?" Serin asked through a stifled smile of her own.

Amirra tried so hard to stop her uncontrollable laughter and speak, but she just sounded like someone blabbering underwater. Riddick shrugged like he had no idea what was making her laugh so hard which only spawned another stint of blabbering laughter from Amirra. Shaz couldn't help but laugh and Serin too was finding the exchange amusing.

"Come on in, do you want a drink," Riddick said.

"What are you drinking?" Serin asked.

She was positive Shaz didn't have any ale or alcohol in the castle. He was vigilant in never giving the shadow an easy way to overtake him, so that wouldn't be the case.

"Don't worry this is totally safe, no alcohol for me either," Riddick said.

"Riddick was telling me a funny story," Amirra managed through several deep breaths.

"And it's late so everything is far funnier than they really are," Turkill said.

Riddick grabbed two glass mugs from a cupboard and poured a bright orange drink from a pitcher and handed them one. Serin sipped carefully as to ease into the flavor first and to her surprise, it was a very light flavor, but she couldn't place it.

"What is it?" Serin asked.

"Miote, a ceremonial drink made of the miote fruit and sweet ginger from our homeland," Shaz said.

He took several large swallows and gasped after holding his breath nearly through the entire glass.

"Don't drink it all at once, I'll have to grow more miote," Riddick said.

"Oh man, this is amazing, I haven't had this in so long. How did you find the fruit here?" Shaz asked.

Riddick pointed to a medium-sized bush in a pot sitting in the corner.

"I grew one, it grows alright, but it needs more humidity than there is here, I think it needs a little more salt too, but it was the best I could do for now," Riddick said. Serin wriggled her finger and a miniature rain cloud formed over the bush. "Not too much, just enough to add moisture to the air not constant rain," Riddick said.

"Like this?" Serin wriggled her fingers and the rain cloud softened to a mist so fine you could hardly notice.

"Yes, perfect," Riddick said.

Riddick touched a few leaves and a bright orange fruit emerged and filled to a plump form. The oval-shaped fruit hung on the branch and swayed with its own weight. Riddick picked the miote and took it to the counter where he skinned the thick skin and sliced the soft creamy orange meat of the fruit into slices. He handed a piece to each person who ate the fruit. The delicate fruit was so juicy a round of slurps circled the kitchen.

"Wow, this is amazing," Amirra said.

"What is that persistent thudding?" Serin asked.

"Oh, that? It's my rock man," Riddick said.

A small man-made of floating rocks kept running into the wall. Riddick picked it up and turned it around and patted its rock bottom sending the wobbly rock creation in a new direction.

"What else can you do?" Amirra asked.

Riddick smiled big showing his bright white teeth and grabbed the small sticks he had in his mouth earlier. The polished surface of the wood grew in his hand and changed texture back to the roughness of the original bark. When the wood was about the length of a stem a bright blue flower popped open and the leaves unfolded. He handed the flower to Amirra who blushed.

17-That Would Have Been Nice to Have

The rain of the last few days had created a landslide in the ravine they came through on their way to the caste. Riddick and Bowen returned to the castle as the sun crested the tops of the mountain range in the south. They had spent most of the day and into the night growing logs big enough to make a retention wall to push back the fallen soil. Shaz and Serin tried to pull the water from the grassy areas around the castle and redirect the water that was closing in on the castle.

Amirra spent several hours making as many enchantments to help with the crew's future travels. Bowen was able to talk her into enchanting his favorite set of gauntlets with extra speed for hand-to-hand combat and Turkill gave her his dart gun with a very long list of things he wanted to empower it with. She tried her best but only managed a little more than half of his list. Turkill hurmpfed his usual but had a huge smile underneath his scowl.

Ladtwig wanted her to add extra storage to his satchel, so he could pack more food. Amirra consulted some books Shaz had in his library and was able to find the perfect enchantment. Ladtwig tried several times to pack his bag and each time found he could pack more and more things. He was so pleased with packing it full of food the Whispmother had to banish him from the food compartments.

Amirra slumped into the blue velvet high-back chair. She closed her eyes and drifted off to sleep but the rest didn't last long. The heavy thud of the back entrance of the castle echoed through the open ceilings. She hurried down the corridor to find Riddick slam his fist into the table.

"Riddick, what's wrong?" Amirra said.

"Nothing," Riddick said. He rubbed his fist and Amirra stepped back. Fear crept up her expression and Riddick frowned. "I'm sorry, I'm just frustrated," Riddick said with a softer tone.

Amirra wasn't sure what to do, she had never seen Riddick as much as scowl and her heart raced like when Semias would be mad at her. Riddick took a few steps toward her but found it hard to keep from slipping on the slick stone floor. His boots were encased in a thick layer of mud and debris. He took another step and sloshed against the floor and started to laugh. Amirra smiled but kept her distance.

"I guess you're going to have to come to me," Riddick said holding his arms out.

"Are you going to be mad at me?" Amirra asked.

"At you? Goodness no, why would you think that?" Riddick asked. Amirra shrugged, she couldn't think of a reason why he would be, but Semias never had much reason to be mad at her, but he always was. "I'm not Semias, and I want to give you a hug to show you, but I think I am a little stuck to the floor right now," Riddick said gently.

Amirra went to him and he embraced her gently.

"So, what happened?" Amirra asked.

"The rainfall is so heavy I can't make the stupid ground cooperate. The landslides are all over and I can't make them rescind, it's coming toward the castle at a steady pace and I can't figure out what to do," Riddick said.

"Oh, that would be irritating," Amirra said.

"And the fact I'm stuck," Riddick said.

Amirra melted as he flashed her his amazing grin. She smiled in return and pulled the stray cinnamon lock of hair from her face.

"I'm sorry I'm weirded out when people are angry," Amirra said.

"You have every right, after what that nasty insect of a human did to you. I would so kill him again if I could," Riddick said.

"You would?" Amirra asked.

Riddick nodded and Amirra smiled.

"Can you help me out of these boots?" Riddick asked.

Amirra nodded and pulled a chair from the table for him to sit on and started unlacing one boot as he did the other. Heavy gusts of wind hurled rain at the windows sending a loud clatter through the castle.

"I need to talk to Inelius and see if he has a book or something to help me figure out what to do with this soggy earth, where is he?"

"Last I saw him he was in the senate room," Amirra said.

"Aye, thanks," Riddick pulled his soaked feet out his boots and crossed the kitchen floor in no time. Amirra hurried after him, and they rounded the corners until they reached the senate room. Inelius wasn't there, so they continued searching the castle. They found Inelius sleeping in his oversized padded chair in the library.

"Sorry to wake you, but I need help figuring out what to do with all this wet earth," Riddick said.

"Oh yes, Master Riddick, let me see, oh yes, on that shelf over there," Inelius pointed to a shelf across the room. Riddick moved to the books and pointed until Inelius nodded. He pulled out the soft leather-bound notebook and opened the flap. "Perhaps in the middle of the notes," Inelius said.

Riddick turned the pages until he reached the middle and started scanning through the scribbles. Most of it made sense but there were a few markings he had never seen before.

"Ah, here, it says to treat extra wet dirt like a spoiled child. Be stern, restrict its privileges and use excessive force if necessary."

"What does that mean?" Amirra asked.

Riddick shrugged and scanned the next few pages.

"I'll take this in case I need to refer to it again. Where are the Minca?" Riddick asked.

"I know they were out securing the animals and then I think they were in the entertainment room working on their newly enchanted pieces. Turkill's dart gun now has enhanced accuracy and sudden burst and Ladtwig's satchel can hold more stuff, I think he was shoving food into it," Amirra said.

"You did that?" Riddick asked.

Amirra nodded and smiled. The soft glow from her eyes wafted into Riddick's brain, and he found her incredibly attractive. He wanted to kiss her, he wanted to be with her, but she wasn't allowed out of the castle unless she was going back to the Mountain Temple. In fact, she had only one more night at the castle, and he was stuck dealing with the stupid rain. Amirra watched as the thoughts crossed his mind and wondered what they all meant. One thing she was not good at was interpreting other people's body language. Riddick cleared his throat and put the book into his pocket.

"I better get back out there," Riddick said.

"I wish I could help more," Amirra said.

"You know what, I think you can," Riddick said.

"How? Tell me," Amirra said.

"I could use a cloak that doesn't soak in the rain," Riddick said.

He pulled back his long red wet locks. Amirra grabbed his hand and pulled him out of the library toward the wardrobes where the castle had extra clothes and bedding. The room was organized with shelves and hooks. She rummaged through a box and pulled out a rust-colored cloak.

"Here, I think you will like this one," Amirra said.

She reached onto her tiptoes and swung the coat around his broad shoulders. Riddick quickly wrapped his arms around her waist and pulled her tightly to him. Amirra nearly dropped the cloak and started to squirm but found his eyes were soft, warm and the glint was undeniable. She stared not knowing what to do.

"May I?" Riddick asked.

"May you what?" Amirra whispered.

"Kiss you," Riddick said softly.

"Ummm, I don't know what to say," Amirra said.

Her pink cheeks began to heat up and her stomach twisted.

"Say yes?" Riddick asked.

"Alright," Amirra said.

Amirra was tall enough so Riddick didn't have to bend too far. Riddick leaned into her and touched her lips with his. Amirra's heart thudded against her chest, and she sank into his embrace. She closed her eyes and focused on the sensation his lips gave hers. She rested her arms over his shoulders and kissed him back. The energy was warm and moved around their bodies in a fluid motion. Amirra pulled away and gazed into his eyes.

"I don't know what to say," Amirra said.

"Then don't say anything," Riddick said.

He kissed her again.

"What about the rain?" Amirra managed.

"It stinks," Riddick said.

"I mean, don't you need to go help Shaz and Serin?" Amirra asked.

Riddick pulled away and released her back to the floor.

"I suppose," Riddick said.

"I mean, I don't want you to go either, but-" Amirra started.

Riddick smiled.

"So, what is so nifty about this cloak?" Riddick asked. He shifted the heavy wool over his shoulders and slipped his arms into the long sleeves. "Hey, the sleeves are even long enough," Riddick said.

"This cloak has *repel water*, I found it while I was exploring for trinkets to practice on."

"How can you tell?" Riddick asked.

"See, here," Amirra pulled the bottom corner up and showed him the markings the enchantment made in the garment.

"You are so smart," Riddick said.

Amirra turned bright red.

"I'm not sure how well it will work, so you can tell me if it needs more when you return," Amirra said. Riddick nodded and started toward the door. "Oh yeah, I think you will need a pair of these,"

Amirra held up a clean and dry pair of boots. Riddick took the boots and they returned to the entry.

"I'll look for more cloaks to enchant for the others," Amirra said.

He cinched the laces and wrapped the belt of the cloak around his waist. Riddick gripped the latch and was about to open the door when Amirra took his shirt and pulled him toward her. He smiled as she planted a full-sized kiss on his lips.

"Wish me luck," Riddick said.

"Good luck," Amirra said.

The wind pushed against the door and Riddick had to catch it before it hit the wall. He pulled the heavy wooden door shut tightly and hurried through the soggy mud to the stable. He shoved one boot into the stirrup and swung the other over the horse. Riddick gripped the reins and dug his feet into the horse's sides. The horse leaped into a quick gallop and splattered mud and mush all over the castle wall as it ran by. The rain was careening to the ground at such a speed Riddick had a hard time figuring out where he was going. A shiny coating appeared on the cloak as the rain pelted the exterior and rolled off. Riddick's legs were soaked but the rest of him was dry, and he wasn't a bit cold like he would have been.

He made his way toward where Shaz and Serin had been, but they had gone. He maneuvered the horse around several substantial puddles and over a solid stream of water running along the edge of the road. A deafening crack rippled across the sky and the rumble that followed hit his senses. Riddick slowed the horse and stopped in a place with enough ground for him to search. He found Shaz and Serin near where he had left Bowen and jumped on the horse and started out in the same direction.

Shaz, Serin, and Bowen were so wet their clothes stuck to their bodies and made their tasks nearly impossible. Shaz cursed and slung his over cloak from his body. Serin had given up trying to shield them from the rain and was now working on moving the water toward the ditch Shaz and Riddick were making. Riddick pulled up and jumped off the horse. Shaz and Serin peered out from under drenched hair and glared at the shiny exterior of the wool cloak.

"Amirra found it with and enchantment of *repel water*, see nice and dry," Riddick said showing a section of his tunic underneath.

"That would have been nice to have," Bowen scowled.

"She is working on making everyone one," Riddick said.

Riddick picked up the stick he was using before and dragged the now pointed tip along the side of the road. The earth moved at a sloggy pace, but the line he made gradually became a trench. He slipped over the uneven ground several times but was able to make the trench all the way to the once dry riverbed which was now half full. Serin continued to direct the water into the new trench and Bowen and Shaz moved several jumbo tree trunks into place.

The earth *was* as annoying as a spoiled child and Riddick thought about what the notes meant. He slapped his hands together and stomped on the ground with one foot. Shaz and Serin stopped what they were doing and turned to find Riddick pointing his finger at the ground.

"Now, look here, you *are* going to do as I tell you and do it now. Don't make me get mad," Riddick said.

Riddick pulled the calming earth energy from his chest and imagined it spanking the earth like a spoiled child. The earth shook then it leveled out. Riddick put his hands on the logs.

"This is not me asking, I'm telling you to hold back the earth and do it now," Riddick said.

Shaz and Serin smirked at his new approach but when the tree trunk rolled up against the earth and didn't move a single length, they appreciated his new methods. Serin slipped in the mud and landed on her hiney and slammed her fists into the ground. Muddy slop hit her in the face, and she gasped. Shaz turned to her trying to pick herself up.

She was covered in mud and had the worst scowl on her face. He couldn't help feeling guilty again and tried to push out the regret. Serin always got after him when he blamed himself for the mishaps, but he couldn't help it. Riddick helped Shaz secure another robust log against the others.

"You sure told that earth what to do. Do you think it will hold?" Shaz asked pulling on the lashings.

"Aye, and now that we have the water funneling into the river, I think we need to bring up the banks. No telling how long the river will last before it might overflow," Riddick said.

Bowen held out a hand to Serin who was about to slip again. She took his hand long enough to steady herself and waited for Shaz to make his way to them.

"This is insane, I can't believe how much rain this is. I sure hope the storm stops soon, or we won't be able to cross the valley to reach to Ebassia," Serin said.

She pointed to the valley below the castle where the road traveled. The puddles were now one immense body of water.

"Does the castle have a boat?" Riddick asked.

Shaz shrugged, and Bowen wiped water from his face. Shaz and Riddick trudged to the riverbank and Riddick stuck his hands into the mud. Several rocks wriggled to the surface and formed a barrier along the lower parts of the bank. It didn't take long for the rocks to move into place and Riddick noted the rocks responded to his commands better than the dirt did. When they were confident the barrier would hold, they returned to the castle.

The Whispmother made sure to have a banquet of hot food ready when they arrived and Amirra was happy to keep herself busy helping the Whispmother with the cooking. Amirra hummed an upbeat tune she made up when she was a child as she dumped a pile of white roots squared into a boiling pot of water.

The stove was hardly used but Amirra was determined to change that. Nitida had taught her many things, one of which was cooking, and she found a soothing comfort in it. The Whispmother didn't argue, even though she didn't need traditional methods for cooking, as she found a certain comfort in Amirra's presence. Amirra jumped as the door flung open. A gust of wind whipped through the kitchen blowing out the fire under the stove.

Shaz, Serin, Riddick, and Bowen hustled through the doorway and slammed the door shut. Amirra cursed and started to search for the lighter stick. Shaz sent a burst of flame into the fire and trudged through the kitchen. Amirra's surprise turned to sadness when she saw how miserable they were.

Riddick shook his head behind the others backs and Amirra stifled the words about to come out of her mouth.

"Master Shaz, hot water for baths is waiting for you all, and we have warm food for you when you're ready," the Whispmother said.

Shaz nodded and unlaced his boots. Serin searched for a place she could deposit her soaking overclothes. Bowen too, questioned what to do with his things.

"Leave them on a chair, I will tend to them," the Whispmother said.

"Thank you, you are most kind," Serin said.

Bowen nodded and pulled his cloak off. Shaz shoved his boots out of the way and crossed the floor with a heavy foot. The water usually energized Serin, but she was beginning to wonder if too much water drained her with similar effects as running a race. Either way, she was tired and moved carefully over the now sick floor from Shaz's wet socks. Bowen followed and they disappeared into the corridor.

"Well, how did things go?" Amirra asked Riddick.

"I can't complain with this amazing cloak and all, but the others are not so happy," Riddick said.

Riddick slipped off the cloak and hung it on the hook next to the door. His clothes, all except his trousers, were completely dry.

"Wonderful, I copied the enchantment and made a cloak for everyone, but I think I might need to make trousers too," Amirra said her expression gleaming.

Riddick smiled and pulled her into a hug.

"What are you doing?" Riddick asked.

"Cooking!" Amirra said.

"I didn't know you cooked, what are you cooking?" Riddick asked.

"Potatious rombus smooshed," Amirra said.

"I'm totally intrigued by how you can smoosh those, they're hardened roots," Riddick said.

"Yes, but if you boil them, they soften and smoosh really nice, Nitida taught me," Amirra said.

"I'll help," Riddick said.

18-Boy, Is That Thing Ugly

A soft drizzle crossed the countryside in waves as the clouds sat in a holding pattern over the castle and surrounding valley. Lightning shot across the sky sending the ricochet rumbling through the air. Serin stood at the window in the upper level of the castle and watched the now lake grow. The once deep jade green grass of the rolling hills was now completely underwater, and the river was now part of the growing body of water. The hillside behind the castle had been secured and the water obeyed and followed in the trenches they had made.

The lights in the castle were bright which added to the comfortable atmosphere but Serin couldn't help the uneasiness settling into her chest. Shaz walked up behind her and wrapped his arms around her waist, and she rested her head on his chest. Serin was getting used to the soft silk dresses and overdresses the Whispmother kept fresh in her wardrobe. Every time she tried to find her tunic and leggings the Whis-pmother wouldn't be able to recall what happened to them. Serin decided she didn't even have them anymore and wondered if she was going to have to wear a dress to Ebassia.

"I can't believe this rain hasn't stopped in over a week," Serin said.

"Aye, Inelius was just delving into the record books and found the last time the castle had this much water was over two hundred ro-tations ago. Not long before I was born," Shaz said.

"How long did it last?" Serin asked.

"Nearly a full moons time," Shaz said.

"Wow, we could be here for quite a bit longer. Which also means the now lake will continue to rise," Serin said.

"Umhm," Shaz said.

"How much of the land did the storm cover? Do you think this is happening all over?" Serin asked.

"According to the records, the whole region was affected, but no settlements have been here since the End of the Realms. I don't think the storm goes clear out to Barrick and Helen's if that's what you're worried about," Shaz said.

"You know me so well," Serin said.

Shaz kissed the top of her head.

"Well at least Nitida has decided Amirra will be safe here and has let her stay longer, and Riddick has moved the gardens into the lower level of the castle. We should have enough food to last long enough," Serin said.

"She has definitely been a big help with all her runecasting and all," Shaz said.

"And keeping Riddick busy, I mean, helping Riddick in the gar-den," Serin said.

Shaz chuckled,

"I'm happy for them, they're happy," Shaz said.

"Me too," Serin said.

Shaz gave her a gentle squeeze.

"I don't like being in one place this long, but at least we are here together," Shaz said.

"You don't like being in one place or you feel responsible for the trouble happening," Serin asked.

"You know *me* so well," Shaz said.

Serin patted his arm wrapped her arm around his. The rain against the window picked up and the sky darkened. They could hear Bowen and the Minca in a heated game of castle siege in the entertainment room and wondered what the cleanup would be this time.

"I've been thinking," Shaz said.

"A dangerous thing to do," Serin said.

"At least no smoke is billowing from anywhere and you know I *am* capable of heating things up like that," Shaz said.

Serin chuckled.

"Alright, what have you been thinking about," Serin asked.

"I am obsessed with you," Serin smiled, "I understand we are bonded by Synmagic, and maybe I'm an old-fashioned romantic, but I want more, I want to marry you," Shaz said.

A flutter ripped through Serin's stomach and her body tingled. Serin turned around to face him.

"What are you saying?" Serin asked.

"Will you marry me?" Shaz asked.

Serin stared into his blue eyes and was sucked into their mesmerizing power.

"I would like nothing more than you marry you Shaz," Serin said.

Shaz smiled and kissed her. His kiss was strong, powerful and gentle as he released a certain part of his soul he had never explored before. Serin found herself struggling to breathe with the strength of the energy and pulled away. A rippling of the colorful hues of his magic encompassed them, and she understood a whole new level of his powers. Serin couldn't speak, she had no words for what was unfolding. She understood he was capable of great things but now she understood exactly how magnificent he really was. A force that encompassed eons of time, a force that mingled with every nation, realm, and creature. A force that was truly unique.

"Are you alright?" Amirra asked.

Shaz and Serin turned to Riddick, Amirra, the Minca, and Inelius staring at them, and realized they were now floating in the air. Inelius grinned and Shaz sensed his understanding of what had happened. Shaz let go of the magic, and they settled to the floor.

"What just happened?" Riddick asked.

Shaz and Serin shared confused glances.

"Not sure what you mean," Shaz said.

"The whole castle shook. The lights flickered and went out and came back on and when we came to check on you, we find you floating in the air in a mist of colored magic," Riddick said.

"I'm not sure myself," Shaz admitted.

Serin was still processing what she'd witnessed but couldn't explain, so she shrugged. Riddick gave her a squinted *I think you do* but left it alone for now.

"Since everyone is alright, let's make a sweep of the castle and make sure there's no damage from the ground shaking. Where is Bowen?" Riddick asked.

"We will go find him," Turkill said.

They dispersed and left Shaz and Serin standing staring at each other at the window.

"I suppose we should go and help," Serin said.

"Naw, they can manage," Shaz said.

"SHAZ, COME NOW!" Amirra screamed.

The pitch in her voice wreaked havoc throughout his whole body and Shaz darted toward the staircase. He took several stairs at a time and hurled himself around the sturdy banister. Serin gripped her dress and held the long lacy hem up as she hurried down the stairs after him. Shaz wished he had the sword, but he hadn't needed it in weeks and had left it in his room. Now he wished he hadn't. Amirra saw Shaz coming and dashed down the corridor. Shaz began his full-scale assessment of the castle and detected an enormous darkness coming from the portal room. His heart jumped and the hairs on the back of his neck stood out, a sensation he hadn't had in a long time. The pit in his stomach reached a new peak, and he swallowed hard through deep breaths as his body moved at impeccable speed passing Amirra.

He rounded the next corner with so much speed, he leaped onto the wall and took several steps before he was able to level out and once again move to the floor. He found Riddick at the doorway holding his hands out. The burnt orange color of Riddick's magic emanated around is whole body. A deep reverberation of the earth element echoed down the corridor. Serin grabbed the bottom of the dress and tucked it into her silk belt and grabbed the dagger she kept on a thigh strap. Turkill and Ladtwig ran from the adjacent corridor.

"Get my sword!" Shaz yelled.

Ladtwig shoved his foot into the floor and turned his head around which caused his little body to follow. He shot back down the hallway toward the bedchambers. Bowen barreled around the corner behind Serin and raced to the doorway. Shaz lit his hands and lower arms on fire and skidded to a stop next to Riddick. The strain in Riddick's face and the way the veins of his neck nearly popped out was impressive. Shaz peered around the corner and found Inelius also holding a shield of magic. It had never occurred to him Inelius was magical, but why wouldn't he, he was Mathieu's brother.

Shaz scooted past Riddick and with two long strides stopped next to Inelius. Shaz threw up his hands and ignited the shield Inelius was holding into a flaming inferno. The darkness behind the shield shriveled and backed away.

"What happened?" Shaz called.

The rushing of the fire particles made a loud hum and it was hard to make out anyone's voice.

"I do *not* have such information," Inelius said.

The additional energy the fire element gave Inelius's shield allowed Inelius and Riddick to relax some. Serin stood back with Amirra next to her. Turkill rounded the corner with his dart gun in his lips, but he shielded his face from the flames.

"This is shadow magic of some kind," Shaz said.

"I believe it is a Shadow Selket," Inelius said.

"A Selket? The beast the Gryphton's defeated for the orb?" Shaz asked.

A sick sensation ripped through his guts as he remembered he had taken the orb off and left it in his room with the sword. A sudden fear hit his mind the sword could have been taken also. Taken by who or what, how did it breach the castle's defenses? If this was a Shadow Selket, *he* would have been the one to bring it inside the castle. But why would it attack now, and or how could it have gotten out?

"How do you know?" Bowen asked.

"Because it looks like one," Inelius said.

"Which is what?" Shaz asked.

"A shadow of an enormous scorpion with wings and giant pincers and a tail with venom of the most dreadful sort," Inelius said.

"Oh, great something else with pincers," Serin said.

Serin mimicked the pincers with her fingers at her mouth and Shaz smiled. It had become one of her signature expressions, after fighting the Shade Beetle moons ago.

"Yes, but this is a shadow," Inelius said.

"Not anymore," Riddick said.

Riddick pointed to the enormous black scorpion on the other side of the flames.

"We can't let it out of this room," Shaz said.

A clang hit the floor and bounced around the room. Shaz searched for where the noise came from and found it was indeed the orb from the Gryphton's.

"We need that orb," Shaz said.

"Oh, you mean the one underneath the belly of a dark-as-night flying Shadow Scorpion with razor-sharp fangs?" Riddick asked.

"Yeah, that one," Shaz said.

"Shouldn't be too hard," Riddick said.

The flames were dying out and Inelius was sagging under the weight of his shield.

"Take over, Riddick," Shaz said.

Riddick stepped in front of Inelius and rededicated his efforts on his part of the shield. Inelius released his shield and Turkill grabbed his hand and pulled him into the hall. Loud claps rippled around the stone walls as the critter slammed its sharp-pointed legs against the floor. An irritating rattle escaped the scorpion's stinger at the end of its tail as it shook it violently. The scorpion's black glassy eyes reflected the fire and drool dripped from the fangs.

"Boy, is that thing ugly," Serin said.

"Are they usually good-looking?" Amirra asked.

Riddick blurted a ga-fa and Amirra smiled. Serin grimaced but smiled at Amirra's attempt at making a jest.

"How do you suppose we do this?" Riddick asked.

"I'm betting the weakest points will be in between the joints, so if we strike there, we can disarm it," Shaz said.

"Aye," Riddick said.

The scorpion struck the shield and Riddick recoiled from the force. Shaz stepped out around the shield and threw several fireballs in succession. Each ball hit the thick armored plates and oozed all over the surface. The shadow scorpion hissed and skirted to the side. Turkill slid along the wall with his dart gun loaded and sticking out of his clenched teeth. He sucked in a strong breath and shot the dart through the tunnel. The speed the dart was propelled far exceeded his expectations, but what surprised him was the dart gun released three darts one right after the other.

All three darts hit the same location and Turkill smiled an enormous toothy grin. The understanding of the dart gun's new enchantment that made one dart into three overloaded his senses, and he found himself jumping with excitement. Turkill loaded another dart and blew again, this time he moved his head to one side and the three darts sank into the soft crease between the shoulder plate and the neck plates in a precise row. All the scorpion's legs moved in sync as it rotated its body and scooted back toward the wall.

"Close the door, so I can let down this shield," Riddick called.

"No, way! I have to be able to see you in case I need to heal you," Serin said.

"Well, then get in here, but I'm shutting the door," Riddick said.

Serin, Amirra, and Bowen hurried into the room and Bowen gripped the heavy iron latch.

"Wait!" Ladtwig yelled.

Ladtwig hustled through the door and Bowen closed it tight. Shaz took the sword and Ladtwig's little body shuddered under the exhaustion of carrying the heavy sword and so quickly. Riddick let down the shield and started to reach for the earth element. He realized there was little earth elements to gain access to. There were no roots, vines, dirt, or loose rocks, and he wasn't sure if Shaz would appreciate him ripping his castle apart. Then he remembered his little rock man he made and summoned it, plus a few more rocks from the garden to add to the golem's size.

"Ladtwig, I need you to fetch that orb, I'll keep it busy," Shaz said.

Ladtwig nodded and pulled his dagger from his belt. Ladtwig crouched low to the ground and utilized his already small frame which made him a very hard target to hit. He huddled tightly and crept very slowly toward the gold sphere. Ladtwig could see one side of the sphere was trapped under the hind leg of the scorpion. A knock at the door broke through the humming and Riddick opened it letting in the stone golem.

"What are you going to do with that?" Bowen asked.

Riddick smiled and tightened his fists. The small group of rocks which formed the little man's head and body began to spin into a vortex. The vortex grew in strength as Riddick propelled the forces of the minerals. He opened his fists and released the energy from his chest through his arms and into the vortex. Rocks began to escape the vortex and slashed the air. The scorpion screeched as the rocks pummeled its hard-outer shell. A crack echoed as the concentration of the rocks split the armored plate.

Shaz threw another series of fireballs aiming his efforts at the face. The scorpion dipped its head and the fire hit the helmet-like covering instead. Serin studied the insect-like creature and noted several small etchings on the underbelly.

"Amirra, can you see those markings?" Serin asked.

Amirra scooted closer to Serin and tried to search the area Serin indicated.

"They look like runes of some kind. Hang on, I know what that is, it's a script. A series of identifiers of strengths and weaknesses. Sorcerers put them on when they attempted to transfer their magic into another being," Amirra said.

"Do you mean that creature has been fortified with a sorcerers magic?" Serin asked.

"Yes, that's exactly what that means," Amirra said.

"Does it say what kind of powers it has?" Serin asked.

"Umm, give me a second and I'll tell you," Amirra said.

Amirra moved behind Riddick and lowered to the floor.

"What are you doing?" Riddick asked.

The rocks fell to the ground with a clack and began rolling back toward Riddick.

"I need to read those marks on the belly," Amirra said.

"Why?" Riddick asked.

"If you give me a minute, I'll tell you," Amirra said.

Riddick sensed the irritation in her tone and focused on his rock man instead. Shaz sidestepped and crossed Riddick and gripped the Honor Blade in his hand tightly. Shaz parried right up to the scorpion and swung with a downward strike but the physical form evaporated into thin air.

"Where did it go?" Riddick asked.

"I have no idea, but it can't be good," Shaz said.

The lights in the portal room faded and darkness overcame them.

"What's happening?" Turkill asked.

A bitter cold emerged and a rancid mineral odor pelted their minds. Several holes the size and height of three men formed standing upright and scattered the distance. The portal room was gone and replaced with a deserted and dreary wasteland. One of the holes in the distance gleamed and wobbled. The scorpion leaped out of the hole at such speed that most of the crew didn't even see it until it had hit Bowen square in the chest with its stinger. Bowen cried out but hit the ground paralyzed. The scorpion disappeared into another hole. Serin ran to Bowen and searched his frame for the cause. She understood the poison quickly and revered the effects.

"What in the blazes, where are we?" Serin asked.

Amirra brushed her knees and stood tall.

"I can tell you that we are in the Shadow Realm. Well, an extension of it anyway," Amirra said.

"The Shadow Realm?" Riddick asked.

Shaz had recognized it immediately but didn't want to tell anyone.

"Why, what is this thing?" Serin asked.

"This is more than a Shadow Selket, this one has been enhanced with the powers of an ancient Necromancer that had the ability to port himself wherever he wanted," Amirra said.

"How?" Turkill asked.

"That I don't know," Amirra said.

"How do we kill it?" Riddick asked.

"We don't, that is why it was locked in the orb, only another Necromancer has the kind of magic needed to remove the enhancement," Amirra said.

A sudden understanding of the process came into Shaz's mind. He shuddered because the cost would require an innocent life. But why did he all of a sudden have access to this information?

"Well then we need to get it back into that orb," Shaz said.

"And not get stung in the process," Serin said.

The Selket ripped out of another hole and rammed into Riddick knocking him several lengths. Serin shot Riddick with a burst of wind magic rolling him over, so he could land on his feet. Riddick scowled and called his rock golem. The rocks reassembled and formed the little man. Riddick searched for another few rocks to add to him but there was nothing useful. Turkill hurried to where Ladtwig was and began searching for the orb. Bowen eased himself off the ground.

"Shaz, watch out!" Serin cried.

Serin threw her wind at the insect as it reappeared behind Shaz. The shards of wind ripped through the armor and the beast recoiled. It scurried at near lightning speed and was gone into another hole.

"Did you see that? Serin's wind ripped the armor," Riddick said.

"Aye, so it's weak to wind. It withstood my fire attacks so that won't be useful, the rocks did some damage, so Serin, you, I think, are going to be the most powerful against this thing," Shaz said.

"We haven't seen what the blades will do because we can't get close enough, this thing is wicked fast," Bowen said.

"True," Shaz said.

A hole rippled and then another. The scorpion launched from a third hole and took a swing at Turkill and Ladtwig, but they jumped out of the way. The scorpion crawled into another hole.

"We need to figure out when and where this thing is going to come from," Shaz said.

Shaz sidestepped his way over the uneven surface. The ground started to become sticky, and he had a harder time pulling his boots from the ground.

"Be careful, the ground is getting sticky,"

"Great, just great," Turkill grumbled.

Shaz tried to inspect the darkness with his night vision and found a faint image of the scorpion crawling around the outer perimeter on the *other side* of the blackness, but it moved so quickly he had a hard time deciphering where it was going to go next. A hole behind Serin rippled which caught Shaz's eye, and he shoved his foot into the murky bottom surface. His boot, however, didn't release as he expected it to, and his motions were slowed drastically. The scorpion emerged from the black hole behind Serin and sliced her arm with its pincer and leaped into another hole.

Serin cried out and grabbed her arm. Shaz's heartfire surged to a whole new level, and he broke from the sludgy bottom.

"Are you alright?" Shaz asked.

Serin winced but sent a cooling surge of her magic into her arm. The blood ceased and the wound healed almost instantly.

"I'm alright," Serin said.

"I'm sorry, I-" Shaz started.

"Don't do that Shaz, focus on getting out of this stupid place," Serin said.

She smiled gently at him, and he knew she wasn't angry with his failed attempt at keeping her out of harm's way.

"Alright everyone, create your shields, we need to keep from getting hit," Shaz said.

Amirra and Ladtwig closed in next to Riddick who cast his earth magic around them. Turkill hurried to Serin who whipped a hefty gust of wind around them. Shaz and Bowen covered under his force of fire.

19-Let's Not Do That Again, Shall We?

The Shadow Selket lunged from a hole right behind Shaz and Bowen and flung his pincer which sliced Bowen's shoulder blade. Bowen cried out but gripped his long blade and thrust the steel into the scorpion's side. The blade slipped off the armor plating of the beast's outer shell but sank into the softer flesh between the protective plates. The scorpion side scooted and leaped back into a hole on the other side. Serin felt Bowen's pain and released her wind shield and shot him a dose of pain magic. Bowen grimaced and threw her a thumbs up.

"What do we need to do to make this thing shift from its portal mode?" Riddick asked.

"Umm, well if it's unconscious then it wouldn't be able to use the dark magic," Amirra said.

"This is proving a bit hard since we can't even see the blasted thing before it strikes," Riddick said.

Serin pulled her wind magic around her but couldn't make a full rotation before the scorpion lunged from an adjacent hole. She flicked her wind so quickly the gusty surge formed into the razor-sharp edges of hundreds of tiny blades. The wind pelted the beast head-on as the force whipped over the entire surface of the creature. Dark red blood oozed from the surface of the armor and a harrowing squeal escaped the scorpion's tiny mouth and hit the crew with a deafening sharpness. Shaz pulled the force of the combustion energy and rolled the sizzling energy into a ball. He stepped out from his fiery shield and pulled his hands out and slapped them into the force. The magnitude blasted the scorpion back into a hole. The darkness rippled and wobbled and faded. The castle walls emerged, and the Shadow Selket vanished.

"We did it," Ladtwig said.

Everyone dropped their shields and Serin checked Bowen's wound.

"I don't think this is over yet," Shaz said.

Ladtwig scowled.

"Amirra, how does the shadow realm work?" Riddick asked.

"I'm not sure I understand your question," Amirra said.

"How can this creature bring us to the shadow realm?" Riddick asked.

"Oh, I understand. I don't know how it works, but the theory is if the necromancer's magic was that they had access to the portal magic, they can make a portal appear anywhere they want. That was one of the things Gavin Rhill was trying to secure. We used to have meetings all the time with the promise of rewards for anyone who could figure it out," Amirra said.

"You went to Velshari meetings?" Riddick asked.

"Yeah, they were so exciting, a bunch of humorless necromancers milling about the dessert table trying to make jest," Amirra said.

Riddick's brows wriggled from confused to interested and back to not sure if she's telling the truth. The corner of Amirra's lip twitched and Riddick broke into a hearty ga-fa.

"Alright, so if one could make their own portal, what would they be able to do?" Shaz asked.

"I suppose they would be able to port anywhere they want to at any time, without the need for an actual portal," Amirra said.

"Alright, so someone figured it out, and tried to obtain the orb from the Selket in the first place," Serin said.

"They only partially figured it out," Shaz said.

"How so?" Riddick asked.

"So far the only place that we've been ported to is the Shadow Realm," Shaz said.

"Unless because this creature only knows of the Shadow Realm and therefore only takes itself there," Serin said.

"That would make sense, but if a person were to use the magic, they would know of all the realms and therefore could transport there," Shaz said.

"Well, anywhere actually, not just from realm to realm but also within a realm too," Amirra said.

The lights in the portal room began to dim and the darkness covered the corners of the room.

"Get ready, it's coming back," Shaz said.

Shaz half-stepped-half-crouched around the room. He scoured the corners of the room and anywhere there was a clump of darkness. Nothing manifested and the pit in his stomach grew.

"Do you see it?" Turkill asked.

Shaz shook his head.

"I don't see the orb either, where did it go?" Ladtwig said.

Everyone started to search for the orb, but it wasn't in the room.

"Do you think the bug took it into the Shadow Realm?" Ladtwig said.

"Quite possible," Shaz said.

Ladtwig grumbled.

"I guess we need to go back into the Shadow Realm," Riddick said.

"I knew you were going to say that," Bowen said.

A rattle came from the back of the room and the clicks of the sharp feet against the floor grew louder.

"There," Serin said.

A set of red eyes followed by the reddish tint of the black-armored body materialized from the shadows.

"Does that stupid bug look bigger to you?" Riddick asked.

"Aye, it sure does," Shaz said.

"Bigger!" Ladtwig said.

"Great, just great," Turkill said.

The scorpion lowered its head and lunged the spiky stinger over the long body. Shaz ducked and sidestepped the strike. He shoved his foot into the ground and launched himself upward and caught the stinger with his arms. The scorpions tail flailed about and Shaz flew through the air like a rag doll. Serin sent a blast of air after Shaz to cushion him, but the tail slammed him into the floor. Shaz hit the ground hard and pain ripped through his entire body. Serin blasted him with her healing magic, but he couldn't move. Serin hurried across the room and Riddick propelled his rock golem into a vortex. The spinning rocks created a suction and Ladtwig had to hold onto Amirra's leg. Turkill loaded his dart gun and searched for a soft spot to aim for. He spotted the hole in the undercarriage, that he had noticed last time. He filled his lungs and shot the darts and loaded another dart and shot them quickly. The darts stuck into the thicker skin but didn't penetrate as deep.

Serin put her hands on Shaz's body and scanned with her magic. A majority of his bones were broken throughout his body and a surge of panic raced to her chest.

"Hold still," Serin said.

Riddick let go of his vortex and the rocks slammed into the scorpion with a rapid succession. The force scooted the scorpion several lengths but didn't break the armor as before. Bowen had crept behind the scorpion and hoisted his long-blade high above his head. He dropped the weight of the sword and used as much of his own strength to slash the stinger. The blade penetrated the tissue between the armor and blood sprayed him and the wall behind him. The tail crashed to the floor and the insect lurched forward with the sudden release of balance.

Riddick threw out his earth energy force and covered Shaz and Serin as the beast lost balance and fell onto them. Riddick shoved the earth force hard, and the insect fell back onto its hind legs. The bug twisted and swung at Bowen who was trying to move in the slippery ooze. Turkill rammed his bulky but small frame into the front leg and snapped the appendage in half. The scorpion swung back and Turkill leaped into a somersault and rolled out of the way.

Serin sucked in a deep breath and ran her hands over Shaz's chest. Cracks and pops rippled through Shaz's body, and he grimaced. Even with Serin's pain block, he could still feel the irritated tingle of the bones returning to normal. The scraping sensation on his insides made his teeth hurt, and he shuddered. Serin hurried to his arms and legs and back to be sure she didn't miss any.

"Let's not do that again, shall we?" Serin said.

"Yeah, let's not," Shaz said.

He snuck a quick kiss and jumped up and Riddick released his shield over Shaz and Serin. The scorpion pulled back into the shadows and the room went dark.

"Here we go again," Riddick said.

"Ladtwig find the orb," Shaz said.

Ladtwig nodded and scrunched his face as the rotten stink of minerals emanated from the Shadow Realm. The murky daylight of the Shadow Realm casted a set of shadows that danced in the radiating fumes from the uneven ground.

"Stay close, Riddick can you determine where the bugger is?" Shaz asked.

Riddick put his hand on the ground and shivered.

"This is one nasty place," Riddick said.

"I agree," Amirra said.

"I can't tell, I'm not finding anything. Hold on, we are on top of a hive of sorts," Riddick said.

"A hive, but this is an insect," Serin said.

"Alright, more like an anthill then," Riddick said.

"That would make sense, so how do you suppose we access the tunnels then?" Shaz asked.

"No clue, there's a shield of some sort, I can't make the earth move or do anything," Riddick said.

"Shadow magic," Shaz said.

"Yeah, probably," Riddick said.

Ladtwig made his way halfway around the circular realm and couldn't find the orb. He lowered to the ground and peered into the surroundings. A tiny glint reflected the dim light and Turkill started toward the object. A black hole flashed, and the scorpion lunged from the empty space and snapped his large pincer a tiny length above Ladtwig's head. Ladtwig rolled to the side and pulled his blade. He lunged at the scorpion but the fine hairs on the scorpion's leg brushed against Ladtwig's skin and a sharp pain pricked his senses.

The scorpion scurried back into another hole and disappeared. Serin sent a cooling mist to Ladtwig who threw a thumbs up and started after the orb. He found the opened gold ball, but the edge of a gritty green rock had fallen onto it pinning it to the ground. Ladtwig gripped the stone and heaved but the rock singed his flesh, and he hissed and pulled away.

Shaz and Serin grouped with Riddick, Amirra and Bowen, and huddled in a tight circular formation and scanned the black holes.

"The scorpion is using the tunnels underneath to move from hole to hole, if we break up the tunnels, we might be able to isolate the thing into one area," Riddick said.

"Aye," Shaz said.

"But how are you going to do that?" Serin asked.

"Riddick, when I say, close off those tunnels in the center," Shaz said.

"Aye," Riddick said.

Shaz crept to the center of the circular area and brushed the hair from his face. He dropped his inner shield he always kept and allowed the shadow access to his thoughts.

"Shaz NO!" Serin shouted.

Shaz kept his focus on the darkness inside his chest, the dread he experienced made him shiver. The dark ground beneath him began to crawl up his feet and onto his legs. Serin focused on their shared magic and monitored his heartfire and the drain the shadow magic was taking. The ground around Shaz turned a dark brown and then a light brown.

"Now Riddick," Shaz said.

Riddick stomped as hard as possible and slammed his fists into the dirt. A heavy echo ripped through the cave-like realm and then shook the earth. Ladtwig steadied himself and sucked in a deep breath. He heaved his shoulder into the rock and pushed frantically. Turkill barreled into the rock and winced as the sharpness of the stone cut into his shoulder. The rock shifted as the earth moved and Ladtwig gripped the gold orb. He yanked and Turkill shoved again. The orb popped out from under the rock and Ladtwig fell on his hiney. Turkill helped Ladtwig up, and they raced back toward the others. Shaz struggled to let go of the shadow magic and Serin's heart raced.

"Riddick, get him out of there!" Serin shouted.

Riddick turned and lunged at Shaz toppling him to the ground. Shaz shook his head and Riddick rolled to a crouch.

"You alright mate?" Riddick asked.

"Aye,"

"Watch out!" Amirra shouted.

The scorpion crawled out of a hole in the floor and shook the dirt from its battered frame. Serin gritted her teeth and dug her toes into the ground, the anger in her raged through her arms and into a battering of wind shards. Shaz and Riddick leaped out of the way as the torrent ripped over the earth and consumed the scorpion. The creature screeched as the knifes cut through the hardened armor. Serin twisted in a circle as the motion carried her around and launched another full-on assault. Shaz and Riddick crawled out from under her attack and circled back. Amirra began a runecast to strengthen Serin. Shaz hurled several fireballs and Riddick released his vortex of rocks.

Ladtwig and Turkill scurried behind them and set the orb on the ground. The gold ball was half their size and it was hard to carry for too long. Serin's blast of slicing wind pummeled the scorpion and caused blood to ooze from the insect's entire body. Shaz extracted the fire elements' combustion forces and formed the chaotic energy into his hands. The heat gave off a wavy array of energy, and he slammed his hands together. The blast shocked the airwaves and sent the insect flying into a hole. The darkness faded and the castle emerged once again.

"Is everyone alright?" Shaz asked.

Everyone nodded or gave an affirmative. Ladtwig and Turkill rolled the heavy gold orb to Shaz's feet.

"That thing is huge," Bowen said.

"Are you sure that thing will fit in there?" Riddick asked.

"We need to figure out a way to force the Selket back inside," Serin said.

"I'll have to use shadow magic again," Shaz said.

"Shaz, be careful," Serin said.

"I will, as long as we force the scorpion back in before we are sucked back into the Shadow Realm I won't have to use as much magic," Shaz said.

"So, what do you propose?" Riddick asked.

"We need to act fast," Shaz said.

"Do you think it will be bigger again?" Riddick asked.

"And healed again," Serin said.

"Blast, I hate this thing!" Shaz said.

"Shaz, use your bang thing you do and knock the scorpion unconscious first," Riddick said.

"I have to be holding the orb," Shaz said.

"How do you fight a shadow?" Ladtwig asked.

"Well, I sleep with a light on, so, there aren't any shadows in the first place," Amirra said.

Serin thought about Shaz's nightmare and how she made the shadow release him and allowed her light magic to grow from her chest.

"I could use my light magic," Serin said.

"But how would that make it go back in the orb?" Shaz asked.

"You could make a flash-bang bomb," Ladtwig said.

"A what?" Bowen asked.

"A bomb made of a rock with the combustion force and light rays inside, aim the bomb a few lengths in front of the beast, then while it's blind and deaf, Shaz sucks it into the orb. Easy peasy," Ladtwig said.

Everyone looked at the little man with interest, and he shrugged with a 'what' kind of shrug.

"Well, that might work, I suppose," Riddick said.

"I suppose," Shaz said.

Riddick dropped his vortex of rocks and grabbed the largest one. He gripped the edges and broke the rock in half and handed one half to Bowen. Riddick wriggled his fingers and the inside of the rock shook and broke into gravel-sized chunks. He dumped them out and then repeated the process with the other side. Shaz rolled his hands around the atmosphere and the hot wavy energy pulsated into a ball.

"Close your eyes everyone," Serin said.

She pictured the brightness of the sun come from her chest and move down her arms and sit in the palms of her hands. Shaz eased the hot force into one-half rock and Serin pushed the light into the other half.

"What happens if the force reacts and explodes in my hands?" Riddick asked.

"Don't put them together until we find the Selket again," Shaz said.

"I'll shield you with my healing magic," Serin said.

"Alright I'm ready then," Riddick said.

The room began to darken and Shaz picked up the orb.

"Get ready," Shaz said.

"I don't know if I'm going to be able to see where it is," Riddick said.

"I'll tell you when," Shaz said.

Pitch black filled the corners of the room and oozed over the walls. Serin steadied herself and Amirra and the Minca moved toward the door. The Selket's red eyes emerged from the gooey blackness and Shaz carefully moved toward the side of the room.

"Serin, you're going to have to make the Selket move closer to you, so I can squeeze behind it," Shaz said.

"Really?" Serin said.

Serin gripped the air element and threw the blades at the scorpion. The shards careened the darkened air and hit the Selket in the face. The irritating rattle of the new stinger ricocheted off the walls and made everyone cringe.

"You were right, that thing does heal itself," Amirra said.

"Almost there Riddick," Shaz said.

Serin blasted the scorpion again and the critter ducked but the wind still managed to rip across the spine. The rattle shook harder and the noise deepened.

"You better hurry," Riddick said.

"Do it now," Shaz said.

Riddick quickly but gently moved the two halves and fused the rock together. He blinked several times to adjust to the new darkness and searched for the beast. He spotted the red eyes and gently tossed the rock bomb to land a few lengths in front. Amirra, Bowen and the Minca closed their eyes and turned into the stone wall of the castle. Riddick leaped out of the way and Serin turned away from the blast. A deafening boom and a blinding light shattered the darkness. The Selket flew backward and Shaz reached into his chest and called the shadow magic. The rigid energy surged through his core and the orb activated. A grungy orange mist swirled around the orb and with a hand-like energy the orb reached for the scorpion. The scorpion's eyes widened and lunged toward Serin and the others. Riddick thrust his vortex and hit the insect in the face. Serin called her light and directed a solid beam into the critter's eyes.

The scorpion screeched and frantically scraped at the floor as the magic dragged it toward it. The enormous bug gnashed its pincers and lifted its tail to strike Shaz, but the magic began to wrap around the tail and the rest of the body as the force pulled the extra-large insect into the orb. Shaz was sweating heavily and Serin sensed the amount of shadow magic he was using, and a spike of fear ripped through her. The scorpion thrashed about and Serin grabbed Riddick's hand. She pointed to Shaz and focused her energy into Riddick's hand. He focused on his own magic, and they sent a strong surge of combined energy. The added boost allowed Shaz to finally suck the critter into the orb, and he slammed the two halves together and locked the latch. The darkness fell from the room and the normal lights in the castle left a soft glow. Shaz pushed the orb into the tiny ball he had been wearing and gripped it in his hand tightly.

"We did it," Riddick said.

"Is everyone alright?" Serin asked.

"Let's not do that again," Shaz said

20-There Are Actually Seven Elements

Shaz secured the orb onto a new chain and put the chain and orb around his neck. The sense of responsibility doubled now that he fully understood what was inside the orb. He tucked it into his tunic and slipped the fang over his neck, the once tingling hot and cold sensation now barely made an impression. Shaz wrapped the leather straps of the slate which had the inscription of the Sev-Rin-Ac-Lavah around his wrist with the markings facing his skin. He slipped the dream ring onto his small finger and another ring Amirra enchanted which gave him added stamina. He liked the extra source of strength he received, and he now would never take them off. Shaz ran his hands through his hair and stared into his reflection of the mirror on his wardrobe. The overwhelming dread settled in his chest, and he heaved a heavy breath.

"Things will be alright," Serin said.

Serin came up behind him and rested her hand on his arm.

"I wish I could believe that," Shaz said.

"I know, but I do," Serin said.

"We're not even safe in my own castle, which reminds me, I need to make sure no one can even get to the front door," Shaz said.

"So, about that," Serin said. Shaz braced himself. He was certain she was going to give him a lecture on his carelessness. "I have an inkling Bowen may have been the one to let the Selket loose," Serin said.

Shaz turned and studied her gaze.

"What makes you think that?" Shaz asked.

"He was the only one not accounted for when everything started," Serin said.

"But what reason would he have to do that?" Shaz asked.

"That I can't figure out," Serin said.

"Is that what his intentions tell you?" Shaz asked.

"Unfortunately, no, but who else would do this?" Serin asked.

"That *I* can't figure out," Shaz said.

"Do you think someone snuck in and out but didn't make it? I mean why did this happen in the portal room, to begin with?" Serin asked.

"I've been thinking the same thing, but who?" Shaz asked.

Serin handed him the medallion.

"Maybe this will help," Serin said.

Shaz stared at the medallion for a minute and then placed it on his belt.

"How would this help?" Shaz asked.

"I'm not certain it will, but if Gavin Rhill placed a charm on the portals to read the magic imprint of those who travel through them, then maybe your portals do too or maybe the portals have a history log of some kind and you might need this to figure out the details," Serin said.

Shaz smiled and wrapped her into a hug. "Are you sure you're doing alright?" Serin asked.

"Aye, I am," Shaz said.

"I don't believe you," Serin said.

"I know," Shaz said.

"The Shadow is what makes you feel the despair, not your own thoughts," Serin said.

"I know. Come on, let's go find Inelius and see what he can tell us about the imprints," Shaz said.

The rain was still coming down steadily and Amirra was explaining to Inelius about the chimes in the portal room at the Mountain Temple when Shaz and Serin walked in.

"What about the Mountain Temple?" Shaz asked.

"Oh good, you're here. I was just telling Inelius about the chimes we have at the Temple and how they work, well I don't exactly how they work or rather how to install them, but they are very loud and go off when someone is coming through the portal," Amirra said.

"You're quite clever, but how would we go about doing that?" Inelius asked.

"I could ask Nitida for some help if you like?" Amirra said.

"Yes, I think that would be an excellent idea, Master Shaz?" Inelius said.

"Sure, sounds good,"

"Didn't you tell me to, the portal wouldn't open at the temple without a passkey?" Serin asked.

"Yeah, but you came through so you must have one," Amirra said.

"She had the medallion yes," Shaz said.

"Maybe we need to change the passkey into the castle," Riddick said.

"I agree with that for sure," Shaz said.

"How would you go about that?" Serin asked.

"There is a book here somewhere," Inelius said.

"I'll take care of that," Shaz said.

Inelius nodded and Amirra scribbled a bunch of marks onto a paper and sent it through the portal to the Mountain Temple.

"Inelius, do the castle portals have a log of some kind or an imprint detector?" Shaz asked.

"Humm, I am not sure, that was something your father always took care of, and no one has used them since then, but if there is a way to find out, this book would tell you," Inelius pointed to a book on the table.

"Nope, I've already read that cover to cover."

"I'm afraid I don't have an answer for you then?" Inelius said.

"What did you find out about the Shadow Selket?" Shaz asked.

Shaz walked around the room and Serin helped Inelius into a soft chair.

"This is quite ingenious of a cast for sure. We found out the sorcerer that initially performed the ritual was Rhoefeus, who was the greatest of his time. This cast is a millennium old, and some of the marks are of the ancient language so without those I can't complete the cast," Amirra said.

"However, a few books at the Ebassia Castle are known to have this kind of information that might give us some insight," Inelius said.

"What was the intent of this Rhoefeus, why did he do this, you said he was a sorcerer, not a necromancer," Shaz said.

"The legend is, he was trying to make his own portal because the Velshari had made their own. He was supposedly under the direction of the Bairr Tiornecht, but they were unable to complete the transition before a mighty war broke out," Inelius said.

"War with whom?" Shaz asked.

"The Selket. Rhoefeus was using the underground tunnels of the Selket for his experiments and was unaware of the turmoil brewing between the Selket and the Bairr Tiornecht. The legend says a Selket soldier ran into the caverns Rhoefeus was using at the same time he was about to transform his portal spell," Inelius said.

"What happened to the Bairr Tiornecht?" Riddick asked.

Riddick fiddled with the pebbles he was spinning around his fingers.

"Sadly, they were all destroyed," Inelius said.

"Sorry mate," Shaz said.

Riddick nodded and shoved his hands in his pockets.

"Amirra, could you write down the symbols of the ancient language you saw?" Shaz asked.

"Some of them, but I didn't get a good look at all of them, but this book seems to have it all," Amirra said.

Amirra handed him the book and pointed to the section on the page the scribbles had been made. Shaz skimmed over the content and understood what Rhoefeus was trying to do.

"Rhoefeus didn't have the entire incantation," Shaz said.

"Oh, what was he missing?" Serin asked.

"A passkey, but not one linked to these portals. The key to this kind of magic, is the user needs to have an element from all the elements. This shows here he had five elements, Earth, Fire, Water, Air, and Shadow, but there are actually seven elements," Shaz said.

"Seven?" Inelius asked.

"Time and Soul are missing and in order to travel through space and time, one needs to understand how they both work and how they work together. Whoever created the original portals understood and possessed these elements," Shaz said.

"Oh my, that makes perfect sense," Inelius said.

"Who *did* create the portals?" Amirra asked.

"The ancient sages of the Tooatha De Dannon," Inelius said.

"Aye, when the realms were created to organize the creatures sent by the God of Glory to plague the inhabitants of the world," Shaz said.

"That's kinda harsh," Riddick said.

"So, is there any literature on how that was done?" Serin asked.

"Not that I am aware of, the oldest documents are a few millennia old, but this occurred *many* millennia ago," Inelius said.

"How can we be certain that this happened then if nothing is written?" Riddick asked.

"I was wondering the same thing," Amirra said.

Images of the wyverns came into Shaz's mind, and he understood the *wyverns* were the ancient sages of the Tooatha De Dannon, not humans. Sweat crested his brows and the heat around his body swelled. His heart thudded against his ribs and Serin turned to find him running his hands through his hair.

"What's wrong Shaz?" Serin asked.

"I need some air," Shaz said.

Shaz hurried from the room and started down the long corridor.

"Is he alright?" Amirra asked.

Serin nodded and followed him. Shaz reached the back of the castle and opened the heavy wooden door. The cool humid, rainy atmosphere pelted his senses, and he sucked in a deep breath. He walked to the edge of the covered patio and stared blankly into the distance. Serin opened the door and the gust of wind blew her hair. She pulled a cloak off the hook and slipped her arm into the soft fabric as she closed the door behind her.

"The wyverns are the sages of the Tooatha De Dannon," Shaz said.

"I wasn't going to ask, I just want to be here with you," Serin said.

"Why? Do you think I am going to do something stupid?"

"No, but I don't like being alone, so I thought maybe you didn't either, I can leave though if you like," Serin said.

"No, please stay," Shaz said.

Serin slipped her hand into his and gave a squeeze. The chaotic energy inside him was back and Serin's heart sank. They listened to the rain hitting the roof and drizzle off the edges.

"I'm starting to get quite irritated with all this rain," Serin said.

"You, irritated with water?" Shaz asked.

"Yes, I love the water and all, but this is getting out of hand. Why does the rain behave like this, I mean what is it trying to say?" Serin asked.

"Maybe the rain isn't trying to say anything, sometimes things just happen," Shaz said.

"Maybe, but I am getting tired of this nonsense. I've tried to tell the clouds to stop, but they aren't listening to my instructions."

"Maybe they will listen to mine,"

"How so?"

"With this being my castle and all, so maybe it has to come from me," Shaz shrugged.

"That would make sense,"

"I don't have a clue on what to do though,"

"I can help with that,"

Serin put the hood over her head and stepped out into the rain. The cloak she grabbed was Riddick's waterproof one and the rain dripped off. Shaz followed behind her, and she moved out to the edge of the hilltop. The clouds were low and dark, and the rain made such a ruckus on the surface of the water. Serin raised her arms out and up to the clouds. She would normally do a little dance as she focused on the power within her. Shaz moved up behind her and rested his hands on hers. He thought about his magic, the colors were always connected, and he had a hard time sifting through the right one.

"What do I do now?" Shaz asked.

"Just let your energy follow my arms and focus it on the clouds," Serin said.

Shaz allowed his energy to follow her arms and it merged with hers. The forces combined and a bright blue ray of light shot into the clouds. They focused their energy for several lengths and the clouds began to lighten.

"It's working," Serin said.

"Aye,"

They lowered their hands and the blue sky emerged from the murky sky. The rain stopped and the whole sky lightened. Riddick and Amirra came from the doorway onto the patio.

"That was impressive," Riddick said.

"You two make such a good team, you're so in sync, you could do anything," Amirra said.

Shaz wasn't sure what to say and Serin blushed.

"Have you found anything on the portals yet?" Shaz asked.

Riddick shook his head. Shaz let go of Serin's hands, and she smiled at him, and he returned to the castle with Riddick.

"You two really are special," Amirra said.

"How so?" Serin asked.

"I can't explain exactly, but you two have something most of the world would die for," Amirra said.

Serin's brows twitched and her lips scrunched. Amirra chuckled.

"I'm still not sure what you are talking about," Serin said.

"LOVE! Silly girl, real actual love, not the fake love, the kind of love most other people never have," Amirra said.

"How do you know so much about love?" Serin asked.

"I don't know anything about love, in fact, the only thing I truly understand is hate, but that is why I can tell when I see it,"

Serin hugged her tightly.

"I'm so glad we have you now," Serin said.

Amirra hugged her back and smiled.

"I'm still not sure why you think that, but I'll take it," Amirra said.

"Come on, let's go see if we can help the guys," Serin said.

21-You Have Now Come Full Circle in Time

The blue sky darkened as the sun fell behind the mountain range and a soft padding of nightfall encompassed the castle. Now that the rain had stopped, Serin and Amirra busied themselves with gathering equipment and supplies for their travel to Ebassia. They discussed the different items and what enchantments might be useful and Turkill and Ladtwig chimed in. Amirra made each of them rain gear and fortified the satchels to be able to carry more things, which made Ladtwig happy. Turkill and Ladtwig argued, as usual, about how much stuff Ladtwig was allowed to take with him and Jagwynn hissed every time Ladtwig started to pack his satchel with things he didn't need, being they would be riding on her back. Bowen spent time in the stable polishing the saddles and reworking some harnesses. Shaz and Riddick went to the library and started searching for anything they could find on the castle portals.

"This is starting to be very annoying. We have been searching for hours, and we can't find a thing," Riddick said.

"Aye, I guess we just won't find out if anyone came through the portal," Shaz said.

"Maybe we're going about this the wrong way?" Riddick said.

"Perhaps I might be of service," Nitida said.

"Please tell me you have something," Shaz said.

The little silver-haired Minca woman crossed the library and set a very old wooden box on a table.

"What is this?" Shaz asked.

"A box left in the Mountain Temple by the black mage," Nitida said.

Shaz's surprised expression moved to intense intrigue.

"What's inside?" Riddick asked.

"This hasn't been opened since the black mage left it millennia's ago," Nitida said.

"How old are you?" Riddick asked.

Nitida gave him a sideways glare.

"Not that old. No one has had the proper magic," Nitida said.

Riddick blushed as he realized what he had said. Shaz ran his finger along the old copper fittings at the corner of the box. A sharp tickle pricked his senses, and he perceived the ancient magic. A part of his soul related to the energy, and he was sucked into a memory.

Shaz stood in the center of a runecircle. The lines carved in the hardened ground were chiseled with precision, only magic could make those clean lines. The circle was divided with two lines crossed at the center and spanned the entire circle. At each of the four marks was a symbol. The outer edge of the circle was lined with smaller marks and symbols Shaz had never seen. The lines began to glow a dark amber and Shaz searched the room, but he wasn't in a room as he had expected. He wasn't anywhere. There were no trees, mountains, rivers, or buildings. No moons, a sun, or stars. He was surrounded by veins of glowing particles glittering between all the colors. The strands of energy formed a dome-like structure and Shaz's first thought was he was in the Teorran Belt. The energy, magic, life force of the planet Edenocht. Deep thuds echoed over his shoulder and Shaz turned to find the black mage appear.

His strong features stood out under the black robe he wore. Shaz recognized him from his dream as Alisdair, the Black Wyvern. The mage carried the Honor Blade on his hip and Shaz's heart raced. Alisdair crossed the circle being careful not to step on the lines. Shaz looked at his feet to make sure he wasn't standing on any lines but found he was floating in the air. Alisdair stopped right next to Shaz and pulled out a circular disc carved out of metal. Shaz had never seen this kind of metal, and he peered at the engravings. The tablet was clearly marked with the ancient language, but the marks were organized in such a way Shaz didn't understand completely what they said.

The black mage ran his hand over the plate-like disc and began to read the incantation. The swirling energy particles bumped and moved around as the words flowed from the man's lips. Small energy balls formed around the mage and began to grow. Sweat dripped from Alisdair's brow and the spheres separated into colors and shapes. Alisdair's hands shook and his body began to glow. The colors of the magic surging from the mage merged and blended into each sphere and his speech became labored. Shaz wanted to send his own magic to help the man, but he worried if he tried, he would ruin the memory.

The mage turned to Shaz and stared through him. A ricochet of energy coursed through Shaz's body, and he felt the pull of his magic as it left his frame. The mage blinked and then squinted. Shaz stared into the man's deep blue eyes. Shaz had never seen another person with blue eyes and his heart skipped. The understanding of Shaz's presence surprised the mage, and he blinked again. The spheres began to shrink and Shaz peeled his eyes from the man and could now read all the ancient text. The tablet's amber glow faded and Shaz began to read the words still highlighted.

The mage cleared his throat and started reading with Shaz in unison. The spheres popped with brightness and the center opened. Shaz and Alisdair finished the incantation and the mage placed his hand on the tablet. A deep green glow illuminated his skin and the tablet. The heat of the green magic broke the tablet into pieces and the mage put one into each of spheres and ran his hand over each sphere.

The piece disappeared and the spheres closed and faded away. The mage breathed heavily and Shaz had a hard time standing.

The magic of the casting made Shaz's body feel the same as when he was confronted by Drafang in the forest. A soothing blue force encompassed his frame, and he knew it was Serin.

"Who are you?" Alisdair asked.

"I'm Shazmpt, son of Reinholt," Shaz said.

"We shall meet again, Shazmpt son of Reinholt,"

Shaz nodded and the memory ceased. Shaz blinked a few times as the light of the magic realm left his senses.

Shaz had a difficult time standing. His head wobbled, and he couldn't keep his focus on anything.

"Are you alright mate?" Riddick asked.

"Aye,"

Shaz turned and managed to see everyone standing behind him. He wasn't sure how long the memory took to experience, but he understood by all the concerned faces it was more than a memory for him. Shaz ran his hands through his sweaty hair. His strength was fading, and he was sure he wasn't going to last too much longer. He turned to the box and ran his finger over the latch. The latch clicked with a snap and a puff of air escaped the seams. Everyone took a step back and Shaz lifted the lid. Shaz reached into the heavy energy and pulled out the tablet, the same tablet Alisdair and he read from, to create the realms. He rolled the smooth metal around in his hand and noticed the broken lines.

"What is that?" Riddick asked.

Serin touched his arm and Shaz found her gaze one of caution. Shaz was certain she had also witnessed it, when she buffed him with her cooling magic and understood her warning meant someone in the group was not capable of handling the information.

"An ancient inscription of the beginning of the portals," Shaz said.

"What does it say?" Bowen asked.

"Our language has no words to be translated into," Shaz said.

"May I be of any help?" Nitida asked.

"I don't think so. Where did you say this box was?" Shaz asked.

"In the Temple, in a room I wasn't aware existed until the doorway started to glow when I returned to search the temple library," Nitida said.

"Was anything else in the room?" Shaz asked.

"No, nothing. Not that I could see anyway. I have learned that the Temple holds secrets even I'm not privy to. Just because I didn't see anything else doesn't mean anything," Nitida said.

Shaz put the tablet back in the box and closed the lid. He wondered if the temple in the Minca realm had secret rooms too. He ran his finger over the latch and the lock slapped shut.

"Can I talk to Serin, alone," Shaz asked.

"We'll be in the supply room," Riddick said.

He took Amirra's hand and led her from the room. Bowen, Inelius, and Nitida followed and the Minca scurried around them. Jagwynn laid on the floor and wrapped her tail around her hind legs.

"So, you don't think your part of everyone?" Shaz asked her.

"No, I don't, plus there is something you need to ask me," Jagwynn said with a deep purr in her throat.

"Did you see what happened?" Shaz asked.

"I did, but I'm not sure that I understand what happened," Serin said.

"I helped Alisdair create the portals. But that's impossible, that happened eons ago," Shaz said.

"And yet you were there, I was there, I witnessed it happen," Serin said.

"Aye, my magic was definitely used. Alisdair saw me, I saw him, but how?" Shaz asked.

"The tablet is an element of time. When you opened the box, you were transported back to the time Alisdair was in the Teorran Belt and used its forces to create not only the portals but the realms too," Jagwynn said.

"The realms too?" Shaz asked.

Serin sent a burst of healing magic into Shaz's weakening body but nothing happened and Serin scowled.

"You have now come full circle in time. You were at the beginning, you are here now, and you will be at the end," Jagwynn said.

The realization hit Shaz so hard his knees buckled, and he fell onto his hands and knees. Serin hurried to him and wrapped him in her arms. His breath stung his esophagus as it tried to escape but his lungs seized up, and he couldn't breathe. Serin sent another cooling burst of magic but still nothing. Shaz wheezed and choked on the frustrated air in his throat. Serin tried again, but her healing magic still didn't work.

"Shaz I don't know what to do, my magic isn't working," Shaz's skin started to turn blue and Serin's heart raced. "Jagwynn, why won't my magic do anything?" Serin asked.

"Because you're using the wrong magic."

Serin grabbed her light magic and hugged him tightly. The light enveloped his whole frame, and he coughed and sputtered as his lungs allowed air to return. Tears burst from Serin's eyes, and she tried to speak but the emotion was too strong to allow any sound to escape. Shaz sucked in slowly and the heat in his lungs eased. Serin rubbed his arms and back and tried to keep his body from shaking. Jagwynn caressed his shivering frame, and she nuzzled her nose into his chest. Shaz gained enough strength to sit on his haunches and rubbed his face. He wiped the sweat and tears away and hugged Serin.

"What happened?" Shaz asked Jagwynn quietly.

"The best way to explain is, you have a new level of magic. An awakening in your mind and soul has opened, and you have gravitated to a higher understanding. You have been to the Teorran Belt itself and now have more magic than before, but your body needs time to adjust." Jagwynn said.

"How much time?" Serin asked.

Serin boosted her healing magic with the light and sent the energy into Shaz's body. His body responded quickly to the new blend of powers, and he sighed.

"Will I always have to use this new combination for Shaz?" Serin asked.

"Not for regular wounds, but for those of a magical nature, yes," Jagwynn said.

Jagwynn nuzzled Shaz and purred loudly.

"Let me help you to your room so you can rest for a while," Serin said.

"I'm alright," Shaz said.

Shaz rose and Serin helped him to a chair.

"You don't look alright. I really think you should lay down for a little bit," Serin said.

Shaz nodded and Serin took his hand. They left the library and Jagwynn padded behind them. At the top of the stairs, Shaz stopped and looked out the large window.

"Looks like the lake has receded some," Shaz said.

"Yes, it does, so, good news there," Serin said.

"Serin, I'm sorry, this has been the weirdest couple weeks," Shaz said.

"As compared to spitting hot earth, a Jaduuk war, and a fire demon?" Serin said.

Shaz smiled.

"I guess that's true,"

Serin took him to his bedchamber and helped him pull off his leather jerkin and boots, then tucked him in. She pulled the curtains over the large windows.

"I know you are concerned about something, and this time it's not me," Shaz said.

Serin turned around and found Shaz watching her.

"Yes, but that will have to wait," Serin said.

"Unless its bad news," Shaz said.

"Something the man that came to the castle said keeps bugging me,"

"What did he say?"

"He said, Isot is getting close to figuring out the scroll and you need to hurry and intercept it. But you can't be of any good to anyone like this and you need sleep to reset your body, that I know, and I won't take no as an answer, now go to sleep," Serin said.

Serin reached the doorway and touched the pad on the wall which indicated someone was in the room. The lights dimmed until they shut off completely and Serin closed the door and made her way to the top of the stairs. She found Riddick and Amirra quietly talking and Turkill making darts and Ladtwig was wiping down his dagger.

"Where is Bowen?" Serin asked.

"He's gone to bed, why?" Riddick asked.

"Come close, I don't want to have to speak loud," Serin said.

The crew perked up with glances of concern. Serin sat on a chair and quietly explained what had happened.

"I don't want Bowen to know any of this, he doesn't have the propensity to understand it all and I fear he will unwittingly share things he shouldn't. We need to leave quickly but there is still too much water. Did you find any boats at all?" Serin said.

"No, nothing, but I can make one," Riddick said.

"Good, first thing in the morning start working, I need to check out something Inelius said the other day but be ready to leave by the day after. I think our time here has come to an end. Amirra I am going to ask Nitida if you can come with us, I think your skills as a runecaster will be needed. Try to think of a way to make yourself an undetectable spell or something. I have a feeling our next task won't be fighting only physical adversity, and we need to have everything at our disposal," Serin said.

"You're kinda twigging me out right now," Riddick said.

Serin's face twitched into a curious glance.

"What do you mean?" Serin asked.

"You sound too much like Shaz and I'm not sure what to do with that," Riddick said.

"I wasn't going to say nothing, but I think so too," Ladtwig said.

Amirra and Turkill nodded.

"I don't mean to twig you out, but things have jumped a notch on the ladder and I'm afraid we might be getting in over our heads," Serin said.

22-A Long Line Of Dodjen

The thick weaved drapes covered the tall windows and a wafting of freshly baked bread circled the room. Oladesni shifted in her padded chair and fiddled with the tightness of her over-gown. The claps that held it together was digging into her skin, and she didn't want to be wearing it. Isot had gone to dressing her for everything she did and made her stand and sit properly. Oladesni didn't want to disobey, but she wondered if there was really a reason for it all or if it was Isot's way of controlling things. The days grew since her father's passing and Isot's kindness had begun to wear off.

Heavy footsteps sounded outside the door and stopped. Isot motioned for the doorman to open the door and a muscular man with four tightly dressed soldiers entered the room. They bowed to Oladesni who stood and bowed her head, and they nodded to three men sitting at the other end of the table and to Isot who returned the gesture and motioned them to sit. The four military officers sat on one side of a long-polished table and waited for the meeting to begin. Isot stood and organized a few parchments at the end of the table and sat in the chair next to the Queen. She pushed a paper in front of the Queen and Oladesni read the heading.

"Thank you for coming, we are here to discuss the matter of security for the city and the castle grounds during the coronation. The Grand Vizier has suggested we need to show the people of Ebassia that there is a strong leadership in the castle and has suggested we open the coronation to the public and hold it on the grand staircase in the main courtyard. What do you feel would be the biggest hurdles to overcome for this to happen? Lorn?" Oladesni said.

Lorn cleared his throat.

"Majesty, we have never done such a thing, I don't think we would have enough soldiers to cover that many people. I don't think that is a good idea," Lorn said.

"What about adding new forces?" Oladesni asked.

"We don't have the budget for that," the tall lanky man at the end of the table said.

"What about a temporary force, one that will only be needed for the coronation?" Oladesni asked.

"We don't have time to train new recruits," one of the other officers said.

"What if they are trained at the most basic levels and are really only there to signify to the people that the castle is clearly prepared," Oladesni said.

"Like ushers but only in uniforms?" the other officer asked.

"Yes," Oladesni said.

"I suppose that would work," Lorn said.

"Great, make it happen," Oladesni said.

Lorn nodded but Oladesni could tell that he didn't like the idea.

****

Garrison pulled the latch and opened the door. The office building was dark, and Garrison fumbled around until he found the switch that illuminated the glow stone in the ceiling. It was one of the perks that remained from the old days, when magic encompassed every part of living. There were few buildings or structures for that matter, that held onto anything from the old world. A world that Garrison spent his whole life dreaming about having again. Stairs that moved on their own, lights that came on when you walked in and so much more. Everyone he talked with about the old days always laughed at him, and he was getting tired of it. He knew the stories were true, especially once he started working with the Dodjen. He had seen the special glow stones, remnants of the rolling stairs and others. In fact, it was part of his job at the Dodjen, to find and secure any relics that could cause confusion for the people now.

Garrison set his satchel down next to the leg of the side table next to the door and looked around the room. He decided with the council out of the way, he would make himself at home and spend as much time as he needed to learn everything, he could about the Tooatha De Dannon. He sucked in a deep breath and started to run through every idea he had about where Mathieu would keep any information on the mysterious magical people from the North. They were said to have blonde hair nearly white with blue eyes and be able to harness all the elements. They say that is where the War Wizard's come from, and Garrison wanted to find the portal that would take him to where they had hidden themselves from this world.

Garrison started toward a shelf at the far side of the room and began reading each heading. He skimmed his finger over the embossed gold lettering that was on most of the spines and pulled out the ones with no titles to read the covers. There were two books that didn't have a title on the spine or on the cover, and he pulled them out and made his way to the desk.

Garrison set the books down and pulled the soft padded chair close to the table. He lifted the top corner of the book carefully and listened as the old glue in the binding cracked. Garrison had learned that many of the books hadn't been read in many rotations and might never have been read. The Dodjen collected as much as they could on the inner workings of the days of Queen Ambrosia and the Realms, but not always as a means to learn but as a way to keep the information hidden.

Garrison was from a long line of Dodjen and had grown up with the stories but when his great-grandparents mysteriously disappeared his father became bitter and obsessed and when he died, Garrison picked up the torch. He skimmed the letters and were thankful they were legible. He skipped a few pages but found the book was not going to be what he was looking for and set it aside and opened the next book.

The soft parchment pages were a good sign as that meant it was old enough to come from before the End of the Realms or E.O.R. for short. Garrison lifted each page carefully until he found the first set of text. But was quickly disappointed when it was only a collection of recipes. He returned the books and continued to the next shelf and pulled out a few books to flip through the pages but returned them when he didn't find what he was looking for. Garrison slowly studied the little statues and trinkets that either sat on the surfaces or were hanging on the walls. Garrison rubbed his hands over his misty gray hair to calm the frizz from the natural curl that wasn't actually curly. If he didn't keep his hair short, it grew into a tight ball around his head, and he looked like a seeded dandelion plant.

The hours passed and Garrison had made his way through all five of the offices with no luck. A surge of anger and frustration ripped through his core, and he slammed his hands on one of the walls in the last office. The sound wasn't solid like he had expected, and he stood up quickly. He stood back and realized that there was nothing in front of the wall in the space the size of a door would be. He ran his hands along the wall but the texture on the wall was slightly rough, and he couldn't tell if there was a seam anywhere.

Garrison picked up a solid wood chair and slammed it into the wall. The textured surface fell off the wall and revealed a polished wood behind it. Garrison quickly started to peel away the wall covering and unveiled a solid polished wooden door. He reached for where a handle would normally be but there was nothing. Garrison turned around and searched for a blade or shiv or anything he could use to pry the door open. He didn't find anything in that office, so he searched each one until he found the fire stoker and hurried back to the secret door.

Garrison stuck the tip into the seam of the door and the wall and wriggled it around until he made a hole in the wall, and he was able to shove the point to the other side of the door. He gripped the iron pole and shoved it toward the wall hoping the counterbalance would pop the door open, but it didn't budge. He moved the poker around the edges and continued to maneuver the lever. After what seemed like forever, he found the latch that bound the door shut and shoved on the poker which broke the lever inside, and the door opened. Garrison threw the poker down and heaved the door open shoving the pile of debris out of the way.

A stiff odor of stifled air hit him in the face, and he coughed. He found the switch and the glow stone illuminated the room. The room didn't look much different except that the books were replaced with scrolls of fine parchments. There were metal bowls and jewels of all kinds with strange markings and symbols and Garrison didn't know what they meant. The fire in his chest was now replaced with a childlike glee, and he had a hard time keeping his excitement in check. He quickly made his way through the parchments, delicately opening each one to read the headings. Even though he was searching for the one particular scroll that explained where the War Wizards Keep was, he had a great love for all things old and knew he needed to be careful with their delicate nature.

23-Nix, An Irritating Little Bugger

Shaz woke early and pulled his tunic and jerkin on, ran his hands through his hair and hurried to the kitchen. The Whispmother was leaving warm biscuits and honey on the table and Shaz popped one into his mouth and grabbed one to take with him. His pace was filled with urgency and excitement. He jogged down the long corridor to the portal room and lifted the latch. The lights came on quickly, and he found several portals were now active. A slight flutter in his stomach churned, and he stepped up to the portal that went to the Olorim Realm. He knew this portal was safe and he would be able to return, after visiting with Azrack first of course.

He wanted to try his upgraded forces first so, he took the tablet and examined the broken lines. Shaz wondered at what point the tablet pieces had been returned to their current state and if he were to break it again what would happen. Even though Serin had been stern for him to sleep, sleep didn't come for many hours. He had spent much of the night sorting through his new memory of his time in the Teorran Belt and Alisdair.

He read the entire tablet. The amount of magic in the tablet was overwhelming and was far too dangerous to be allowed to fall into the wrong hands. Shaz placed his hand on the tablet.

"Shido'ah ray machina chadarr ha no'ha la tenta no me' vina," Shaz read.

A green glow wrapped around his hand causing his skin to glow. The lines in the tablet's engravings glowed and the tablet broke into pieces and floated in the air.

"I had a feeling you would be awake," Riddick said.

"Aye, kind of hard to sleep at a time like this," Shaz said.

"Aye. What is that exactly?"

"This is the tablet of Alisdair, an element of time."

"So, that controls time?"

"Not controls time, makes time. Which is why it can't be in one piece, at least not for this time and place," Shaz said.

Shaz held out a piece to Riddick. Riddick took the smooth metal piece and turned it over a few times and handed it back.

"Serin's is really concerned about you,"

"Aye,"

"She wants me to build a boat, so we can reach Ebassia, she's convinced we need to go fast,"

"Aye. I think there is another way to travel though,"

Riddick's brows rose, and he shoved his hands in his pockets. Shaz touched the edge of the portal wall. Hundreds of tiny symbols illuminated that hadn't before, and he scanned them with his fingers.

"This is the way the portals log those who have traveled through them, but only if the person has a magic imprint," Shaz said.

Shaz pointed to the detailed inscription of symbols.

"So, that's how Gavin Rhill did it,"

Shaz nodded. He traced the lines of symbols for a minute and mumbled as he read them.

"Ah, here, this might give us more information," Shaz said.

Shaz held his hand in front of the shimmering surface but didn't touch it.

"Ano tay re nada' shento may'ha vi say na marri she'late narata," Shaz said.

The portal rippled and bounced as though tiny raindrops were pelting the surface. A deep hum wrapped around the room and the portal illuminated an image of a Grey Tailix.

"You have got to be kidding me!" Shaz snarled.

"Oiy, mate, what is it?" Riddick asked.

"That little bugger, I knew he was going to be trouble. What else did he take?" Shaz asked.

"Who?" Riddick said.

"Machina ha no'ha la no me' vina" Shaz said.

The portal projected several small trinkets and some gold coins. Shaz studied the trinkets and found nothing of importance.

"How did it get through? Does it have a medallion?" Riddick asked.

"Nada' may'ha na she'late," Shaz said.

The portal illuminated an image of the creatures that did not require a medallion in order to travel through a portal. The Grey Tailix and two other rodent-like creatures Shaz hadn't encountered yet, illuminated.

"Serin is not going to believe this," Shaz said.

"Why, who is that?"

"Nix, an irritating little bugger that steals shiny things," Shaz said.

"Is that Nix?" Serin asked.

Serin pulled her blue gown up and crossed the floor.

"Yes, and he was the one that tried to take the orb," Shaz snarled.

"Shaz, how can you say that?" Serin said.

"This, right here and to make things worse, the Grey Tailix is not required to have a passkey!" Shaz said.

Riddick snickered at Shaz getting so worked up over the whole thing.

"Shut it mate, that little monster is the worst pain," Shaz said.

"Shaz, you're being ridiculous. Nix is a very nice little fellow," Serin said.

Shaz through up his hands.

"I'm taking this is quite a story," Riddick said trying to keep from laughing.

"What portal did he come from, I thought we left him with Orand, nowhere near that sanctum," Serin said.

Shaz's brows were so tight on his face Serin was sure he was going to explode.

"It is that exact portal. I guess he decided he didn't want to stay with Orand and went back," Shaz said.

"The portal isn't too far from Ebassia and opens in the forest, so we would have good coverage. We could use that to get to Ebassia," Serin said.

"And when I get back, I'm going to find that nuisance and end it,"

"Shaz, you will do no such thing," Serin said.

"Watch me!" Shaz said.

Shaz stormed toward the door.

"Maybe you should secure the portals, so they can't travel through them anymore before you storm off," Serin said.

Shaz stopped and spun around on his toes. He stomped back to the portal, his hair steaming, and not in a figurative way. Actual steam radiated from the top of his head he was so angry.

"Noshari senate shat yo'ha. Mevina charlata mo'ha, latenta no mevina somella no 'me tere," Shaz said.

Shaz spun on his heel.

"And put the tablet away," Serin said.

Shaz turned around and took the tablet and put it in the box. Serin smiled at his scrunched face, his childish disdain for Nix and how much of a tantrum he was throwing. She did understand, Nix was a sneaky critter and even she was angry at first. Shaz locked the box and stormed out of the room.

"You better let me in on this," Riddick said.

"Nix is a critter with an intense need to collect shiny things. He took the medallion when we escaped Ebassia, and he gave Shaz quite a run. Shaz has hated him ever since. I guess you don't have to build a boat after all. Looks like we are going to the Shifting Woods," Serin said.

"And I was actually looking forward to building a ship," Riddick said.

"Let's go tell the others," Serin said.

She and Riddick left the room and filled everyone in on the new plans. The Minca were happy they wouldn't need to ride in the boat and Jagwynn even seemed pleased. Riddick returned to the portal room to wait for Amirra to return from making their arrangement with Nitida. Serin found Shaz in the armory. He was sharpening a small blade he kept in the small of his back. Serin touched the weapons sitting in a row as she made her way to him.

"Don't say anything Serin," Shaz said.

Serin shook her head and lifted her leg and rested her foot on the stools tiny section between Shaz's legs. Shaz straightened and Serin slowly lifted her blue gown revealing her bare skin up to her thigh and Shaz scanned her soft skin up her leg and landed on the delicate features of her illuminated face. The flirtatious gleam in her eyes snapped at his emotions, and he swallowed hard. He smiled under his scowl and tried not to let her attempts change his sulking. She pulled the dagger she kept on her outer thigh from the leather strapping and handed the blade to Shaz who took it without taking his eyes off hers, then she dropped her dress and moved to a row of arrows and began to arrange them neatly. Shaz cleared his throat and tried to figure out what her tactic was. He slid her blade along the sharpening stone while eyeing her intently. The soft scrape of the metal moved about the room and Serin finished making her arrangement and then moved on to a row of longbows.

"You're not going to yell at me?" Shaz asked.

His tone half indicated he wanted her to, so he could argue back how he felt.

"Nope, you have every right to be angry with Nix, after all, he is the cause for the Shadow Selket being released. And he did steal the medallion in the first place. Of course, we don't know his side of the story, but he did make a mess," Serin said.

Shaz scraped the blade against the stone and wiped the residue on the cloth he had across his leg. That was the game she was playing, guilt, and of course, it worked. Shaz's anger returned but not because of what Nix did, but because of why he did it, which was what Shaz didn't know, and maybe he did have a reason, although not a good one that was for sure.

"Blast it all Serin," Shaz said.

"I didn't say anything, you asked," Serin said.

Serin turned to face Shaz who was still scowling. Her soft but flirtatious eyes reassured him she understood how he felt, and her smile was kind as she walked gracefully toward him. She leaned down and ran her fingers through his hair and lifted his head, so she could kiss the top of his head. Her caress was tantalizing and his anger suddenly dissipated. He both smiled and scowled realizing she had so much sway on his emotions, which he decided wasn't so bad. Serin sensed his diffused anger and ran her fingers through his hair. Shaz relaxed and sank into the stool he was sitting on.

"Is everyone ready?" Shaz grumbled.

"We're waiting on Amirra, she should be here soon," Serin said.

"We leave as soon as she arrives," Shaz said.

"I'll go and change then, if I can convince the Whispmother to give me back my traveling clothes that is," Serin said.

Shaz handed her the sharpened dagger, and she left the armory. Serin returned to her room and found traveling clothes laying on her bed.

"You were right, I did hide them," the Whispmother sang.

"It's alright, I do like the dresses, but unfortunately they aren't very practical for traveling," Serin said.

Serin unlatched the gown and let it fall from her body and draped it on the bottom of the bed. She took her leggings and slipped them on. The insides were soft and fuzzy, and the outside was smooth and slick. She held up the tunic. The lacy layers draped around the tunic and resembled the dresses the Whispmother had picked for her.

"Are you pleased?" the Whispmother sang.

Serin pulled the dressier tunic over her head and wrapped the belt around her waist. She stepped to the mirror and inspected herself.

"I am, thank you," Serin said.

"Now you can be a proper lady, even when traveling," the Whispmother sang.

Serin smiled.

"I don't have to look like a proper lady to be one," Serin said.

"True, but it doesn't hurt either. I have packed more in your things," the Whispmother said.

"I'm going to miss you too, and the castle. I do love this place," Serin said.

"Are there any improvements you would like me to make while you are away?" the Whispmother asked.

"That is a question for Shaz," Serin said.

The Whispmother floated down to be at Serin's eye level.

"Now that you are the lady of the castle, I am delighted to please you,"

"The lady of the castle?" Serin asked.

"Why yes, my dear, we know all about the proposal. I must tell you I am most excited for the union," the Whispmother said.

Serin smiled, she liked the sound of that.

"Me too, if we make it that far," Serin said.

"You will my dear, I will plan a grand event. Keep your hope," The Whispmother said.

"I would hug you, but I would squish you," Serin said.

"My arms wouldn't reach around you," the Whispmother said.

The two laughed and Serin finished dressing. She grabbed her satchel and slung the bag onto her back.

"There is one thing that would be nice," Serin said.

"What, my dear?"

"A bath in my private quarters but separate from the bedchamber. Perhaps a doorway into a private bath, and another window on that wall," Serin said.

"Yes, that would be a lovely addition, I will begin immediately," the Whispmother sang.

Serin skipped down the stairs and hurried to the portal room. Shaz, Riddick, Amirra, and Bowen were discussing the plans for when they reached the shifting woods. Turkill arranged his pack on his back and Ladtwig shoved a very large piece of wrapped cheese into his. Jagwynn cleaned her fur in the corner.

"Oh, good you're here," Shaz said.

"Sorry I'm late, I didn't think I had taken that long," Serin said.

"You didn't, we just all arrived here too," Ladtwig said.

"Did I miss anything?" Serin asked.

"Nope," Shaz said.

Shaz opened the box and pulled out the pieces of the tablet which were now strung onto their own leather tethers. He handed each person a tablet.

"These are never to be shown to anyone, so wear them under your clothing. I've asked Amirra to make a disguise spell, so they don't look like the tablet. These will be our new passkeys. They will work on every portal and they are undetectable. I have disabled the medallions for the castle, so they won't work here any longer, except for the Temple Portal. If in the future anything happens you will still be able to access the castle with the medallion through a temple. Once we get to the Shifting Woods, Ebassia is but a few days ride. Riddick, I need you to stay at the sanctum and rebuild it. Amirra you disguise the building once he's finished. Bowen, you will come with Serin, the Minca and myself into Ebassia. We will make contact with those still loyal and you can begin your plans to take back your army. Serin and I will find our friend Deagan and his brother and hopefully enlist their help. Then we will regroup at the sanctum and figure out the rest then," Shaz said.

"Why do we need your friends help? I'm sure my men can handle things," Bowen said.

"Aye, but they see from different eyes and might know things your armies don't. It's nothing personal," Riddick said.

They could tell Bowen didn't like it, but he nodded.

"I'll go first," Riddick said.

Riddick stepped up to the portal and put his hand into the shimmering mist. The particles rearranged into a dancing array of purple haze. He stepped through and the tightness of the magic stung his skin. Amirra went next and then Ladtwig, Turkill, and Jagwynn. Bowen hesitated and then stepped through.

"I didn't give Bowen a piece of the tablet, the tablet is too much for his non-magical body, so I gave him a separate passkey. I also put a special identifier on it. I don't believe he will do anything on purpose, but like you, I'm not sure he understands enough, and I don't trust those he might come in contact with," Shaz said.

"Thank you. Are you still mad at Nix?" Serin asked.

"Yes, and no," Shaz said.

Serin smiled and stepped through the portal. Inelius walked gingerly toward Shaz.

"I hope to see you again," Inelius said.

"Me too my dear friend," Shaz said.

"I shall do my best to stay alive until you return, and say hello to Merrick and Mathieu for me," Inelius said.

"Merrick?" Shaz asked.

"He is now part of the council and will be waiting for you in Ebassia," Inelius said.

Shaz's smiled and stepped through the portal.

24-I'm A War Wizard

The senate sanctum of the Shifting Woods was just as Shaz and Serin remembered. The late sun left long shadows from the waslick trees on the ruins and rubble. The misty fog began to form, and a chill ran through their bones. Shaz and Riddick scanned the surroundings and between all the guys made a full sweep of the area. Amirra wrapped her purple cloak around her tightly and decided she was going to enchant a warming spell into her things the second she got a chance. Serin stepped around the crumbled stones and stared at the wall-size mural of Shaz's father. The images eyes seemed to glisten and smile at her, as if he were telling her he was pleased she was now going to be part of the family. She shook her head and dismissed it as her own thoughts.

Serin turned around and found the stone pillar they used as a step stool in the same place and was relieved no one had been there or at least moved anything. She flicked her finger and a gust of wind picked up several of the stones and rubble and moved it to the outer edges of the stone floor.

"That is quite the mural. Is that Shaz's father?" Amirra asked.

"Yes, it is," Serin said.

"Do you think he thought a lot of himself?" Amirra asked.

"I guess I never thought about it, why?" Serin asked.

"He has a whole picture of only himself. Semias did too, and he definitely thought a lot of himself," Amirra said.

"I have no idea, but that would make sense," Serin said.

"Shaz seems a bit that way," Amirra said.

"You think so? I think more like he has so much responsibility and everyone relies on his every move," Serin said.

"I like that better, I agree with that," Amirra said.

"As far as I can tell we are the only ones in the forest," Shaz said.

The girls jumped and spun around.

"Shaz-" Serin started.

He looked at them with a blank expression.

"You scared the tar out of us," Amirra said.

"Sorry, I didn't mean to. We don't have too long before the sun sets, but I think we can make most of the way if we leave now and use your wind-walk," Shaz said.

"Alright. Where is Bowen and the Minca?" Serin asked.

Riddick stepped from around the mural wall with several small logs in his arms. He set them on the ground and then touched the mural wall. A pile of rubble bounced and popped as the earth's energy forced the broken pieces back into their original shape.

"Looks like you've got this under control," Shaz said.

"Aye, we'll see you in a few days," Riddick said.

"Amirra, you might want to disguise anything shiny. You don't want the little bugger sneaking off with your stuff in the middle of the night," Shaz said.

Amirra nodded and handed a log to Riddick who wriggled his fingers and the log started to grow. Jagwynn, with the Minca already on her back, came from around the half-fallen wall on the other side and Serin buffed everyone. Jagwynn started out at a quick pace with Bowen following close behind. Serin started after but Shaz grabbed her hand and pulled her back.

"What's wrong?" Serin asked.

"I want to find Nix," Shaz said.

"Shaz, don't,"

"I won't hurt him, but I need to find out why he, or rather his kind isn't scanned by the portals. It doesn't make sense that every creature there is except those three would be detected but not them, were they not a part of the original creatures before the realms? Did they come after? Did someone create them for a purpose and if so, what purpose would that be?

"Wow, you have been busy thinking,"

"Plus, he might be hurt,"

"Hurt! Why do you say that?"

"I found a smudge of blood on the portal wall, which is why I chose that one to inspect,"

"I hope not,"

"I think he might be this way. Remember we were over there when we started chasing him,"

"He should be with Orand," Serin said.

"We really didn't know much about him in the first place,"

"True, and I guess we won't until we ask him," Serin said.

"Look, blood," Shaz said.

Shaz and Serin followed the trail of blood for several lengths and passed the location they had made camp all those moons ago. The forest thickened, and they came to a pile of rubble. Shaz scanned the pile and nodded.

"He's in there, and he's wounded,"

Serin flicked her fingers and the wind moved several rocks until they could see the tunnel.

"Nix, it's me Serin, can you move?"

Shaz shook his head.

"I don't think he's going to make it,"

"Yes, he is,"

Serin threw her arms in the air and the wind picked up the entire pile of rocks and revealed the curled-up body of the furry rodent. Shaz hurried under the rocks and picked him up and returned to Serin who dropped her air and returned the rocks to the ground. A pang of sadness hit Shaz's heart, and he felt bad that he had let the little critter under his skin so much. Serin rubbed his back and sent a boost of magic into his body.

"Looks like the scorpion stung him, the effects of the poison have slowly been causing his body to shut down,"

"Are you able to heal him,"

"I think so,"

Nix blinked and hissed.

"Hey there, you're alright now," Shaz said.

Nix blinked again and rubbed his eyes.

"Shaz?"

Shaz nodded and Nix leaped onto his neck and wrapped him tightly with his small arms.

"What happened?" Serin asked.

"A very big bug stung me," Nix said.

His body shivered and Shaz had a hard time peeling his little frame off him.

"You're safe now," Serin said.

"Why did you go into the castle in the first place?" Shaz asked.

"I have to, the scary lady makes me," Nix said.

"Tell me everything about this scary lady," Shaz said.

"The scary lady came to me before I met you and told me I have to find everything shiny, or she won't give me back my family."

"Is that why you left Orand?" Serin asked.

Nix nodded and let go of Shaz's neck.

"Why does she want everything shiny?" Shaz asked.

"Nix not know, she is scary and mean,"

"How did you find out about the castle?" Shaz asked.

"The scary lady found me after I left Orand and told me to go to the castle and find the shiny there, but one of the shiny's turned into a meaner and scarier bug and it stung me,"

"Can you tell me what the scary lady is looking for?" Serin asked.

"Your shiny,"

"You mean the one you took before? The medallion?" Shaz asked.

Nix nodded and sunk onto his haunches. His long fur rippled, and his dark eyes filled with sadness.

"Nix, does love shiny's but Nix wouldn't do it if he didn't have to,"

"Thank you for telling me. Can you tell me why you are able to get through the portals without a shiny?" Shaz asked.

Nix shook his head.

"Nix has always been able to go through the misty's,"

"Do you know where you came from?" Serin asked.

Nix shook his head.

"Well, you won't be able to go into the misty's anymore, I locked them," Shaz said.

Nix's heart jumped and his paws gripped one another. His long ears covered his big eyes, and he shivered.

"What's wrong?" Serin asked.

"Nix never found the shiny for the scary lady, now Nix will never see his family," Nix said.

Shaz removed the medallion from his belt.

"Nix, you can have my shiny, in fact, I want you to find the scary lady and give it to her and get your family back," Shaz said.

Nix's ears rose from over his eyes, and he stared at Shaz and then the shiny.

"Nix is confused,"

"I have a different shiny now, and you need this more than I do," Shaz said.

"Nix *is* grateful,"

"We will be staying in the city, but we have friends at the misty, when you are done go to them, but don't take anymore shiny's, alright?" Serin said. Nix nodded and scurried away. "I guess that explains a few things," Serin said.

"Aye, a few, but not everything. We're still not certain who the scary lady is. I'm guessing Isot, but with the Shadow ever-increasing, I have no idea how many Velshari are lurking about," Shaz said.

"I have been thinking the same thing," Serin said.

"Come on, we better get moving and catch up to the others," Shaz said.

The sun had set, and they found it a little harder to find their way in the darkness and slowed their pace. When they neared the end of the forest Shaz found the others near the border.

"What took you so long?" Turkill grumbled.

"They were kissing," Ladtwig said.

Ladtwig and Turkill laughed and Serin gave them a stern glare. Shaz dropped his pack next to Jagwynn and sat down. He wished they were kissing, but there was little time for that with the Shadow lurking everywhere. Serin released her backpack and lifted the top and pulled out a portion of dried meat and bread.

"I guess we're back to travel food," Ladtwig said.

He pulled out a large white cheese wheel, dried meat and a slice of bread. Turkill glared and ripped a piece of bread from the loaf he unwrapped.

"We won't be here long, maybe a day or two. Once we meet up with Bowen's men and find Deagan," Shaz said.

"I would like to find Mrs. Bailey too," Serin said.

Shaz nodded and yawned. He popped a biscuit in his mouth and released the straps which held his sleeping roll. Bowen rolled out his bedroll and laid on his headrest.

"Bowen, you have been awfully quiet. Is everything alright?" Serin asked.

"What if my men aren't loyal anymore? I have been gone for some time and I have no idea what the Grand Vizier has done," Bowen admitted.

"Then we take them back by force," Turkill said.

"That might not be as easy as you think," Bowen said.

"Maybe not, but we got your back," Ladtwig said.

Bowen smiled.

"Thanks,"

"Let's get some rest and in the morning, we will head into the city and figure things out," Shaz said.

Serin sat next to Shaz and pulled her long wavy brown hair up and secured it with a string. She rolled out her bedroll and fluffed her headrest and laid down. The small fire let off a soft crackle as the flames consumed the wood. Shaz thought about the way the flames danced and flickered and the way the wood popped and sizzled. He found an odd relationship between the two. One destroyed and one created. The wood sacrificed itself to the flames to create heat and the fire used the force to create light. Shaz found the mesmerizing effects of the fire and his relationship with it more soothing than the water sounds and drifted to sleep.

The morning came quickly, and the crew cleaned up camp and started the rest of the way to the city. The trees thinned, and they could see some of the tall building spires in the distance. The sun peaked over the trees making the mist lurking on the forest floor disappear. Ladtwig and Turkill's eyes popped out of their heads as they witnessed the magnificent city emerge. Tall buildings stretched into the sky and appeared to disappear into the atmosphere. Some buildings were encased in square hand-honed stones and narrow arched triangular windows. They had a feel which spanned the lengths of time with crenellations that wrapped around them as though they were the lookout points during times of war. Other buildings brought the shine and glow of a newer era and peaked at the tops with highly polished stone and intricately carved details.

Waterways were lifted high so, as the boats came in off the sea, they could navigate the waterways. The larger ships docked in the pier outside the city waterways but the smaller the vessel the further into the city they could sail.

"It's so big!" Ladtwig said.

"Yes, it is, so you will need to say close," Serin said.

"Where do we go from here?" Shaz asked.

"There's a tavern in the outer district that my men frequent. We'll start there," Bowen said.

"Aye," Shaz said.

Bowen took the lead, and they made their way toward the crowded street leading to the South-southeast gate of the city.

"Do you think the guards will remember us?" Serin asked.

"Why would they?" Bowen asked.

"She blew up their gate," Shaz said.

"That was you?" Bowen asked.

Turkill and Ladtwig gave her contorted expressions.

"They shut it, so I opened it," Serin said.

"You're a legend around here now, and the guards hate it, because the country folk that are mad with the city folk try to mimic it," Bowen said.

"Really," Shaz said.

Serin cringed and everyone chuckled and moved into the crowd. The street was busier than they had remembered and wondered why there were so many more people going into the city than out. Serin joined a group of women's conversations as they walked by them and learned the Queen was going to have a grand celebration in honor of her coronation and was going to be held in three days. Serin also discovered the Queen was going to allow a certain amount of people into her outer courtyard as a '*Coming of Age*' gathering in hopes to find a suitor as a new king.

The women explained how they were so excited to have a Queen as a ruler and hoped she would be the means for new changes to the way women were seen in society. Serin couldn't help relating to them. Before she met Shaz, she too felt the lack of equality. Now, however, things were so much bigger than men verse women. They neared the gate and the crowd thickened. A soldier kept shouting over the noise for the people to show their papers.

"We don't have papers," Serin said.

"Aye," Shaz agreed.

"What are we going to do?" Serin asked.

"I'll take care of it," Bowen said.

They stepped up to the guard. The guard started to holler but stopped when he saw Bowen.

"Commander. Sir,"

The soldier threw an instant salute and stood at attention. Bowen returned the salute.

"Relax soldier, my company and I are just passing through," Bowen said.

"Sir, yes Sir," the soldier said.

The soldier held up the gate and let them through.

"I take it, he's still loyal," Shaz said.

"He's only a gate patrol, the one I'm most concerned with is the second in command. He's now in command, and I'm not guessing he will want to give up his control," Bowen said.

They continued through the people until they were able to break away and into a back alley. The slender walkway was cool and under the shadows of the tall aqueducts that led around the outer ring of the city. Bowen guided them through the dingy outskirts of the Working District until they reached the tavern.

"This tavern is a bit different than the one on the outskirts," Bowen said.

"We'll be fine," Shaz said.

"Why, they don't have food?" Ladtwig asked.

Serin shook her head, rolled her eyes and followed after Shaz and Bowen. Serin coughed and almost gagged at the putrid odor of liquor and ale. It wasn't the wreak itself but the amount of it. Turkill ducked as a drunk man threw his hand holding his half-full tankard out. Shaz rounded several men in dark traveling clothes and Serin tried to squeeze through the same crowd. One of the men smiled a toothy grin and looked Serin up and down. Serin glared at him and shook her head telling him he better not even as much as move. Another man didn't see the glare and scooted his chair out and put his beefy leg in front of her.

"Excuse me please," Serin said.

"Where are you going in such a hurry?" the bulky faced man asked.

"Nowhere you are going, that's for sure," Serin said.

Serin tried to move around the man, but he wouldn't move. Serin sucked in a deep breath and stepped back but bumped into another man with a long black beard.

"This lass thinks she's going to get out of here without joining me for a drink," the first man said.

"Well she don't know who's she's messing with now does she," the man with the beard said.

"I don't think you want to start this," Serin said.

The bulky faced man's eyes bulged, and he leaned into her and sniffed her hair.

"Oh, but I do," the first man said.

Shaz grabbed the man on the shoulder and sent a shot of sudden heat into the man's body. The man recoiled and winced.

"Sorry, but this *lady* is with me," Shaz said.

Shaz reached around the man and took her hand and started to pull her out of their block.

"I don't think so, this *lass* belongs to Greederick the Tower," the man said.

"And I suppose you're Greederick the Tower?" Shaz asked.

Serin rolled her eyes and sighed.

"Shaz don't," Serin said.

The man stood up out of his chair and rose to his full height. The man was most certainly a tower, standing nearly three more lengths than Shaz.

"Look at this, tiny little men," the second man said.

Turkill and Ladtwig maneuvered under the man's leg and hurried after Bowen.

"I'm tired of this, let me pass or else," Serin said.

"You really ought to let the lady pass," Shaz said.

"Or else what?" Greederick growled.

The amount of alcohol expelled from his lungs stung Serin's nose, and she coughed and fanned the fumes away. Serin squeezed her fist and the air in his lungs thickened. The man's eyes filled with panic, and he gripped his throat as the lack of air continued to stifle his next breath. The man sat on his chair and slammed his fist into his chest, but the air wouldn't reach his lungs, and he started to turn blue.

Serin stepped around him and whispered in his ear.

"Never ever speak to me that way again," She released her fist, "Someone help him, he's choking."

The man with the long beard hurried to Greederick and banged on his back as Greederick wheezed and sputtered. Shaz pulled Serin in front of him and kept her close to him as they headed to where Bowen was sitting with a fellow comrade.

"You weren't going to kill him, were you?" Shaz asked.

"No, of course not, but a little bit of pain and panic wouldn't hurt," Serin said.

"I never even thought about you being able to restrict the air in a person's chest," Shaz said.

"I didn't either until we dealt with Semias," Serin said.

"*That* is crazy attractive," Shaz said.

"Shaz! How can you think that?" Serin asked.

"I'm a *war wizard*," Shaz said.

"So, what is that supposed to mean," Serin asked.

"What do you think I'm here for?" Shaz asked.

Serin stopped suddenly making Shaz nearly run into her. She turned around and studied his eyes. Her heart skipped a beat as she realized what he was saying.

"I guess I never took it that way," Serin said.

"I can't keep fighting the purpose for my existence," Shaz said.

"I never thought about that either," Serin said.

"I'm alright with it," Shaz said.

"I suppose I'll have to think about that too," Serin said.

"Over here," Bowen said.

25-This Is An Initiation Ceremony

Riddick took his boots off and wriggled his toes into the soft dirt. The rubble of the old building scattered the surroundings for several lengths leaving an eerie tale in its wake. The sun drifted over the treetops lazily and the soft sprigs of amber light created a warm and soothing atmosphere. Amirra pulled out her notes she had made at the castle and started to run the glyphs through her mind. Riddick pulled his long red hair back and secured it at the back of his head with a tie. He rolled the sleeves of his dark green silk shirt and pushed them up onto his muscular arms. The veins on the tops of his hands bulged as he allowed the earth's energy to enter his body.

A low rumble crossed the old ruins and the stones started to shake. Riddick closed his eyes and focused on the image the old remains gave his mind. He circled the stone foundation in his mind as he interpreted the imprint of the last footings. Amirra jumped and scurried out of the way as a sizable pile of dirt shifted and bounced. Several medium-sized hand-chiseled stones emerged from under the dirt and started to roll with a thump every time they landed on their flat side. Riddick dug his toes deeper into the dirt and held his hands out to steady himself. He had never focused this much of the earths magic and was starting to sag with the weight on his frame.

Amirra found a tree stump and climbed onto it, so she wouldn't be on any earth that might need to be moved. She tried to keep an eye on the surroundings but couldn't deny her attraction to Riddick and what he was able to do. His tall slender and muscular frame was trim and pleasing to gaze at. Amirra blushed at finding herself staring at him. A line of pebbles formed on the far side and began to grow into the shape of the larger hand-carved stones. When the rock had returned to its original shape it started to roll toward the ruins. A bead of sweat dripped down the side of Riddick's face, and he was thankful for a soft breeze blowing in from the east.

The largest stones rolled with a thud and some scooted as if someone were pushing them. They lined the outer edges of the sanctum and moved in tightly. Riddick breathed heavily as the energy surged from his core and into the earth and back into his body. He opened his eyes and exhaled. Several rows of stones lined the perimeters and waited to be organized into new walls.

"That was amazing," Amirra said.

Amirra jumped from the log and scaled the new rows and piles of stones. Riddick smiled but sagged a little and wiped the sweat from his face.

"Thanks, but I hope we can get most of this done before the sun sets," Riddick said.

"How can I help?" Amirra asked.

Riddick shrugged and looked at all the heavy rocks.

"I'm not sure you can, but if I think of anything, I'll fill you in," Riddick said.

Amirra smiled and nodded and then returned to the tree stump. Riddick lifted his hands out in front of him and the energy of the rocks eased into his skin. Riddick first wriggled his fingers the way he did to make his rock golem move, but the stones only twitched. Riddick scowled and puckered his lips tightly. He realized these stones were not the same as his little golem. They were much heavier because of their density and it was going to take more force to get them to rise into the air.

He thought about when he was in the desert with Yerild, Sebastian and Batovi, and they would throw rocks at him. Back then he had to use his whole body to 'throw' the rocks away from hitting him. Riddick slapped his hands together and focused on one large stone. He bent at the knees and raised his hands over his head. The stone raised into the air and hovered at waist level until Riddick moved his hands in the direction, he wanted the stone to go.

When the stone was in the proper alignment, he lowered it down and scooched it into place and dropped the energy connection with it. Riddick repeated the process with each of the largest stones around the bottom creating the foundation of the walls. He then organized the cornerstones for the walls into sizes and the rest would be used in the middle. He wasn't sure yet if he would have enough stones because he didn't know what the structure looked like prior to its demise. Did it have windows, was the roof made of stone or did it have woodwork and planks?

The sun was beginning to wane as it slipped below the tree canopy. It wouldn't be long until it would fall behind the horizon and it would soon be dark. Riddick hadn't made as much progress as he had expected and found a bit of irritation sitting in his chest.

"I'm going to go gather some wood to make a fire for the night before it gets too dark," Amirra said.

"Alright, but don't be long," Riddick said.

"I won't," Amirra said.

Amirra hopped off the stump and rounded the outer edge of the rocks. She wrapped her cloak around her snugly and tied the belt around her waist. The forest was calm and one of the night insects had already started singing its annoying sounds. The leaf people rustled about the tops of the waslick trees and Amirra amused at how well they scurried around the branches. The leaf people weren't people exactly, they were insects, and they have small heads at the tops of their bodies which of course look like leaves with tiny arms and legs that surround the edges of the leaf. They feed on the lichen and moss which grows on the bark which helps keep the trees healthy.

Amirra searched for the larger sized branches, so they wouldn't have to put so many onto the fire to keep it going. The sunlight faded so gently she hadn't realized it became so dark. She hadn't found as many logs as she had wanted to, but she started back toward the sanctum. Amirra stopped and listened and confirmed in her mind the noise was in fact, voices. She quickly made her way over the forest floor trying to keep her footsteps quiet but found it difficult as the fallen leaves were heavier in this section of the forest.

"Amirra, is that you?" Riddick asked.

"Yes, but we're not alone," Amirra said.

"What do you mean?" Riddick asked.

"I heard voices and hurried back here," Amirra said.

"It's probably Shaz and Serin," Riddick said.

"No, they are Velshari," Amirra said.

"Are you sure?" Riddick asked.

Amirra gave him a sideways glare.

"Of course, I'm sure, I know what they sound like," Amirra said.

"I wasn't saying... I know you... well, alright, so we need to find out what they are up to then," Riddick said.

"No, we need to hide," Amirra said.

"But," Riddick started.

Amirra's pale face was even paler and her body began to quiver. Riddick grabbed her into a hug and squeezed her tight. It was obvious she wasn't handling this very well.

"The building isn't finished, and you haven't disguised it yet," Riddick said.

The voices came into earshot and Riddick froze keeping Amirra tightly in his arms. She buried her face into his chest, so she wouldn't cry, and he stroked the back of her head.

"I know, hang on tight, and whatever you do, don't make a sound," Riddick said.

Amirra looked up with a confused glance and wrapped her arms around his waist tightly. Riddick closed his eyes and imagined himself turning into a tree. Amirra gasped but shut her mouth quickly and closed her eyes. A crackling ripping sound crested the late evening air and Riddick's body mutated into the shape and appearance of a medium-sized waslick tree. Amirra opened her eyes and found herself sitting in the branches of a the tree. The leaves were so thick she couldn't see out around her, and she hunkered close to the main trunk.

"Riddick, are you there?" Amirra whispered.

"Aye, I'm the tree you're in, don't move," Riddick whispered back.

"You're a tree?" Amirra whispered.

"Aye, now shush," Riddick whispered.

The voices grew and Riddick stood as still as possible, which was actually easier than he thought and surmised it was the strength of the bark that helped him. Two people in dark red robes rounded a couple of trees a few lengths away and Riddick hoped it was dark enough to keep the partially built building out of sight.

"I think we're about to the place the little rat is supposed to meet us," a female voice said.

"Are you sure, I think we went too far," a male voice said.

"Shut up you idiot, you're always contradicting me, I thought you said you trusted me,"

"I do, but I counted the trees on the first visit, and we have gone more than last time," the man said.

"This is just like you, to always be whining and selfish, I don't even know why I bring you along," the woman said.

"I can-" the man started.

"Shut up, someone is coming," the woman said.

A bristling of leaves grew, and Riddick understood it was a small rodent-like creature. He couldn't detect the people, so he closed his eyes and searched the earth. The image the earth energy gave him was even stronger than when he used it in the Realm of Yune to spy on Crolos. A clear image of a small thin woman and a stalky man sat in his mind. Amirra gripped his branch harder as he started to move. Riddick felt her heart thudding in her chest, and he wished he could comfort her more. He grew a few extra branches around her just in case and crept closer.

Riddick opened his eyes and was surprised to be able to see with his human eyes. He noticed the little critter scurry out from under a bristly bush and stop in front of the two people.

"About time you got here. Do you have something for me?" the woman said.

"Yes," Nix said.

Nix handed her the medallion and Riddick had to stifle a gasp. The woman looked around but when she didn't find anything, she snatched the medallion from his little paws.

"About time you found this," she said.

"Now, can Nix have his family back?" Nix asked shakily.

"Are you an idiot, of course not, they are locked in the dungeons and no one ever gets out of there," the woman said.

"But you said all Nix needed to do was find the shiny," Nix said.

"I never said you would get your family back, you assumed that you filthy rodent," she said.

Nix lowered onto his haunches and pulled his long ears over his eyes. Riddick crept a little closer and found the man and woman were within reach of his longer branches. Riddick snapped the tip of the branch against the man's cheek, and the man yelped. Nix scurried back under the bush.

"What are you doing, you fool," the woman spat.

"Something just bit me," the man said.

"There is nothing out here that would bite you,"

"Then what was it?"

The man rubbed his cheek and showed it to the woman who barely paid attention.

"Come on, let's go meet the others," the woman said.

The woman whipped her robe out of the way as she turned sharply. Riddick slid a few lengths and covered the building from view as they moved back to where they had come from. Riddick let them move ahead several lengths and then began to move after them.

"What are you doing?" Amirra whispered.

"We need to find out what they are doing and why they need that medallion," Riddick said.

"No, we need to get as far away as possible," Amirra said.

Riddick stopped.

"Amirra, I am *not* going to let anything happen to you, I promise. They can't even see you and with me being disguised as a tree we can figure out what they are up to," Riddick said softly.

"Alright," Amirra said hesitantly.

Riddick moved a small branch inside her cocoon of leaves and brushed her cheek. Amirra smiled and rested her head on the trunk. She allowed her body to relax and move with his soft swaying motions as he moved his root-like feet through the forest floor. Riddick followed the residue of their essence through the forest and stopped at the edge of a clearing.

"They are over there," Riddick said.

Amirra pulled the small branches away and peeked out but didn't find anything.

"The *other* over there," Riddick teased. Amirra turned to the other side of her cocoon and peeked out. The man and woman were now mingling with a group of about fifteen other Velshari members. "I don't see a dessert table," Riddick said.

Amirra shoved her hand over her mouth a second before she blurted a ga-fa. Riddick smiled and wondered how his smile would look as a tree trunk.

"I'm going to get closer," Riddick said.

"Be careful," Amirra said.

Riddick slowly pulled out of the tree line and merged back into the darker shadows of the other trees. He moved quicker once he was behind the other trees, which was still at a very slow pace. He wished he moved faster, so he didn't miss anything. Riddick rounded a large boulder and came to a stop close enough to make out most of the details of faces but still not close enough to hear what they were saying. The night moons drifted in and out of the lazy clouds crossing the sky. Each time they disappeared Riddick took another step closer. Amirra kept a tiny hole pulled open, so she could tell where they were going. After a sufficient amount of time, Riddick found a comfortable place close enough and pushed his toe-like roots into the ground.

"It won't be much longer," the woman said.

"I think I know that woman," Amirra whispered.

"Who is it?" Riddick whispered back.

"I'll tell you in a minute after I make sure," Amirra said.

The woman rolled the medallion in her fingers and gazed around the crowd. Several of the other members watched with wide-eyed expressions and Amirra understood them to be the newer ones to the cult. She remembered her first moons-light ceremony, but she was much younger than anyone there now, and she didn't have a choice which made her shudder. Maybe these people didn't either. That was the way the Velshari operated. They tell you everything you want to hear. They promise you, if you are faithful to the end you will inherit eternal life. If you obeyed every command, the Shadow would secure you a safe passage through the Shadow Realm and allow you to enter the heavens as a God with the leader Gavin Rhill.

The only problem was after they beguiled you with their kindness and flattery and you are completely at ease with them and share all your darkest secrets and desires, they switch into a mean and unforgiving creature. The sudden shift blinds you and makes you feel like somehow their bad behavior is your fault. Then just when you think it's time to move on, they turn on the love and flattery again and suck you right back into their clutches. Then the cycle repeats over and over with no end in sight. Over time, you lose your soul and become like a mindless being with only one goal, never make them mad at you.

Riddick felt her shudder and a hint of regret formed at the back of his throat. He hadn't realized how much damage they had done to her, and he was asking her to do something that was very scary for her.

"If this is too much, we will leave," Riddick whispered.

"No, I'm alright, but if this is what I think it is, this is going to get very uncomfortable," Amirra said.

"Why?" Riddick asked.

"This is an initiation ceremony," Amirra said.

"What does that mean?" Riddick asked.

"There will be blood," Amirra said.

"How much blood?" Riddick asked.

"Shhhhhh," Amirra said.

26-That's A Bit More Complicated

Serin and Shaz finished the distance to Bowen's table and sat in an open seat. The tavern was dark and dingy with scattered nutshells all over the floor mixed with a dark gooey substance Serin guessed to be tobacco spit. She cringed with the idea and tried to think of something else, but the only thing that kept coming to mind was Shaz's admission. *I know he is a war wizard, nothing new there, but what does that actually mean? A wizard designed for war? A wizard designed to kill? A wizard meant to plan, strategize, organize and fulfill war? War is killing, innocent people die in war. But Shaz didn't start the war...he didn't create the reasons for war... But he must finish them. He must go up against Necromancers, creatures, darkness, deceit, cruelty, anger. His existence is predestined, he didn't ask for this. Everyone wants to control him or hurt him.*

I guess he has to accept his role, so if that's his role, what is my role. I love him more than my heart can express. He has shadow magic. I have light magic. He uses the destructive magic of fire. I use the restorative magic of water. He has a short temper; I have more patients. He is impulsive, methodical, and has chaotic energy within him. I am calm, caring and soothing. We're perfect opposites. I guess we <u>*are*</u> *both stubborn and adventurous, spontaneous, and desire to do the right things, which makes us perfect equals.*

"Serin, you ready?" Shaz asked.

Serin lifted her head from resting in her hands.

"Yes, of course, sorry," Serin said.

Shaz was standing next to her and Bowen and his friends had already started to the door. Turkill and Ladtwig stood as tall as they could and started toward the door. Serin rose from the chair and Shaz followed behind her. Shaz pointed to go around the bar the other way, and she turned. Serin eyed Greederick the Tower and found he was back to drinking his ale and slobbering all over himself. *That's one nice thing, I don't have to deal with Shaz and Riddick getting drunk and looking and acting like an idiot,* she thought.

The sun was now overhead, and they shielded their eyes as they adjusted to the brightness. Bowen waved them to his location, and they maneuvered around the crowds.

A tall dark-haired man dressed in the traditional formal suit one would find in the inner business buildings bumped into Shaz's shoulder as he passed and the hair on the back of Shaz's neck stood out.

"We have company," Shaz said.

"Who?" Serin asked.

"Velshari," Shaz said.

"How many?" Serin asked.

"I'm not sure yet and with all these people I might not be able to tell, plus I don't think they wear a calling card to identify themselves as Velshari," Shaz said.

Serin cringed at the thought.

"Follow me, and stay close," Bowen said.

Shaz let Serin and the Minca in front, and they followed Bowen through the people-packed walkway. They exited the working district and made their way into the commerce district. The odor of metal and pitch was replaced with warm loaves of breads and meats and Ladtwig found it hard not to stop and stare at all the food markets. Serin gave him a sideways glare and gripped his shirt to keep him moving. Bowen led them through a cross-section and into a tailor's shop. Shaz recognized the shop and looked for the owner. The man pulled the cloth from the backroom door and made his way toward them.

"Welcome back sir, what can I help you with today?" the shopkeeper said.

He stuck his hand out and Shaz took it in a handshake. Shaz wasn't sure why they had stopped, so he turned to Bowen. Bowen turned around and the shopkeepers' jolly smile turned sour.

"What do you want?" the shopkeeper growled.

"Nice to see you too Sam," Bowen said. Sam crossed his arms across his chest and glared at Bowen. Shaz and Serin witnessed a very unpleasant moment of silence. "I see you are still holding a grudge," Bowen said. Sam didn't even as much as blink. "I'm just here to collect my mending," Bowen said.

"You haven't paid a single bit, you're not getting a thing until you pay your entire bill," Sam said.

"I don't have any money, but I really need my uniforms," Bowen said.

"Why can't you make the castle to pay for it?" Sam said.

"You know why, and I will pay you as soon as I can," Bowen said.

"How much does he owe?" Serin asked

"Who are you?" Sam snapped.

"She's with me, they're all with me," Shaz said.

Sam uncrossed his arms and stared at Shaz.

"Well, then you have gotten yourself into a lot of trouble, sir if you're hanging out with that man," Sam said.

"You have no idea," Turkill grunted.

Sam looked down at Turkill with a confused scowl.

"Sam, I'm happy to pay his bill, and I am sorry for the trouble, but we *are* in need of his things," Shaz said.

Sam studied Shaz for a moment and then nodded and went to the back room. He returned with a large pile of uniforms, handed them to Bowen and Shaz gave him the needed money. Shaz held out his hand

and Sam shook it, but with less enthusiasm. Bowen pulled open the door, and they started out of the shop.

"Sir, you better watch your back and don't trust him at face value," Sam said.

Shaz waved the others on and closed the door.

"Why do you say that?" Shaz asked.

"Anyone who works for the castle is no one to trust," Sam said.

"Thank you for your advice, we are going to try, and change that," Shaz said.

Shaz opened the door and left the shop. He met Serin on the other side of the courtyard where they were waiting. Shaz remembered that this was the courtyard he first met the witch and his stomach turned.

"Bowen, is there any other surprises we should be made aware of?" Shaz asked.

Bowen shook his head and shrugged as a sheepish grimace crossed his lips.

"There is another task I need to do," Bowen said.

"You go ahead and take care of that and meet us here," Shaz said.

Shaz gave him the address of Mrs. Bailey's and Bowen put it in his pocket.

"Do you think we have a minute to stop at a shop near here, I have a few things I would like to buy," Serin asked.

"Like what?" Shaz asked.

"Girl things," Serin said.

Shaz blushed and nodded.

"Then can I stop and get something too?" Ladtwig asked.

Shaz rolled his eyes and sighed. Ladtwig scurried toward the shop filled with meats and cheeses and Turkill hurried after him.

"Do you want to come, or wait for me?" Serin asked.

"I'll wait over there," Shaz said.

Shaz pointed to a group of tables near a café and Serin nodded.

"I'll hurry, thank you," Serin said.

Serin turned in the direction of the shop and Shaz waited until she was on her way then started toward the café. Halfway to the tables, a hand touched his arm and sent a wave of dread surging through his body. The hairs on the back of his neck stood out and the pit in his stomach lurched.

"Reinholt?" a tall dark-haired woman half-said-half-asked.

He shielded his mind as Grandfather had taught him and examined the woman's dark eyes which gave off a youthful anticipation but didn't match the gentle lines of age on her fair skin. Alarm bells ripped through his mind, but he quieted them, so he could think.

"I'm sorry, who did you say?" Shaz asked.

The woman stared into his eyes and examined them with intensity. The awkward silence suddenly overcame the atmosphere added to the sinking in his guts.

"I'm sorry, I thought you were someone I used to know?" the woman said.

"Oh?" Shaz asked.

"Reinholt, do you know him? You look almost exactly like him, with such blue eyes," Shaz felt the tug of the woman's efforts to search his being and pushed back, "it's quite a rare trait," the woman said.

Shaz shook his head.

"I'm sorry, I can't say that I do," Shaz said.

The woman's youthful gaze faded and Shaz watched the signs of age return to her being. Shaz understood she was someone from his father's past and wanted to find out who she was.

"Too bad," the woman said.

Who did you say you were?" Shaz asked.

"I didn't," the woman said.

"That would explain why I didn't hear it then. Well, it was nice to…umm… not meet you, have a nice day," Shaz said.

Shaz started to turn but the woman gripped his arm. Shaz sensed Serin leave the shop and look in his direction.

Stay where you are, he instructed silently. Serin heard the words and stepped back into the shadow of the shops' roof. Serin searched the surroundings and found Shaz and the woman wearing a light blue day dress with delicate lace around her collar and wrists. Serin scanned Shaz's energy and found he was shielding his mind and his alert level was on high. She thought of the Minca and hurried through the crowds to the shop they had gone into.

"Can I help you …whoever you are?" Shaz asked.

"My name is Isot," Isot said. Shaz held back the lump suddenly stuck in his throat. "Are you from around here, or here for the coronation?" Isot asked.

Shaz understood she was attempting to figure out who he was. An unsettling tickle in his mind made him think she was certain he was at least related to Reinholt. Now, in addition to getting inside the castle, he wanted to figure out how she knew his father. The look in her eye indicated that she had a romantic attraction to him as some point.

"I'm here for the coronation, I was supposed to be on the guest list, however, it would seem there was a mistake and my ticket is nowhere to be found," Shaz said.

"I might be able to help you with that," Isot said.

Isot's attention never left his eyes, and he knew she was probing his mind.

"Well, thank you," Shaz said.

"Where might you be from, so that I can inquire as to what happened to your invitation, that is," Isot asked.

"I'm here on behalf of the Grasslands, I'm also here to find out why the Queen has ceased aid to the farmers," Shaz said.

"I see, that I cannot answer, however, I can inquire and try to secure a meeting with the Queen," Isot said.

"How is it that you can do all that?" Shaz asked.

"I work at the castle and know a few people. Where are you staying?" Isot asked.

"I haven't figured that out yet," Shaz said.

"There's a man at the Northern Citadel Hotel named Henrick, tell him I sent you and he will make accommodations for you. I will send you word," Isot said.

"Thank you, your generosity is very kind," Shaz said.

Isot nodded and turned and walked into a group of soldiers disguised as high-class city folk, and they escorted her from the market square. Serin waited until she was out of sight, and she and the Minca hurried to Shaz.

"Who was that?" Turkill grunted.

"Isot," Shaz said.

"Serious!" Ladtwig said.

Ladtwig's eyes bulged and a partial sneer peaked the corner of his mouth.

"What did she want? How did she find you?" Serin asked.

"Let's keep moving," Shaz said.

Shaz directed the others through a small ally at the side of the square and down a long corridor.

"Where are we going?" Turkill asked.

"Away from the square," Shaz said.

Shaz crossed the ally and into another at a quick pace and Serin and the Minca had a hard time keeping up. The pit in his stomach eased, and he was confident he had moved far enough away from the presence of shadow magic. His mind raced around the details of why she was in the square, he was sure Inelius said she couldn't leave the castle and figured that the shadow magic allowed her to from time to time. He found a small nook and pulled Serin in after him. The Minca followed and huddled tightly at the back of the nook.

"She called me Reinholt," Shaz said.

Serin's green eyes scanned his eyes with full intent.

"Isot knew your father?" Turkill asked.

"It would seem so. I think they might have been more involved by the way she looked at me," Shaz said.

"How did she look at you?" Serin asked.

"Like she was expecting me, or rather Reinholt, to be excited to see her," Shaz said.

"That makes things a bit more complicated," Turkill said.

"She was trying to find out where I was from and why I was here. I think she was trying to figure out if I am me,"

"You didn't tell her, did you?" Turkill asked.

"Of course not. I told her I was here on behalf of the Grasslands. I don't think she bought it though, and she also told me to go to an Inn, and she would help me get into the coronation," Shaz said.

"You're not considering it are you?" Serin asked.

"I'm not sure yet, I might have to. We have no idea how I'm going to make my way into the castle, and this might be the perfect opportunity," Shaz said.

"I thought so," Serin said.

"For now, let's get to Mrs. Bailey's and keep on task and let things work themselves out," Shaz said.

Serin nodded but Shaz could tell she wasn't happy about it. He wasn't exactly thrilled either.

"We're in this together," Shaz said.

"I know, it's just-"

"We'll be alright," Shaz said.

Serin lifted on her toes to give him a kiss, but he hurried out of the nook. Serin wasn't sure what to think and wondered if he didn't notice or if it was something else. Serin didn't press but felt a pang of something, anger, jealousy, frustration, she couldn't tell. She tried to put it aside as they turned the corner and started toward the docks of the waterways.

✱✱✱✱✱✱✱✱✱✱✱✱✱✱✱✱✱✱✱✱✱✱✱✱

Isot paced the floor wringing her hands together tightly. A pit in the bottom of her stomach etched at her guts, and she was sure she was going to be sick. The sting of seeing someone who looked nearly exactly like her first love, but wasn't, was sending her emotions into a frenzy. Dread settled in, and she both longed for Reinholt but reveled in her being his ultimate demise. *He chose her over me, he deserved what he got*, Isot thought. Heavy footsteps outside the door brought her from her memories.

"Come in," Isot said.

A bulky soldier came through the door and greeted her.

"How may I be of service?" the soldier asked.

"Something has been brought to my attention and I wondered if you could take care of it for me," Isot said.

"I'll certainly try mam," the soldier said.

"Today in the square, I met someone that resembles someone I used to know, and I fear he is going to be trouble for our new queen. I need you to dispose of him and quickly," Isot said.

"Are you refereeing to the younger man with light hair?" the soldier asked.

"Yes, precisely, and everyone he is associated with, I don't trust any of them," Isot said.

"They were with Bowen the General, mam," the soldier said.

"I understand that, but that means he will have to go as well," Isot said.

"But that is the General mam, and my good friend," the soldier said.

"He used to be the General, and it seems he has picked a new group of friends, and they are not to be trusted, is that clear," Isot said.

"But-" the soldier said.

"Lorn stop being an idiot, do you want to stay the captain of the guard forever or do you want to be the King?" Isot asked.

"King? How would I become King?" Lorn asked.

"It is custom for the Vizier to help chose the spouse for the Queen so that the blood of the next heir stays as pure as possible. You do this for me, and I will make sure you are selected," Isot said.

"So, all I have to do is get rid of Bowen and his new friends and you will make me the King," Lorn asked.

"Yes, that is what I said," Isot said.

Isot rolled her eyes at his lack of intelligence and waited for him to run through whatever he was thinking.

"Alright, I'll do it," Lorn said.

"Good, let me know when it is done," Isot said.

Lorn slammed his hand on his chest and closed the door behind him.

27-Hurry, Come In And Shut the Door

They took the stairs to the lower pathway and noted the passenger boats as they made their way through the canals.

"Shaz, Serin!" Deagan shouted.

Shaz and Serin turned to the familiar voice and found a bright-eyed Deagan pushing his boat quickly toward them. Serin waved energetically and hurried to the edge of the stone platform. Deagan docked his boat and threw the mooring line over the hook and hopped across to the wet stone. His black hair was slicked back in his usual fashion, and he wore the same neatly pressed trousers and shiny shoes. Deagan screeched and jumped up and down. Turkill jumped back with a mix of surprise and terror. Shaz chuckled.

"Oh Deagan, it's so good to see you again!" Serin said.

"Oh girl, you look amaaaazinnnng!" Deagan said.

Deagan grabbed Serin in a tight hug and lifted her off the ground then set her back down. Deagan turned to Shaz and Shaz held out his hand, but Deagan shoved it aside and pulled him into a hug. Shaz wasn't sure what to do and lightly patted his back. Serin chuckled.

"How have you been my friend?" Shaz asked.

"Never mind about me, tell me everything, I can't wait to hear it all!" Deagan said.

"I don't think we have time for all that," Shaz said.

"Oh, come on, I have to know," Deagan said.

"Can you take us to Mrs. Bailey's?" Serin asked.

"Of course, of course," Deagan said.

Deagan motioned to his boat and Serin moved to the edge. Deagan held his hand out, and she took it and stepped in. Turkill and Ladtwig hefted their satchels into the boat.

"Oh, I didn't even notice you two, who is this?" Deagan asked.

Deagan hunched over and Turkill gave him a hearty hurmpf. Deagan's smile was bigger than life and Turkill narrowed his eyes and his brows scrunched into the center of his face.

"This is Turkill and Ladtwig, they are of the Minca nation," Serin said.

"The where?" Deagan asked.

"We'll fill you in as soon as we reach Mrs. Bailey's," Shaz said.

Deagan nodded and the Minca and Shaz climbed in the boat. Deagan unlatched the mooring line and hopped into the back and onto the small platform. He shoved the pole into the murky bottom and the boat slipped away from the cobblestone pier. There were quite a few more boats than Shaz had remembered and Deagan delicately maneuvered the six-passenger boat around the slower boats and into the waterways that took them to the part of town Mrs. Bailey lived.

The mid-day sun was hot and the hint of moldy moss from the waterways sat on their senses. Ladtwig sat in the front of the boat and leaned over the edge and watched the rippling water pass along the hull. He even got his hands wet and wriggled them in the water. Turkill gripped the center strap in the middle of the center seat and tugged tightly. He focused his attention on the horizon and tried to keep from retching. Shaz snickered, but he wondered why he was showing signs of being seasick this time and not when they went to the Mountain Temple. Shaz calculated it could be all the other boats and the number of people that were his full height taller than he was and not actually the sway of the boat.

"Do you think she will be there?" Serin asked.

"I hope so. We need to find out if she knows what the council is up to," Shaz said.

"What do you mean by that?" Serin asked.

"I really don't think they want to find out what I can or can't do," Shaz said.

"What do you think they want then," Serin asked.

"I'm not sure, but my gut says that something isn't right, and I need to find out what. I also need to find out what they have on the scroll," Shaz said.

"Alright," Serin said.

"I know my father and grandfather are in the council, and I know they all know about you, but I get a bad feeling about it all, and I think it might be better to have you stay with Mrs. Bailey, at least at first, the last time I talked about you, you were taken to the dungeons, and I'm not about to do that again," Shaz said.

Serin now understood why his affection for her seemed to change. He didn't want to make her a target. She wanted him to hold her, but she smiled with the understanding that this was one of his ways of keeping her safe.

"I hope it won't take long," Serin said.

"Aye, me too,"

Shaz smiled at her, relieved she understood him and gave her hand a tight squeeze. Deagan was intent on the two and smiled as he found them secretly holding hands. The taller buildings of the inner sections of Ebassia left a shadow on the waterways which was a welcomed relief. Deagan rounded the last bend and slowed the boat until he reached the next pier. He shoved the pole into the thick bottom in front of the boat to stop it completely and moved it up against the dock. He secured the pole into the latches on the side and strapped them down with a secured rope. Deagan slipped the mooring line over the hooks and hopped out onto the pier.

Shaz stood and helped Serin and Ladtwig out of the boat and waited for Turkill's head to stop spinning. Turkill's normal dark bronzed skin showed a hint of green as he slung his pack over his back and climbed out of the boat.

"I always knew you had a thing for her?" Deagan said to Shaz.

Deagan winked at Serin and smiled. Shaz smiled and slapped Deagan's shoulder. Deagan leaned in close to Serin.

"You *have* to tell me *everything*!" Deagan whispered.

Serin chuckled and latched her arm in his and started toward the ally between the buildings. Turkill's green eased and his usual hurmpf scowl returned. Ladtwig investigated everything he could, from the little pots on the edges of the windows to the knockers on the doors. Shaz counted the numbers he remembered and started down another ally. They continued down the last few lengths until they came to the soft pink curtains hanging in Mrs. Bailey's door window. There was a dim light on the other side of the door and Shaz lifted the knocker and tapped the metal ring three times. The light brightened and the pink curtain shifted. A round eye peeked from the corner of the bottom of the window and then the curtain dropped. The latches clunked and the door opened.

"Oh, my goodness, I can't believe it! Come in, come in," Mrs. Bailey said in a raised voice.

"Mrs. Bailey, I'm so excited to see you!" Serin said.

Serin stepped into the house and gave Mrs. Bailey a tight hug, followed by Shaz.

"Mrs. Bailey these are our friends, Ladtwig, Turkill, and Deagan," Serin said.

"Hurry come in and shut the door," Mrs. Bailey said.

Her bright eyes quickly changed to worry with a hint of fear. The crew moved into the house and Mrs. Bailey shut the door and locked the latches.

"Mrs. Bailey, what's wrong?" Shaz asked.

"Keep your voices low and follow me," Mrs. Bailey said.

Mrs. Bailey navigated the furniture toward the back of the house. Shaz and Serin exchanged concerned glances and Deagan bit the cuticle off his first finger. Shaz knew once he started, he wasn't going to stop biting them until he had bitten each finger. Mrs. Bailey's small and round frame bobbled as she quickly made her way up the stairs at the back of the house. Serin took each step and Shaz skipped two at a time. Mrs. Bailey stopped at a door which Shaz hadn't seen the time he was there and hushed them inside. The room was in the shape of a square circle with shelve on three of the six walls and a window on one. Shaz figured it was one of the lookout towers from rotations past made into a room. The heavy weaved curtains draped from the ceiling to the floor covering every inch of the wall the window was on and even puddled onto the floor.

Shaz recognized some of the artifacts like those he had seen in the large officers' buildings on Turob.

"What is going on?" Shaz asked.

"Oh, goodness, things have been such a mess, I can't think of where to start," Mrs. Bailey said.

"Is it safe in here?" Shaz asked.

"As safe as I can make it," Mrs. Bailey said.

"Hang on," Shaz said.

Shaz rubbed his palms together and rusty orange sparkles emerged. Deagan jumped and scooted close to Serin and shoved his hands under his armpits and bit his lower lip. The misty dust started around the room and made it halfway when it came to a round object sitting on one of the shelves near the ceiling. Shaz reached up and took the silver ball off the shelf. He ran his hands over the surface and understood it to have an enchantment on it.

"What is this and where did it come from?" Shaz asked.

"I've never seen it before. I'm too short to have ever seen that high up there," Mrs. Bailey said.

"It definitely has an element of shadow magic in it," Shaz said.

Shaz called the energy of the fire element with a hint of shadow magic and a red-hot green-tinted flame burst from his skin. Deagan shrieked and Serin shushed him. Shaz set the ball on a table across the room and let the flame heat the metal until it melted into a pile of ooze. A black puff of smoke smoldered off the remains. The rusty orange sparkles drifted around the room in their search for anything else of an evil magical nature. The particles didn't find anything and fizzled into nonexistence.

"Alright, we're safe now. Whoever placed it here did it with the intention to spy on you," Shaz said.

Mrs. Bailey gritted her teeth, tightened her fists and grunted under her breath. Deagan wobbled a little and tried to find something on the wall to steady himself.

"Deagan, I think you better sit down," Serin said.

Serin helped Deagan to a chair by the table and Mrs. Bailey fidgeted with her dinner apron.

"What just happened?" Deagan asked.

Deagan's frame shook and his dark eyes studied Shaz and Serin.

"Shaz, you're not safe here. The city is crawling with Velshari. Seems as though a signal was given, and they have come in droves. You have to get out of here as fast as you can," Mrs. Bailey said.

"Aye, I have been sensing them since we arrived," Shaz said.

"The who?" Deagan asked.

"It would seem we might be more outnumbered than originally thought," Shaz said.

"What about Riddick and Amirra, they're still in the forest?" Turkill asked.

"Aye, I think they'll be fine," Shaz said.

"So, when you say crawling, how many is that?" Serin asked.

"Too many to even count," Mrs. Bailey said.

"What does the council think about all of this?" Shaz asked.

"I haven't heard from the council in weeks," Mrs. Bailey said.

"Who's the council?" Deagan asked.

"I think they are mad at me for sending you away," Mrs. Bailey said.

"You didn't send me away. I chose a different path at the time. Who said that to you?" Shaz asked.

"Garrison, he's the leader, as of now anyway. He's a bit of a pompous...individual," Mrs. Bailey growled.

Mrs. Bailey's soft creamy skin turned a hot red, and she breathed in several deep breaths.

"What do you suppose is going on then?" Serin asked.

"Is anyone going to answer my questions?" Deagan asked.

Serin turned to see his deep sun-bathed skin nearly white.

"Oh dear, you don't look well, I have some tea that will help," Mrs. Bailey said.

"I'll take care of it," Serin said.

Serin pulled off her long gloves and put her hands on his face and sent a cooling mist of magic into his frame. The soft blue hues danced from her hands and her silver tattoos delicately entwined on her hands and arms glowed as her healing magic enveloped Deagan's shaking body. Deagan's eyes brightened with the peaceful energy but shivered as he internalized the sensations.

"That is magic!" Ladtwig said.

Ladtwig smiled and nudged Deagan who gawked at him.

"Serin, I should have known you were an elemental healer," Mrs. Bailey said.

"Speaking of magic, Shaz you have used yours so now we are going to have the sqwalls too," Serin said.

"Blast," Shaz said.

Shaz ran his hands through his hair. Serin understood his chaotic energy inside was now even more so and bit her lip. A faint knock at the door sounded.

"I'm guessing Bowen," Serin said.

"I'll fetch them," Turkill said.

"Who's coming?" Mrs. Bailey asked.

Turkill gripped the door and slipped out and pulled it closed. Turkill hurried down the stairs and rounded the corner as Bowen banged on the knocker. Turkill yanked the latch and pulled open the door. Bowen peered into the doorway and then down at Turkill who had his arms crossed over his chest and a scowl.

"Hurry, inside," Turkill grunted. Bowen pushed the door open enough for him and another man to slip through. "Don't say a word and follow me."

Bowen nodded and the other man closed the door and locked the four latches before catching up to Bowen on the stairs. Turkill practically ran up the stairs and Bowen skipped two at a time. Turkill opened the upper door and they hurried inside.

"This is Lorn, my second in command," Bowen said.

"Nice to meet you," Serin said.

Lorn turned to Serin and his heart skipped a beat. He couldn't help but find her beauty remarkable and his whole body shifted into a suave swagger. He eyed Serin with a bright look of eagerness and Serin gave him a curt nod but wanted to role her eyes, which she didn't.

"Welcome," Shaz said.

Lorn peeled his eyes from Serin to shake Shaz's hand and jumped at how hot it was. Shaz's steely glare sent a very clear signal to Lorn that Serin was off-limits, and he pulled his hand away and shook it out. Turkill smirked and Ladtwig fidgeted with a statue on the desk.

"This is Mrs. Bailey, whose home we are in, and has welcomed us to stay, however, we need to come up with a plan and quickly," Shaz said.

"Pleasure, mam," Bowen said.

"Were you followed?" Shaz asked.

"I don't think so, but I wasn't expecting to be," Bowen looked around and saw everyone in the small room. "What did I miss, it feels like a funeral," Bowen asked.

"Things are a bit more complicated than we expected," Serin said.

"Why, what's happened?" Bowen asked.

"The city is crawling with Velshari," Shaz said.

"Does it have to do with the scroll?" Bowen asked.

"Aye, we think it might be because Isot has figured it out," Shaz said.

"What is this scroll?" Lorn asked.

"It binds the crypt making the holder immortal," Shaz said.

"It does more than that," Mrs. Bailey said.

Shaz shot her serious but surprised glare, and she pulled back.

"What do you mean, it does more than that? What else does it do?" Shaz asked.

"It makes the beholder immortal, yes, but also anyone they seem fit to add," Mrs. Bailey said.

"So, they are planning on making all the Velshari immortal?" Turkill asked.

"That's what I think they are doing, but without having inside information I can only guess," Mrs. Bailey said.

"How many are we talking?" Bowen asked.

"Too many to count," Mrs. Bailey said.

"If only we knew what the council was doing about all of this," Serin said.

"I bet that Isot has done something to them," Turkill said.

"Yes, that would make sense, and also why I haven't been to any meetings," Mrs. Bailey said.

"I'm so confused," Deagan said.

"We'll explain everything in a minute," Serin snapped.

Deagan slunk into the chair and Serin patted his shoulder.

"I'm sorry Deagan, I'll summarize quickly. Shaz is a War Wizard, I'm a Water Mage and the evil Shadow is controlling a secret organization called the Velshari. The Binding of the Crypt scroll is a powerful object we believe has been infused into the walls of the Ebassia castle. Shaz needs to get into the castle, restore the incantation of the scroll and find out what happened to the council, which is a group of people trying to stop the Velshari. We need to keep the artifacts hidden and restore the realms and we need to find out if the Queen can be an ally," Serin said.

"Oh, is that all?" Deagan asked.

"Now it's even more important that I find the council," Shaz said.

"If they didn't kill them, they would have taken them to the dungeons," Bowen said.

Serin studied Shaz's expression as the dread ran through his being, knowing that Merrick, and Grandfather were both a part of the council.

"Well, if they are in the dungeons, we'll just break them out," Shaz said.

"Impossible, once you go in you never get out," Lorn said.

"You mean the dungeons that *we* escaped from?" Deagan asked.

Lorn stared blankly at Deagan. Bowen's face twisted through the memories his brother Barrick told, and now understood it was true.

"Aye, and exactly what we are going to do again if we need to," Shaz said.

"I was worried you were going to say we were going back in there. Wait, what? Did you just say what I thought you said?" Deagan asked.

"I did, do you think Lucien and his thugs will help?" Shaz asked.

"Oh, no, no, no, no," Deagan said.

"Give him your medallion," Shaz said. Serin slipped the chain from around her neck and dropped the old medallion into Deagan's hand. Deagan put the necklace on. "You better keep that hidden, with so many Velshari around, you don't want to become a target," Shaz said.

Deagan gulped and quickly shoved it into his shirt.

"I haven't seen Lucien since you left, he's been angry at me and you for that matter," Deagan said.

"Why?" Serin asked.

"You never got him what he wanted from the dungeon," Deagan said.

"Oh yeah, well, I guess we'll pay him another visit," Shaz said.

"And we need to figure out what to do about the sqwalls," Serin said.

"Sqwalls? Great," Bowen said.

"What are sqwalls?" Lorn asked.

"Trouble," Bowen said.

Lorn squinted with a new curiosity.

"If the sqwalls are on the move, so are the Ukari," Shaz said.

"I'm worried we might have an issue with the Jaduuk," Turkill said.

"Bowen make it known that your soldiers are not to attack the Ukari," Shaz said.

"What are the Ukari?" Lorn asked.

"We'll take care of the Jaduuk," Bowen said.

"Are you sure, they have been increasing in hoard sizes," Serin said.

"What are you talking about?" Lorn asked.

"I'll fill you in later," Bowen said.

"When and where do you suppose Isot is going to do this spell thingy?" Turkill asked.

Deagan jumped out of his chair.

"The coronation!" Deagan said loudly.

He covered his mouth and sat down.

"Of course, that would certainly be a place that all those people could be at once," Bowen said.

"When is the coronation?" Serin asked.

"In two days," Bowen said.

"I'll have to hurry and find the council and figure out what is going on," Shaz said.

"And go shopping for a dress for Serin," Everyone stared at Deagan. "What? It's the coronation. I already have my outfit," Deagan said.

"What can you tell us about the Queen, will she join forces?" Shaz asked.

"What kind of hold does Isot have on the Queen?" Mrs. Bailey asked.

"Quite a bit, in fact, she is the one who made the queen make her the Grand Vizier," Bowen said, "but the army is with us."

Serin perceived Lorn's deception and gave Shaz a slight nod and Shaz noted her thoughts. The mid-afternoon sun baked the heavy curtain and caused the heat to radiate heavily through the room.

"Alright then, I think that's all we need from you," Shaz said to Bowen.

A flash of curious defeat crossed Bowen's face until Shaz stepped toward him where Lorn couldn't see his face and Bowen nodded with understanding.

"I'll walk you two to the door," Serin said.

Lorn smiled big and Serin tried not to gag. Lorn followed her out of the room and down the stairs and Shaz put his hand on Bowen's shoulder.

"Be careful, Lorn isn't committed to you like he used to be, and he has his own agenda. Do what you can with the Jaduuk, but most of all stay safe," Shaz said.

Bowen nodded.

"I was hopeful, but I guess you're right," Bowen said.

"I'll fill you in on the rest of the plan later," Shaz said.

Bowen nodded and he left the room. Serin returned and rolled her eyes around her head and put her finger in her mouth like she was gagging and Shaz blurted a hearty full-bellied rumble.

"I think we need to have a backup plan," Shaz said.

"I know where we can find some help," Deagan said. Everyone turned to Deagan who shoved his hands under his armpits. "They aren't soldiers, but they do know a few things about the city that most people don't, not even the guards," Deagan said.

"Like what?" Shaz asked.

"Things like secret tunnels and such," Deagan said.

"Are you referring to the travelers, the group of lower-class people that move from place to place trying to stay hidden from those of magic?" Serin asked.

"You know about the travelers?" Deagan asked.

"Yes," Serin said.

"How?" Deagan asked.

"Never mind, we can talk about all that later. Right now, we need to see if they'll help," Serin said.

"Turkill, you and Ladtwig go back to Riddick and Amirra and fill them in, bring them here as soon as they're finished," Shaz said.

"I met Isot in the market square, and she thought I was someone else, and invited me to attend the coronation," Shaz said.

"Who did she think you were?" Mrs. Bailey asked.

"Reinholt," Shaz said.

"Oh my," she patted her chest and waved her plump hand in front of her face to keep the blood from making her faint.

"What's wrong?" Serin asked.

"I forgot that they knew each other," Mrs. Bailey said.

"How *well* did they know each other," Shaz asked.

"I wasn't there of course, but what I heard, was your mother won his heart and Isot didn't," Mrs. Bailey said.

"Oh, one of those kinds of things, how comforting," Serin said.

"I guess that explains why she looked at me the way she did," Shaz said.

28-Yeah, She's A Real Peach

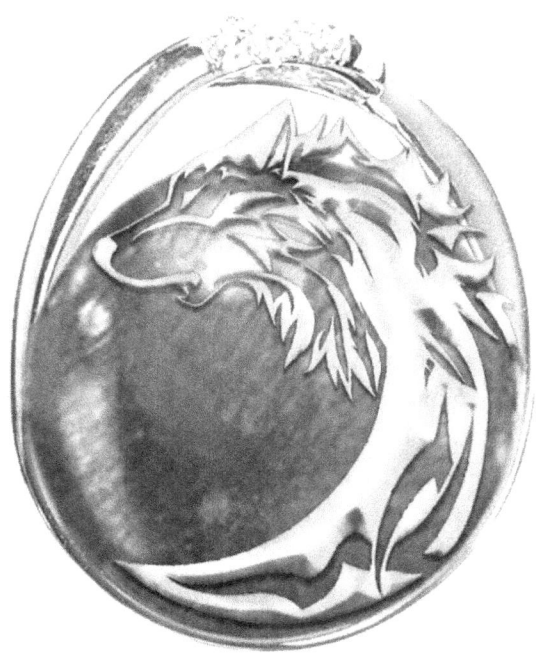

Riddick inched a few lengths closer and ended up only a few lengths from the last member of the Velshari. The man fidgeted with his robe and crossed his arms over his chest to keep his hands from shaking. Riddick dropped a seed from the tree into the small opening at the back of the man's robe. The cold round nut touched the man's skin, and he jumped and reached for the object. The man wriggled and turned, and Riddick could see the red welt on his cheek. Amirra shoved her foot into his, well she wasn't sure what part of the tree was what part of his body.

Riddick quietly giggled to himself and dropped another nut onto the man's head. The man brushed off the annoyance and took several steps away from the tree. Riddick slowly lowered a very small branch and touched the shoulder of another man. The man turned but didn't see anyone or anything and looked back. Riddick did it again and the man brushed off his shoulder and stepped closer to the other man. Riddick scooted a few tiny lengths. The largest moon eased the last few lengths and the second moon rested to the left side and the smallest moon sat slightly underneath and to the right. The woman moved into the center of the group of people and Amirra gripped the branch she was holding tighter and her skin grew pale.

"We are gathered here to welcome our newest members. Tonight, is also a special night as we have reached a pivotal moment," she held out the medallion and half of the crowd gasped. "Tonight, we will be able to talk to the moons and call down the powers of the elements. We have not had this opportunity in over a millennium, not since the Council stole our access to the elements," the woman said.

The woman held up another amulet which hung on a chain around her neck and let the moon's light reflect the light. Riddick recognized its description as being the Sistine Moon the Ukari spoke of.

"I have to get that amulet," Riddick whispered.

"What?" the man with the welt asked.

The man next to him shook his head and put his finger on his lip. The man with the welt shook his head to clear the fog that was setting in.

"New members, please step forward," the woman said. Seven or eight people stepped toward the woman. "Cover your heads and faces," she said.

The whole group pulled their hoods over their heads and pulled out long white masks and covered their whole faces except their eyes. The woman took out a blade and bent down. With the tip of the bade she drew a circle in the dirt. She stood and held out her hand and slid the sharp edge against the skin of her palm. She winced with the pain and then squeezed several drops and let them drop onto the dirt inside the circle.

"Hold out your hands," she said.

The recruits held out their hands with their palms face up and Amirra gripped her hand tight. Riddick's heart sank and a red-hot flame erupted at the core of his being. The woman took the first hand in her bloody hand and Riddick could tell it was another female. She sliced the skin and squeezed several drops over her own blood, then moved on to the next member until she had finished each one. The woman wiped the blood from the knife onto a handkerchief and returned them both to the inside pocket of her robe.

With the medallion in one hand and the Sistine Moon in the other, the woman lifted them until she caught the moon's rays and then angled them, so the rays met each other. A bright light flashed the crowd and they shielded their eyes. The woman angled the moon rays reflecting from the medallion, so it was shining on the circle. The etched line started to glow and crawl along the dirt floor in an outward circle.

The woman held the Sistine Moon at the right angle to shine the ray of light into the center. The pool of blood started to sizzle, and pop and smoke flared and rose in a spiraling motion. Amirra leaned close to the main trunk hoping it was closest to Riddick's ears.

"We can't let her finish the spell, we need to block the moon's rays," Amirra whispered.

Riddick grew a branch at the very top and moved it carefully into position to block the moon. The light on the ground faded and the sizzle and pop lessened. The woman realized the infraction and shifted the medallion and retook the ray. The circle grew again, and the sizzle intensified. The woman started to chant the spell and Amirra's body tightened. She hadn't realized her own initiation rotations ago would still be active, and she closed her eyes. The pain in the back of her head gnawed into a throb, and she pulled in a long and slow breath.

Riddick used a branch and snuck into her pocket and pulled out the ring she had made to block the Velshari's magic access to her mind. Riddick tapped her on the shoulder, and she opened her eyes. She quickly slipped the ring onto her finger and the throbbing instantly ceased. Amirra sighed quietly and tried to relax. The woman started to shake as the energy of the moons beam went into the Sistine Moon and then came out at a stronger rate.

The woman started to move the amulet toward the blood and Riddick eased the branch over the moonlight. The amulet softened and the woman looked up. She saw the branch and scooted a few lengths to one side and regained the moon's light. Riddick tried to ease the branch over, but the woman moved the stones again. The light beam shot out of the amulet and onto the blood and then sent individual light rays into the members' bloody hands. The people cried out with the pain it caused as the new power ripped through their bodies.

"Now Riddick," Amirra said.

Riddick flung the branch with a snap and stung the woman's hand holding the Sistine Moon. She yelped in pain and dropped the amulet, but it didn't fall as it was secured to a chain around her neck. Riddick cursed and snapped the other hand. She yelped again and dropped the medallion which did fall to the ground. Riddick readied his branch to reach for the chain around her neck. The woman rubbed her hands and bent to pick up the medallion and Riddick slipped the tip under the chain as she bent down and lifted it off of her as she stood up, but before anyone could see the branch stealing the amulet Riddick took several other branches and slapped the behinds of the closest members.

A chaotic rustle ensued as people yelped and rubbed their back-sides. The woman reached for the amulet, but it wasn't there. Riddick slapped her on the backside, and she yelped again.

"Everybody RUN!" Amirra screamed.

Riddick continued to slap people as they panicked and started to run. The woman tried to call them back, but Riddick slapped her again. She grabbed the medallion tightly and the neck of her robe and ran after the rest of the Velshari. Amirra had a hard time containing her sudden amusement. She had daydreamed rotations ago at something just such as this happening. The tightness in her hand eased as the large moon moved out of the alignment. Riddick started to move his way back toward the building as quickly as he could, so if anyone came back, they wouldn't be there. He handed the amulet to Amirra who put the chain around her neck and shoved the jewel into her shirt.

Amirra rested her head again on his trunk and closed her eyes. She thought back to her own initiation. Images of Semias's handsome face surfaced, and she remembered back when he was young and captivating. A flick of angry heat ripped through her chest as she remembered she once had a young girl's crush on him. She tried to push past that part and focus on the ceremony itself. Something wasn't sitting right, but she couldn't figure out what it was. Riddick's movements stopped and Amirra sat up.

"Hang on," Riddick said. Amirra wasn't sure what to hang onto but didn't end up having time anyway. Riddick released his earth magic and the tree form faded from around his human form. Amirra gulped as the sensation of falling churned her stomach. Riddick gripped her with his warm soft skin and kept her from falling as her feet touched the ground. The swaying in her head stopped and she wobbled. "Are you alright?" Riddick asked.

"Yes, I think so," Amirra said.

She shook her head clear and blinked a few times. A small ray of moonlight lit up part of Riddick's face, and she could see him give her his gentle smile. She hugged him and he squeezed her tight.

"I'm sorry I made you do that, I never want you to experience that again," Riddick said.

"I know, but I have to start facing my demons and figure out how to manage them. If I keep running from it, then I will never overcome them," Amirra said.

"When you're ready will you tell me what the tarnation that was about," Riddick said.

"I will, there's something different about it though, and I can't figure it out yet," Amirra said.

Riddick grabbed her hands, and she realized she was nervously rubbing them together. She tightened the palm with the scar, but Riddick opened her fingers.

"I want you to be certain, that when you are ready to talk, I will listen and I won't judge you, I understand you are a different person than what they made you be," Riddick said.

Amirra smiled and kissed him. He returned her kiss and his soft warm lips eased the pit in her stomach.

"Let's find our stuff and make a shelter for the night, and we can talk tomorrow or when you're ready," Riddick said.

"Thank you," Amirra said.

"For what?" Riddick asked.

"Giving me a good laugh at the Velshari's expense," Amirra said.

Riddick gave her another squeeze then let her go and started to search for his pack. A bristling of leaves under the bush startled him, and he froze. Nix's dark eyes glistened, and Riddick's heart skipped a beat. Nix slowly came out from under the bush.

"Are you Shaz's friend?" Nix asked.

Riddick pulled back and realized it was the little critter from earlier that evening.

"Aye, but who are you?" Riddick asked.

"Nix. Don't be mad at Nix, Nix had to do it, and then the scary lady said Nix wasn't going to get my family anyway. That stupid lady, she lied," Nix said.

"Why did you give her the medallion?" Riddick asked.

"Shaz told me to, he said Nix was to give the shiny to the scary lady and then find you," Nix said.

"Why would he do that?" Amirra asked.

"He said he had a different shiny and didn't need it," Nix said.

"I bet he put a tracking spell on it, or something," Riddick said.

"Ah, cleaver," Amirra said.

"That scary lady put your family in the dungeons," Riddick stated.

Nix nodded and wrung his hand-like paws together.

"Nix is very, very angry with the scary lady," Nix said.

"The scary lady's name is Gitre, she's one of the leaders and I bet she's under Isot's command," Amirra said.

"She is a scary lady," Riddick said.

"Yeah, she's a real peach," Amirra said.

Riddick chuckled.

"We have a lot to do tomorrow, let's get some sleep," Riddick said.

A distant crack rippled across the sky and a coolness crept into their skin.

"And looks like rain too," Amirra said.

"I'll take care of that," Riddick said.

Riddick picked up his pack and slung it over his shoulder and Amirra grabbed hers. They made their way to a small section where there had been a pile of stones. The dirt was soft now that the stones were gone, and he molded it into the cradle-like trough like the one he had slept in the desert. He motioned for Amirra to take the first one, and he made a second next to it. Amirra pulled out her bedroll and laid it in the cradle and climbed in. She was surprised to find how soft and cozy it was and succumbed to the instant weight of drowsiness. She yawned bigger than she had in a long time and Riddick grabbed several branches from a nearby tree.

He fashioned a weaved canopy as they had used in the jungle but this time, he used his magic and made the leaves and twigs weave themselves. The covering grew as it weaved in and out, and he placed it in a dome over their new beds. He made a second one and placed it in the opposite direction and secured them together. He took a few smaller sticks and shoved them through the edges of the leaf tarp, climbed inside and secured them to the ground. Riddick was about to unroll his bedroll when there was a small scratch on the covering.

Riddick lifted the edge and found Nix's big eyes drooping in sadness. Riddick sighed and opened the dome so Nix could climb inside and secured the edges. Nix pawed at the dirt and wriggled himself into a small hole of his own and Riddick slipped into his bedroll.

29-Has Anyone Ever Been To One Of These Before?

The air was clear, and the large moon was high overhead as the men and women gathered at the edge of the forest. There were fifteen women and sixteen men gathered at the outer perimeter gate of the location they had been instructed to meet. A gust of wind picked up a smattering of leaves and tossed them through their hair on the way by. The trees swayed and moved about creating an eerie set of shadows on the dirt path.

"Has anyone ever been to one of these before?" a scrawny pink-nosed lad asked.

"This is an initiation into the Couvetry, so no, of course not," a fairly built middle-aged man said.

"I mean, I know that, but I just thought maybe someone might have heard what happens, is all," the red-nosed lad said.

"I guess we'll find out soon," a woman about the age of the lad said.

The night cooled down and some people tightened their coats and cloaks around them tightly and some bounced in place to keep warm. A creek from a nearby gate stung the night and the crowd turned to find a small dark figure. The hood of a long dark robe draped the ground and covered the woman's head and wrapped over nearly covering her eyes. The shadows were so dark none of her features were visible and the lad wasn't sure it was a woman until she spoke.

"You will now be escorted into the Couvetry where you will receive your entrance into the Velshari and receive your gift. Make sure you have with you your tools, and in a single file line, follow my assistant. If you speak even one word, you will be eliminated," the woman said.

Her voice was strong and eerie at the same time and the lad gave the young woman a grimace. The young woman took his hand and gave it a gentle squeeze, and they fell into the line together. The assistant was taller and had a stronger gate to their walk and the lad supposed it to a man. The lad took in as many details of the path they were on, the trees they passed, and the smells in the air. He couldn't place them all, but he did pick out the bitterness of dockweed, and the sweetness of ginger root as the most dominant. The long thin clouds in the sky shifted over the moon several times making the trek a little hard at times, and the lad was thankful they weren't moving very fast.

An old wooden plantation estate emerged from the distance and the lad could see the tall stained-glass windows illuminate as the lantern light inside grew brighter. The plantation had several fireplaces and a balcony on the upper level with pillars supporting it over the main entrance. The lad expected they would turn toward the main doors, but they veered to the side and back of the house instead. Dogs barked in the distance and a cold wind sank into their bodies. Someone's teeth began to chatter from the back of the line and the lad's stomach lurched into his throat, and he wanted to gag.

"Wait here," a woman said.

The lad jumped as the woman's voice came from behind him, he hadn't noticed her following them. The assistant unlatched the lock of a basement door and pulled the heavy chain off. The clanking of the chain seared the night and the lad wanted to leap into a dead run. He turned to find the young woman and was able to make out her delicate features from the light of a nearby lamppost. She smiled gently and his nerves eased. The door opened and the assistant pointed to a man and pointed to the right, then pointed to a woman and pointed to the left.

The man at the front of the line entered the house and turned right and the first woman turned left. The lad peered into the light as he waited for the line to move forward. He turned to the right and the young woman turned left.

They were led down a long hall which had several pictures of what he supposed were previous leaders and the not in his stomach tightened. The line stopped, and he tried to look around the taller man in front of him but couldn't see anything. He took in a deep breath and shook out his shaking hands. The line began to move again, and he emerged into a long skinny room which had been fitted with rows of hooks and shelves.

"You will remove all of your clothes and dress in the ritual garments and place your dagger and tools on the altar, so they can be sanctified. You will receive them as part of the ritual, and when you are done, you may sit and meditate to prepare your minds. You will not speak a word until later in the ritual," the man said.

The lad looked around and found the man was now in the front of the line. Several of the men began to disrobe, even down to their nothings and the lad gulped. He quickly pulled off his coat and hung it on an empty hook and unlaced his boots. He shoved them under the bench beneath his coat and pulled off his tunic and nickers. He pulled the black robe over his head and let the heavy wool drape his body. The robe was several sizes too large but at least he wasn't naked, and he wrapped the extra's in his hands and hugged himself.

He wanted to cry but sucked in a breath and filled his lungs and remembered his dagger and removed it from his coat pocket. He waited behind a stout fella and placed his knife on the red velvet altar. He made note of the other knives and was at least pleased with himself because his was one of the largest ones. His thoughts turned to the young woman, and he wondered if they were being made to do the same. He tried to sit at the edge of the room and clear his mind. The lad could tell there was a soft commotion coming from the other room, and he listened as hard as he could.

A full-figured woman dressed in a dark green lace collared dress which draped off her curves in a delicate flowing motion, dipped a long wick starter into the flame of a candle at the end of a mantle on the wall. The flame engrossed the starter showing her lace wristbands were snug against her puffy hands. The woman's rosy cheeks glowed in the flickering of the flame and her warm brown eyes glistened in the twinkling of its light. A man in the corner of the dark-wood paneled room struck a drum with his fist and listened to the hum it made as it faded into the night's silence. He struck the drum again and repeated the strike in a rhythmic pattern which echoed off the high arched ceiling. The woman moved around the room in a calculated manner lighting each of the hundreds of candles to the beat of the drum.

The lad jumped at the sound of the drum and the irritating nauseousness in his guts ripped through his body. He took in several deep breaths and his head started to feel wobbly. The lanterns on the walls started to dance and sway as his head became heavy. The man with the dark robe appeared at the end of the room.

"You will now be led into the ritual. Remember, no talking. When it is your turn you will be asked to speak your new name. You will be united with your dagger and the ritual will be complete. Now form a line starting here, you will walk slowly to the beat of the drum until you are told to stop," the man said.

The man motioned to the mark on the floor and the group of men formed a line. The lad tried to get into the middle of the line but was shoved toward the back, and he nearly fell over the long foot of another man.

The woman in the other room nodded and the door at the back opened. A warm amber light filled the room until the row of women and men cast their shadows as they walked to the beat of the drum into the spacious area. The rosy woman pointed to a mark on the floor for each of the new recruits and each one took their place as indicated. The door closed and the person at the door came behind the first woman. She pulled a black cloth draped over her arm and tied it over the woman's eyes and proceeded to the next woman. A man at the other side of the room tied the same black cloth over the eyes of the men and stepped back and next to the woman.

The woman stepped to the side of the mantle as the small woman in the dark robe entered the center of the room. She waved to her assistant who brought the red velvet platform the knives were on and placed it on the wooden altar at the head of the room. She waved to the other assistant, and they brought a second velvet platform and sat it next to the first. The woman took out her own dagger and drew a circle in the sand on the floor. She made several lines crossing the center of the circle and took each blade and stuck the tip into the sand, so they stood up next to each other but not touching any of the lines. She dipped her finger in a bowl of water and touched the butt of each knife and started to chant.

The words were unfamiliar to the lad, and he struggled to peer through the black shroud covering his eyes. Even though he didn't want to know what was happening he wanted to know what was happening. He could make out where the woman was but not what she was doing. The sound of the woman's voice sent shivers through the lad and the hairs on his body refused to lay down. The breeze under the wool drape caught him off guard, and he shifted his weight several times. His nerves relaxed when faint sniffles of one of the women crossed his ears, and he was relieved that he wasn't the only one scared to death.

The dark-robed woman ended her chanting and replaced the knives on the altar. She put one foot on each side of the circle at held out her hands.

"Who beseeches this place, the Couvetry of Ebassia of the Velshari?" the woman asked loudly.

"I bring you many who wish to know the mysteries of the Velshari and who wish to be of service to our master, Gavin Rhill," one of the assistants said.

"Bring them forth," the woman said.

The assistant took the arm of the first woman and led her to the center of the room in front of the altar.

"Necrophant, by what name will you be known within this sacred circle?" the woman asked.

The woman repeated the name she had chosen for herself in a shaky voice. The woman took the water and dripped a few drops on her head and the assistant escorted her to another mark on the floor. The assistants did so for each of the members and when the lad was finished, he sighed with relief. The dark-robed woman motioned for the assistants to remove the black shrouds and the lad blinked a few times until the room came into view. He now found they were standing in a circle around the circle and altar. The candlelight now illuminated the woman's features from under her hood and the lad was surprised to see her black hair and small squinted eyes, until she caught him looking at her and her flash of murder crossed her eyes. The lad gulped and he tried not to pee himself. The assistants picked up the platform with the daggers and each took their own knife.

"You will now prove your loyalty with no less than your own blood and a sworn acknowledgment of your fidelity to the cause," the woman said.

The lad began to sweat, not because the room had grown warm but because he was going to have to cut himself. The dark-robed woman picked up a long stem of a plant the lad had never seen and ran it through the flames of the candles that were now sitting on the altar instead of the daggers. She stepped around the circle and with each pass through the flames she flung the smoke at each Necrophant. The intoxicating aroma filled their lungs and a soothing ease sank into their chest. The lad realized the drug-like effect made him not even care he would be opening his skin with a sharp knife and was actually thankful for the effect.

The robed woman took out her own blade and sliced her palm slowly and carefully to follow the previous cut, so she would only have one scar. She gritted her teeth as the pain hit her brain and dripped her blood into the sand of the circle. She motioned for the Necrophants to do the same, and they each took their knives and drew a line through their palms. She motioned for them to, in turn, drip their blood into the circle. The lad happily squeezed his hand and dripped blood into the circle after watching the young woman drip hers.

The woman took a skull and set it on the circle. The lad assumed it was a human skull but didn't seem to mind anymore. The woman dripped a black substance over the skull and then sand and the lad supposed it to be tar. The woman took a candle from the altar.

"Deity of the Shadows and master of the underworld, master of the living, I have found these Necrophants to be worthy of your blessing in serving you and your cause. Necrophant's hold out your hand,"

The woman touched the flame to the black substance, and it ignited instantly and consumed the tar on the skull and headed to the sand. The lad mesmerized by the flame, watched it feed off the tar and jump to life when it hit the blood in the sand. A flame shot out from the circle and ripped into the open wound of each member. Screams of pain wreaked havoc around the room and the lad hit the ground with the sudden pain that sank into his awareness.

30-Dust?

Mrs. Bailey fidgeted with her cooking apron as she had been for the last few hours and waved a small fan in front of her face. A gentle glow radiated from her rosy cheeks.

"Mrs. Bailey, how far to the Council's main meeting place?" Shaz asked.

"Not far, I can take you to the inner-city buildings," Mrs. Bailey said.

"I'm going with you," Serin said.

Shaz started to object but felt a prick in his brain and knew she was not going to allow it this time. He rubbed his temples and nodded.

"I'm going to go and make us some refreshments," Mrs. Bailey said.

"I'll go with you," Deagan said.

Deagan pulled the door behind him.

"Aren't the traveler's your people?" Shaz asked.

"Yes, why?" Serin asked.

"Do you know about the secret tunnels?" Shaz asked.

"No, I traveled with my father too much, so I was never privy to that information, so if Lucien can get it, that would be best," Serin said.

Shaz nodded.

"I'm going to go help Mrs. Bailey," Serin said.

Shaz nodded and sat in one of the chairs sitting next to the desk and put his face in his hands.

Mrs. Bailey quickly set out a pitcher and popped the lid from a jar and poured a dark amber powdery substance into the container. Serin gathered enough glasses and pulled the large tray from a cupboard and arranged them. Deagan followed Mrs. Bailey's instructions and gathered some sweet biscuits and tarts and organized them onto a tray. Mrs. Bailey twisted the lever and began to fill the pitcher with water.

"Mrs. Bailey, things are going to be alright," Serin said.

Mrs. Bailey looked up from the overflowing pitcher and quickly shut the valve off. She poured the excess out and set the full pitcher on the counter. Serin put her hand on her shoulder and gave her a compassionate smile.

"Oh, Serin dear. I don't want anyone to get hurt, and this is all too much, you are too young for this," Mrs. Bailey said.

"Shaz and I have seen much worse than this, and you haven't met Riddick and Amirra yet," Serin said.

"Yes, tell me about you and Shaz, my dear," Mrs. Bailey said.

"I knew you were going to ask," Serin said.

Deagan perked up and leaned toward them to hear what she was going to say and Serin smiled. Mrs. Bailey's eye twinkled with expectant delight and Serin poured more powder into the pitcher.

"You were right, he's a handsome man…and much, much more," Serin said.

Mrs. Bailey's wise little eyes were bright and dreamy, and her grin covered half her face. Serin smiled and stirred the herbal tea.

"Is that all you're going to tell me?" Mrs. Bailey asked.

Serin handed Mrs. Bailey the pitcher and took the glasses while Deagan took the plate of soft sweet biscuits. Serin picked up the tray and started up the stairs. They returned to the room at the top of the stairs carrying a tray and set the refreshments on the desk. Mrs. Bailey's demeanor was a little grumpy as she poured the glasses and handed them out. Ladtwig popped a biscuit into his mouth and licked his fingers and Shaz crossed the room. Shaz took one of the sweets and Serin handed him a glass of the cold tea. Shaz intentionally touched Serin's hand as he took the glass from her, and she smiled.

"Deagan, do you think you can go to your friends and talk to whomever you need to?" Shaz asked.

Deagan nodded.

"We don't have a lot of time, so we better get moving. Turkill, Ladtwig, instead, meet us at the Inn with Riddick and Amirra when they're finished, tell them to hurry," Shaz said.

Shaz handed them a piece of torn parchment with the Inn's name and Turkill tucked it into his belt.

"I'll take you as far as the last pier," Deagan said.

The Minca nodded and the three hurried out of the house. Shaz and Serin helped Mrs. Bailey clean up quickly and waited for Mrs. Bailey to pack her day bag.

"You ready?" Shaz asked.

Serin stuffed another couple of Mrs. Bailey's pain relief jars into her bag and tucked the flap of her satchel into the notch and threw it over her shoulder.

"I am," Serin said.

Serin followed Shaz from the room and down the stairs.

"Are you ready?" Shaz asked.

"I think so," Mrs. Bailey said.

The three left the house and managed their way through the crowded afternoon streets toward the city center. Mrs. Bailey hurried as quickly as her small frame would go until they reached the correct courtyard, and she started toward the building. Shaz grabbed her shoulder and stopped her and she froze.

"We need to be careful. Shadow magic has been used here," Shaz said.

"That's not good," Serin said.

"Aye," Shaz said.

"Oh my," Mrs. Bailey said.

"Wait here," Shaz said.

Shaz moved up against the wall and scooted along its smoothness until he was at the corner. He peeked around the corner and studied the shadows and surfaces of the buildings around the courtyard. He spotted a few finely dressed gentlemen and a man and woman sitting on some benches in the courtyard. The smooth stone of the plaza reflected the sun in several places and Shaz had to move around a platform and plant stand to do a full inspection. He waved his hand and the ladies followed his path until they met up with him. They finished the distance to the building and the cold steel handle of the outer building tingled as Shaz yanked it open. Shaz held the door open for Mrs. Bailey and Serin. Shaz made a quick assessment of the structure, noting the exits and levels as well as any nook or crannies there might be. Serin also made note of the exits and places she could hide or take shelter behind.

"There's not many people here today," Serin said.

"Must be the coronation, everyone is taking their holiday for the celebrations," Mrs. Bailey said.

Mrs. Bailey pointed to the stairs, and they hurried up to the upper level. Mrs. Bailey's breath turned heavy and her pace slowed the higher they went.

"How many levels are we going," Shaz asked.

"Ten, so we're almost there," Mrs. Bailey said.

They rounded the next few levels and started down the long corridor. Mrs. Bailey stopped at the tapestry and pulled the side and revealed the tall ornately carved wooden door. Mrs. Bailey held the tapestry and Shaz, Serin and herself slipped behind the hidden opening and into the nook. Mrs. Bailey maneuvered the pattern and the door unlocked.

Garrison came around the corner of the hallway and stopped at the tapestry. The bag of lunch he had in his hand wafted an aroma of roasted meat, but his stomach lurched as he noticed the tapestry ripple slightly which meant someone had just entered the secret passage. He held his breath and quickly put his bag on the floor on the other side of the hallway and leaned his back against the wall next to the tapestry and listened.

Mrs. Bailey pushed on the latch and the door opened. Shaz shut the door quietly behind them and the lights lit up. Garrison waited for several lengths and peeked through the edge of the hanging rug. The nook was black as it should be, and he slipped into the darkness. Mrs. Bailey opened the first door and Shaz and Serin searched the others around the circular lobby.

Serin came out as did Mrs. Bailey, but they didn't see Shaz. Mrs. Bailey crossed the room and into the one Shaz was in and Serin followed.

"What is it Shaz?" Serin asked.

"Dust," Shaz said.

"Dust?" Mrs. Bailey asked.

Shaz ran a finger across the table and collected a small pile of dust.

"It looks as though no one has been here for at least a moons cycle," Shaz said.

"About how long it's been since I last saw anyone," Mrs. Bailey said.

"Who is the last person you saw?" Serin asked.

"Garrison, Patriza, Valida, Merrick, and Ceros but Mathieu was on some errand as usual," Mrs. Bailey said.

"Does he go on errands regularly?" Shaz asked.

"Oh, yes, but no one has any idea of where he goes or why," Mrs. Bailey said.

"Who else knows about this place?" Shaz asked.

"Not entirely sure, but what I understand, only those I mentioned, myself and Yerild. I suppose anyone from the old days would also know, this has been the council's headquarters for centuries," Mrs. Bailey said.

Shaz walked through the room and down a long hall. Shaz heard a click and stopped and listened, but he didn't hear anything else. Shaz found the pile of wall compound and the secret door slightly ajar and slowly pushed the door open.

****

Deagan eloquently maneuvered the boat around the crowds and Turkill found the ride less nauseating than the last time. The cool mist the waterways let off eased the uncomfortableness of the heated afternoon and Deagan wiped his forehead several times as he shoved the long skinny pole into the sandy grit at the bottom of the waterways. Turkill was impressed with the speed he was able to maintain and paid careful attention to the directions they were going.

Turkill noted specific stores and corner lamp posts as well as markings of chiseled stone or worn off edges to make their return easier. The boat reached the last pier and Ladtwig and Turkill could see the outlines of the forest and secured his pack over his shoulder. Ladtwig wrapped his on his back and as soon as the boat scooted against the wooded dock, they hopped out and waved at Deagan and ran down the pier scooting around the other passengers. A group of ladies getting out of another boat near the end of the pier squawked and gasped as they darted through them.

Turkill was getting grumpier as they had to weave and dodge through the heavy traffic of people. They spent half of their time waiting for wagons or horses to pass. After what seemed like forever, they finally found the path they had come through in the forest and hustled as quickly as they could to the tree cover. The shade of the trees felt good, but they knew it wouldn't take long before the sun would set behind the buildings and cause the forest to darken, so they kept a fast pace. Turkill came to a screeching halt and Ladtwig nearly barreled him over.

"Shhh," Turkill said.

"What is it?" Ladtwig said through heavy breaths.

"I'm not sure," Turkill said.

Turkill crouched to the ground and tiptoed to a tree stump and Ladtwig followed. Turkill pulled his dart gun and pointed in the direction the noise came from. Ladtwig slipped in behind him and pulled his dart gun. Turkill peeked out from around the stump and searched the distance. Jagwynn padded out from behind a large tree and crossed the distance.

"Blasted Jagwynn, you scared the tar out of me," Turkill said.

Jagwynn purred loudly and ran her soft but hefty hide against him nearly knocking him over.

"Where have you been?" Ladtwig scolded.

Jagwynn rubbed up against him too and licked his face.

"We need to hurry back to Riddick and Amirra," Turkill said.

Jagwynn came eye-to-eye to the little men, so she lowered, and they climbed onto her back. They settled into their usual riding positions, and she padded at a quick pace, which was twice as fast as they could move on their own. They didn't take too long to reach the sanctum and the Minca jumped off Jag's back. They searched the surroundings but didn't find Riddick or Amirra.

"Where do you think they are?" Ladtwig asked.

"I have no idea, the building isn't finished yet, so they must not be far," Turkill said.

Jagwynn jumped onto a branch and leaped onto a higher branch of a tree.

"Ouch," Riddick yelped.

Riddick transformed from the tree that Jagwynn leaped into, and she and Amirra tumbled to the ground. Turkill and Ladtwig jumped out of the way and shot behind one of the walls of the building.

"Sorry, are you alright?" Riddick asked.

Turkill and Ladtwig peeked around the stone wall and watched in horror as Riddick transformed from a tree back into a tall red-haired man with a red scruffy beard.

"Oiy, what in the tarnation was that?" Turkill said.

Riddick rubbed his arm and Amirra brushed the leaves and dirt off her hiney. Riddick pulled up his sleeve and found three long scratches. Jagwynn nuzzled into his leg and purred.

"No biggy Jagwynn, we heard you coming and didn't know who it was," Riddick said.

"Who did you think we would be?" Turkill asked.

"Velshari," Amirra said.

"Why?" Ladtwig asked.

"They have been here in the forest for the last two nights, and we have been watching their initiation ceremonies," Amirra said.

"What kind of initiations?" Turkill asked.

"They are making elemental mages with shadow magic," Amirra said.

"Oh, that sounds very bad," Ladtwig said.

"What are you doing here?" Riddick asked.

"Shaz needs you to hurry and finish the sanctum and get to the city, things are worse than we thought," Turkill said.

"How so?" Amirra asked.

"We believe Isot has reconstructed the scroll and is going to use it at the coronation," Turkill said.

"That would make sense," Amirra said.

"How so?" Riddick asked.

"The Velshari focuses on the arts of necromancy, or the undead, which is why the Binding of the Crypt spell is so important to them. They also believe that the more human sacrifices offered the greater the incantations will be. In order to secure their place among the undead, they must offer a living soul to take their place in the underworld, so having all those people there for the coronation would secure the needed offerings," Amirra said.

"How comforting," Riddick said.

"How much more do you have on the building?" Turkill asked.

"Not much, a few more timbers in the roof and the runecasting," Riddick said.

"It's already late in the afternoon, looks like we will be working late into the night," Amirra said.

"Aye," Riddick said.

"What can we do to help?" Turkill asked.

"You two and Jag can be lookouts," Riddick said.

"We're on it," Turkill said.

Turkill and Ladtwig tightened their cloaks around their bodies and split in different directions and faded into the forest. Jagwynn rubbed against Riddick's leg and leaped over a rock and into the distance. Riddick hauled large tree limb and focused his efforts on the size of the opening in the roof. He had already measured out the structure in length, width, and height, but he hadn't figured out the area of the rise and fall of the slope of the needed roof. He took several steps away and ran toward the wall. Riddick shoved his foot into the groves of the larger stones at the bottom and leaped upward. His hand caught the top of the wall, and he shoved his other foot into the building and lunged upward. The momentum carried him upward enough, and he gripped the top of the wall with his arms and climbed into a sitting position.

Amirra lifted the flap of her satchel and removed a purple velvet pouch and set the bag on a tree stump, then pulled out a gold instrument with a few levers and arms and a dial in the center. She took the instrument and placed the center lever in the middle of the stump and pushed the sharp point into the wood. Amirra adjusted the levers in a pattern to make a perfect circle in the wood. She twisted the contraption and chanted the runecircle incantation as she twisted. A faint green line illuminated under the surface, and she twisted it around a second time. She repeated the process several more times each time adding the needed instructions to add the future, past, current, and cause and effect dials of the runecircle.

The green light brightened each time she etched the new symbol until she had completed all the runecircle. Riddick finished his calculations and while still sitting on the edge of the wall he reached for the limb. The limb sprouted new branches and lifted the main tree branch toward him. He directed the branch to center itself and grow to the appropriate length to reach from one end to the other. The branch settled into the cutouts he had made for them in the peaks of the walls. The new sprouts organized themselves in even lengths and reached out toward the other two walls and settled into their grooves.

Riddick scooched in between the cross beams and counted out the new measurements pointing to each one as he went. The new sprouts sprouted even newer sprouts and started to intertwine themselves into a delicate design across the top of the center and cross beams. Riddick climbed down the wall as the heavily weaved roof came closer to him. He inspected the tightness of the weave around the underneath side and made certain there were no holes.

Amirra slid the clasp from the tie of the pouch and opened the top. She reached into the bag and emptied the stones into her palm before pulling them all out of the bag. She closed her eyes and focused on the symbols on the stones and the symbols that came to her mind. Amirra studied them as they appeared onto the backs of her eyelids, contemplating the meanings and implications of each. After evaluating all the runes, she opened her eyes and gently tossed the small runestones onto the circle.

The runestones made a dull clack as they hit the aged wood and Amirra arranged the pieces into the sections of the circle they fell into. She pulled out a small notebook and a writer's stick and quickly sketched the symbols and the circle, making notes by each as she remembered them. She ran her hand over the casting and the faint green lines brightened highlighting the runes. Amirra wrote the symbols in order and then again as an instructional. She started to gather the stones but paused as one of the stones shifted slightly on its own.

This kind of thing wasn't completely unheard-of, but it was rare that a stone would change its tale during a casting. Nitida had told her this was because the circumstances in the current time had been affected drastically and therefor changing the current and the future. She quickly made the notations and changes and gathered the stones and returned them to the pouch. She secured them and the implement into her satchel and locked the flap. Amirra engaged her mind with all the rituals she had learned from Nitida and decided on the one she wanted to use then scoped out the perfect spot to stand while she evoked the enchantment.

Riddick tossed a few more branches onto the roof and wove them into the thinner sections. The sun was now setting behind the last bit of horizon they could see through the forest and Amirra started her cast. Her voice was soft and soothing with a hint of excitement and Riddick found the rhythmic beat soothing. He listened mindlessly as her tone fluctuated up and down louder and softer. Amirra read from her book the first several times until the words flowed off her tongue with ease.

Riddick shifted the last few branches overhead and reached out with his earth energy. The vibrating pulse ricocheted off the four walls and returned with a complete image of the structure. He then examined the portal and secured several small stones into the missing sections of the frame. Turkill and Ladtwig returned as the last of the stones rested into place. Amirra's singsong faded into the night chill, and she put her book into her satchel.

"Is it finished?" Turkill asked.

Riddick nodded and smiled.

"Won't be long now until the Velsheri start coming out," Amirra said.

"What are you going to do?" Ladtwig asked.

"Interrupt them of course," Amirra said.

"I thought you might say that," Turkill said.

Riddick laughed and Amirra smiled.

"You can stay in the sanctum and wait for Jagwynn if you want," Riddick said.

"Then we will head out first thing in the morning," Amirra said.

Ladtwig and Turkill nodded and helped Riddick and Amirra gather their camp and move it into the new sanctum. Riddick had spent a little extra time organizing the elements to reflect the details of Shaz's castle as well as their homeland of Turob, the swirls from Serin's tattoos, and the Mountain Temple. It was warm and comfortable with slender pillars along the inside walls that connected to each other with pointed arches that were inlaid into the stone of the walls. Tall long thin windows were spaced between the arches and were stained-glass murals that were in the same artists' style as the mural of Reinholt which was on the back wall. The portal sat in the center front of the building, and had a new appearance that resembled the castle.

Turkill tossed his bag into the corner and slumped onto the padding of his pack. Ladtwig finished his tour around the generously sized room and then plopped next to Turkill and made himself a makeshift bed. The door crept open and bright yellow eyes popped out from the darkened outside.

"You know, this is really annoying that you are pitch black and scare the tar out of me at night," Turkill said.

Jagwynn crossed the floor silently and nuzzled her enormous nose into him. Turkill rubbed her behind the ears, and she laid down next to them and purred softly. The Minca were nearly asleep when Riddick and Amirra made their way into the building. Amirra tiptoed across the floor and Riddick secured the door shut and then made his way to where she had left her bedroll.

"Well, what did you see?" Turkill asked.

"No dessert table, that's for sure," Riddick said.

Amirra snorted a throaty laugh and Riddick snickered.

"I don't understand," Turkill said.

"Never mind, we'll tell you everything in the morning," Riddick said.

****

Shadow's crippled the alleyways and the stench of pitch and ale wreaked havoc on Isot's nose hairs. She cinched her dark robe around her neck and rubbed her hands together. The cold night air stung her lungs as she hadn't been outside the castle, at night, in such a long time. This part of the outdoor courtyard was the only place she could go to be outside and it was the worst part. She hissed at the thought of all her rotations being stuck to the castle and her suppressed rage surfaced. She held her breath and clung to the black wall and listened as the heavy footsteps rounded the corner several lengths away.

A soldier with a medium build emerged into the light of the torches of the balcony above them and his chainmail armor clinked. Isot reached out and grabbed his arm as he was about to pass her. The man startled and went for his sword.

"It's just me you fool," Isot said.

"Sorry mam," the soldier said.

"You better have good news for me, Lorn," Isot snarled.

"I am working on it," Lorn said.

"You said, you knew what their plans were," Isot said.

"I do, but it's going to take some time," Lorn said.

"We don't have time, get it done," Isot said.

"I'm working on it," Lorn said.

"You are the Captain of the Guard, don't you have hundreds of soldiers at your disposal?" Isot sneered.

"Yes, mam," Lorn said.

"Then use them," Isot said.

Lorn nodded and continued on his path of securing the outer perimeter of the castle and Isot slipped back into the shadows.

31-So, What Are We Looking For?

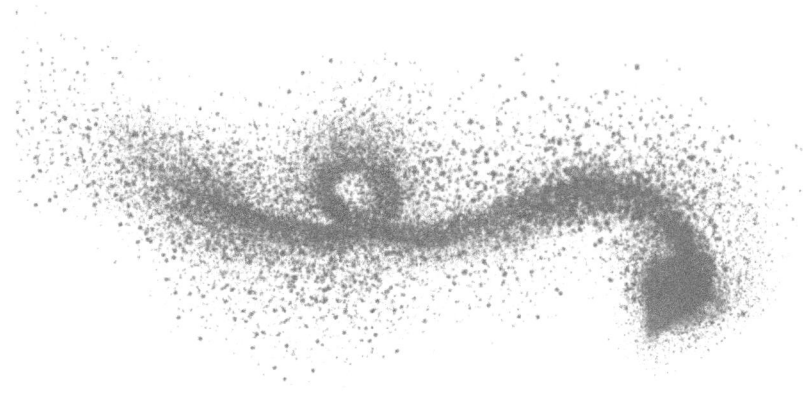

"Oh my, what happened here?" Serin asked.

"I have no clue," Shaz said.

Shaz ran his hands through his hair and sucked in a deep breath. An odd feeling sat at the back of his mind, but he couldn't quite place it. The room was larger than the others and full of shelves and stacks of books and parchments that now sat in a pile of rubble. Artifacts of varying types laid strewn about the floor and papers nearly covered the entire surface. There was something familiar and the first thing that came to mind was Alisdair, but nothing jumped out at him. Serin wandered around the room and examined the little figurines and book titles as she came across them. Shaz picked up a shelf and gathered some parchments and tried to set them on the top shelf.

"Someone was looking for something that's for sure," Shaz said.

"But what?" Mrs. Bailey asked.

Shaz clapped his hands and the orange sparkles popped into existence.

"What was the person who did this trying to find?" Shaz asked.

The sparkles hovered for a second and started toward the door. Shaz and Serin followed it down the hall to another room. The door was shut, and the sparkles waited for Shaz to open it then hurried into the room. The sparkles maneuvered into an arrow and pointed at a picture hanging on the wall behind a desk.

A sickening feeling crawled up his spine, and he realized someone was in there and listening to them. Shaz hurried out of the room and back down the hall and heard footsteps and the door click shut.

"What is it Shaz?" Serin asked.

"Someone was in here listening to us," Shaz said.

Shaz pulled the door open and searched the hallway on the other side of the tapestry. He looked around for a minute and scanned with his magic but didn't sense anyone of a magical nature. He listened but the building was quiet and the knot in his stomach faded. He returned to the offices but locked the door with his magic and returned to the picture on the wall.

Shaz realized it wasn't a picture but a map. The map was old and secured inside a flat box with a clear covering over the top. He picked it off the wall and set it on the table. He searched for the latch or lever to open the top. The box didn't have any levers that he could find, and he tried to lift the top straight off, but it wouldn't budge. He turned the box over and found a small thumb hole. He placed his finger in the crevice and tried to lift the back off, but it wouldn't open. He ran his hand along the side seam and called his magic to release the bond and then tried again. The panel opened and he lifted it from the lid. The map stuck to the back panel as Shaz flipped it over and set it on the desk and propped the picture box against the leg.

"What is it?" Mrs. Bailey asked.

Shaz ran his finger over the map but didn't touch the surface. He allowed the energy the parchment gave penetrate his skin, and he could tell it had an element of the same energy as the Teorran Belt. The paper was a myriad of shades of tans and the ink had darkened in spots but lightened in others. He gently touched the corner and found that paper was still in fair condition. He lifted the delicate paper slowly off the panel and turned it over carefully. A series of symbols scattered the back of the map.

What does it say? Serin asked in her mind.

It's a map to the Wizards Keep and a very dangerous spell, but we can't tell Mrs. Bailey, Shaz replied in his head.

Shaz shook his head as a gesture to Mrs. Bailey.

"The symbols are all jumbled, this makes no sense at all," Shaz said.

"Is it one of Grandfather's puzzles," Serin asked.

"Oiy, if it is, we'll be here for days," Shaz said.

"Well, maybe we don't need to figure it out right now," Serin said, giving Shaz an out of having to tell Mrs. Bailey anything.

"That's right, it will be here later, but for now we need to focus on getting to the bottom of things," Mrs. Bailey said.

"We still don't know what happened to Grandfather and the others," Serin said changing the subject.

"No, we don't, but I have an idea," Shaz said.

Shaz rolled the map up and slid it into his tunic, he wasn't sure why this kind of document would be hanging in such an open place, but he knew it needed to be kept from whoever was trying to find it. He rubbed his hands together and the burnt orange sparkles popped into life. Shaz sent them on their mission and the glittering rounded the room and then left. The three followed it down the hall and into another room and then back into the hall. It went up and down a couple of times and then headed to the main door. Shaz waved his hand along the surface of the door and the levers and latches clicked and clacked, and he opened the door. They followed the sparks as it led them back down the stairs and out of the building's main doors. It danced around the courtyard for a minute and then fizzled away.

"That wasn't helpful," Serin said.

"Now what?" Mrs. Bailey asked.

"You go back home and stay there, keep your head down and blinds shut. We will call for you when we need you," Shaz said.

Mrs. Bailey nodded and hurried across the courtyard and into the ally and disappeared into the distance. Shaz and Serin hurried back to the building but instead of taking the stairs to the upper floor, Shaz veered to the side and rounded the tall balusters. The wall that supported the spiraling staircase, blocked them, and he pushed Serin into the little nook at the back of the rounded structure. Serin snuck the chance and leaned into his body and he wrapped his arm around her waist and pulled her close as he listened for any noises.

"Are they still here?" Serin asked.

Her voice was quiet and Shaz searched with his magic.

"I don't sense anyone, we must have scared them off, but we need to hurry," Shaz said.

Shaz started to search where the map indicated a door should be. Serin too started to look for any marks that would indicate a secret door.

"So, what are we looking for?" Serin asked.

Serin tried to hide the mischievous glint in her green eyes.

"An invisible door," Shaz said.

The corner of Shaz's lip lifted in a wistful flick.

"But if it's invisible how are you going to see it?" Serin asked.

"I just will," Shaz said.

"How can you, you can't see something that isn't there?" Serin said.

"What are you babbling about?" Shaz asked.

"The invisible door," Serin said.

"Oh yes, that one, I can't find it, it's invisible," Shaz said.

They both couldn't hold in the laughter and took a minute to reminisce their meeting of Turkill and Ladtwig at his castle in what seemed like so long ago.

"Please don't take your shoes off though," Serin said composing herself.

Shaz laughed again and stepped back from the wall. He called the magic in his chest and rolled the energy around in a ball, like he would access an earth portal. The wobbly energy rounded tightly into a nice sphere and he sent the glowing ball toward the door and it sank into the wall. The energy dispersed evenly and illuminated the invisible door. Shaz reached for the glowing handle and it hardened under his grip. He twisted it and a puff of stale air escaped the cracks and Shaz paused. Serin quickly checked around the stairs and gave him a thumbs-up before he pulled it open.

They hurried inside and Shaz closed the door. The latches re locked and a light came on. A hallway opened as they took a few steps into a gray mist. A hint of moss and musk wafted through the mist as it wrapped around their bodies illuminating their auras. The delicate hues of Serin's blues mixed with the intense multi-colors of Shaz's magic and then faded into the now shimmering mist. Serin wondered if this was a different realm, or what it might be. The mist gave her the impression that it was learning who they were as it tickled her energies.

"This is amazing," Serin said.

She moved her hand through the cool fog and watched her magic aura fade in and out.

"Aye," Shaz agreed.

"So, is this the Wizards Keep from the map?" Serin asked.

"Aye," Shaz said.

"What is a Wizards Keep anyway?" Serin asked.

"I guess a place to *keep* stuff," Shaz said.

"That explains a lot," Serin said.

"Aye, I'm just full of answers today," Shaz said.

Serin chuckled.

The hallway wrapped around a corner and started to slope downward and then rounded another corner. The mist began to lift, and their feet sank gently into a soft surface, but as they crossed over the soft floor it began to be replaced with a harder surface and Shaz couldn't tell exactly what it was. Shaz peered through the mist and tried to determine where they were. A soft trickle of water dripped from a high surface and landed in a shallow pond. The ripples left a soothing echo around the cavern-like room. The mist sifted back and forth and settled to the bottom and Shaz and Serin could see a splendid set of stone steps in the middle of a shallow pool of crystal blue water.

The stairs were wide and ascended through a hole in the mist that led to an upper level. Shaz started into the pool, but he didn't sink as he expected and mused at how he was walking on the surface of the water. Serin followed and they moved up the stairs carefully. The hole opened and the mist parted in a way that they were able to see what appeared to be an earth portal several steps away. A scent of the grassy plains eased into their senses and then was replaced with the clean coolness of the mountain air, and then the ocean breeze. The closer they came to the misty wall the mist dissipated, and they could now see that there was no cave-like surface, no mountain, no trees or sky or stars or anything. There were only variations of colored mists that moved around the wall-like surface in soothing waves that exuded a variety of scents that they both recognized and didn't.

"Who was trying to find this place, and why?" Serin asked.

"I have no idea, but I get a feeling if they found it, it would be a very bad thing," Shaz said.

"This is nearly identical to the place we saw Alisdair in," Serin said.

"It is, it has the same energy too," Shaz said.

"The Teorran Belt?" Serin asked.

"It's similar, but not the same. I think maybe this is a place that still has access to the Teorran Belt magic, but it's not the belt itself," Shaz said.

Serin nodded.

"Is it an earth portal?" Serin asked.

Shaz moved close to the array of swirling mist that organized itself into a pattern shaped like a small portal from the castle but with no frame around it.

"It certainly seems like one," Shaz said.

Shaz searched the area for any signs of symbols or etchings that would tell him what it was, but nothing stood out. He lifted his hand to inspect it and the soft caress of the mist danced on his skin.

"Be careful Shaz," Serin said.

"Why, you don't want to be sucked into a realm with an insane witch that will try to steal your magic?" Shaz asked.

"No, not really, kind of already did that," Serin said.

Serin touched his arm to tell him she understood his need to make a joke and he exhaled. Glyphs began to illuminate from the mist and Shaz studied the marks. He took a step back and took Serin's hands in his. Shaz interlocked his fingers into hers and his touch caressed her senses. Shaz started to roll their hands around as he pulled his magic from his core. Serin sent a mix of her magics into his sphere and together they released it into the mist. The energy was absorbed and disappeared.

"Latenta somella ray narra anoto chari la'ta'ya ha no soma tom'me," Shaz said.

The misty portal began to grow into an oval and Shaz and Serin stepped back as it grew to the floor. The wafting substance hardened, and it became clear it wasn't an earth portal.

"This is a portal that we can step through, not just access information," Shaz said.

"Where does it lead to?" Serin asked.

"The Keep," Shaz said.

"Will we be able to come back though?" Serin asked.

Shaz nodded and she agreed. They stepped through together and the surge of the Teorran Belt magic raced through their beings. Serin gasped with its strength and hoped she wouldn't have to go through what Shaz did when he experienced it the first time. An expansive room emerged with bright white stone walls that went for so many lengths Serin wasn't sure she could tell how big it actually was. It resembled a library but included just as many items and artifacts as books and scrolls.

"How would someone find anything in here?" Serin asked.

A puff of blue sparkles jumped into existence and hovered in front of Serin and she jumped. She laughed at herself for letting it surprise her.

"I guess that's how, and your search spell seems to be blue," Shaz said.

"What do I want it to find?" Serin asked.

"Is there something you are worried about or fear?" Shaz asked.

"Well, yes, there are a few things, but how would that make a difference?" Serin asked.

"Something that Grandfather always told me, was when a chance presents itself, start with the thing that is the most pressing in your mind and you will find the answers," Shaz said.

Serin thought about it, but wasn't sure what it really meant. Several ideas came to her mind, but the one that made her stomach twinge was how she could make sure she had what it took to help Shaz. The blue sparkles wriggled and danced and then started off toward one of the shelves. Serin followed it and Shaz followed her. Shaz ran his hand along the shelf and interpreted the ages of time that were in the various items and wondered if anyone would be able to know everything. The glittering specks were diligent in its search and finally stopped and pointed to an intricately detailed armlet made of a type of metal that she had never seen before. Serin stepped close and inspected it but wasn't sure she wanted to pick it up.

"Are you going to pick it up?" Shaz asked.

"I'm not sure if I should," Serin said.

Shaz held his hand over it and was confident it didn't have any shadow magic, so he picked it up. The mineral tingled his skin and he understood it to have the Teorran magic infused in it.

"It's safe," Shaz said.

Shaz held it out and Serin slipped her hand in and he slid it up her arm and over her elbow. The details shifted and the design of her tattoos intertwined with the old marks to become new ones. Serin took a deep breath as a flood of images crossed her vision and she struggled to internalize it all. Shaz held her as her body wobbled with the new sensations.

"Are you alright?" Shaz asked.

"Yes, what is this?" Serin asked.

"The inscriptions say it's a Zemi of the Lavari, a good-luck charm, but I think it's more than that and that you are the only one that can know what it really is," Shaz said.

Serin searched the armlet again and she found she could read the inscriptions this time, but she also understood them to be the language of the Lavari and she smiled.

"What do you think, is it me?" Serin asked playfully.

"It certainly is," Shaz said.

"What about you, are you going to search for something?" Serin asked.

"No, but I am going to leave a few things here," Shaz said.

Shaz took off the Selket Orb and looked around. He spotted a shelf near the back that had a glass covering and a lock and made his way around a tall time-ticker-like thing. Shaz wasn't sure what it was but knew if he stopped to try and figure it out, his brain wouldn't stop until he did and that could take a lot of time. He pulled the glass door open and set the orb on the shelf and then pulled out the map of the keep and set it on the shelf above it and shut the glass door and locked the latch.

He started back toward Serin when he noticed another access point and stopped. He looked around the room and found several places that looked like they could be openings and wondered if the Keep was accessible from all of the realms. His chest heated up with its truth and he hurried back to Serin.

"I think we're done here for now, but we will need this place again," Shaz said.

Serin nodded and perceived his understanding and they made their way back to the entrance they came from. Serin grabbed his hand and pulled him to a stop. He turned around to find her looking at him.

"What's wrong?" Shaz asked.

"Nothing, I just want to do this first," Serin said.

She reached up and wrapped her arms around his neck and

kissed him. He gripped her tight and kissed her back.

"Are you alright?" Shaz asked.

"I am," Serin said.

Serin couldn't explain exactly why she had, what seemed like new feelings for him and wondered if it was the armlet, but she was alright with it and kissed him again, then let him go. Shaz smiled at her and took her hand and led her back to the staircase and the mist closed back into the swirly form. They crossed the water and back through the hallway. Shaz opened the door a tiny bit and peeked out. He didn't see anyone, so he pushed the door open enough for he and Serin to slip out and then locked it. The day had passed into night and was moving back into the morning. They inspected the main floor and then left the building.

32-I Don't Think You Remember How This Works

A tiny spray of early sunlight eased into the sanctum and Riddick stirred and blinked. The dimly lit room left shadows around the edges, and Riddick's search settled on a small lump in one of the corners, and he studied the breathing of the little animal and recognized it to be Nix. He nudged Amirra who stirred and rubbed her eyes.

"Let's pack up and head out," Riddick said.

Amirra nodded, stretched, yawned and climbed out of her bedroll and rolled it up. Riddick secured his to his pack and Turkill woke up to the rustling. Turkill nudged Ladtwig, and he rolled onto his side and Turkill nudged harder. Ladtwig sat up and rubbed his eyes, and they packed their things.

"How long is it to the city?" Amirra asked.

"About half the days walk," Turkill said.

Ladtwig broke a piece of dried meat and shoved it into his mouth. Nix smelled the morsel and his nose twitched. He sniffed a few times and opened his eyes. He spotted the meat in Ladtwig's pouch and made a plan to secure it for himself. Ladtwig stood and turned around

Nix made his move. He scurried out of the shadows and snagged the backpack on his way by and darted into the shadows of the next corner. Ladtwig turned back around to put his blanket in his satchel and screeched at finding his bag missing.

Everyone in the room jumped and looked at Ladtwig with surprise and Jagwynn hissed.

"What are you carrying on about?" Turkill asked.

"My satchel, it's GONE!," Ladtwig said.

"What do you mean, gone?" Turkill asked.

"I mean missing, not where it was, gone, nowhere, taken," Ladtwig said.

"Shhh," Amirra said.

Amirra pointed to the corner and put her finger on her lips. She crept quietly across the floor and faded into the shadows. Nix was so busy unwrapping one of Ladtwig's cheese blocks that he didn't notice Amirra closing in on him. She snatched the bag and yanked it away. Nix startled backward and fumbled the cheese in which he regained his hold and held it tightly to his small furry body.

"I thought it might be you, you can't take that," Amirra said.

"But Nix is hungry," Nix said.

"We all are, but we don't steal things," Amirra said. Ladtwig dropped his blanket and ran over to the rodent that was half his size and snatched the cheese from his clutches and sneered at him. "Now, now, that's not how we act either Ladtwig," Amirra said.

Ladtwig lowered his head and looked at the floor. Nix's big black eyes glossed over and Ladtwig tried not to look, but his soft heart overtook his greed, and he broke the cheese into half and handed the that half to Nix. Nix's smile crossed his face from one ear to the other and then he wrapped his short arms around Ladtwig's leg and took the cheese. Ladtwig quickly stuffed half his piece into his mouth and returned to his blankets.

"Nix, you will need to stay here, you won't be safe where we are going," Riddick said.

"Where are you going?" Nix asked.

"Into the city," Riddick said.

"Is that where the dungeons are?" Nix asked.

"Yes, why?" Riddick asked.

"I need to get Nix's family out," Nix said.

"Your family is in the dungeons?" Ladtwig asked.

Nix nodded and rubbed his paw-like fingers together.

"We have to help him," Amirra said.

"Aye, and I am sure that Shaz has a plan, but we don't know what that is, and we need to make it there to find out," Riddick said.

"I won't be any trouble, Nix promises," Nix said.

Riddick studied the little face and understood completely how Shaz could feel about him. Even though he wreaked of innocence, there was a substantial amount of mischief in the little critter.

"I'm going to regret this, I'm certain, but fine, as long as you stay out trouble," Riddick said.

"And no more stealing my food," Ladtwig said sharply.

Riddick and Amirra smirked as they had never seen Ladtwig have a stern bone in his body. The crew finished gathering their things and Riddick secured the door shut behind them. The sun was still behind the horizon, but the sky was brighter, and it wouldn't be long until it peeked over. They headed toward the city at a quick pace and the Minca and Nix ended up on Jag's back as usual. Jag, however, wasn't thrilled with Nix being there and made her objections noted.

They reached the edge of the forest and Jagwynn leaped back into the treetops where large cats love to sit and stalk their prey. They guessed she was going to wait there and stay out of the city. They stopped at the edge of the tree line and scoped out the best way back into the city. Turkill explained the guards were asking for papers at the gates and suggested that they head toward the docks and piers and Riddick agreed. They skirted the trees and bushes until they ran out of forest. The distance to the shore wasn't very long, but there was nowhere to hide until they got to the first pier.

Riddick watched the few boats pull around a bend and explained they would follow its path toward the docks. The first boat rounded the corner, and they quickly left the last tree. The boat's captain was busy yelling out commands that Riddick knew so well. A pang of longing hit his heart, and he dismissed the homesickness he suddenly felt. Amirra smiled gently and he nodded. Riddick spotted the guard at the end of the pier and when he turned to wave the boat on, they made the break as the boat rounded the next bend that would take the boat to the last docking on the pier.

A few large boulders sat at the edge of the water and the pier and Riddick darted behind them as the others followed. Riddick climbed the first rung and underneath the pier. The overpowering odor of saltwater and mossy seaweed sank into his senses, and he gagged. He loved the saltwater aroma, but it was the stink of the seaweed he had never been a fan of and to have them mixed was chaos on his sniffer. Ladtwig and Turkill held their breath and Amirra tried not to wretch. Riddick scaled the support beams under the pier until he could peek out and find the next guard.

He picked out the next three moves and explained his plan to the others. Riddick waited until the guard was turned and climbed the last support and onto the shore in between that pier and the next, then waved to the Minca who followed then Amirra. They repeated the process until they had made it to the last pier which would be the trickiest. The guard was a large rotund fella and had no qualms with getting vocal if he needed to. In just the last few minutes of them reaching the last pier, he had already barked orders to three individuals.

Riddick gripped the edge of one of the side-supports and wriggled his fingers. Several rocks near the sloping shore wriggled and formed into a golem similar to the one he had made at the castle. Amirra and the Minca smirked and steadied themselves to watch the chaos the little golem was about to stir up. The golem rolled toward the guard who jumped back. Riddick flung a few pebbles at the guard who hollered.

"What in the-" the guard started.

A few more pebbles flew, and the guard pulled out his sword. He parried a few steps toward the golem with his sword in a defensive position. The golem shot toward him and the guard jumped and shoved his sword at the wobbly figure and the rocks moved out of the way and then regrouped. The guard swung again, and the rocks moved out of the way. Riddick moved the golem away from their position and the guard chased it. A second guard hurried to the first. He tried to kick the rocks, and they jumped out of the way and regrouped again.

Riddick signaled to the others, and they climbed up onto the pier and hurried past the commotion. Another guard joined the fray and several people circled around to see what was going on. A group of young boys poked through and started to laugh and cheer for the rock golem. As soon as they were clear of the opening into the city, Riddick sent the golem up to one of the boys who held out his hand. One of the smaller rocks hit the boy's hand in a gesture of comradery and the boys laughed and started to run away. Riddick sent the golem to play with the boys, and they hurried toward the walkway that would take them to the Inn. They could hear the guards shouting at the youth and the people laughing.

The streets were crowded, and they found it hard to maneuver around without getting separated. Turkill had the Inn's name, but they didn't know exactly where they were going, and Riddick stopped for directions twice after the first time taking the wrong turn and getting mixed up. Turkill had his usual scowl but it sank deeper into his face than usual. After an exhausting effort they finally found the Inn but before they went inside Riddick did a full sweep of people and evaluated the surroundings. Amirra had a funny reaction settle in her guts, but she tried to ignore the feeling and passed it off as the excitement of the busy people all around her.

Riddick opened the heavy door, and they entered the elegantly decorated lobby. The floors were a highly polished stone and were decorated with deep shades of woven rugs and tapestries. Tall crystal vases held brightly colored bloomed flowers that gave off a sweet smell. A finely-dressed man rubbed past him on his way out of the Inn and Riddick moved out of his way. Amirra gazed around at all the high-end dresses and suits and a hint of red formed under her skin. Turkill hurmpfed and crossed his arms over his chest.

"This place seems way out of our league," Amirra said.

"Aye, but this is where Shaz said they would be," Riddick said.

"Uh-hum," a dignified looking gentleman at the counter said.

Riddick cleared his throat and made his way around a large round table.

"If you're looking for lodging, you are in the wrong place," the man said.

Riddick ignored his beady stare and tight curled lip but fascinated himself with the man's tightly clipped eyebrows.

"We are here to meet someone, have they checked in yet?" Riddick asked.

The man glared at him and wondered if he had heard him.

"I highly doubt anyone that would stay at this facility would commiserate with the likes of you," the man said.

"I see, so you're one of-" Riddick started.

Amirra stepped beside him and held out her hand. The man looked at her and then at her hand. Her palm was facing up and Riddick noticed, for the first time, a long light-pink scar that ran across her palm. The man took her hand in a grip that Riddick had never seen and nodded and handed her a key. Riddick's stomach lurched and sank as the realization hit his mind, that Amirra really had been one of them. A kind of fear he had never experienced settled in his chest, and he tried not to stare at the man's blank expression. Amirra took Riddick's elbow and moved him away from the desk. They moved behind a large fern growing in an even larger pot, and she let go of his elbow.

"We don't have to stay here, in fact, let's get out of here," Riddick said.

"No, I need to do this. I need to face my past to prove to myself that I have overcome it, plus I can manage insider information that I think we drastically need," Amirra said.

"Are you sure?" Riddick asked.

Amirra nodded, and Riddick and the Minca followed her up the long spiraling staircase to the room number indicated on the key. The room was massive and full of deep-colored fabrics and crystal and silver accents. Amirra set her pack down and pulled out a medallion and strung the lace around her neck.

"What's that?" Riddick asked.

"A charm I made to protect my mind from those that can hack my thoughts," Amirra said.

She pulled out a ring for Riddick and two hair clips that the Minca warriors wear for special ceremonies and handed them to the Minca.

"What are these for and where did you get them?" Turkill asked.

"The Chieftess gave them to me, these will shield your minds too," Amirra said.

The Minca clipped the hand-carved clasps onto their warrior braids and Riddick put the ring on his small finger.

"Now what?" Ladtwig asked.

"I need to go find the dessert table, and you need to stay out of sight," Amirra said.

The Minca shared confused glances and Riddick chuckled.

"I'll stay a distance away, but I'm coming with you," Riddick said.

Amirra nodded, and she grabbed her backpack and took it into the washroom that was separate from the sleeping quarters. She shut the door and clicked the latch. Riddick rubbed his neck and breathed out heavily. He eyed the window and rounded a chair on his way to discover what was on the other side. He pulled back the heavy curtains and the brightness of the late afternoon hit his face. Riddick blinked a few times and leaned into the glass window. Riddick peered down at the city and found that they were several stories high. He knew they had climbed the stairs for what seemed like forever, but it hadn't impressed his mind until now.

Ebassia was a very curious place. Tall polished buildings of a new era mixed with the old rugged stone buildings of times past. He shifted his thoughts to the energy the materials the buildings were made of and a ragged history flooded his mind. A familiar sensation ripped through his frame and understood he was near an earth portal. He couldn't access it, but he had a level of desire that surprised him. The door latch clicked, and Riddick closed the curtain. The darkened room was soothing to his energy, and he loved the intense colors of the decor.

Amirra examined herself in the mirror that covered most of the wall over the washbasin. An odd acceptance of the outfit filled her being, and she was both comfortable and ashamed. She cleared her mind and smoothed her cinnamon waves behind the back her head with a clasp and arranged the wispy fringe around her face. She took a deep breath and gripped the latch and turned the handle. Amirra came out of the washroom and Riddick stifled a gasp. Her tall curvy shape was accentuated by the tight black leather pants and corset she was now wearing. The black silk blouse tucked in nicely to the edges of the corset and draped down her arms and rested at her wrists. Riddick couldn't help his intrigue, and he found her both frightening and alluring.

"I'll be back later, stay here," Amirra said.

Ladtwig climbed up onto an overstuffed lounge and propped a pillow under his head and Turkill sat next to the fireplace and pulled out his blade and a sharpening stone. Riddick followed Amirra out of the room and down the long corridor. Amirra had an air of authority and tension Riddick hadn't seen since he met her in the Minca's village. He couldn't help the aching gnawing in his gut, but he had to trust her. A gently aged man on his way up the stairs scooted over and bowed a slight bow as she moved passed. Normally Riddick would nod or make eye contact and smile or some other gesture of kind acknowledgment, but Amirra kept her head taunt and left no expression on her face at all. The youthful glee he was used to seeing was sitting somewhere behind the surface, and he hoped she wouldn't get in over her head.

They reached the main level and crossed the lobby to an adjacent room that was decorated with a similar feel as their room. Long drapery hung from the windows and intricately carved details lined the walls a few lengths below the vaulted ceiling. Riddick slowed his pace and let Amirra gain several lengths and veered off the other direction that Amirra was headed. Riddick pretended to examine some old hand-painted images of persons he assumed had some significance to the Inn.

A group of finely-dressed men and women stepped to one side as Amirra entered another room toward the back of the Inn. The men nodded and the women curtsied. Riddick was surprised at how much respect she received and supposed she must have a high rank within the organization, which only sparked another stint of energy to ripple through his core. He gently made his way around the couch in the first room and skirted the edges into the other room. That's when he saw it, the dessert table! A hefty toothy grin encompassed his face, and he coughed to regain his composure.

Three men, one so old that Riddick wondered how he was even standing on his own and one young enough Riddick thought he should still be in school and the other middle-aged, all mingled at the table filled with small or devours and treats. Riddick noted there was a bit of resemblance between the three and guessed them to be related. Two women mingled at the end of the table and a third woman casually gathered some refreshments onto a small plate and took a tiny fork from the stack at the end of the table. Amirra eased into the lady's conversation.

"This is so exciting, don't you think?" one of the women asked the other.

"It is, I'm not sure though if it's really going to happen," the other said.

"Why is that?" the first asked.

"I overheard one of the leaders talking about needing the prisoners but one of them died while being tortured," the second said.

"Which one?" Amirra asked.

The first woman turned to Amirra and was about to answer when she realized who she was.

"Oh, your greatness, please forgive my negligence, I didn't see you there," the woman said.

Amirra wanted to give the poor woman a hug but had to keep her soulless demeanor in check, so she waved her hand and dismissed the infraction with a dark expression.

"I overheard, I mean from what I know, the prisoner was a woman," the other said.

"What a pity, women are always such fun to torture," Amirra said.

The women nodded in agreement, but Amirra could tell they knew very little about the real darkness of the Velshari.

"I presume she has them in the dungeons here in Ebassia with the Interrogator," Amirra half-stated-half-asked.

The woman nodded and stuffed a sweet biscuit in her mouth.

"Excuse my insolence, but may I ask, is it true that the scroll has been found and the ceremony will include the Pact of the Everlasting?"

Amirra's thin brow raised, and she gripped the dread that crept up her chest. Her suspicions were correct, and she understood now what Isot was going to do at the coronation.

"Yes, that is correct, the *ritual* will be a magnificent one," Amirra said.

The woman blushed and shrunk a little with the correction.

"Excuse me, mam, what can I get for you?" a servant boy asked.

Amirra turned to the lad and eyed a small framed woman in the corner and her already ridged frame tightened. Riddick rounded another fern taller than he was and positioned himself so that he could keep an eye on Amirra. Amirra turned to the woman and waved off the lad. Riddick recognized the woman to be the same one from the last few nights initiation ceremonies and shivered.

"Amirra, what a surprise to see you," Gitre said.

Amirra rolled her eyes with indifference and a small flame ripped across Gitre's dark pupils. Riddick instantly understood there was history between them, and he had to shove his hands in his pockets to keep from unleashing a branch from his hand and strangling the woman. Amirra made direct eye contact and felt the tug against her mind, and she refocused her efforts on her mental shield.

"Gitre, your still around, what a shame," Amirra said.

"Oh, come now Amirra, you're not sore that I was advanced, and you were not," Gitre said.

Gitre glanced around the room checking to make sure the rest of the members were watching and inadvertently picked up the medallion that was hanging around her neck. Amirra recognized it as the ones Shaz had given Nix and the others, including herself, and smirked.

"Please, shows how little you know," Amirra said. Gitre's self-adorned expression faded and turned to sharp disdain at the lack of admiration Amirra showed. "So, what does that make you now, a Crypt Theda?" Amirra asked.

"Yes, it does, and that is a higher rank than you will ever reach," Gitre said.

Amirra pulled out the medallion Shaz had given her and dropped it onto the soft creamy skin of her bare neck. Gitre sneered with a mixture of rage and jealousy. Amirra then pulled out the crest Semias used to wear around his neck and dropped it over the medallion. Shock compelled Gitre to stifle her horrified glare. Since defeating Semias, Amirra had earned the right to wear the rank of Zunda-sune-voiant, the third-highest rank in the Velshari, making her four ranks higher than Gitre. Amirra smiled with a flash of disdain across her features. Riddick couldn't hear what they were saying, but he could tell that Amirra just outranked Gitre and that it didn't sit well.

"I guess, you get to do what *I* tell you to do," Amirra said.

"I answer only to Isot. I will *never* do as you command," Gitre said.

"I don't think you remember how this works, with this touch you will be forbidden to ever to speak my name or anything about me, and that is a *direct* command," Amirra said.

Gitre began to pull away but Amirra touched Gitre's arm who flinched and crumpled to the floor. The two other women shrunk away with the understanding that they could have faced the same punishment, and the other members in the room backed up and scooted out of the way. Gitre's body convulsed several times as the pain of the shadow magic thundered through her. A flash of remorse and guilt surged into Amirra's chest and then total satisfaction.

Amirra did a full inspection of Gitre's mind and tears flowed from Gitre's eyes. Amirra made a mental note of the details and released her hold on Gitre. Gitre slumped to the floor and panted through the pain still in her body. Amirra turned and started out of the room. She stopped and turned around, waved her hand and commanded that the entire room remember nothing of her being there and left the room. Her strong vibes echoed through the lobby and people sitting in a dining hall nearby turned to see her ascend the stairs. Riddick quickly skirted the outer perimeter of the room and caught up to Amirra a couple of floors up the stairs.

Amirra fell into Riddick's arms, and he hugged her shaking frame. The tightness in her chest squeezed her breath, and she struggled to fill her lungs. Riddick helped her the rest of the way up the stairs and into their room.

"What happened?" Turkill barked.

"She's alright, she's just having an endorphin letdown," Riddick said.

"A what?" Ladtwig asked.

"You know, when after you do something really hard or scary and your body releases the chemicals that helped you do the hard thing," Riddick said. The Minca shared blank looks. "Never mind," Riddick said.

Riddick helped her to the bed and sat her down. He tried to comfort her but there was nothing he could do, and he wished Serin was there.

Realms of Edenocht

33-It Gets Worse

The door swung open with a BANG and Deagan jumped. He had forgotten the old rickety door barely hung on its hinges the correct way. The odor of tobacco and ale hit him in the face, and he puckered his lip in a sideways gag.

"What are you doing here Deagan, I thought Lucien was very clear you were never to come back here," a husky thug said.

"Yeah, yeah, is he here, I need to talk to him," Deagan said.

Deagan shoved the door back into place and started toward the bar at the back of the room. The thug shoved his oversized muddy boot into the pathway and Deagan pulled back.

"I'm not convinced you two are brothers," the thug said.

"You and me both, now just go fetch him," Deagan said.

"My, you think your such a tough guy now do you," the thug said.

Deagan searched the room and made note of all the patrons sitting around. The men and women here were the kind the rest of the world wanted nothing to do with. Some had markings all over their bodies, including their heads and some were disfigured from either birth or the result of severe injuries. He used to be friends with them all, at one time. But he and Lucien had a falling out when Deagan wanted to live in the city and take a job driving the boats. Lucien disowned him, mostly that is.

"He wants to hear what I have to say, so just go tell him," Deagan said.

"I aint goin no where, and not by the likes of you neither," the thug said.

The burly man pulled a chair from a table nearby and sat his large frame in the walkway. Deagan tried not to obsess with the leftover food stuck in the man's dusty brown beard which covered most of his face. Deagan skirted the table and started toward the back door and another man stepped in front of him.

"LUCIEN, I can tell you're here, now come out I have to talk to you," Deagan hollered.

The man in front of him covered his ear and rose his fist as though he was going to pummel him for shouting in his ear. Deagan darted under the blow and rounded another table. The other patrons started to laugh and casting bets whether Deagan was going to make it to the back hallway. Deagan shoved a table to one side and leaped over the chair but got stuck by yet a third brusk man.

"Really?" Deagan said. "Fine I won't tell you who is back in town," Deagan yelled.

Deagan slipped under the third man's raised arm and gagged at the amount of body odor that emanated from him. Deagan turned on his heel and ducked the grasp of the second man.

"Who, who is back?" Lucien asked.

Lucien gripped the lapels of his tailored vest and squinted his tiny eyes making his face almost disappear. He was not tall enough to reach the top shelf in normal places.

"I knew you couldn't help yourself," Deagan said.

Deagan slipped under the table and crawled away from the second man's attempt to catch him and the derelict tavern's crowd roared with laughter.

"Well, who is it?" Lucien said.

Deagan jumped over another chair and sidestepped two not so womanly looking women.

"Shaz," Deagan said.

"ENOUGH!" Lucien shouted.

The tavern silenced immediately and Lucien hurried his short bald self to where Deagan was.

"What do you mean Shaz is here?" Lucien asked.

Lucien peered up at Deagan who was nearly three lengths taller than he was.

"Shaz and Serin, and their friends, and boy do they have a story to tell," Deagan said.

"Does he have my merchandise he promised me?" Lucien said.

"Well, no, but he did promise to get it for you this time. Things got a little out of hand last time," Deagan said.

"Why did you tell me this if he doesn't have my merchandise?" Lucien asked.

Deagan swallowed the lump in his throat.

"Well, he needs our help again, but this time we will have a much bigger score," Deagan said.

"You mean, I will have a much bigger score," Lucien said.

"Yeah, what I said," Deagan said.

"What is the payoff?" Lucien said.

"The castle treasury," Deagan said.

Deagan nodded, raised his pointed brows several times and motioned to entice the notion more. Luicen scrunched his round face and studied Deagan for several minutes.

"What are you talking about? Have you gone mad? How is this Shaz guy going to get us into the castle treasury, and why? What does he want for it?" Lucien asked.

The three thugs were now standing close to Deagan, and he pulled at his collar and shoved his hands into his pockets.

"Well, you see, there is an evil necromancer who is going to cast a spell on the loyal subjects of Ebassia at the coronation of the new queen making them immortal and Shaz needs us and the travelers, to create a distraction," Deagan said.

The whole place burst into laughter and Deagan started biting his fingernail.

"Your serious?" Lucien asked.

"Come on boss, of course, he's not serious," one thug said.

Lucien understood his adopted brothers' idiosyncrasies and was sure he was telling the truth.

"Come on," Lucien said.

Lucien walked briskly back to his office and Deagan followed him. Lucien shoved Deagan into his office and shut the door.

"You better not be pulling my leg," Lucien said.

Deagan shook his head rapidly.

"Oh, I'm not, so, you'll help?" Deagan asked.

"I didn't say that tell me everything," Lucien said.

Deagan rehearsed his encounter with Shaz and Serin and the others leaving out the parts about the magic and tried to make sense of how to describe Isot and her plans to immortalize the secret organization and then explained what their job would be and how to enlist the travelers, so they could gain access to the secret tunnels of the castle.

"How are you going to make the leader give permission to ask the travelers to give up their secrets?" Lucien asked.

"Serin's mother was Ambrosia," Deagan said.

"Alright, now you've gone too far, there is no way, she would have to be over three-hundred rotation's old," Lucien said. Deagan nodded, "You can't be serious," Deagan nodded.

Lucien sat back into his oversized chair and looked up at the ceiling. He was tired of looking at the bent and twisted beams and the leak in the corner dripped even when there was no rain. *It would be nice to be able to fix this place up.* Lucien thought.

"What will we have to do?" Lucien asked.

"We need to meet up with Shaz and Serin to find out the details, but from what I can tell, we need to help them breach the castle without being detected and create a distraction while Shaz finds the scrollythingy," Deagan said.

"What kind of distraction?" Lucien asked.

"I was thinking, the performers haven't performed for the new Queen, maybe we could crash the coronation and give her a spectacle she's never seen before," Deagan said.

"I like it, but it will be a hard sell to convince the performers to be willing to do it," Lucien said.

"How come," Deagan asked.

"Did you forget the last time they performed, things didn't go well," Lucien said.

"Oh, and we'll have to break into the dungeon again," Deagan said.

"Oiy vay, you never stop do you," Lucien sighed.

****

Shaz and Serin moved their way through the crowded streets and stopped every so many streets to reassess their directions until the found the Inn. Shaz opened the door for Serin and she stepped inside. The instant relief from the sun's heat was welcoming, and she breathed in the soft aroma of the mixed flowers sitting in the large vase on the side table next to the front desk.

"Are you sure this is the right place?" Serin asked.

"Aye, why?" Shaz asked.

"It's just so nice, I guess I expected it to be a hole in the wall," Serin said.

Shaz chuckled and started toward the man at the main desk. Shaz stopped and turned and waved for Serin to follow him up the stairs.

"We're not going to check in?" Serin asked.

"Not yet, we'll check in on our way out, to throw them off our trail," Shaz said.

"Do you know where Riddick and Amirra are then?" Serin asked.

"Not entirely, but I think they are up here somewhere," Shaz passed the first-floor exit and then the second, "Ah, yes down this way," Shaz said.

Shaz hurried down the hall and stopped and knocked on the door. Riddick opened the door and let them into the room.

"Wow, this place is so nice, how did you get a room like this?" Serin asked.

Riddick wasn't sure if he should say anything but Amirra was in the washroom changing.

"It would appear after defeating Semias, Amirra is a very high-ranking officer in the Velshari," Riddick said.

Amirra came out of the little room and burst into tears when she saw Serin.

"Oh, my goodness, what happened," Serin asked.

Serin hurried to Amirra who tried to pull herself together but couldn't seem to get a grip on her composure. Shaz looked at Riddick with a 'what in the tarnation happened' look and Riddick shrugged.

"Unfortunately, she had to face one of her biggest rivals and inflict pain on her. It was quite unreal, and it rattled her pretty good," Riddick said.

Serin boosted her with a dose of healing magic and the panic left Amirra's chest, and she stopped crying.

"You don't have to talk about it yet, but at some point, you need to tell me everything, so we can make sure we have the right precautions, alright?" Serin said.

Amirra nodded and wiped her eyes.

"Is it safe to ask what you found out?" Shaz asked.

Amirra nodded and Serin took her hand and gave it a squeeze.

"Isot is indeed going to use the coronation as the focus point, but she is also going to utilize the Pact of the Everlasting," Amirra said.

"What does that mean?" Shaz asked.

"The Pact of the Everlasting is the spell which each member agrees to when they join the Velshari, which is what binds them to the ruler's commands. It forces them to go against their will and succumb to whatever the current leader requires of them. It also means the members don't have to be here to receive the benefit, but in order to do it, a live human sacrifice is needed for each member," Amirra said.

"You're saying for each member of the Velshari there is, a live person will die to give them eternal life?" Shaz asked.

"Yes, that is exactly what that means, and they don't have to be near the member, it can simply be someone they name," Amirra said.

"That's the most horrible thing I have ever heard," Serin said.

"Aye, that's pretty sick," Riddick said.

"How many people are we talking?" Shaz asked.

"Thousands," Amirra said.

Shaz ran his hands through his hair and paced the floor.

"It gets worse," Amirra said.

Shaz turned to her with an exasperated grimace.

"I won't be able to fight it this time," Amirra said.

"Yes, you can," Serin said.

Amirra shook her head and held out her palm. Serin took her hand in her own and felt the shadow magic inside the scar.

"I am bound by the agreement I made rotations ago," Amirra said.

Amirra's voice was soft and broken and Serin's heart sank.

"I understand how you feel Amirra, but worse, I have shadow magic inside me and for a long time I thought I had to fight it, but what I learned was by accepting the fact I was always going to have a part of me be evil, didn't mean *I* was evil. And then I learned I could *use* my evil for good and that was quite freeing," Shaz said.

"Use bad for good, that doesn't even make sense," Amirra said.

"Yes, it does, look at it this way, when you have to do something really hard, like when you punished Gitre, you had to have a level of anger in order to do it right?" Shaz said.

"Yes," Amirra said.

"Well, some would argue being angry is considered bad, right?" Shaz said.

"Yes," Amirra said.

"So, if the punishment was to help the person learn what they were doing was going to hurt themselves or others, then it was a good punishment, yes?" Shaz asked.

Amirra nodded and her expression lightened.

"I see what you're saying, but how does that apply to me," Amirra said.

"Well, you can be certain the pain won't affect you because it hurts more to see innocent people be sacrificed for the selfishness of others," Shaz said.

"I understand that but I'm not sure I have the ability to make it effective in my life, but I'm willing to give it a try," Amirra said.

"Atta girl," Riddick said.

Amirra smiled at him, and he saw her childlike gaze return, and he kissed her.

"Now, what is the plan?" Turkill asked.

Shaz and Serin rehearsed the meeting with Bowen and Lorn and Riddick and Amirra filled them in on the initiations and the rest of the details of the encounter with Gitre and the Velshari.

"We can't trust Lorn, so we need to expect some kind of betrayal on his part, and there are going to be a great deal more guards than we expected," Shaz said.

"We need Lucien's help to get into the dungeons and search for my father and grandfather," Shaz said.

"We can use the secret tunnels to sneak into the castle and find the scroll before the coronation," Riddick said.

"If they even agree to help us," Shaz said.

"Well then I guess we have our next move," Riddick said.

"Where did Deagan say he would meet us?" Serin asked.

Turkill rehearsed the message and meeting spot from Deagan.

"Alright, then let's go," Shaz said.

34-Please, Make Yourself At Home

"Shaz, over here," Deagan said.

Deagan waved his arms over his head to show his whereabouts and Shaz veered to the side. Deagan leaned against the back wall of the city and a small crack popped open. Deagan looked around and hushed everyone inside the secret passageway. The passageway was dimly lit and cold. Shaz realized they were underneath the wall's turrets and walkway the guards used to see over the borders. The dim light grew, and they were able to see Lucien standing a few lengths away with an exceptionally cross scowl. Shaz wondered if his face was going to be stuck like that permanently. Grandfather used to always tell him the more he scowled the longer his face would stick that way.

"You have the nerve to come back to *my* city *and* without what *you* promised me?" Lucien said.

Shaz tried not to laugh, but he was right, he didn't get the item from the dungeons he said he would, and he did feel bad about that.

"Yes, and I am sorry, things just didn't work out the way I planned," Shaz said.

A flash crossed Lucien's eyes as he wasn't expecting an actual apology but kept his face stern.

"And, *then* you ask me to take you into *my* people and ask *them* to reveal all of *their* secrets," Lucien said.

"Well, when you put it that way, it does sound bad," Shaz said.

"*And*, you want *me* and *my guys* to give *you* a distraction so *you* can do what, *exactly*?" Lucien said.

Shaz was impressed Lucien was able to emphasize so much in such a short exchange.

"You have every right to be angry, and we're sorry," Serin said.

"And, who do think you are?" Lucien barked.

"I'm Serin Svirtari, and you had better change your tone," Serin said.

"You expect me to believe that? I don't do business with women," Lucien said.

Lucien waved his hand in front of Serin to dismiss her and Shaz stepped back, he was most certain she was going to unleash something on the short man, and he didn't want to be caught in the middle. Riddick, Turkill, and Ladtwig also stepped back which made Deagan step back. Lucien glared at her and found Amirra had her scarily-cross Velshari face on and was standing behind Serin. Serin sensed the anger inside him jump to max and her patients was about to end abruptly.

"Excuse me!" Serin barked.

"I don't know what you think you are doing, but you don't just throw that name around, especially when you have no business speaking it in the first place," Lucien said.

"I will speak my sir name anytime I please, and who do you think you are to tell me who or what I am," Serin said.

Shaz wanted to reassure her Lucien wasn't worth the energy, but he had learned that by this point, it was better to let the flames fizzle on their own instead of trying to throw water on them. Riddick crossed his arms over his chest and made ready for the fireworks he was sure was about to be unleashed on the partially bald squirrelly man. Lucien looked from Serin to Deagan and back to Serin.

"What is a Svirtari?" Turkill asked.

"It is the name of *my* clan, but if *he* doesn't believe *me* then *who* needs him," Serin said.

Her tone was cross, and she threw her arms over her chest and stared into Lucien's eyes. Her energy sank into his being, and he began to feel itchy all over. Shaz tried to stifle the chuckle he had for the emphasis she was doing to make fun of Lucien.

"The Svirtari are a very old family of travelers which have been gone for rotations and rotations, they are the closest things we have to royalty, but there haven't been any that we know of for decades, there's only rumors that they return from time to time, but I think it's just our peoples way of not forgetting our King," Deagan interjected.

"It is true, my family has been gone for some time, but you have no right to insult me as you are, and I will speak when I want to and to anyone I choose," Serin snapped.

Lucien started to squirm as Serin's energy etched at his being.

"Alright, let's all calm down, I think there is an explanation to this, but we can't talk about it here," Shaz said.

"Well, we are not going another foot unless I get some answers," Lucien said.

"I guess we don't need you, Deagan let's go," Serin said.

Lucien grabbed Deagan by the arm and kept him from going anywhere.

"I don't think you understand, no one just walks into a traveler village," Lucien said.

Serin tightened her fists and Shaz grabbed her shoulders and turned her around to look her in the eyes. Shaz shook his head.

"Serin don't let him rattle you," Shaz said.

"I can't believe the nerve of this man," Serin said.

"You're right, he is a pompass and arrogant man, but he's not worth getting this upset," Shaz said.

"But Nix is?" Serin snapped.

"You're right, but do I need to tell you what you tell me?" Shaz asked gently.

Shaz's gaze was kind and understanding and Serin sucked in a deep breath and let it out slowly.

"I'm sorry, I've just never been treated that way from another traveler," Serin said.

"You have been here before?" Deagan asked.

"Yes, but last time *I* came by a green *earth wyvern* named *Medrith*," Serin said.

Lucien and Deagan stared blankly at her not knowing what to say.

"Come on, I can find it myself," Serin said.

Serin turned and started down the corridor. The tall walls flanked a passageway and rounded inside the outer wall of the city. Deagan pulled out of Lucien's grip and ran to catch up with the others. Lucien threw his hands up and followed them. The outer wall stopped and was replaced by a row of thick hedges the height of the wall for several lengths and resumed for another length and another hedge and so on. Shaz inspected one of the hedges and found a gate of thick iron rods in the center and found the next several hedges to be the same. He guessed the hedges were placed on purpose and wondered if it was used as a trick to make a possible enemy think they would be an easy access point into the city.

Deagan stopped at a hedge and gripped some branches and moved them out of the way and a small lever appeared. The lever was attached to a rugged rock which sank under the dirt floor and was about as tall as Shaz. Deagan heaved the lever and the hedge swung open. Shaz nodded with acceptance and Ladtwig jumped with enthusiasm. The early morning sun was fresh on their skin and Serin soaked in its energy. Turkill and Ladtwig hurried through the door and Deagan followed. Deagan found the lever on the other side and yanked it downward which closed the door.

Shaz's guess was confirmed when the door had shrubs on the other side which covered every inch and tried to find something to use to find it again, but it was nearly undetectable. Shaz thought the dirt would tell him since the door swung open but there was no trace in the gravel which was strongly mixed with dirt and grass. Shaz looked back down the wall and counted the same amount of shrub sections but there were more than on the other side, and he guessed the access on the inside was in the middle which meant there might be another passageway on the other side of where they met Deagan.

His mind started running through new scenarios of ways to defend the city and how many secret passageways there might be. Deagan started down a hill and Lucien hurried to be in front. Shaz knew he shouldn't listen to Serin's thoughts and usually tried not to, but when he tried to get her attention, he learned she was busy thinking of the many ways to hurt Lucien without leaving any marks. He found her methods invigorating and a bit sexy, which of course he wasn't going to ever tell her that. Small tents peeked over a hill as they rounded a bend. The tents were fashioned onto the tops and sides of the brightly decorated traveling wagons. Shaz understood the wagons were used for selling goods and wares made here in the 'village', which of course, traveled from town to town

Shaz took in the details and was impressed by the diverseness of the people. Many were dark-skinned and dark hair and eyes, but others were lighter skinned like Deagan and had a variety of light and dark brown shades. There were many people that had been left behind by society, people with deformities, illness, and or mental limitations. They followed Lucien through the wagons and Shaz found the same little squat man who kicked his shin the first time he came with Deagan, and he scowled.

The little man laughed and pointed his finger at Shaz who patted his blade and shook his head at him. The short-legged man backed away but still laughed at Shaz, until he eyed the Minca and frowned. Shaz wondered why the Minca would change the man's demeanor. Amirra rounded a wagon and tried not to be surprised by the two women who shared a pair of legs and Shaz chuckled. He had the same reaction a rotation ago and was happy it wasn't just him. Amirra blushed and nodded at the women who giggled behind the lace fan they each had in their separate hands. A sudden prick stabbed at Serin's heart, and she stood up straight and started looking over the people and around the wagons.

"What's wrong?" Shaz asked.

Shaz's alert level shot to fight or flight, and he gripped the hilt of the blade. Deagan saw her and stopped. Lucien stopped only when Deagan slapped his arm.

"Someone I know is near," Serin said.

Serin looked around, she gripped the familiarity and moved through the people quickly. A tall wall-like man stood several lengths above everyone else but was nearing the edge of the market. Serin started after the man and Shaz moved in close behind her. Turkill and Ladtwig moved in behind Shaz and secured the flank side, while Riddick and Amirra took the other side. Serin's pace was quick and Shaz's heart was starting to turn into panic. Serin rounded a long wooden pole that secured one of the market tents and found the man near another trading booth.

"Asher?" Serin asked.

The man stood up straight and gained another length or two. He turned around slowly. His dingy traveling cloak and boots were worn, and his aged face was kind but showed rotations of wear. The man blinked and looked at Serin and then at Shaz who had half the sword drawn. The man studied Serin for a minute and then a light came on inside and his face brightened.

"Serin?" Asher said.

Serin ran to the man and leaped into his arms and was swallowed up in his embrace. Tears escaped Asher's eyes at a sudden force and Serin gripped him tightly.

"What just happened?" Turkill asked.

Shaz put the blade back in place and rested his thumbs in his beltloops.

"I get the distinct impression they know each other," Shaz said.

Turkill grunted and Ladtwig snickered. Riddick and Amirra mused at the size of the man and how much of Serin you could no longer see. Lucien's mouth gaped open and Deagan smiled. Asher put Serin back on the ground and put his hands on her shoulders to inspect her.

"I can't believe it," Asher said.

"How can it be, how are you still alive?" Serin asked.

Asher noticed Shaz and the crew staring at them and started to move Serin to another location.

"No, it's alright, they're with me," Serin said.

Serin motioned for Shaz to come to her.

"This is Shaz, Turkill and Ladtwig, Riddick, Amirra, Deagan and," Serin wasn't sure if she was going to acknowledge Lucien, "Lucien," Serin said.

Shaz held out his hand to shake Asher's but the man's friendly glance became stern. Shaz's heart skipped a beat. Even though the man had some rotations on him, his sheer size would squish Shaz like a bug.

"Uncle stop, we all know you're the biggest softy on the planet," Serin said.

"Uncle?!" Lucien said.

"This is Asher, my mother's brother," Serin said.

"You're Asher Svirtari," Lucien said.

Lucien's mouth dropped open again and he stared.

"Does he always look like that?" Asher asked.

"I'm not sure, I just met *him*, but Deagan I trust," Serin said.

"Come 'little one', we need to find a better place to talk," Asher said.

Asher led them from the market and further into the rolling hills of Ebassia. They all found it hard to keep up with the man's gate and as soon as they were at a safe distance, Serin stopped and air buffed everyone. Lucien and Deagan panicked and Turkill quickly barked instructions, and they caught up to Asher.

"Where is he taking us?" Turkill asked.

"To our deaths for sure, out in the middle of nowhere, where no one will ever look for us," Deagan said.

Shaz chuckled and Serin gave him a sideways glare. They rounded a bend and a small group of tents emerged. A few people moved about the tents and wagons pulled by horses, but they stopped and inspected them as soon as they realized their presence. Asher made his way to the center of the wagons and looked around.

"Father," Asher called.

An older man turned around. His dark hair was almost lost in the gray and his eyes were a soft deep-brown. He wasn't near as tall as Asher and Shaz wondered how they were related. The older man looked at Asher and then Serin who had stepped out from behind Asher. The man's face contorted through a range of emotions and disbelief and peered at Asher who nodded.

"Yappa?" Serin asked.

"Serin?" Motavo asked.

Serin nodded and the man's knees went weak. Stunned without words he gripped Serin tightly. Tears flooded his eyes, and he blinked several times to focus.

"How can this be?" Motavo asked.

Motavo's voice cracked through the knot in his throat, and he stared up at Asher.

"I have no clue, but that is why I brought them here," Asher said.

Motavo pulled away and stared into Serin's eyes. He raced through as many scenarios as possible but came up empty. Motavo's expression quickly turned as soon as he saw Shaz and the others, and Serin could tell he was filled with instant fear and aggression.

"Yappa, this is Shaz, Ladtwig, Riddick, Amirra, Turkill, Deagan, they are with me. That is Lucien, and he has yet to decide if he is with me or not," Serin said.

"How long have you known them. Can they be trusted?" Motavo asked.

"Yes, Yappa," Serin chuckled, "Shaz is the war wizard, and my lo-" Serin started but thought she should save that for later.

Motavo's eyes widened and his heart skipped a beat.

"You mean, *the* war wizard?" Motavo asked.

Shaz reached out to shake Motavo's hand. Motavo hesitated and took Shaz's hand in his. Shaz smiled and shook his hand with a tight grip. Shaz bowed at the waist and dropped his head and stood up. Serin remembered that was the official greeting for anyone who wanted to seek an audience with a clan leader, and she smiled. Lucien had a hard time closing his mouth and Deagan snickered at how ridiculous he looked. Motavo returned the greeting with a nod of dignity.

"I'm Shaz of the house of Reinholt," Shaz said.

"You are Reinholt's son?" Motavo asked. "So Reinholt had the war wizard," Motavo said quietly with his hand on his chin.

"You knew him?" Shaz asked.

"I never met him, but he was a great man, he was kind to our people when most people were not," Motavo said.

"I'm Riddick the earth sage," Riddick said.

Riddick bowed the way Shaz did and shook Motavo's hand.

"I'm Amirra, the Runecaster," Amirra said.

Amirra also bowed.

"This is Turkill and Ladtwig, they are Minca," Serin said.

The Minca bowed.

"I'm Deagan from the clan Tann, and this is my brother Lucien," Deagan said.

Jagwynn padded up behind Shaz and rubbed against his leg. Deagan jumped away startled and Lucien turned green. Motavo flinched and Asher swallowed hard.

"Oh, and this is Jagwynn," Serin said.

Jagwynn walked slowly to Motavo and bowed her head and Motavo stared but returned the greeting with a bow.

"I am Motavo Svirtari, leader of the traveler people," Motavo said.

"You're Motavo?" Lucien stammered.

Lucien had never seen such a thing. A traveler clan leader never bowed to anyone, ever, let alone the King of all the clans. Motavo looked at Lucien who was about to fall over.

"You might want to sit down before you hurt yourself," Motavo said.

Lucien gripped Deagan's arm who shoved him off and Lucien stumbled and found his way to a stool. Ladtwig's stomach grumbled and he smiled sheepishly.

"Oh, my, please, you must be hungry," Motavo said.

Motavo wrapped his arm around Serin and led them into his tent.

Deagan and Lucien hesitated but Motavo waved them in, and they found a seat in the corner of the tent. The tent was pleasant but didn't have too many decorations. It was left light for easy transportation and Motavo didn't spend much time there anymore. Shaz and Serin sat on a sofa and Shaz leaned over and whispered into her ear.

"When were you going to tell me about your family?" Shaz asked.

"I haven't seen them since I was a small child and finding out how many rotations had passed in this realm, I assumed them to be long passed," Serin said.

Her tone, even in a whisper was filled with agitation.

"Fair enough," Shaz said.

"If you make my 'little one' angry, you'll have me to deal with," Asher said.

Shaz looked up with surprise. He hadn't realized Asher had been watching them.

"I believe that," Shaz said.

Asher came and started to sit between them and Shaz jumped off the couch before he was swallowed up by the enormous man. Asher smirked and Shaz shoved his hands in his pockets. Riddick and Amirra also snickered but Riddick stood next to Shaz to show his allegiance. Jagwynn prowled around the tent as though she were inspecting it for something and Motavo turned around with a tray of fresh vegetables and meats and set it on a table.

"Please, make yourself at home," Motavo said.

Ladtwig hurried to the table and climbed onto a chair and had a piece of food bulging in his check before Turkill even made it to a chair. Shaz walked around the outside of the tent around a few chairs and picked a roll and began to pull open the insides. Deagan was about to get up but Lucien held him back and shook his head and Deagan scowled.

"We're not worthy to eat at the king's table," Lucien whispered.

Lucien was right, it was an honor to be able to be inside the leader's home, but there was a hierarchy which was strictly adhered to by the traveler people and Lucien was not going to risk his being cast out. Even if Motavo didn't do it, others who ranked higher than him could.

"Tell me, what has happened?" Motavo asked.

"Why don't you tell me what you know since I have no idea where to start," Shaz said.

"Let's start with, how did you meet my Nipotina," Motavo said.

Motavo had a 'you better give me the right information or your dead' tone and Shaz gulped.

"Here in Ebassia actually. I saw her in a town square but met her at Mrs. Bailey's," Shaz said.

"When was this?" Motavo asked.

"It was nearly a rotation ago, for Ebassia that is, but we spent a bit of time in the realm of the Minca, and at my castle before returning. So, about two rotations now," Shaz said.

Shaz felt Serin watching him, and he turned to see her smiling at him with her 'you're so beautiful' smile she always gave him, and he smiled back.

"I see there is some chemistry between you two," Motavo said.

35-Let's Go See What the Choovino Has to Say

"I can fix that," Asher said.

Shaz gulped, and Motavo chuckled.

'Do I have to ask permission to marry you now?' Shaz asked in his mind.

Serin shrugged.

'I was too young to learn all the traditions so maybe,' Serin returned.

'How am I going to do that?' Shaz replied.

'I remember the story of my parents, and my father had to dance with my mother at the campfire to show his intent to court my mother and her father had to approve.' Serin replied.

'So, I have to dance with you in front of him?' Shaz asked.

Serin nodded and Motavo and Asher studied their faces. They could tell something was being said, but they couldn't figure out how when they weren't speaking out loud.

"Is there something I should know?" Motavo asked.

Serin stood up and walked to Shaz and wrapped her arm around him. Motavo nodded and his eyes smiled, but his brows and jaw tightened.

"Yappa, Shaz and I-" Serin started.

"We can talk later. Where is your father? Where is Jerim?" Motavo asked.

"I was hoping you could tell me," Serin said.

"Why did he leave you, and not with us?" Asher asked.

"He told me he wouldn't be long, but then I met Mrs. Bailey and Shaz and things went from there," Serin said.

"Is this Mrs. Bailey a Choovina?" Motavo asked.

"I guess you could say so, she's with the Dodjen," Serin said.

"They should just keep their noses out of this, I mean, who better than to teach you than your own family. Why are they always the ones to make the rules?" Asher asked.

"Maybe because we weren't here. If it was only a rotation or so ago, we would have been traveling through the underground," Motavo said.

"Jerim knows about the underground, why didn't he come find us?" Asher asked.

"I guess that is a question for Jerim," Motavo said.

"Are you referring to the secret tunnels and passageways through the realms?" Shaz asked.

"How do you know about them?" Motavo asked.

Shaz sensed the urgency and fear in his voice.

"My Grandfather, I mean, Mathieu, told me all about them, but he always made them out to be stories and I never thought differently until," Shaz hesitated, "I got the Honor Blade, went through a hurricane, met a sea creature, came through the portal on the ocean from Turob, met Serin, rescued Serin from the dungeons here in Ebassia, met the Minca, met Azrak and the gryphtons, rescued Serin from the witch, closed the rift, found out my pet jaguar is an ambassador to the Sun Goddess, my best mate is an earth elemental, closed a crevasse in the earth, defeated a fire elemental necromancer," Shaz counted on his fingers as Motavo and Asher nodded with each addition, "what else," Shaz said.

"Fought the Jaduuk," Ladtwig said.

"And the sqwalls," Turkill said.

"And the Ukari," Serin said.

"Stopped a volcano," Riddick said.

"Saved our people," Turkill said.

"Met the old and new Runecaster," Riddick said.

Riddick smiled at Amirra.

"Created a new Mountain Temple," Amirra said.

Motavo looked back and forth from everyone with a curiosity which seemed to overload his mind.

"Wait, you have the Honor Blade!," Motavo asked.

"Yes," Shaz said.

"And the sheath?" Asher asked.

"Yes," Shaz said.

Shaz patted the blade at his hip and both Motavo and Asher turned to see the blade.

"We were aware Mathieu had the blade, but we were moving the sheath around. We weren't aware he raised you or even where you were being hidden. In fact, we didn't even know for sure you had been born. No one did," Motavo said.

"How did you acquire the sheath?" Asher asked.

"Semias the Fire Necromancer had it," Shaz said.

"Maybe Patchi is still alive," Asher said.

"I wouldn't think so, not if a Necromancer took the sheath, we have no way to fight against magic users," Motavo said.

Shaz studied their expressions and energy and figured Patchi was another uncle. He turned to Serin who nodded with sadness.

"I can change that," Amirra said.

Motavo and Asher shot her a look of both intrigue and fear.

"How?" Asher asked.

"It's not hard, the Rangers used this technique to fight magic users. It was one of my first big lessons with Nitida, all I need is a few of your weapons and, or, I could enchant your jewelry or both if you like," Amirra said.

Motavo stared. Amirra hesitated and looked at Riddick who gave her a thumbs up and a smile of pride, which made her smile.

"That is an excellent idea, Amirra you and Riddick get with Asher and start working right away," Shaz said.

Shaz could sense Motavo's hesitation with Shaz issuing orders when it was always, him making the orders. Shaz could tell he didn't mind, but did mind at the same time.

"If you are alright with that, and we won't intrude in your space, so we will find other arrangements, but we have to stop Isot from enacting the Binding of the Crypt spell, and we could use your help," Shaz said.

"Binding of the Crypt!," Motavo said loudly.

"No one has seen the scroll since before Ambrosia had it," Asher said.

"That is because it has been infused into the Ebassia Castle where the mages were supposed to destroy it, but they didn't know a page was missing and the magic took Isot as the missing page and now she is trapped inside the castle," Serin said.

"That would be why we never found it," Asher said.

"How do you know about the scroll," Shaz asked.

"We are the Teorran Travelers, we are the secret, secret group her mother set up to move the artifacts around," Motavo said.

"I thought the Dodjen did that?" Shaz said.

"They move all of them except the real Sev-Rin-Ac-Lavah. Those were entrusted only to us. Which we did a fantastic job until the realms were cut off from one another. The underground doesn't move through every realm," Motavo said.

"Interesting, so are there fake items which look like the Sev-Rin-Ac-Lavah?" Shaz asked.

"No, but it was under strict order no Dodjen was ever to look inside the pouch, satchel or box they were transporting, so they were told they were transporting an item which might not have been what it was said to be. That way no one could be manipulated or used," Motavo said.

"I guess that's why Crolos never found the staff then," Serin said.

"Crolos?" Asher asked. "He's still around?"

"He was in the Realm of Yune searching for the Kar-ka-dan-non," Riddick said.

"Kar-ka-dannon? Why?" Motavo asked.

"We aren't sure, but we think Gavin Rhill is trying to *recreate* the Sev-Rin-Ac-Lavah, at least that's what Semias said and why he re-incarnated Luthrous to make a new Honor Blade," Shaz said.

Motavo rubbed his chin and paced the floor.

"Did he succeed?" Asher asked.

"He did until I destroyed it and sucked up all of its power," Shaz said.

Shaz rubbed his chest and shared a moment with Serin who returned his troubled glance. Her sadness for the pain he had endured suddenly weighed on her mind and chest unlike never before. Serin's gift of intuition was teetering on overdrive, with all the new people she now sensed, and she was having a hard time keeping it separated from the emotions of her healing powers, and Shaz's powers. She turned and walked toward the door and Jagwynn rubbed against her. She breathed in a deep breath and rubbed her ear.

"How did you get to the Realm of Yune, did you use a portal?" Motavo asked.

"Aye, but it was under a waterfall several lengths underwater, we found it by mistake, or rather the great big ginormous crazed gorilla made us find it," Riddick said.

Motavo wasn't sure whether he should believe him, but with everything else, they had said he figured it just might be true.

"Makes sense, we have found a few portals which were in very difficult places to get to, not like they used to be, for sure," Motavo said.

"Is that what you have been doing all this time?" Serin asked.

"It is, we have been searching for your mother, the islands of Srinna Vossa or anything to tell us where she is," Asher said.

"I need some air," Serin said.

Serin started toward the tent door and Shaz understood she meant literally and followed. The sun hit them in the face with force, and they shielded their eyes.

"What's wrong?" Shaz asked.

"I suddenly sense everyone's feelings at the same time, and I have no clue what to do about it. I usually only perceive our crews, but now everyone's affect me.

"Is it my fault?" Shaz asked.

Serin turned to him with her thin delicate brows raised over perplexed green eyes.

"Why would it be your fault?" Serin asked.

Shaz shrugged.

"I don't know, just I usually do something stupid and you have to fix it," Shaz said.

"No," Serin took his hand and gave it a squeeze, "no, this is not your fault," Serin said.

Her voice was soft and reassuring and full of adoration for Shaz. Yes, he did always seem to find a way to blow something up but that was one of the things she liked about him. He is impulsive and charismatic and his passion for getting the job done was exhilarating.

"No, it's in her blood, this is part of who she is. It was the hardest thing for her mother to deal with too," Motavo said.

Shaz and Serin turned around and found Motavo standing behind them.

"How did she manage?" Serin asked.

"The Choovina helped a great deal but I think your Synmagic has helped quite a bit too," Motavo said.

"I love your nipotina Motavo," Shaz pulled Serin into him, "the Synmagic isn't the only force that causes my love and loyalty to her. She's a remarkable woman and I would be nothing without her," Shaz blurted.

Motavo's thick partially gray brows raised and his deep brown eyes squinted. Sweat started to peak at Shaz's hairline and Serin noted his heartfire jump several degrees and smirked. She had never known anyone to make Shaz be this kind of nervous.

"I can see that, and I wouldn't have it any other way," Motavo said. Shaz relaxed, "*But,*" Motavo pointed his finger at Shaz, "we still have traditions around here and not even *the war wizard* can get out of," Motavo said.

Shaz swallowed the sudden knot in his throat.

"Does it involve walking on fire, because that one I can do really easily," Shaz said.

Motavo blurted a hearty ga-fa and slapped Shaz on the shoulder.

"Let's go see what the Choovino has to say," Motavo said.

Shaz smiled at Serin who was beaming up at him, and he squeezed her. They made their way through several tents and the people gawked with wonder, it was evident Motavo had a great deal of respect from everyone. It seemed though only a few of them knew who he actually was, and the rest just knew he was a 'high ranking officer' of sorts. Shaz tried to get a read on everyone and most people he found it easy but a few of them were perplexing just as Motavo and Asher were, and he guessed they were also from the old days.

The heat of the afternoon sun left its mark on Shaz as the sweat dripped down his back. He pulled off his leather jerkin and slung it over his arm. The warmth bathed the ragweed and a bitter odor sifted through the slight breeze. Serin unwrapped her ties that secured her new cloak the Whispmother had made her in the same fashion the Minca women had, and she put it into her satchel. They reached the edge of the valley and a group of trees encased a small hut. The shade felt good as they maneuvered the debris along the path.

"I'll wait out here," Shaz said.

Motavo nodded and pulled open the door to the Choovino's tent. A sudden blast of rosemary and mugwart filled their nose and Serin puckered from its sharp stink. An old man sat in a worn-out rocking chair in the corner of the hut. His dark eyes sat under rotations of heavy skin which made long lines across his being. The man looked up from what Serin guessed was sleep and blinked.

"Motavo, what a nice surprise," the Choovino said.

"Choovino, sorry to bother you, but I have an urgent matter," Motavo said.

"You're the leader of all the clans, you can bother me anytime you wish," the Choovino said.

"This is my nipotina Serin, she is Ambrosia's daughter," Motavo said.

The delicate framed man gripped the handle on his chair and tried to scoot himself to the edge. Serin wasn't sure what to do, but she had the urge to help him. She moved to his side and took hold of his arm. Her cool touch on his skin surprised him, and he blinked again. Serin helped him scoot to the edge of the chair and the man pushed against it but found his body didn't move.

Serin sent a boost of healing magic into the man's body and his eyes opened wide. Motavo stared at the soft hue of blue mist which emerged from her hands and absorbed into the Choovino's.

"A water mage?" the Choovino asked with confused enthusiasm.

The Choovino motioned toward a small padded bench and reached for his healing stick. Serin handed him his staff and the man gripped it gingerly. He turned to Serin and his deep brown eyes traveled up and down her body and stopped at her eyes. Serin gazed into his face, but it was what she understood in her chest that made her almost gasp. The amount of experience this man had was astounding, and she received a clear picture of his soul.

The Choovino studied her more deeply, then took his stick and waved it over her head. Serin wasn't sure if the man had the strength to keep from falling over and used her wind magic to create a buffer around his body. The Choovino's eyes widened even more, and he put his staff on the ground. His old frame shook more, and she wanted to heal his old body. He was closer to death than she had ever seen, but he was completely at peace.

The Choovino slipped a set of bells onto his healing stick. He jingled it slowly around the room, muttering at each corner. Tinks and clanks echoed off the thick wooden walls. Charms, amulets, and talismans sounded against the coin necklaces he wore as he moved. His old wrinkled skin showed through his sheer overshirt. A pot of boiling water rested over the fire and emitted steam and mist into the room. Serin found it hard to breathe with all the mixed scents and odors. Her mind raced around the room as she tried to settle her senses.

"Unsavory spirits begone, do not attempt to partake as you are dead and cannot inherit the blessings of the healing powers I hold," the Choovino said.

His voice was soft and raspy as it moved in a sing-song pattern. With a crinkled hand, he pinched some salt from a copper-tin and tossed it about the room sealing the edges of the door and window. Small eddies of salt sprang to life as the wind from outside seeped in through the cracks. He closed his eyes and muttered in the native tongue of the traveling peoples and slowly spun in a circle. After several minutes he opened his eyes and peered into Serin's pale face.

"The daughter of Ambrosia," the Choovino said.

Serin nodded.

"What have you come here for?" the Choovino asked.

"I have come to ask for your blessing to use the travelers to help defeat Isot the Necromancer, and help with my powers of intuition," Serin said.

The Choovino closed his eyes and spun in a circle. He stopped and spun back the other way several times. He raised his hands over his head and spoke into the dancing light the sun made as it came into the cracks in the hut.

"That is not all," the Choovino said.

"Then I am sorry I don't know," Serin said.

"The child beseeches the truth; she needs to call upon those who would guide her on her path."

A small crystal rested in the center of his healing stick and refracted the light from the sprigs of sunlight onto the ceiling. Serin watched his face contort from grins and frowns and back to grins. This time his voice uttered no sound as he communicated with the spirits on the other side. Serin couldn't see them, but she understood their presence which surprised her. Her body raced with sensations, everywhere from pain and sorrow to pure joy. Serin jumped as he took his tambourine and slapped it against his thigh. His old frame started to sway and rotate at the waist. His body stilled, but his already shaky hand shook more. He rested the tip of his staff on her arm, and she jumped at the zing of energy that shot through her body.

"Serin, daughter of Ambrosia and Jerim, you are a direct descendant of the missing daughter of the Lavari from your mother and a direct descendant of the Travelers from your father. You have powers you alone in this world possess. You will be hunted and desired for your ability to detect a being's true intentions. It will be a blessing and a curse to you. You are to inherit the throne of Srinna Vossa and rule the people as your mother did. You are a chosen daughter of the Travelers and inherit all their blessings, but you will also be their protector and secure the secrets of the Dodjen. The Sun Goddess is pleased with you. You and the war wizard will emerge triumphant with wisdom and intuition and reign over this great kingdom."

Serin's heart swelled as the power of the mysterious spirits words sank in. Motavo wiped the small tear from the corner of his eye as he thought of his beloved daughter. The little blonde blue-eyed baby that captured his heart so many rotations ago and his heart both, swelled and broke.

"Do you have your mother's talisman?" the Choovino asked.

Serin pulled out the necklace the Wyvern Priestess gave her but the Choovino shook his head. Serin removed the ring her father had given her as soon as she was big enough to wear it and handed it to the Choovino who nodded. He took the ring and held it tightly in his palm and closed his eyes again. The man did his dance once more and opened his eyes.

"Ambrosia is not in the land of the dead, neither is Gavin Rhill," the Choovino said.

"What do you mean?" Serin asked.

Motavo perked with intense attention.

"Queen Ambrosia is not dead, but she is not alive either," the Choovino said.

"How is that possible?" Motavo asked.

"They are in a void, a place of in-between," the Choovino said.

"Where is that? How do I find it?" Motavo asked.

"The spirits do not know, only that they are not in the realm of the dead," the Choovino said. "As for your powers, come."

Serin stepped close enough for the man to touch her, and he put his first finger at her temple. A sudden burst of energy ripped through her body, and she started to crumple. Shaz shot through the door and caught her before she hit the ground. Motavo jumped back with surprise, he had never seen someone move so fast. Serin's eyes rolled into the back of her head and Shaz held her head from flopping. He knew she wasn't dead, but she wasn't responding to him either.

"What's happening?" Shaz demanded.

"She is receiving instruction from the Lavari, she is being elevated to a higher place of being, she needs more magic to keep up with you, do not fret, she will be alright," the Choovino said.

Shaz held her tight and his heart raged with feelings he couldn't explain. He remembered how he felt when he reached a new level, and he sagged with the fear of it causing her pain. Her body started to get cold and Shaz searched for a heartbeat. Shaz was relieved when he found it and called his fire element and his body heated up around hers. Motavo stepped back as the heat radiated onto his face. Shaz tried to keep his heat at a comfortable level to keep her from freezing but not too hot as to burn her. Shaz tried to be patient but it seemed to be taking a long time and his worry increased. He noticed the inscriptions of her armlet were rearranging and wondered if it was a way for her to re-member what she was learning. Serin finally gasped, and she regained control of her eyes and then her limbs.

"Serin?" Shaz said.

Serin blinked a few times to clear the mist still in her mind. A sensation rippled over her body and Shaz observed her tattoos on her arms climb a little higher. The gloves she wore wouldn't cover them anymore, and he wondered how things would change for her. Motavo stared in awe but didn't want to ask.

"You're roasting me," Serin said.

"Oh sorry," Shaz said. Shaz turned off his heat and the room fell a few degrees instantly. Shaz hugged her tight. "You scared the tar out of me, if I lost you," Shaz said.

Serin hugged him back and nestled her face into his neck. Motavo could now see just how much they meant to each other and his heart burst with overwhelming joy. Motavo pondered on the idea he was going to be related to the *legend*, the *oracle*, the *prophecy*, the *war wizard*, and for a minute the excitement to see *all* of Shaz's powers overcame him, then he thought of his beloved Finmay, and how ecstatic she would have been and smiled.

The Choovino slouched heavily as the spirits he had been chan-neling left his being. Small beads of sweat crested his temples. Motavo helped him back to his chair and Shaz helped Serin stand. Serin boosted the Choovino's frame with a dose of healing magic which surrounded him with a soft blue hue that sank into his body. He blinked and smiled at her.

"In all my rotations I have never seen two people who love as you two do. I believe our world is in good hands," the Choovino said.

Shaz and Serin smiled but it didn't make them feel any better. Shaz didn't let go of Serin until Motavo motioned for them to leave the hut, and he closed the door behind them. The afternoon sun had shifted a few degrees in the sky, and it wouldn't be long until night would be upon them.

"What are we going to do for the night?" Serin asked.

Shaz turned to Motavo.

"You are all welcome in my home, nipotino," Motavo said.

"Yappa!" Serin said.

Serin gripped Motavo into a tight embrace.

"You still have to follow the traditions," Motavo said.

"I can totally do that," Shaz said.

Shaz held his hand out to Motavo who pulled him into a hug.

"Can you really walk on fire?" Motavo asked.

"Yes, he can and blow things up really well," Turkill grunted.

Motavo looked down at the little man. He hadn't seen him or heard him make his way to where they were and for an instant, his heart jumped. Turkill snickered through his hurmpf glare and Shaz and Serin smiled.

"Does he always show up out of nowhere?" Motavo asked.

"Yep, he sure does," Shaz said.

"I'm standing right here," Turkill said.

Everyone laughed and Turkill grunted.

"Jagwynn has a report for you," Turkill said.

Shaz nodded and Serin motioned for him to go with Turkill and she returned to the camp with Motavo.

36-With This Medallion

Isot hurried down the corridor and rounded the corner but stopped in time to avoid hitting square into Lorn.

"Do you have news," Isot asked.

"Yes, mam, they are outside the city with the scrounges, I have an attack party planned for tonight," Lorn said.

"The Coronation is tomorrow and there better not be any surprises," Isot said.

"Yes Mam," Lorn said.

The tone in his voice was full of irritation but Isot let it slide and glared at him instead. She waved at him to dismiss, and he turned on his toe and barreled down the hall. Isot turned to see the early moon was peaking, through the gray sky.

Gitre stood at the palace gate and waited for the guard to open the man door at the side of the large drive. Gitre admired the smooth white stone and ran her finger along one of the cracks. The stones were of the old-world construction but with a certain quality that gave the impression, it came even before that. Gitre snarled at the guard as he fumbled through the keys to open the man gate. The heavy iron bars clicked open and swung on hinges that made no noise at all and Gitre shoved her way passed the guard shoving her shoulder into him as she went by. The guard rolled his eyes and pulled the door shut and locked the gate again. Gitre's long black traveling cloak flowed in the wake of her strong gate as she thudded over the cobblestone toward the side tower.

Gitre studied the guards on each of the vantage points around the peaks and spires of the castle and noted there were twice as many soldiers as the last time she was there. The man at the door opened the latch and let Gitre inside the side tower. The darkness shaved her brows, and she blinked a few times to acclimate her eyes to the new darkness. She hurried up the rounded staircase and across a bridge that was suspended over the main gate and down another set of stairs on the backside of the main wall. Gitre's thick boots clunked against the smooth stone of the courtyard as she hurried across and into a small opening at the backside and behind a tall shrub.

The fading sun cast several shadows off the many tombstones that encompassed the grassy field and Gitre sucked in a deep breath inhaling the acrid odor of the cemetery. Gitre eyed the fresh dirt of a new grave but didn't see its headstone and guessed the passing was recent. She wondered if that was the poor sap Isot had arranged for their sacrifice. She passed the large crypt that held the royalty and rounded the corner of the intricately carved pillars. Gitre counted the stepping-stones on the backside of the crypt and stopped at the thirteenth stone and turned to the east. She stomped on the stone three times and the latch underneath clicked and the stone sunk a tiny length. She hopped off the stone and hurried to another building that was adjacent to the larger one and pushed the door open.

The acrid odor of a rotting corpse stung her nose, and she swallowed the gag in her throat. Even though it was the nature of a Necromancer, she couldn't get used to the smell of the dead bodies. This was going to be her first introduction to the art of casting a spell with a full corpse as a Crypt-Theda, and she wanted to make sure she was on time and ready. Gitre closed the door and removed a torch and pulled a flick stick from a small ledge and struck it against the stone wall. The sparks bit at the oil-soaked cloth and a brilliant orange flame jumped into existence. Gitre rounded the room lighting all the torches and replaced the torch on the wall by the door. She rounded the altar at the center of the room that had the dead form under a white cloth and to a long wooden table at the back of the crypt. The table had several small glass jars with different colored fluids sat at one side and small dishes with crushed herbs and a long skinny dagger sat on a black velvet cloth.

Gitre picked up the blade and rolled the metal around in her small hand and admired the gems encrusted into the shiny silver. She smiled knowing that after that night it would become her own athame for when she begins doing her own rituals. She set the blade back onto the cloth and pinched a smidgen of one of the green leafy herbs. The aroma of rosemary and mint wafted into her senses, and she smiled. The flames on the walls flickered, and she jumped and spun on her toes. Isot closed the door behind her and walked carefully but solidly toward the altar. The door opened again, and three men and a woman cloaked in the red robes entered. Their hoods covered their faces and Gitre lifted her hood over her head and situated so that she could see but that her face was hidden.

Isot lifted her hood and situated it over her dark hair and clasped the latch at her throat. Isot stopped at a long gold chain hanging on the wall and lifted it off the hook. She held it over her arms keeping it from hitting the floor and walked to the body on the altar. Gitre swallowed and scrutinized every move Isot made taking as many mental notes as she could. She was after all the next highest-ranking officer of the Velshari until she remembered Amirra. Her stomach lurched and the blood under her cheeks heated up. She had tried so many times to tell Isot about Amirra but every time she had tried her tongue swelled up and her mouth went dry, and she couldn't speak.

Gitre rehearsed the events with Amirra one more time and the hot anger seeped into her chest. Her breath filled her rib cage and she exhaled slowly. Isot gave her an irritated sideways glare and Gitre shoved her hands into the large openings her robes arms had. The other members rounded the altar and gripped hands and Gitre stepped aside letting Isot stand at the head of the cold stone. Isot handed one end to Gitre who took the soft golden chain and secured it to the hooks in the side of the altar. Gitre carefully reached across the body and laid the chain over the chest. Gitre found the body was that of a male, and she lowered the chain so that it rested on his sternum. Gitre walked around the altar and picked up the chain and snugged it and hooked it on another hook. She laid the chain back over the body and across the chest at the neck and rounded the altar. She hooked the chain and crossed the body again, each time she secured the chain to the altar and placed the chain in the correct placement so that it would cross over the body ten times. When she came to the wrists, she wrapped the chain around the cold rigid form and a shiver ran down her back. Gitre hadn't expected the body to feel that way and wasn't sure what to think of it. At first, it was uncomfortable, but it became alluring and even arousing.

Isot let out the length each time Gitre crossed the body. Gitre tried to stay focused on what she was doing but Amirra's face kept popping into her head. Isot growled under her breath and Gitre cleared her throat and rearranged the chain at the ankle and moved to the next hook. Gitre finished the last length and breathed out with a little puff, she hadn't realized she had been holding her breath, and she blushed. She looked out from under her hood, but she couldn't tell if the others were watching, and she moved to the table. Isot pointed to the empty dish and Gitre set it in the center of the black cloth. Isot pointed to the dish with the rosemary and mint and pointed to the bowl and mallet. Gitre pinched the herbs between her fingers and dropped it into the bowl and picked it up and started to smash the leaves.

The now powdery substance began to clump in the bowl and Isot pointed to a jar of brown goo. Gitre popped the stopper out and the pungent odor of black mushroom slime pelted her nose hairs, and she wriggled her nose to stifle the unpleasant feeling in her sinuses. Isot smirked but returned to her expressionless features and pointed to the bowl. Gitre dropped several clops into the bowl and mixed it into the powder. The green and brown mixed to become an uglier green brown and Isot pointed to the dish with bright yellow powder. Gitre wondered what the color would become now and nodded ever so slightly when she dumped the powder and started to mix. The new concoction was just green brown and yellow yuck and the mint was now covered up by the tangy grit of the dockweed. Gitre had spent several days studying the needed elements for this spell and was well familiar with the protocol, but she had never done it in practicality, so she didn't know exactly what to expect.

Isot pointed to another jar and then another dish and Gitre continued to mix all the elements. After several minutes the potion was ready and Isot picked up the blade. She ran the sharp edge across the palm of her hand and the bright red of her blood oozed to the surface. Gitre took the knife from Isot and repeated the cut on her own hand and hissed as the sting of shadow magic released into her veins and then she set the blade back on the cloth. Isot smeared a glob of the position onto the cut and Gitre followed. The others in the room started to sway back and forth and hum a harmonizing group of sounds.

Isot turned to the body on the altar and squeezed her hand. The bright red mixed with the grungy brown and splashed onto the pale skin of the body's forehead. Gitre squeezed her hand next to the spot Isot had and then squeezed again on every point the chains overlapped or touched itself. Isot mimicked it and the chanting grew and softened in waves of sound. Gitre's heart pounded and her body heated up with the excitement. An unusual sensation radiated through Gitre's head as the shadow magic fed off her own energy. A faint glow found its way to the forefront of her mind, and she blinked and squinted.

The spirit form of the dead body emerged and Gitre understood it to be the late King of Ebassia. She wondered why she hadn't noticed before and made a note to ask Isot later. The chains on the body reflected in the misty glow of the spirit and Gitre could tell they were becoming tighter and tighter. The entity wriggled and gripped at the chains, but they wouldn't budge. Gitre's guts churned as she came to the realization that he hadn't been bound until now, and she smiled.

The euphoria of control stiffened her resolve and her greed for ultimate power surged through her frame. Isot picked up the parchment that was next to the black cloth and unfolded it and held it in front of Gitre.

"With this medallion, I summon the spirit of this body and command the powers of the shadow world to bind it to me. Give me strength and infuse my form with the deathly energies to strike fear into the hearts of those who dare defy me," Gitre said.

The body on the altar shuddered and writhed with what Gitre assumed was pain, but wondered how the dead could still feel pain. A dark glow formed around the spirit form of the king and his dark eyes became darker. The glint of a new reflection appeared and Gitre's blood quickened in her body. The new sensation of the evil magic coursed through her body and at first, she smiled with the satisfaction of a new completeness, but the pain began in her stomach and churned her guts. She struggled to keep from lurching as the pain swirled around. She breathed in heavily, and she gripped the edge of the altar. Her fingernails broke as her fingers dug into the cold stone.

The chanting continued and an irritating buzz sat at the back of Gitre's mind. A hot burning surged up her esophagus, and she coughed blood from her lungs. Gitre's eyes widened, and she turned to Isot who stood motionless. Gitre wiped the blood from her lips and closed her eyes as a new rush of pain she recognized as the shadow magic slammed into the back of her mind. The crawling tingle of the energy moved through her soul, and she understood it to be searching for a reason she might not be worthy of this binding. Gitre tried to steady her breathing but the pain was so intense her knees became wobbly and her mind started to fade. Gitre's body fell completely weak, and she hit the edge of the stone altar as she went down.

****

The flicker of the candle in the sconce on the far side of the room left little light to decipher the images on the paper. Bowen rehearsed the plan in his mind as he traced the lines that he had drawn of his plan to get into the queen. He shoved the paper into his pocket and mumbled the events as he strapped the leather bracer on his arm. The rundown inn he was staying was least to be desired, but it gave him the advantage of not being detected by anyone of importance. He pulled the curtain of the small window back and searched the darkened lower alleyway and courtyard. He counted the four men he stationed outside, studied the night sky, and rubbed his nose.

Bowen secured his sword onto his belt and swallowed the last few chugs of brew left in his mug and set the empty vessel on the side table. He yanked the iron handle and the door creaked open. The hallway wasn't much brighter, and he made his way down the narrow passage. Bowen rounded the corner and descended the rickety staircase. His large boots clunked as he crossed the old wooden floor. The noise was impressive for being a dive bar, and he tried not to make eye contact with anyone. At the edge of the smoky room, a barmaid stopped in front of him.

"I don't have time for this," Bowen said.

He pulled her hand off his arm and started to shove her out of his way but a large man with a dark beard stepped in behind her.

"I think the lady wants your attention," the man said.

"So, it would seem, but I'm not interested," Bowen said.

The man let a profound belch of brewed odor and Bowen coughed and gagged. The woman laughed and Bowen shoved her aside and slammed his shoulder into the man's chest. The burly fellow was so drunk that the force knocked him over, and he tumbled to the floor. Ale went flying and Bowen snuck past him as he went down grabbing onto the table next to him. Bowen pulled the door shut behind him and crossed the alley with only a few large steps.

"Everyone ready?" Bowen asked.

"Yes, Sir," the soldier replied.

"Good, let's go," Bowen said.

Bowen started down the alley and the four soldiers fell into place behind him. Their armor clanked in the quiet night, and they tried to be as light on their feet as possible while carrying several pounds of steel over their bodies. The cobblestone path was uneven, and Bowen found it annoying that he had to focus on the stupid path, so he wouldn't trip and fall. The men made their way out of the lowest class district and slowed their pace as they came to the entrance of the commerce district. Bowen held his breath as he saluted the guards that were minding the entrance to the commerce district, and they saluted in return.

He wasn't sure why he was nervous, after all, he was the real general and knew everything about the castle and the royal family, except now that Isot had changed things, he was left a certain feeling of unrest.

The small entourage crossed the commerce district and rounded the bend to the outer gatehouse of the main house of the castle grounds. One of the guards pulled out a long solid wood stick and ran it across the iron gate and shoved it back into his holder on his belt. The guard in the gatehouse gruffly yanked the inner door open.

"Who goes there, what do you want?" the man barked.

"The General, now open the gate," the guard said.

The soldier peered through the dim lights of the streetlamps across the corridor and started to stammer when he caught sight of the generals' crest on Bowen's shoulder. He fumbled with the key but managed to open the iron gate.

Bowen started through the gate and the other four men followed. The first man slammed his shoulder into the gatekeeper's shoulder and glared. The gatekeeper slunk slightly but returned the glare. Bowen maneuvered the hallways and passageways until he came to the inner housing section of the castle.

"I will be back with the queen, make sure you wait here until I come back and don't let anyone up these stairs," Bowen said.

The soldier nodded and stood at attention and the other three found their place in the corridor. Bowen quietly took two stairs at a time until he reached the top and rounded the corner. The queen's quarters were on the other side of the building, and he needed to pass the quarters of the viziers and the chamber help before he would come to the queen's quarters. At the end of each hall, Bowen slowed and stopped, and checked around the corner before leaving the safety of the current hallway. He gripped the clanky parts of his armor with a strong grip and steadied it as he hurried down the hallway of the servant's rooms.

Bowen stopped and let out the breath he was holding in and tried to fill his lungs quietly. The sound of the whooshing air entering his lungs sounded much louder in his head, and he feared someone would hear his breathing. He gripped the latch to the queen's door and pushed the lever with his thumb. Bowen caught a whiff of a dead body and puckered his nose. His mind raced through the options, but he shook his head to clear his thoughts.

"I see you have returned to the castle Bowen," Isot said.

Bowen froze and his stomach flipped inside his guts.

"Isot, you're still here making a mess of things," Bowen said.

"Oh, no, you see, things are going quite as planned, and I have you to thank for it," Isot said.

Bowen's brain frantically searched every reason why he would have been any part of her evil plan, but he came up with nothing.

"I'm not sure I follow," Bowen said.

"It doesn't really matter," Isot said.

Isot lifted the amulet which hung at her navel and rubbed her skinny fingers across the smooth surface. A green mist emerged, and Bowen took a step down the hallway. Bowen wanted to get out of there as quickly as possible, but he was certain he wasn't going to make it far before Isot sounded the alarm. Isot muttered under her breath and the mist grew. Bowen took a few more steps but felt each one become harder until his feet became completely stuck to the floor.

Panic raced through his frame and his hands shook as he gripped the hilt of his blade and tried to turn back around to face Isot. His feet wouldn't move, but he was able to rotate enough to see the mist seep into her nose and mouth and her eyes became black and glassy. He swallowed the bile back into his esophagus and winced at the pain the acid made in his throat.

Bowen heard the clanking of guards, and he tried to yell but his mouth was glued shut with a force he couldn't understand.

37-Dance, Dance, Dance

Asher pulled a long satchel from a storage container behind the tent and heaved it over his shoulder. He moved to a suitable location next to his and Motavo's tent and set it on the ground. He unlatched several ties and the top flopped onto the ground. Shaz and Riddick helped him unroll the heavy canvas and straighten and smooth out the corners. They pulled the heavy spikes out of the bag and secured them into the corners. Asher picked out several smooth wooden poles and explained the process to assemble them together and then started on the main pole which would push the center of the tent up.

"Blast, the main pole is broken," Asher said.

"Oh, I can help with that," Riddick said.

"There is nothing you can do, even if you try to repair it, it won't hold the weight of the tent for long," Asher said.

"Let me see," Riddick said.

Asher handed him the poles with an expression that said, 'suit yourself'.

"Where does it go?" Riddick asked.

Asher pointed to the hole and crossed his arms over his chest. Riddick rubbed his hand along the smooth surface and examined the pieces. Shaz picked up the canvas and climbed under and held up the center high over his head. Riddick stepped underneath and after estimating the needed length and thickness, he wriggled his fingers and the pole shot to the proper length.

"Oiy," Asher yelled.

The tent popped up and into place in a matter of a second and Motavo came running out of the other tent. Riddick smiled and blew on his clenched fist and rubbed it on his tunic.

"Don't get cocky," Amirra said.

Riddick turned and shoved his hand into his pocket and Asher blurted a full-bellied laugh.

"What is going on?" Motavo asked.

"I can't even explain it," Asher said.

Motavo scrutinized them as they busied themselves with staking the corners down. Motavo shrugged and helped them with some extra bedding. Serin and Amirra organized the bedding around the outer edges leaving the center open for moving about. They all helped prepare supper and Riddick and the Minca went for firewood. Jagwynn prowled around the camp and inspected the contents of the crates and boxes that were around the tents. Shaz noticed Serin rest a few times while trying to help Amirra with some supplies. Shaz decided she would need to soak in water after her ordeal at the Choovino's, but he also knew how stubborn she was and that she needed to come to her own conclusions, so he kept a close eye on her. Serin stumbled over the rope holding down the edges of the tent and caught herself before she fell.

"Serin, are you alright?" Shaz asked.

"I'm fine, I'm just tired," Serin said.

"I think it's more than that, come on," Shaz said.

Shaz took her hand, and he led her away from the tents.

"Where are we going?" Serin asked.

"I found a stream earlier, and I think it might help for you to soak in some water and see if you can regain some of your strength," Shaz said.

"Yeah, maybe you're right," Serin said.

Shaz showed her were the stream was and turned his back to her. Serin pulled her boots off and stepped into the water. It was cold but it was the energy surge through her body and crawl up her spine that made her shiver. She bent down and dipped her hands into the liquid and let it fall out of her hands and back into the stream. The last bit of day cast a rainbow of colors over the surface and Serin smiled at its beauty. Serin wiped her face and shook off her hands and climbed out of the stream. She found a rock big enough for her to sit on and made her way over a slippery patch of mud and grass.

"You can turn around," Serin said.

Shaz turned around and made his way over to the rock and sat next to her and wrapped his arm around her shoulders.

"Feel better?" Shaz asked.

"Yes, thank you. You didn't have to turn around," Serin said.

"I thought maybe you wanted some privacy," Shaz said.

Serin leaned into his warm body and rested her eyes.

"Do you think your father will like me?" Serin asked.

"I assume you mean Merrick," Shaz said.

"Umhum," Serin said.

"Yes, I think he will like you a lot actually," Shaz said.

"Why is that?" Serin asked.

"You have spirit and you don't put up with my nonsense," Shaz said.

Serin laughed.

"If he's still alive that is," Serin said.

"He is, he's too stubborn to die. I think he'll be a million rotation's old before he gives up," Shaz said.

"I like that," Serin said.

"Me too. Motavo is calling a council of the eldest, those which are from your mothers' era, and then they will call a council with the rest, I hope they will agree to help," Shaz said.

"I think they will, but if they don't, you go in as the invited guest, and we will find another way in. Maybe we can throw Ladtwig over the wall," Serin said.

Shaz blurted a laughter and looked at Serin with surprise. Serin returned the look with a mischievous grin.

"Lorn isn't going to be an ally, and I think he is already working for Isot," Shaz said.

"He definitely doesn't want Bowen coming back into the picture, maybe Jagwynn will eat him," Serin said.

Shaz stifled the laugh.

"With more soldiers in the castle, getting around might be tricky," Shaz said.

"Maybe the travelers do have some secret passageways like Deagan said," Serin said.

"Let's hope, it feels like we are wasting time, and we're running out of it," Shaz said.

"Me too, but what more can we do?" Serin asked.

"I've been asking myself that all day, we have to rely on others now, I guess," Shaz said.

"We should head back, maybe there is news," Serin said.

Shaz stood up and handed Serin her boots, and she put them back on, and made their way back to camp. The people had been mingling about most of the day and were now starting to gather around the large fire pit in the center of the tents. Serin's heart jumped with excitement as she eyed the fiddler pull out his violin case from his tent and start toward the center.

"Oh Shaz, you are going to love the fiddle, it's so beautiful," Serin said.

Shaz smiled at her enthusiasm and found the childlike gleam in her eyes endearing, but he couldn't shake the need he was feeling to do something. Amirra's brows were tight on her face and her lips puckered in an alarming manner as she barreled across the grass toward them.

"What's wrong?" Serin asked.

"I'm not sure how to handle something?" Amirra said.

"Is something wrong?" Serin asked.

"I was told by a few of the other women that the *women* aren't allowed to sit with the *men* at the fireside. Is that correct?" Amirra asked.

Serin studied Amirra's nose flare with exasperation each time she said a word and if steam could be rising off the top of her head, it would be.

"Unfortunately, that is their custom, so yes, we will have our own section that we sit and visit with the women," Serin said.

"I can't believe that, I thought the Velshari was bad," Amirra said.

"Shhhhh, Amirra, I agree, believe me, I think that is the dumbest thing on the planet, but we need to respect their wishes, plus, we won't be here long," Serin said.

"Fine, but I don't like it," Amirra said.

"You might find some value in listening to the women. My mother used to tell me of her mother, who she thought was very wise. It was because she talked and listened to the other women around her which helped her gain knowledge. You'll see, it won't be so bad," Serin said.

Serin took her hand and gave her a squeeze and Amirra relaxed some. Riddick and the Minca returned with a very large pile of wood which Shaz knew didn't come from the twigs in the nearby trees and made his way over to them. Asher started to arrange the pile and Deagan and Lucien mingled nearby. Jagwynn laid down next to Deagan who shifted a few lengths but hesitantly reached out and tapped her head. Jagwynn rolled onto her side and Deagan rubbed her belly.

"What's wrong mate?" Riddick asked.

"I can't just sit here while my family could be in the dungeons," Shaz said.

"Let's go get them now then," Riddick said.

"I have to wait for Motavo, and I have no idea how long that could take," Shaz said.

"We will go tonight," Turkill said.

"You'll need someone to distract the guards," Shaz said.

"Take Lucien, he did it last time, yah?" Riddick said.

"No way," Lucien said.

"So, you are listening," Shaz said.

"You *will* go, and you will do it *now*, and that *is* a direct order," Asher said.

Lucien threw up his hands and stomped off. Shaz found his pack and pulled out the map Lucien had given him and showed Turkill how they got in and out last time. Serin took out a couple of glass jars and handed them to Turkill.

"What's this?' Turkill asked.

"This is a healing potion in case you need to heal anyone," Serin said.

Turkill nodded and took the jars and Ladtwig gathered the rest of their things from Motavo's tent and Jagwynn leaped toward them and Deagan jumped, and the three disappeared into the late evening.

"Look Motavo's back. I'm going to go see what the decision is," Shaz said.

Serin nodded and walked with Amirra to where the other women were gathering. Shaz half-ran-half-walked over to Motavo and the other men.

"Ah Shaz, this is Barsoli, Kaven, Lashi, and Ruslo. My oldest friends, and members of the Teorran Travelers," Motavo said.

"Pleasure to meet you all," Shaz said.

"The pleasure is ours," Barsoli said.

"Can you really walk on fire?" Lashi asked.

Shaz chuckled.

"Yes, but I will have to show you another time, but now, I am sorry, but I do need to know what you have decided," Shaz said.

"He gets straight to the point, doesn't he?" Kaven said.

"We will help, but we will need to ask the other councils, which I am sure they won't object," Motavo said.

"They can't, you are the king, and they all know that," Ruslo said.

"We will go make the announcement and make plans to begin first thing in the morning. What will you need exactly?" Barsoli asked.

"I need all the secret tunnels in and out of the castle and a distraction to put off the coronation as long as possible to give me time to get into the castle and find the scroll."

"I think we can manage that. I have a wonderful show of acrobatics and the street performers would love to show off for the new queen. Maybe they will get some acceptance," Lashi said.

"That is what Deagan had suggested, so that sounds perfect," Shaz said.

"You know Deagan? He's my great, great, great, umm…" Lashi tried to count on his fingers, "well he's my nepitino many generations later," Lashi said.

Everyone laughed.

"We'll be back later," Barsoli said.

Shaz bid them farewell with their traditional greeting and the men nodded with a sense of respect they hadn't had in a long time. Shaz returned to the campfire with Motavo and found Riddick tending the fire. He had arranged the logs into a triangle with the tips all leaning in on each other and a bunch of kindling and smaller logs in the center. It wouldn't take long for the fire to be large and warm.

Shaz watched Serin and Amirra sitting with the women and Serin was having a conversation with an elderly woman who was showing her some kind of needlework, while Amirra was sitting quiet with a gentle scowl on her face. Shaz felt bad, he hadn't ever realized how often women get shafted, and he wondered why when they had so much to offer and how much he himself relied on them. Riddick sat next to Shaz and Shaz filled him in on the details. Serin looked up from the artistic display the woman was showing her and found Shaz and Rid-dick deep in conversation. Motavo and Asher joined, and she could tell they had worked out many of the details.

One of the women rose and beckoned the others to begin dish-ing out the food and Serin and Amirra helped. Amirra was having a hard time and struggled to keep her mouth shut as she figured it would be the safest thing for her to do.

"I can see that you do not share our ways, and that is alright, but there is a kind of satisfaction in being able to tend to the men who work so hard to give us everything we have," a woman said.

Amirra looked up from the ladle of the soup she was dishing into a bowl and found the soft gaze of the elderly woman. Amirra didn't have a clue what to say or do, so she smiled and nodded. Amirra took the bowl and a spoon and headed toward the fire.

"Does she always act this way?" the elderly woman asked Serin.

"No, Amirra has a violent past that haunts her, and she is trying to figure out how she wants to think about this new life she is now experiencing," Serin said.

"That sounds dreadful," the woman said.

"She has come a long way, but like us all, has a long way to go," Serin said.

"Well said my child," the woman said.

Serin helped the woman with her bowl and followed her to the men where Serin handed Shaz the bowl and the older woman handed hers to another man sitting around the fire. Shaz smiled but gave Serin sad eyes. Serin smiled and nodded to tell Shaz it was alright, but she could tell he didn't agree either. The women returned and gathered their own dishes and sat together. The evening passed and the women cleaned up and the storyteller began to tell his tales.

The middle-aged man was a bit round and had deep red cheeks under tan skin giving his face a rust-colored look. The elderly woman pulled a long scarf that had been mended together to reflect the many colors of the fabrics of the travelers, and she motioned for Amirra to stand. Amirra stood slowly and the woman rose and draped the scarf around Amirra starting at her shoulder and wrapped around her chest and then her waist. The gold dangling coins tinkled against themselves and stood out from the hushed conversations.

"This scarf represents *all* of the beautiful things of this life. We all have demons and secrets that haunt our past, but you are beautiful in every way, never forget that," the woman said.

Amirra witnessed the twinkle in the old woman's eye, and she burst into tears and wrapped her arms around the woman. The woman, a little surprised, hugged her back and stroked her long cinnamon hair.

"Oh, I'm so sorry I've been cross, I've-"

"No need to explain yourself," the woman said.

"I have been so rude, I don't even know your name," Amirra said.

"My name is Mergita," Mergita said.

"Thank you Mergita, I will treasure this always," Amirra said.

Serin gave Amirra a squeeze when she sat down and Amirra beamed as she inspected the delicate and sparkly cloth. Serin turned to the fire and found that the storyteller wasn't standing anymore, but the fiddler was pulling his violin out of the case.

"Amirra, you're going to love this part, it's my favorite," Serin said.

The man pulled the bow and tightened it and with careful pressure, gripped the strings with the course hairs letting a wonderful sound ripple from the instrument. It was first soft and slow, but the music began to intensify. Motavo stood and swayed back and forth as the music leaped from the strings. Serin sat listening, imagining what the music was telling her, just as she did with her mother when she was young. It was one of the few memories she had of her and her mother. She remembered her long pale blonde hair and for the first time realized her mother had blonde hair, just as Shaz did. She hadn't realized she had forgotten so much of the little bit she had left.

"Dance, dance, dance," Asher said.

Asher nudged Shaz in the ribs and Shaz was convinced it was hard on purpose. The rest of the men joined the chant and Serin knew she was supposed to go out and dance, but she didn't have the faintest idea how. A young woman took Serin and Amirra's hands and led them to the fire. She clapped her hands at the side of her face and Serin and Amirra followed. She then clapped on the other side and the girls repeated. The young woman then began to move her feet and lifted her long colorful skirt, so her shoes showed. Neither Serin or Amirra was wearing a skirt but the girls tried to follow the steps and found it harder than they thought and started to laugh at themselves. The fiddler made his fingers dance on the neck of the violin and were moving so quickly that the notes seemed to be flying off. The sound was wonderful and soon there was a jolly sound coming from everyone.

Motavo nodded to the fiddler, and he slowed the pace of the music. Serin and Amirra were relieved and started back toward where the rest of the woman were but the young woman stopped them. Motavo stood and the fiddle halted.

"Who here dares dance with my daughters?" Motavo asked.

Serin stepped back as the deep voice gripped her attention. If she didn't know better, she would have thought he was angry.

"Who dares dance with my daughter," a middle-aged man asked.

Shaz stood and made his way around the fire and took Serin's hand. Riddick took Amirra and a young man in the back made his way to the front and took the young woman's hand.

"I, Shaz, Motavo sir," Shaz said.

"I, Riddick, sir," Riddick said.

"I, Kallum, Bricker sir," Kallum said.

"Let it be," Motavo said.

"Let it be," Bricker said.

The fiddler began his soft slow tune and Shaz pulled Serin into his grip. Shaz started to move Serin across the dirt just like they had done in the Minca realm. Serin gazed into his deep blue eyes and a flicker of her mother's flashed before her, and she had a sense of peace about her mother that she hadn't ever experienced before. Riddick and Kallum also began to move the ladies across the dirt and the three pairs took Motavo's breath away. It had been so many rotations since he gave his blessing to Jerim and Ambrosia and his heart swelled.

"Motavo, you're crying," Barsoli asked.

"Leave me alone, I'm a sappy old man with new hope," Motavo said.

"I remember her mother and Jerim looking so much the same way, I can't believe how much time has passed since then," Barsoli said.

"Me either. Have you made the necessary plans?" Motavo asked.

"Yes," Barsoli said.

"As have I," Lashi said.

"Excellent," Motavo said.

Shaz and Serin's movements were in perfect rhythm and the gentle glow of their magic started to emanate from their beings.

"What is happening?" Barsoli asked.

"*That* is what Synmagic looks like," the Choovino said.

The three men turned and stared at the old man.

"Choovino, what are you doing here? Shouldn't you be home in bed?" Barsoli asked.

"And miss the war wizard ask permission to marry a traveler, no way," the Choovino said.

The Choovino hobbled on his cane and Motavo helped him into Motavo's chair. The wrinkles on the man's body were staggering but the smile on his face and the glint in his eye was refreshing. It was the way Motavo felt too.

38-I Have A Matter to Settle

Turkill lifted his dart gun to his lips and pursed them tightly over the end of the bamboo shoot. He steadied his breath and counted the thunks the heavy-soled boots made on the thick stone floor. Ladtwig hunkered onto his haunches and rested his back against the cold stone. Ladtwig reached up and gripped the iron latch and waited for Turkill's signal. The thunks grew but now were accompanied by a second heavy-footed person. Turkill pulled in a long slow breath and nodded to Ladtwig. Ladtwig pulled on the lever and shoved his body weight against the door. The wooden door swung open and Turkill rolled into a crouched position and quickly blew his dart gun. Three poisoned darts crossed the distance in a blink of an eye and landed nearly on top of one another and sank into the pudgy skin of the first guard's neck.

The second guard looked around the full-bellied guard as the man began to slump. His gruff expression flashed into a contemptuous glare. Turkill let go of another burst of darts which sank into the less than stout man's neck. The man gripped his neck and yanked out a dart and studied it. Turkill watched with a focused stare as the poison coursed into his blood. The man began to sway and wobble, and then he fell backward and hit square against the floor with a slap. Ladtwig rounded the corner in a squatted crawl and Turkill loaded another set of darts. Ladtwig made his way to the guards and checked for a pulse. He shook his head and the two leaped over the bodies. They hurried down the corridor several lengths and then scaled the wall as they approached another corridor. Turkill peeked around the corner and checked both directions before moving on. Ladtwig followed keeping his eye on the hallway behind him. The brothers were small but fast and highly skilled in the art of combat and stealth. When it was time for no-nonsense, they understood the concept to a level no one would expect. Turkill slowed at the end of the corridor and peeked around the next bend. He shot across the opening of the intersection and moved down the next pathway. Three more turns and he stopped and hugged the wall. Ladtwig pulled his dart gun and licked his lips.

The door across the hall was the entrance to the first level of cells. They had the layout of the dungeons but wasn't sure where Mathieu and the others were being held. Ladtwig hurried across the intersection and gripped the latch. Turkill nodded but the latch didn't release. He shook his head, and they hurried back down the corridors until they reached the two bodies. Ladtwig searched the guard and found a steel ring with keys big enough to slide onto his arm, and they hurried back.

Ladtwig shoved a key into the lock but it didn't open, and he tried another and another until he found the one that opened the lock. He shoved the key ring into his side pouch and lifted the lever. The door swung open and Turkill repeated his lunge and roll but there was no one to shoot. He waved at Ladtwig who rounded the corner closely to the wall. The stink shot into their senses, and they had a hard time not retching. The dimness of the cell block meant they would have to search each one. Ladtwig took the cells on his side and Turkill the other. They hurried through the cells giving each other hand signals to explain their findings.

Turkill stopped at the next cell and reexamined it.

"Miss. Patriza, is that you?" Turkill asked. A woman stirred from the back of the dark cell. "Councilwoman Patriza, is that you?" he said.

"Who's there?" a deep raspy voice asked.

"Merrick, is that you?" Turkill asked.

Turkill moved to the cell across the aisle and Ladtwig kept searching the surrounding cells.

"Who are you?" Merrick asked.

"Are you Merrick?" Turkill asked.

"That depends on who's asking," Merrick said.

"I'm with Shaz," Turkill said.

"Aren't you kind of short?" Merrick said.

Turkill hurmpfed and Ladtwig snickered.

"Are you Merrick or not?" Turkill grunted.

"Aye," Merrick said.

"You'll have to prove it first," Turkill said.

"Shaz is my son, and we met Ceros in the Screaming Siren Tavern in the Turbulent Reef," Merrick said.

Ladtwig reached onto his tiptoes and unlocked the door. Turkill swung it open, and they hurried and unlatched the shackles at his ankles. Turkill bent down and Ladtwig stood on his knee to unlatch the ones on his wrists. Merrick's arms fell to his sides and his knees went weak, and he struggled to loosen the leather straps that wrapped around his chest and waist. Turkill took out the glass jar Serin had given them and popped the cork stopper off. He gave it to Merrick who gave him a wary eye.

"It's magic water and will heal you," Turkill said.

Ladtwig hurried out of the cell and kept looking.

"How did you come by magic water?" Merrick asked.

Merrick took a swig and handed it back to Turkill who replaced the stopper.

"Serin is a healer, and she sent it,"

Serin had buffed the water with a serious dose of her healing and light magic fearing that they might need to counteract the shadow magic, and she was right. The magic tickled as it eased into his core. His chest zinged, and he sighed as the pain in his entire body eased. A small smile crested his eyelids and Turkill put the jar back into his pouch.

"When we return to Serin, she will do a full exam and you will feel amazing," Ladtwig said.

"I already do," Merrick said.

The fog in his mind cleared and for the first time in who knows how long, he had all his faculties.

"Where are the others," Turkill asked.

"Mathieu is there, and Patriza is there," Merrick said.

He pointed to the cells respectively and Ladtwig hurried to the one he was closest to. Ladtwig opened the lock and he and Turkill released Mathieu. Merrick helped hold the old man's unconscious body while Turkill dripped the healing water onto his lips. Mathieu's eyes flickered and then blinked.

"Mathieu, are you alright?" Merrick asked.

Mathieu blinked a few more times and tried to understand the details he was seeing. Turkill dripped a few more drops and Mathieu licked his lips.

"Go find Patriza," Turkill said.

Turkill held Mathieu's head and helped him take a few sips. The energy ran through his body quickly and Mathieu's eyes focused.

"Who are you?" Mathieu asked.

"Turkill, I'm here with Shaz," Turkill said.

"You're a Minca?" Mathieu half-asked-half-stated.

"Yes," Turkill said.

Turkill rolled his eyes, he figured at least Mathieu would know about them.

"Are you fit to travel?" Turkill asked.

Mathieu wriggled his fingers and examined his body. He took another swallow of the water and handed it to Turkill who corked it and shoved it into his pouch. Mathieu smiled as the magic removed the aches and pains in his body, and he stood up. Turkill hurried out of the cell and found Ladtwig waving to him across the block. He darted to the cell and began giving the last of the water to Patriza.

"Aren't there five of you?" Turkill asked.

Merrick shook his head.

"Not anymore, we haven't seen Valida or Ceros," Merrick said.

"I can't sense their presence," Mathieu said.

"We passed another cell block, maybe they are in there," Ladtwig said.

"I hope so," Mathieu said.

"How are you feeling?" Merrick asked.

"I don't know, I'm not in pain, but I'm not sure if I can make myself move," Patriza said.

"Give it a try," Merrick said.

Patriza wriggled her fingers and then her toes. She lifted her arms to push herself up and to her surprise, she moved easily.

"What is going on, what is this?" Patriza asked.

"These are Shaz's friends, and they are here to break us out," Merrick said.

"And the others?" Patriza asked.

Merrick shook his head.

"Come on, let's go," Turkill said.

Patriza followed Mathieu and Merrick followed her. His anger grew as he eyed the long-jagged marks on her back from whatever torture they had done. They followed the Minca through the passageways and Merrick was highly impressed with the Minca's meticulous and calculated moves and understood why Shaz would trust them with such a task. They moved to the next block and each hurried along the lengthy rows of cells. Close to the end, they found Ceros and Valida, and Ladtwig opened the cells. Turkill pulled out a second jar and helped each of them. Mathieu helped Valida while Merrick went to Ceros.

"Ceros, are you alright?" Mathieu asked.

"I am now, what is that stuff?" Ceros asked.

Ceros' nearly black skin blended into the darkness of the cells but the whites of his eyes and teeth shined off the small lantern on the other side of the aisle.

"Magic," Merrick said.

Ceros' face contorted through the range of emotions and thoughts the others had and settled on the same self-satisfying smile.

"How are we going to make it out of here?" Mathieu asked.

"We need to find your things, do you all still have your medallions?" Turkill asked.

"We did, why?" Merrick asked.

"They are the passkey and will get you out of the dungeons," Turkill said.

"Why, I never thought of that," Mathieu said.

"I must be in shock, there are Minca in our realm," Ceros said.

Turkill rolled his eyes again and hurried out of the cells. His short but muscular frame ran with a stalky swagger and the others found it hard to keep up with him. He and Ladtwig stopped at the door and listened. Turkill put his finger on his lip and the others nodded. They pulled their dart guns and Turkill peeked around the corner and lunged and rolled to his crouched position and let go of the rapid-fire. Three darts lodged into the neck and chest of a guard several lengths down the hallway.

The guard's body slumped, and his eyes rolled into the back of his head as the poison ripped the life from him. Turkill waved the group on, and they followed him down the hall. Ladtwig stopped, shoved his foot into the floor and spun around. He narrowed his vision and let go of a blast of darts. A guard that had barely rounded the corner behind them slapped his neck and then went weak in the knees and fell to the ground. Patriza gasped at the sudden movement and looked behind her to see the guard falling dead.

Her heart thumped against her ribs so hard she wondered if they would break. Merrick gripped her hand and squeezed it tight, and she started to jog-run to catch up to the others. Turkill led them around a few more corners taking out two more guards and then came to a tall door. Ceros tried the latch, but it wouldn't open and Ladtwig handed him the keys. Ceros tried them all but none of them worked. Ladtwig rummaged through his backpack and pulled out a long metal stick. Merrick knelt and Ladtwig climbed up on his knee and jammed the stick into the hole and rolled it around until he found the latch inside, and then he yanked on the bell of the lock. The pin slipped and the latch popped off, and he jumped down from Merrick's knee. They rummaged through the aisles of personal belongings until Mathieu snapped his fingers.

A dusting of red sparkles burst into existence and it floated around the room until it had sniffed out their belongings. Ladtwig stood watch at the door until everyone had dressed and gathered their things. Merrick moved the ladies between Ceros and Mathieu, and he took up the rear. Ladtwig and Turkill started out of the locker and Merrick grabbed Turkill's shoulder. Turkill turned around and found Merrick's large frame rippling with the vibes of revenge.

"I have a matter to settle, get everyone out and I'll catch up to you soon," Merrick said.

"You'll need this," Turkill said.

Turkill removed his hair clip and stuck it on Merrick's tunic, and gave him his blade.

"Aye," Merrick said.

It wasn't near the right size for the giant of a man, but he nodded with a thankful smile and stuck it into his belt.

"Merrick, you don't have to do this," Patriza said.

"Oh, but I do, and nothing will stop me," Merrick said.

His voice was gruff with a load of angry revenge in it, but his eyes were soft and caring. Patriza nodded and kissed his cheek. Merrick waited until they had disappeared down the corridor and turned in the direction, he figured the guards would be. Merrick didn't even try to be quiet, in fact, he barreled down the corridor like thunder ripping through the atmosphere. A guard rounded the corner and saw the brute of a man only a few lengths away and started for his sword, but Merrick closed the gap faster than he was able to fully draw it from the scabbard.

Merrick tightened his fist and slammed it into the man's face knocking him unconscious before he bounced off the wall and landed on the ground. Merrick stepped over the man and continued on.

He found the barracks and slammed his fist into the door sending wood fragments flying and the guards that were milling about ducked for cover and started for their weapons. Merrick scanned the room quickly but didn't find the guard he was looking for and pulled the remaining door closed. He moved at a quick pace and found the interrogation rooms adjacent to the ones he believed held Patriza. He kicked in each door causing such a ruckus that many of the prisoners woke and were calling for their release. A door at the end of the hallway opened and a small pinched face man peeked out. Merrick recognized the man and he gripped his fists together.

The scrawny man pulled the door shut and Merrick gripped the latch which was locked. He stepped back and shoved his boot into the center of the wood door knocking it clean off its hinges. The door flew across the room and the man squealed like a girl. Merrick stepped inside and gripped the quaking man's collar and lifted him off the floor.

"Where is he?" Merrick asked.

"Who exactly?" the man asked.

"I know, let's do this instead," Merrick said.

Merrick picked up the scrawny man who man wriggled and squirmed fiercely and put him in the chair with the spikes. Merrick blocked the man's feet from kicking him and yanked the strap over his chest and lap. The man yelped as the spikes in the seat began to bite at his skin. Sweat formed over his now pale face and he breathed heavily.

"Now before I start sending these spikes into your skull, tell me where he is," Merrick said. The beady eyes that were filled with sheer terror relaxed when he found several guards standing at the doorway. Merrick turned to find them armed and ready to pounce. "Don't worry, this won't take long," Merrick said.

The pinched face man smiled but an element of fear hid just below the surface. Merrick pulled the little blade and started for the first man in line. The guard lunged and Merrick ducked to one side and grabbed the back of the man's head and slammed it against the wall knocking the man out. The next man stepped forward and brought his sword up in an uppercut, but Merrick blocked it with the blade and rammed his fist into the man's stomach. The man lurched forward with the sudden force to his gut and gasped for air that was unable to fill his lungs. Merrick brought his elbow down on top of the man's head, and he hit the floor. The next guard gripped his blade, but Merrick could tell he was nervous and stepped over the last man and toward him.

The guard gulped and with both hands gripping his sword started toward Merrick who sidestepped and gripped the back of the man's head and slammed his face into his knee. The man hit the floor and the next man started to back away, but Merrick swung the blade and sliced the man's arm as he turned. The shock of the pain halted his movements and Merrick used the flat of his palm and pounded the man's sternum sending him flying down the hallway. Merrick returned to the room with the scrawny man and his face drained of all its color.

"Now, where were we? Oh, yes, I am now going to do to you what you do to everyone else, only I don't care if you give me information, I'll find out what I want anyway and you will be dead," Merrick said.

"Now, now, I'm sure we can work something out, I know people in high places, I'm sure I can find something you want more than killing me," the man said.

"No, I don't think so, but you can first tell me where is *your* friend that took such pleasure with *my* friend," Merrick said.

"Oh, he no longer works here, he's been sent to a different department," the man said.

Merrick chuckled and the man smiled nervously.

"Wow, you think I'm that stupid? Well, have it your way," Merrick said.

Merrick picked up a spike and twirled it around in his fingers. The spike was about a hand and a half long and made of sharpened steel. Merrick ran it along the man's cheek, and he squirmed while sweat dripped down the side of his face.

"You wouldn't, you're not like us, you're better than that. If you do this, you'll be no better than I am," the pointy faced man said.

"You think you understand me? You haven't a clue about what I am or am not willing to do," Merrick said.

Merrick took the spike and stabbed it into the man's leg just above the knee. The man hollered with pain and pulled and squirmed against the restraints.

"Now, see we are both the same, I'm going to go look for my friend and I will be back," Merrick said.

The man hissed through gasps of pain.

"If I tell you where he is, you let me go?" the man asked.

Merrick nodded.

"He's on patrol at the end of the next corridor that way,"

The man tilted his head in the direction and Merrick left the room and shut the door kicking one of the disabled guards out of the way. Merrick followed the corridor and found the area in the next set of cells. He searched the group of cells and found the man on the far side of the block. Merrick calculated the distance and the nearby exits as well as the route to and from where the man was. He decided on the most direct route and started across the aisles. He took the blade and ran it along the iron bars of a cell and the man jumped.

"What in tarnation, how did you get out?" the guard asked. Merrick continued to slowly drag the blade along the iron bars. "I'm warning you," the man said. Merrick took another step and one more bar. "You know you can't escape right, and even if you kill me, you won't be able to beat all of the guards, this prison is huge,"

The man reached for his blade and a murderous glare flashed across Merrick's eyes. The guard fumbled the blade and Merrick took another step. The guard pulled his blade and sidestepped toward the side of Merrick. Several prisoners roused and started taunting the guard. The guard lunged at Merrick, but he blocked the blade's strike and slammed his fist into the man's face. Blood spurted from his cracked lip and cheek. The guard stumbled backward and hit into an empty cell. Merrick circled the man and waited for him to shake off the sting of the hit. The man wiped his mouth and spit the extra blood out. He circled Merrick who ran the blade along another few bars. The clanging echoed around the room and left an irritating vibe in the man's chest.

The guard brought his blade up at an angle and crossed his body as he lunged at Merrick. Merrick slammed the little blade into the longer blade and rolled his wrist over. He stepped toward the guard and plowed his fist into the man's stomach. The guard doubled over as the wind was forced from his lungs. Merrick walked around the man as he coughed and heaved. He gripped the man's moppy hair and yanked his head backward. The inmates cheered and the noise encompassed the cell block. Merrick brought up the blade until it touched the man's skin. The guard quivered and tried to swing his sword at Merrick. Merrick dodged the swing and shoved the small hilt into his side. The man's body recoiled, and Merrick thought he heard a crack.

"What do you want?" the guard managed.

"I want you to suffer the way you made my friend suffer," Merrick said.

"Then you'll have to go after the Interrogator, we're not allowed to touch the victims, I'm just doing my job," the man said.

"Oh, see I think you are, just *after* he has done what he wanted to do," Merrick said.

The fear in the man's eyes confirmed Merrick was right and Merrick drew the blade slowly, but not deep, across the man's neck. The man cried out with the pain and went weak in the knees. Merrick let the man fall, and he landed on the cold ground and rolled into a ball. The man cried and Merrick picked him up and opened the gate of a cell. He dropped the man on the hard floor and slammed the door shut.

"Maybe when your coworkers find you, they might let you out, if you don't bleed to death first," Merrick said.

The other inmates cheered and begged to be released. Merrick turned and moved back to the corridor. He hurried to the Interrogator and stepped over the men still laying on the floor. The Interrogator looked at Merrick with a pleading and pained expression.

"I will do anything," the Interrogator said.

"I bet you will, but you don't have any chances left, see, you have been doing this for too long as it is, and I think your time has come to an end," Merrick said.

"Wait, wait, I have information, what do you want?" the Interrogator said.

"What is so important that you find Shaz?" Merrick asked.

"How do you know about Shaz?" the Interrogator asked.

"You forgot, I'm asking the questions," Merrick said.

Merrick picked up another spike.

"Alright, he escaped a rotation ago and I need to find out how he did it and where he is," the Interrogator said.

"Why?" Merrick asked.

"Because Isot wants to know and because no one can escape the dungeons, not even the guards can leave," the Interrogator said.

"So, if you can find Shaz, not that you can go ask him yourself, then you can find out a way to get out yourself," Merrick said.

The Interrogator nodded and closed his eyes.

"How do *you* know Shaz," the Interrogator asked.

"He's my son," Merrick said. The shock and surprise surged through the Interrogator. "I'll pass your message on, but you won't be here long enough to get a response," Merrick said. Merrick gripped his head and twisted, snapping his neck. The Interrogator's body fell limp against the restraints. "Now to find Garrison," Merrick said.

Merrick dropped the spike on the table and left the room.

39- All I Need Is Shaz To Come Quietly

The music filled the night and the crowd engaged in the dancing and talking. Amirra and Riddick decided to go for a walk and Shaz and Serin kept dancing. The fiddler shifted his tune to a slow nighttime lullaby and Shaz gripped Serin close. He breathed in heavily and Serin looked into his eyes and found the 'things are going to get bad' look.

"We're about to have company," Shaz said.

"Who, how many?" Serin asked.

Shaz took a long step and Serin followed as he swung her around.

"Not, sure, they're coming from several fronts," Shaz said.

"Several, so Jaduuk?" Serin asked.

"Aye, and horses, my bet is on Lorn," Shaz said.

"That rotten," Serin said.

"We need to move your family to safety," Shaz said.

"You're going to have to let me go then," Serin said.

Shaz pulled her tight and sighed.

"Oh fine," Shaz said.

Serin smiled and kissed him, and he kissed her in return. Serin hurried to Motavo and Shaz jogged several paces until he wasn't in direct earshot and whistled. The crowd startled and the fiddler stopped playing.

"What's wrong?" Motavo asked.

"We are about to have company and not the nice kind, we need to move all the travelers to safety," Serin said.

"What do you mean?" Barsoli asked.

"Jaduuk," Serin said.

Riddick stopped and grabbed Amirra's hand.

"What is it?" Amirra asked.

"Shaz, come on, hurry," Riddick said.

Riddick spun on his toe and pulled Amirra behind him as he made his way back toward the camp. Riddick stopped and dropped to the ground and pulled Amirra down. Amirra slunk next to the cold earth and shivered.

"What is it? Amirra whispered.

"Jaduuk, and a lot of them," Riddick said.

"What are we going to do?" Amirra said.

"Run," Riddick said.

Riddick jumped up and Amirra darted after him. She found it hard to keep up with his long strides and stumbled a few times trying to navigate over the uneven terrain without much light.

"I don't have time to explain, you need to get everyone out of here," Serin said.

"We don't have anywhere to go," Lashi said.

"Yes, we do, the old underground," Motavo said.

"Is that still around?" Barsoli asked.

"I checked on it earlier today, it's old, but it will work," Motavo said.

"Alright then, follow me," Barsoli said.

Lashi and Kaven followed Barsoli at a fast pace and started to maneuver the people from the fire and into the darkness of the night.

****

Turkill hurried down the hall and stopped at the edge of an intersection. He peeked around the corner and waved for Ladtwig and the others to keep moving. Ladtwig held onto Valida's hand and ran quickly down the next hallway. Mathieu, Patriza, and Ceros followed and Turkill took up the rear. Ladtwig slowed and pushed Valida up against the wall. The cold stone gave her chills, but she relished in the soothing it had on her torn and dry skin.

Ladtwig scanned the vaults of the vast opening and examined each of the sizeable pillars that held the vaulted ceiling. He gripped Valida's hand and shot across the room and hid behind the nearest pillar. He stopped Valida at the pillar and put his finger on his lip. Valida nodded and sucked in a slow breath as she tried to calm her shaking body. Ladtwig held up his hand to Patriza who stopped at the edge of the hallway. He puckered his lips and blew a low steady whistle. A low steady whistle replied and Ladtwig pointed to the next column and shoved Valida, who darted across the opening holding her torn dress the best as possible, but the energy of fear and freedom pulsed from her core with such magnitude that she barely kept her feet moving underneath her.

Deagan reached out and grabbed her with all his might and pulled her into the passageway. She gasped a fearful squawk and Lucien's thugs pulled her into the next corridor. The thug shooshed her and nodded with a friendly smile, one he probably only showed his mother. Valida nodded and ran to the next thug who was waving her on frantically.

Ladtwig waved to Patriza and she too shot across the empty lobby of columns. Ladtwig waved her to keep moving and signaled to Mathieu and Ceros. Ceros didn't wait for Mathieu but reached under his arm and gripped him tightly. They hobbled quickly and as soon as they passed Ladtwig, Ladtwig followed behind backward keeping an eye on the many intersecting passageways. He spotted Turkill rounding the corner at a fierce pace. Turkill's dark skin glistened with the sweat that warmed his frame and his little arms were swinging at full range of motion. Ladtwig understood this to mean, 'coming in hot' and

Ladtwig hopped in place ready to take flight until Turkill caught up with him. Three gray rabbit-like rodents scurried behind him and Ladtwig gave him the 'did-you-get-it' look and Turkill nodded. The Minca brothers skidded around the corner and into the darkness a second before the guards' shouts reached the echo of the vaulted lobby.

One of Lucien's men heaved Valida into Deagan's gondola with such strength that she felt like she might overshoot the side. She gripped the edge tightly and breathed heavily. Her heart leaped when she saw Patriza and the others emerge from the darkness. The clean air filled their lungs, but it was harder to process than they expected. The thug eagerly helped Patriza into the boat and the women hugged each other.

"This everyone?" Deagan asked.

"For now," Valida said.

Deagan jumped onto the back of the boat and waited until Mathieu and Ceros were in then shoved off hard. The thugs darted into the night and melted into the shadows. Mathieu observed Deagan's deep concentration which complimented the Minca. It became very clear to him that these people would do anything for Shaz, including sacrificing their lives. Mathieu's soul rejoiced and a calmness overcame his frame.

Deagan pushed hard against the bottom and sides and got the boat moving at a fast clip. His execution was impeccable, and everyone was impressed but kept silent. After reaching the larger waterways and a good distance from the dungeons, Deagan slowed the boat to a comfortable but quick speed.

"Is everyone alright?" Deagan asked.

Everyone replied with soft affirmatives and quietly examined each other.

"Where are we going?" Mathieu asked.

"To my house, Mrs. Bailey is waiting for you there," Deagan said.

"Very good, thank you," Mathieu said.

"Where is Shaz?" Ceros asked.

"I don't know, but I'm sure it won't take long to meet up with him and the others," Deagan said.

"Others?" Ceros asked.

"I'll fill you in when we are safe," Deagan said.

"Drop us off at the main intersection," Turkill said.

Deagan nodded and moved his pole to the other side of the boat and made ready to turn the boat slightly to the side and move against the cobblestone pier. The boat neared close enough and the Minca hopped out and Turkill nodded to Deagan and then to Mathieu. Mathieu nodded back with a glint of appreciation only a grandfather could give. The Minca raced into the darkened alleyway and Deagan thought he saw a large set of yellow eyes and blinked, but when he searched again nothing was there. He shook it off and pushed the boat faster.

****

The heavy thuds of the soldier's horses broke through the night and Shaz stood with his thumbs in his beltloops. Serin turned around and counted twenty horses and more coming. A surge sank into her stomach and her throat tightened. It wasn't that she was worried to take on so many, but that she was going to have to hurt people. It's one thing to fight the Jaduuk or even Semias, but these are innocent men, doing the bidding of a bad person.

"Ah, look what we have here," Shaz said.

Lorn brought his horse to a trot and stopped a few lengths away from Shaz. Motavo walked up next to Shaz.

"What can I do for you soldiers?" Motavo asked.

"This doesn't concern you, old man," Lorn said.

Motavo looked around.

"Old man, I don't see an old man?" Motavo said.

Shaz smiled, but he knew there was a sizable pack of Jaduuk coming, and he didn't have time for the nonsense.

"What do you want Lorn?" Shaz asked.

"You, actually, dead or alive, it doesn't matter. As long as you're out of the way," Lorn said.

"I'm going to have to disappoint you," Shaz said.

"I don't think you understand, I have over fifty men, and you're coming with me," Lorn said.

"Fifty, that is impressive, but the answer is still no, now move along before you get hurt," Shaz said.

Lorn laughed a hearty belly roll and a couple of the men near him also laughed. Shaz sent his energy out to try and find Riddick, but he didn't sense him near and wondered where he was.

"You are trespassing on the travelers land, I suggest you leave," Motavo said.

"Travelers land? You can't be serious, this land belongs to Ebassia, and hence Isot," Lorn said.

"I suggest you listen to the man," Asher said.

"And what are you going to do about it?" Lorn asked.

Asher gritted his teeth. He could easily take on three men at a time without even breaking a sweat and this man was getting on his nerves.

"All I need is Shaz to come quietly and no one gets hurt," Lorn said.

"Be ready," Shaz said.

Serin listened and heard the faint pounding of the Jaduuk's hooves and nodded. Lorn noted Serin's head tilt, and he turned in his saddle and scanned the darkness and turned back around. Asher slammed his fist into Lorn's face and knocked him clean off his horse as he flipped over and landed on his back. A loud gasp escaped his lungs as the air was expelled from the sudden hit. The soldier next to Lorn gripped the hilt of his sword but Asher yanked the scabbard off the man's belt and flung the blade out of his grip. Another soldier kicked his horse and the horse lunged toward Asher who jumped out of the way and grabbed the billet strap and snapped the buckle that held the saddle in place. The saddle loosened and the man fell as the saddle landed on the ground. Motavo shoved his boot into the man's throat and started to press and the man squirmed and tried to wriggle out of the choke.

"Where's Riddick and Amirra?" Serin asked.

"I have no idea, I scanned for them, but they must be too far away," Shaz said.

"How close are the Jaduuk?" Serin asked.

"About a minute or so," Shaz said.

The ground rumbled and everyone moved into alert mode.

"What is that?" Motavo asked.

"Jaduuk," Serin said.

Motavo's brows raised and his eyes widened as the earth shook. There was a sizable hoard and Shaz settled on the best plan he could think of.

"No magic Shaz," Serin said.

"Sorry love, but that's not going to happen," Shaz said.

"I figured, but it was worth a try," Serin said.

Serin threw out her hands and gripped the air element. She whipped the air around Shaz, Motavo, Asher, and herself and boosted everyone with her wind-walk. Shaz soaked in the power of the air but Motavo and Asher's face went pale. They threw out their arms to steady themselves and Shaz dug his toe into the ground and shoved off. His body hurled across the open field, and he yanked the Honor Blade from the sheath. The blade hummed with eager energy and a sharp grinding from the blade running along the sharpening stone on the inside of the sheath echoed in his ears.

"What in tarnation is happening," Asher bellowed.

"This is wind magic, it will help you move faster," Serin said.

"What?" Asher asked.

Asher couldn't understand how he was now sitting a tiny length off the ground. Motavo pulled his whip stick from the inside pocket of his traveling cloak, and he moved faster than ever before. A soldier jabbed the side of his animal with the heel of his boots and the horse launched into a run. The man pulled the reigns against the horses' neck and the animal steered toward Shaz. Several men followed and Serin darted toward Shaz.

Motavo turned to watch Shaz slide under the large arm of a Jaduuk and slice the back of the creature's leg. Bile shot into his esophagus as his mind processed the size and fierceness of the beasts. The long fangs wrapped upward toward its eyes and the long snout dripped as the red eyes flared. They had long thin ears that flicked around as they searched for the sounds around them and their bodies were covered in patches of scraggly black and brown tufts of what Motavo assumed was fur. Asher steadied himself and dug his toe into the air pocket and his body moved freely. He yanked a solder off his horse and hit the man in the face. His arm moved so quickly that he didn't even see it himself, and he smiled.

Another soldier moved his horse toward Asher, but Asher stepped aside and shoved the man off. Serin yanked the air from the lungs of a Jaduuk and held it until the beast fell to the ground. The animal grappled at its throat, but it couldn't make its lungs fill with air. Motavo wasn't sure what to think. He had never witnessed a fight with magic, and he was both fascinated and terrified. Motavo didn't have any weapons. He had given them up for a life of secrecy as he tried to find Ambrosia.

"Serin, over there," Shaz said.

Shaz pointed to Riddick who had several Jaduuk entangled in a thorn bush. Serin did her little dance and cast her wind-walk on Riddick who gave her a thumbs up and smiled. He stomped on the ground and the ground opened into a maze of large holes. Motavo squinted and tried to make out what he was doing. Five large Jaduuk grunted as they barreled toward him and Motavo's heart skipped. The Jaduuk, however, disappeared into the earth and Riddick stomped again and the ground closed over the beasts. Motavo ran his hands through his hair and tried to understand what he just saw.

The soldiers yanked on the reins as they came closer to the Jaduuk and saw just what they were. They pulled their swords and began to fight the oncoming creatures. Shaz jumped and rolled from the downward strike of a battle-ax and gripped the sword and slashed it through the Jaduuk's shoulder. The blade severed the main tendon and the animal dropped the ax. A hissy growl escaped its sharp teeth and it lunged at Shaz. The beast's open snout was nearly big enough to snag Shaz's whole head and Shaz parried out of the way and shoved the sword into its belly under its rib cage. Shaz felt the blade sink into the softer innards and swung his arm upward pulling the blade through the tough skin. Blood splattered everywhere and Shaz puckered from the pungent odor the Jaduuk's blood left in his nostrils.

Shaz ran to the next animal and threw out his empty hand. The fire element erupted from his palm, and he shot a multi-blast of sizzling balls at three more Jaduuk. The fireballs encompassed the creatures and dripped all over their bodies as it consumed everything it could. Howls rang from nearby as Riddick launched several spear-like projectiles into the Jaduuk. Riddick stepped on the tip of a spear and it flung into the air, and he gripped it and threw it straight at another large Jaduuk. The spear missed its target but sliced the shoulder and sank into the upper leg of one behind the first. Amirra huddled into the brush Riddick had made to hide her but Serin could see her chanting and was certain she was trying to cast a bonus skill on someone.

Serin hurled a blast of air shards which sliced the air so fast it left a thunder-like sound in its wake. The air blades tore through the flesh of the oncoming Jaduuk, and they jolted backward from the force. Asher grabbed the reins of a horse and through the soldier off and shoved his foot into the stir-ups and swung his leg over the horse. The horse balked at his weight, but he gripped the reins and nudged the animal forward. The horse started out toward the others and Asher leaned into the stallion. Asher came up behind a soldier and clocked him in the back of the head with the butt of his ax. The man fell from the horse and his horse peeled away. Asher swung the butt of the heavy ax again and landed it in the back of another soldier. The man crumpled and cried out in pain as the bones in his back crushed.

A soldier shoved his foot out from the stir-up and kicked Mo-tavo in the side of the head. Motavo had been watching the crew take on the beasts and didn't see the soldier. Pain hit his brain and he stumbled backward. Serin shot another surge of air-blades then boosted Shaz over a Jaduuk. Shaz flipped the sword backward and sliced the back of the Jaduuk's neck. Shaz felt the tug of the blade as it sliced the bone in its spine and the beast fell forward with a thump. Serin spun around and released a wave of healing magic that sank into Motavo's body. The instant pain relief eased his mind, and he was able to think. The soldier was about to kick Motavo again but Jagwynn's huge white claws flashed as she lunged over the horse and sank them into the soldier's flesh. The momentum carried her over and she took him to the ground.

Motavo touched the side of his head where the metal of the stirrup had hit him but there was no blood. Turkill gripped Jagwynn's soft fleshy skin of her neck and jumped onto her back as she pounced off the soldier. Her long strides crossed the field toward the Jaduuk in no time and Turkill loaded and released several blasts of his rapid-fire poisonous darts. Ladtwig scurried onto an empty horse and yanked the reins. The horse darted toward the Jaduuk and Ladtwig loaded his dart gun. Ladtwig steered the horse around the two Jaduuk his darts had just hit and began to load more.

Turkill jumped off Jag and she lunged onto a Jaduuk. She released her claws and sank her teeth into the neck of the beast. The beast recoiled and tried to shove her off, but she gripped tighter. Jag threw her weight toward the ground and her large size was enough to off balance the large male Jaduuk. It toppled the ground and Jagwynn pounced again. Ladtwig came up behind Turkill and he jumped and grabbed the saddle and pulled himself onto the horse behind Ladtwig. Ladtwig gripped the reins tightly and pulled sharply to the side avoiding the battle ax of a smaller female Jaduuk. Turkill blasted it with another dart and went to load his gun but found he was out. He reached for Ladtwig's supply and loaded the last three darts.

Shaz released another multi-burst flame and the singed skin and fur wreaked through the atmosphere. Shaz shot a bolt of fire into the sky and searched the surroundings. His heart sank at the oncoming number of Jaduuk. Shaz whistled and Riddick finished wrapping a large vine-like limb from a thorn bush around the neck of a smaller Jaduuk and hurried to Amirra. The two ran full speed over the clearing and made their way to Shaz and then back to Serin. Asher spotted them in the corner of his eye and steered the horse toward them. Ladtwig sounded a battle cry and Jagwynn released the next beast she had in her jaw and raced back toward them.

"There are too many of these, there is no way we are going to be able to take them all," Shaz said.

"If we can make it to the underground, we will be safe there," Motavo said.

"And, then what, will the Jaduuk attack the city?" Serin asked.

"I don't think so, but if you send our scents on the wind away from the castle, we can divert them for a time. Riddick, can you make a barrier that will slow them down," Shaz asked.

"Aye," Riddick said.

Riddick stomped on the ground and a long trench opened. The ground rumbled as it tore open quickly. Riddick moved his hands around and scrunched his nose as he made the earth on the side closest to them, grow several lengths into the air. A handful of soldiers that were still mounted noticed them and one shouted a charge. He kicked his horse and started after them. The Minca jumped off the horse and Shaz turned it toward the soldiers and slapped its rump. The horse darted away and ran straight for the oncoming men.

"Alright, let's go," Shaz said.

Asher jumped off the horse and slapped it on the butt and the horse lunged away. Motavo led them toward the secret passageways and Serin blew their tracks off the dirt and sent it into the distance. A powerful howl crawled over the dark night, and they knew the Jaduuk had reached the barrier. Another howl sounded the alarm and the hoard veered to one side. The clops of the horse's hooves digging into the soft earth crawled through their minds, and they ran faster. Serin's air spell gave them the advantage they needed, and they maintained enough distance that Motavo was able to pull a tree limb and then another and hurried to another tree and pulled another branch. They neared a grassy hill with an old wooden staircase that rose to the top of the hill and Shaz was about to scale the steps two at a time, but the staircase lifted and revealed an entrance. Motavo ushered them into the mound and hit the lever on the other side and the stairs lowered and sealed shut.

"Shh, stay still," Motavo said.

Everyone stopped and stood still and listened. The horses nickered and huffed, and they could tell the soldiers were trying to figure out what way they had gone. A few minutes passed and the noise passed as the soldiers moved down the path away from the hill. Shaz lit his hand on fire and the tunnel lit up.

"Do these tunnels lead to the castle?" Shaz asked.

"They do, but there are many to navigate through and it will take a while to reach it, but we need to find the meeting place and make sure everyone is alright," Motavo said.

40-We're Running Out OF Time

"We must be as quiet as possible, there are several sections of the tunnels that run close to the outside and if we are heard, people will start looking for our tunnels," Motavo said.

Shaz pulled a few torches from an iron rack mounted on the wall, lit them and handed one to Motavo, and Riddick and extinguished his hand. Motavo led them along and several times they heard faint voices from the other side of the wall. Shaz wondered what part of the castle grounds they were at and wondered if on the other side the walls tightly compacted dirt or stone were. After several minutes they reached the end of the dirt tunnel and entered a moderate intersection. Motavo crossed the intersection at an angle and the short passageway opened into a much larger room.

The people were gathered quietly mingling in small groups. Barsoli rushed to meet them and slapped Motavo on the shoulder.

"We weren't sure if you would make it. What were those things?" Barsoli said.

"Jaduuk," Motavo said.

"What were they doing here?" Barsoli asked.

"I'm afraid that is my fault, they hunt me and so indirectly I brought them here," Shaz said.

Barsoli turned to Shaz and studied the regret in Shaz's eyes.

"It's not your fault they hunt you, but thank you," Barsoli said.

"I don't think it would be wise for your people to go back, I have no idea if there are still any out there, but I don't think they will leave and I am sure there will only be more coming," Shaz said.

"He's right, you should take the people to the highlands and stay there," Serin said.

"But, what about the performers, and your distraction?" Lashi asked.

Shaz turned to the man that had joined them.

"We'll just have to get in a different way," Shaz said.

"No, we can do it, besides, we are tired of being treated like garbage. It's time we do something to help ourselves," Lashi said.

Lashi locked eyes with Motavo and Motavo found urgency in them.

"Alright, but if there is any sense of things getting out of control, I'm pulling the plug," Motavo said.

"No problem," Lashi said.

Lashi turned and threw out two thumbs and the performers let out quite spurts of glee.

"Shaz, there is something you need to know," Amirra said.

Shaz turned and found her thin brows tight and gripped with uneasiness.

"What is it?" Shaz asked.

"There are *two* things we need to get," Amirra said.

She wrung her hands tightly and shoved them under her armpits.

"What do you mean?" Shaz asked.

He tried to keep his tone neutral, but he was frustrated that she hadn't said anything yet.

"The corpse," Amirra said.

"What corpse?" Shaz asked.

Amirra sucked in a deep breath.

"In order to enact the Pact of the Everlasting, which is the spell before the spell, Isot has to have a bound corpse that becomes the conduit of the powers to travel between the realm of the dead and living. If she is going to do the spell tomorrow, then she would already have the corpse prepared and ready. But if we can get to the corpse, we can keep the pact from being performed," Amirra said.

Shaz ran his hand through his hair and breathed out heavily.

"Where would she hide a corpse?" Serin asked.

"In a crypt, as close to the ritual as possible," Amirra said.

"There is a crypt reserved for the royal family only a few lengths from the backside of the courtyard," Motavo said. Shaz and Serin looked surprised at his knowledge of it. "It's part of the underground, there is a secret door that goes right into it and out the other side," Motavo said.

"Amirra, do you know what to do?" Shaz asked.

"I do," Amirra said.

Shaz nodded and Amirra wrung her hands together. Riddick took her hands and gave them a squeeze and smiled. Amirra nodded with a forced smile but she appreciated his efforts to help her feel better. Serin categorized her energy and Shaz determined this was going to be a big deal for her. He hoped it wouldn't be too much.

"Riddick, you go with Amirra, do whatever you need to," Shaz said.

"Aye," Riddick said.

"Serin and I will go for the scroll in the castle, but I have a feeling Isot will have it on her, so I'm not convinced we'll find it," Shaz said.

"What about us?" Turkill asked.

"You two help the performers into the city, do whatever you need to," Shaz said.

"Do you have sleeping darts instead of poison? Try and sleep the soldiers instead of killing them," Serin asked.

"No but maybe if we do a very small dose that will work," Ladtwig said.

Turkill agreed and he and Ladtwig headed over to Lashi.

"What are you going to do?" Motavo asked.

"I have a plan, let's get going, we're running out of time," Shaz said.

Riddick gripped Shaz's shoulder and nodded and Motavo gave Riddick the general directions up to the crypt. Riddick took a torch and he and Amirra hurried into a tunnel on the other side. Asher's large frame emerged from the tunnel they had come from and he shook off the dusting of dirt that was in his hair from the constant rubbing along the ceiling.

"All good, but I did have to clear out the bugs, and we will have some repair to make when we can," Asher said.

Motavo nodded and rubbed his chin.

"What is it?" Serin asked.

"Motavo, when do you want us to start performing?" Lashi interrupted.

"Crash the party your way," Serin said.

"The bigger the better," Shaz said.

The excitement exuberated off the dark-haired man's rosy cheeks and Serin smiled.

"How do we get to the castle?" Shaz asked.

Motavo snapped his fingers and a boy half the age of a man, skirted a large woman and hurried to Motavo. He wore a long overcoat that was twice his size and he reminded Serin of Ladtwig. A shot of worry hit the back of her head and she tried to push it out of the way. She knew the Minca were highly skilled, but she couldn't seem to push out the fear that they would get caught.

"This is Moti, he will escort you through the castle," Motavo said.

"You can call me Rat," Moti said.

"Rat?" Serin asked.

"Because no one ever sees or hears me," Moti said.

"Rat it is," Shaz said.

"I'll call you Moti," Serin said.

"Oh, come on, You're Highness, please," Moti begged.

Moti's large warm-brown eyes increased in size as he gave her a long pout. The sound of being called You're Highness startled Serin and she swallowed hard. Shaz liked the sound of it, and Motavo too was pleased. Serin looked at Shaz who gave her a 'why not' shrug and she sighed.

"Oh, fine, lead the way Rat," Serin said.

Moti gave a little hop-jump and spun on his toes and darted into a tunnel. Motavo chuckled and started toward Lashi. Moti popped his head out of the tunnel and waved to Shaz and Serin and they hurried after him.

****

Riddick kept a close connection with the earth's magic as they navigated the tunnels. He ran his hand along the dried dirt walls and a few times he stopped to run through in his mind how the tunnels he was seeing ended up. Amirra tried not to be nervous but the pit that sat in the bottom of her stomach ate her nerves. Riddick knew she was confused with emotions and tried to keep his conversation limited and neutral.

"Watch your step, the tunnel goes up sharply around this bend," Riddick said.

Amirra nodded and Riddick rounded the bend. The tunnel did indeed incline sharply and Riddick found the discomfort of having to slip as he tried to move up the path. Amirra too had a hard time and twice slipped backward several lengths.

"This is ridiculous," Riddick growled.

Riddick put his hands on the floor. He closed his eyes and imagined the dirt arrange into steps. The ground shook gently, and the gritty brown earth bounced and popped as a sturdy formation of steps formed.

"You are quite amazing, I wish I could do cool stuff like that," Amirra said.

"Don't you start young lady, you have an incredible gift, two actually, maybe even a million," Riddick said.

His tone was playful but had a hint of sternness and Amirra understood he wasn't kidding. Amirra smiled and they hurried up the newly formed staircase. At the top Riddick slowed and squashed the torch's flame into the wall. The flame fizzled and hissed as it faded, and Riddick put the wooden handle in the iron rack that was mounted on the wall. The darkness filled their heads and Amirra gasped.

"Hold my hand," Riddick said.

Amirra fumbled for his hand and gripped it tightly when she found it. Riddick slowly moved toward a stone wall. He opened his mind and let the earths' array of forces fill his mind. A picture formed and he detected the altar on the other side of the rock wall. A small framed figure emerged into Riddick's vision.

"There's someone on the other side," Riddick said.

"Gitre," Amirra said.

"How do you know?" Riddick asked.

"She is the new Crypt-Theda, it's her responsibility to protect the corpse, which also means she has been infused with the corpses' life force," Amirra said.

"A corpse doesn't have a life force, it's dead," Riddick said.

"In the normal sense, yes, but necromancy doesn't work that way, there is power in the dead too," Amirra said.

"I have no idea what you are talking about, but I'll take your word on that," Riddick said.

"Maybe if we can release the bonds without her seeing us, we won't have to battle her," Amirra said.

"Battle her?" Riddick asked.

Amirra didn't see his face but by the sound of his tone, she knew he contorted through several expressions and settled on confused amazement.

"Unfortunately, the corpse is now a servitor, and it won't want to let go and return to the dead, so we will have to battle it too," Amirra said.

"You could have mentioned this sooner," Riddick said.

"I know, I'm sorry, I just don't want you to think I'm a sicko or something," Amirra said.

Riddick didn't know what to say, he didn't think she was a sicko, but he also didn't want to know what she knew about the evils of the art of necromancy either. He gave her hand a squeeze and put his other hand on the wall.

"What is your plan?" Riddick asked.

"We wait until Gitre is at the farthest edge of the room and then we go in. We will need to find the last knot of the binging straps which will probably be a metal chain of some kind and undo it. We will have to move fast because a servitor can move very fast," Amirra said.

"What will the servitor do if it catches us?" Riddick asked.

"It will probably try to suck your life from you," Amirra said.

"Lovely, that's all I've ever wanted," Riddick said.

"I'll worry about the servitor, you focus on the chains. Get them off the corpse as fast as you can," Amirra said.

"Alright," Riddick said.

"Oh, and if you find a black dish with a weird goopy substance in it, DO NOT TOUCH IT!" Amirra said as sternly as she dared while still in a whisper.

"Got it," Riddick said.

Riddick watched the small-framed figure crossed the room and back until he was certain he could guess her next moves.

"On, three," Riddick whispered.

Realms of Edenocht

41-Isot Wants You

Rat led Shaz and Serin through the maze of tunnels and Shaz was impressed with how fast he moved and without much light. It didn't take long until they had reached the end of the underground tunnels and were now moving through stone hallways. Shaz admired their construction and wondered why the castle security didn't' use them anymore. Rat slowed his pace and moved up against the wall. Shaz squashed his palm and moved in behind Rat. Rat put his finger to his lip and Serin moved in next to Shaz.

Rat pushed a stone-carved wall open enough for his tiny eye to peek out. The sliver of pre-dawn light crept in and Shaz now was sure of what time it was. He was slightly relieved to know there was still less than half the night to get into the secret lair. Rat pushed the doorway open a little more and then a little more. He waved behind him and slipped through. Shaz and Serin followed and it only took Shaz three long strides to cross the open courtyard pathway. Rat held open another section of the stone wall that separated the courtyards and buildings in the outer section of the city. The stone was rough and it rubbed against their skin as they darted through the opening.

The next passage was the same as the last and so was the next two as they moved toward the main building of the castle. Rat stopped at the next doorway.

"This is the end of the outer walls, from here we will have to be careful. There won't be any covering and if we run into people act like you are supposed to be there," Rat said.

Serin scrunched her nose and was angry that these people would have to *act* like they belonged. Rat opened the door and peeked around. He nodded and they quickly left the security of the tunnel.

Rat was very good at knowing exactly where he was going and led them through the inner building's labyrinth of ally's and half walls. The sun was still a few lengths from the horizon but there was enough light from the few streetlamps and the lights of the shops that they were able to make their way easily. The heavy beat of wings against the air crossed Shaz's mind and he grabbed Rat's slender fame and hurried him against a nearby wall and Serin followed quickly. Rat looked at him surprised but stifled the outcry he was about to make when he found the concern on Shaz's face.

"What is it?" Serin asked.

"A Sqwall," Shaz said.

"I wondered how long it would take for them to get here," Serin said.

"I'm sorry," Shaz said.

"You can't stop being who you are," Serin said.

"Here it comes," Shaz said.

Shaz gripped the hilt of the Honor Blade and lifted it carefully from the sheath. He listened to the vibrations in the air and homed in on the direction it was coming from. The thrill of the hunt filled his body and he smiled a tight grin. Serin was perplexed but didn't figure it was the time to interrogate him. Serin moved Rat behind her and held him against the wall. The vast wings flapped against the night air and Shaz steadied his breathing and eased his grip onto the leather strapping on the pommel. Serin pulled her dagger from her thigh and wished she had her bow, which she decided to leave at Mrs. Bailey's so that she would be less obvious.

The black-bird tilted its head and pointed its razor-sharp beak toward the ground and dove toward them. Rat tried to look around but found it hard to see anything with Serin holding him against the wall. She hushed him sternly and he stood still. The sqwall swooped upward in time to lunge its long skinny legs at Shaz who swung his blade. The beast screeched and blood gushed from its belly onto the blade. Shaz swung the blade in a sideways swing and flicked the blood from it so that it wouldn't get on him, but he didn't manage to escape it all. The beast didn't have time to transform into its human-esque-like-figure and slammed into the outer wall and crumpled to the ground. Shaz hurried to the creature and stabbed the point through its neck. He waited a moment until the creature's limbs stopped twitching and rummaged through its feather-like pockets. He found a few miscellaneous trinkets and some string but nothing important.

"Is there only one?" Serin asked.

"So, far it doesn't appear they hunt in packs, but I don't think it will be long until another one shows up. Come on lets hurry," Shaz said.

"Should we leave it here, or do something with it?" Serin asked.

"We shouldn't leave it here, but what do we do with it, I can't burn it like we should," Shaz said.

"True," Serin looked around, "I know, I'll lift it over the wall, at least that way no one will find it inside town," Serin said.

"Good idea," Shaz said.

Rat got a glimpse of the creature and threw his hand over his mouth to keep from retching. Serin waved her arms around and the wind picked up the carcass and she heaved it over the tall wall and dropped it over the edge. Shaz motioned for Rat to take the lead. Rat managed to swallow the hurl in his throat and started toward the next passageway and rounded a corner. Shaz reached out and gripped Rat's long overcoat and yanked him backward, shoved his boot into the coble stone and twisted at the waist and shielded Serin and Rat from a blast of fire.

The Fire consumed his shirt and the odor of melted leather and burnt fibers etched at the back Serin's mind. Shaz's bare skin absorbed the heat and his head swelled with the influx of energy. Shaz gripped his shield energy and thrust it out and around them as another blast of fire encompassed them. Serin struggled to figure out what was happening and had a hard time breathing through all the heat. Rat through his face into Serin's waist and gripped her tightly. The whooshing of air ripped around her sending her hair in a flailing mess. She called her air magic and a hefty gust of air suffocated the fire and it fizzled to a crackle and evaporated and Shaz rushed Serin and Rat back behind the wall.

"What just happened?" Serin asked.

"Velshari," Shaz said.

"I guess Amirra and Riddick didn't stop all of the initiations?" Serin said.

"Seems so," Shaz said. Serin did a quick assessment and found there were no injuries. "Are you hurt?" Shaz asked. Serin shook her head and Rat shook his but didn't' lift if from Serin's body. "Good,"

"How many are there?" Serin asked.

Serin wrapped her arm around the boy and tried to reassure him.

"Three," Shaz said.

"How did they find us?" Serin asked.

"I have no idea," Shaz said.

"So, now what?" Serin asked.

"Well one of them has the fire element, which won't hurt me, but I don't know about the other two. Rat, you need to get back to the tunnels," Shaz said.

Rat nodded but found his body wouldn't move.

"Well, considering you have all the elements, none of them should hurt you," Serin said.

"That's true," Shaz said.

Shaz rubbed his chin and squished his brows tightly. Shaz peeked around the corner and made out the three members of the Velshari. Two men and a woman stood spread apart waiting in battle positions to make their next attack. Shaz sucked in a deep breath and stepped out from the corner with his hands raised at his sides.

"Hey there, how are things?" Shaz asked.

Serin rolled her eyes but smiled. She knew his snarky sense of humor often got him into trouble, but she loved it anyway.

"Isot wants you," the man in the center said.

"Oh, how nice, but I have other plans, do you think she will take a rain check?" Shaz asked.

Shaz reached his vibes out and scoured their beings to assess how powerful they were.

"Oh, he thinks he's cute," the woman said.

"Sorry, but I'm taken," Shaz said.

The woman sneered and shot a bolt of lightning from the palm of her hand. Shaz braced himself but the force hit him in the chest and lifted him off his feet sending him flying backward and slammed into the wall. A blinding light left his eyes sightless and there were only chaotic confusions of color dancing in his head. His ears thumped with a dull echo and his numb limbs ached from the lack of sensation as he hit the ground and fell. He coughed as the air expelled its presence in his lungs and Serin blasted him with a mix of her light and healing magic. The cooling sensation eased his lungs and the feeling returned down his limbs and into his fingers.

****

Riddick pushed against the heavy stone but found it moved easily. He opened it enough for he and Amirra to slip through and closed it carefully. The green fire in the sconces around the room left an uncomfortable dread in his mind. The stench of the rotting corpse sank into his nose and Riddick swore all his nose hairs had been singed by its potency. He gagged the sudden urge to puke and wondered why Amirra didn't seem bothered by it. Amirra pointed to the end of the alter and Riddick reached the end in three long strides. He found the last knot and started to pick at the binding but found it harder than he expected. Amirra tiptoed to the table and found the black cloth the dishes had been placed on but the dish with goop wasn't there. She searched the surface of the table but didn't find it and spun around.

Amirra froze as the small figure turned and Amirra saw the hollow blackness of Gitre's eyes. Amirra spotted the dish resting on top of the corpse's chest and started to reach for it, but the black coldness of the servitor that was suspended above the corpse gripped her skin.

"Amirra, I figured you would show up sooner or later," Gitre said.

Gitre's voice wasn't the usual soft tones of a human but had a crackling echo to it. Amirra pulled her hand back and sucked in a deep breath. She squared her shoulders and Riddick tried to pay attention to untying the knot.

"Let him go Gitre," Amirra said.

"Or you'll do what? As if you can do anything to me now. That last little stunt of yours made things quite a bit difficult and you think I'm going to give into you now?" Gitre said.

"Yes," Amirra said.

Gitre let out an eerie echoed laugh and Riddick shuddered. Amirra pulled out Semias's talisman from her pocket and slipped the chain over her head.

"That won't do anything here," Gitre said.

Amirra ran her first finger across the smooth gold metal and allowed the power of the talisman to surge into her chest. She had seen Semias do this a million times and even pictured his once handsome face in her mind. It was still a mixture of conflicting emotions, but she had started to accept that she was both a necromancer and a Runecaster. She spent many hours thinking of how she might unite the two powers for good within herself and this was the best time to try. Riddick stopped fiddling with the knot and searched for a metal stick of some kind.

He couldn't find anything bigger than an old rusty nail, so he stuck the small tip into a metal link at the top of the knot and focused on the nail growing until it popped the chain link in half. Gitre noticed

Riddick for the first time and shot a bolt of lightning at him. Amirra jumped in front of the bolt and caught the energy with the talisman. The sudden force of power lifted Amirra off her feet, but she kept a tight hold of the gold crest and steadied herself as she returned to the floor. Riddick ducked and felt the dispersion of the forces rush over his head. Riddick searched the crypt for anything to use to make a shield but there was nothing.

He shoved the nail tip into another chain link and started to grow the metal until another link broke. Gitre hovered over the floor and stopped in the center of the room. The crypt wasn't very large, but it had high vaults and detailed carved pillars around the room. Amirra picked up the dish from the corpse's chest as she stepped around the altar. Amirra dipped her finger into the goop and Riddick winced. He didn't know why she could touch it, but he couldn't, and a spike of fear ripped through his core.

Amirra whispered the beginning of the first chant that Nitida had taught her. The one on choice. Semias had taught her that she didn't have a choice and that a true necromancer obeyed the commands of the shadow, but now she understood there was a side that said otherwise. Gitre raised her hands and clasped them in front of her tightly. The door of the crypt behind Gitre opened and two figures in red robes entered the room.

"You are outnumbered now, it's useless to try and fight me," Gitre said.

"I am not outnumbered, you are," Amirra said.

Gitre laughed again but the menacing tone died out as three black figures emerged from behind Amirra.

"What are you doing?" Gitre sneered.

"*You* are not the only one that can summon a servitor, and I don't need a corpse to do it," Amirra said.

Gitre's eyes flashed as the anger slashed at her being. Amirra pointed to the Velshari and two of the servitors attacked. The Velshari threw out their casts of lightning and fire, but the forces were dissolved into the misty blackness of the partially formed human-like figures of the servitors. Flashes of bright-white light lit up the room and Riddick struggled to interpret his sudden fear and attraction he had for Amirra. Her long cinnamon hair was gently flowing in the unseen forces of the magic that summoned the dead and her fair skin glistened in the green flames. Her curvy figure was strong and powerful, and Riddick had to make himself stay on task with the chains. A few more links and the knot fell from the hook it was secured to on the edge of the altar.

"Has it ever crossed your mind, that you are not that important Gitre," Amirra asked. Riddick snickered at the insult and moved to the next knot. The Velshari moved around the room and dodged the blasts of the green force that Riddick didn't know what it was. Gitre blinked but her stone-cold face didn't move. "That all you are is a pawn in Isot's game. She doesn't care about you any more than you care about me," Amirra said.

"That's not true. Isot needs me," Gitre said.

Gitre took another few steps.

"Needs you, maybe, but cares about you, no," Amirra said.

Amirra witnessed the gears inside Gitre's head churning trying to process the difference. She remembered when she too, didn't understand the separation.

"It doesn't matter, I am united with this spirit and together we form the conduit to the realm of the dead," Gitre said.

A blast of lightning whizzed over Amirra's head and she ducked. The blast hit the stone wall behind her, and shards of broken stone shattered everywhere. A sizeable shard slammed into Amirra's back and she recoiled from the hit. Riddick threw his hand out and summoned all the shards to stop and fall which they did with a clatter. Amirra sucked in a heavy breath and breathed through the pulsing pain.

"You are not so invincible are you," Gitre said.

One of the Velshari leaped out of the way of one of the servitors and rolled to the other side of the room. The man jumped to his feet and turned to blast Amirra with another bolt of electric energy. Riddick imagined the man becoming a tree and the earth force shot up and encompassed his figure. The man yelped at the sudden entombment and

Riddick popped another link off the next knot.

"Blast, this is taking too long," Riddick cursed.

Riddick eyed the table behind him with nails embedded into the frame. He yanked them with his magic and commanded the little army of nails to each find a link. They responded with sharpness and within a minute every nail was breaking links all over the corpse.

42-That Hurt

The man on the side started toward Shaz, and Serin peeked around the corner. *Serin, NO!* Shaz said in his mind. Serin heard him but ignored it and stepped out and sent a heavy barrage of wind shards at the man. The man yelled in pain as the razor-sharp blades of air ripped through his clothes and flesh with ease sending blood splatters across the surrounding stone wall. Serin stepped back around the corner and Shaz threw up his deflecting-shield and managed to stand. Serin peeked around the corner again and noticed that the other two had made their way to the man and were pulling him back toward a short stone wall. Shaz made his way back to where Serin and Rat were and shook out his hands.

"That hurt," Shaz said.

"Well, that didn't go as planned," Serin said.

"No, it didn't," Shaz said.

"So, one has fire, one has lightning, but what about the last one, and how do we defeat them?" Serin asked.

"They don't seem to have very good defenses," Shaz said.

"That's a good thing, and we don't have a lot of time either,"

Serin said.

Serin motioned to the sky. The early dawn was now teetering on morning.

"Alright, we both attack. You take the one on the right, I'll take the one on the left," Shaz said.

Serin nodded and Shaz peered around the corner. The man and woman were crouched behind the partial wall with the wounded man's leg sticking out. The male Velshari peeked over the wall and Shaz stepped out and Serin followed. The two Velshari rose and stepped out from the cover of the wall. The man's deep inset eyes narrowed, and his chin tightened. He was a middle-aged person with a moderate build but with a few extra pounds on him and the woman was curvy with long black hair and a strong nose.

"We don't have to fight you know," Shaz said.

"Oh, but we do," the man said.

"Why? What did we do to you?" Shaz asked.

"It's not what you have done to us, but what you can do for us, if you come peacefully you won't get hurt," the man said.

Shaz snickered but the statement sat at the back of Shaz's mind and Serin dreaded his need to find out what he meant. He had an idea that they wanted him to read the scroll.

"But I don't want to help you, *at all*, so I guess you'll just need to go home now," Shaz said.

The man lifted his hand and the heat of the fire element left the atmosphere around Shaz and Serin indicating that he was about to call on the fire element. Shaz ripped the combustion forces from the man's grasp and slammed them into the man. The force blasted the man off his feet and flung him like a ragdoll across the courtyard. The woman stared in fear as the man slammed into the ground and she turned on her toes and shot back behind the wall. The first man wasn't there any longer and she darted toward the other man and helped him up and they hobbled into the shadows of the alley and disappeared.

"Are we going after them?" Serin asked.

"No, Isot will know we are here in a matter of minutes and we need to get to her lair," Shaz said.

Serin nodded and turned to find Rat huddled behind a stone planter.

"It's alright now, but we need to keep going, you can go back if you want to, but we could use your help still," Serin said softly.

Rat nodded but took a seconded to make his body move. Serin touched his shoulder and gave him a calming dose of energy and his body relaxed. He pointed to a set of stairs and darted across the blood-spattered stone.

****

Isot draped the long blue gown on the bed and smoothed the silky surface. The heavily beaded and jeweled overcoat caressed the floor by several lengths. Isot had the robe made after the fashion of the previous Kings and since this was the first woman in centuries to be coronated as the queen, there were no traditional clothing already pre-pared. Oladesni came out from around the dressing wall wearing the underdress. The cream silk accented her soft olive skin and amber eyes. Isot motioned for her to take a seat in front of the mirror and picked up a brush.

Oladesni sat with her back straight and picked up the dangly earrings she had chosen and amazed at their glimmer in the flames of the wall scones. Isot pulled the brush through Oladesni's warm brown hair until there were no more tangles and proceeded to wrap the long locks up into swathing curls and swoops around her head. It wasn't Oladesni's preferred look, but she didn't object. Isot pulled out a small glass jar and removed the stopper and put her finger over the opening.

"What is that?" Oladesni asked.

"This is a sacred oil, created especially for your coronation," Isot said.

"What is it for?" Oladesni asked.

"This will help call the spirits of old, so they can offer you guidance," Isot said.

Oladesni smiled, but she didn't think that necessary, but the aroma was pleasant so Oladesni didn't object. Isot *had* created the oil, and it was to call upon the spirits, but she didn't say *which* spirits it would summon. Isot ran her finger around Oladesni's hairline and down her neck and dipped the bottle again. Isot rubbed the oil into the skin on her own wrist and put the stopper back and returned the vial to her pocket.

"There is one more thing you need to do," Isot said.

"Alright, what is it?" Oladesni asked.

"Hold out your hand," Isot said.

Oladesni held out her hand and Isot took out her athame blade. The long slender blade reflected the flames and Isot took Oladesni's hand before she pulled it away.

"What are you doing?" Oladesni asked.

The shock and panic caused Oladesni's voice to crack and her adrenaline spike.

"This won't hurt, well only a little. You must show your people you are willing to sacrifice everything, especially your own blood for them," Isot said.

Oladesni searched Isot's face and found a gentle smile but her eyes seemed darker than usual. She swallowed the lump in her throat and closed her eyes and nodded. Isot pulled the sharpened blade across Oladesni's palm and Oladesni winced as the pain opened her skin. Isot squeezed her hand around Oladesni's and the blood oozed from the cut. Isot took out another vial and scooped up the blood until the vial was half full. Isot wrapped a bright white cloth around Oladesni's hand and secured it tightly.

"You are a brave girl, now your people will know you are willing to whatever it takes on their behalf," Isot said.

Oladesni's hand hurt, but she felt better knowing she was willing to whatever it took, or so, she hoped. Isot slipped the vial of blood into her other pocket and helped Oladesni finish dressing. The gown draped down her chest revealing a bit more skin than Oladesni wanted, but she admired how her female frame had grown into a woman and her features were starting to show. The overdress robe was heavy with all the beading and jewels but Oladesni had a sensation of power and pride she hadn't had before. Isot picked up the train of the ceremonial robe and nodded for Oladesni to open the latch to her private chambers. The latch clicked and the door popped open and Oladesni heaved the door. It was one of the heaviest doors in the castle and when Oladesni had asked why she was told it was to add more protection in case of an invasion. The coolness of the early morning in the castle hallways seeped into her lungs as she carefully made her way to the grand staircase. Armed men stood every ten lengths along the hallway and Oladesni didn't like the added security, it made her feel like they were expecting the unthinkable, but it also made her more secure.

Oladesni rounded the last corner and the hallway opened into a vast grand lobby. The staircase was along the far wall and had been covered in deep purple velvet. The banister was polished to a high gloss and the sconces along the upper section of the wall had been lit. The brightness of the morning sun sparkled around the room at every point there was glass, brass, or crystal décor and Oladesni gasped. She had never seen the castle so beautiful and her eyes wandered around the room. Isot cleared her throat and motioned for her to keep moving. Oladesni stopped at the top of the stairs as instructed and waited.

****

Bowen woke to the beating of his brain against his skull. The cold iron straps ate at his wrists and he tried to swallow but his throat closed off with the dryness of the hot air. He peeled his eyes open, but the sting of the heat caused him to shut them. He listened carefully to figure out where he was. There were muffled voices and clanging of pots that sounded like he might be near a kitchen. He slowly opened one eye and tried to peek out of his eyelid. He kept it open as long as possible which caused tears to form at the edge. He blinked a few times letting the cool moisture create a barrier and opened his eyes again. This time he realized he was in the corner of the furnace room that fed the castle kitchens many coal stoves.

Bowen pulled in a slow breath and blinked again. The heat stifled his lungs and he coughed. The pain sat heavy in his chest and he tried to figure out what to do. He searched around the floor and found that the chair he was in was not secured to the floor. He started shoving his weight against the chair at the same time as trying to lift it. The chair moved a few small paces, but he found it much harder than he would have thought.

Bowen closed his eyes and tried to steady his heart rate and tried again. It took several tries, but he managed to reach the small steel grate that was in the center of the wall. The muffled voices were a little stronger now, so he opened his mouth to yell. His throat burned from the dryness and there was no sound to leave his voice box. Anger overtook him and he struggled against the restraints but sank into the chair. He kicked the wall and a hollow echo vibrated through the wall. The voices hushed for a minute and then returned to their normal bustle. Bowen kicked again and again. The echo rolled around the kitchen for several lengths and he kicked again.

Bowen heard the voices get stronger and he kicked again. A loud clang pulsed in his ears and a bright warm light shot across his face. Bowen blinked and was able to make out people on the other side of the firepit in the center of the room. The men rushed into the round room and started to pull at the iron grate, but it wouldn't budge.

One started shouting orders and the others scrambled to find something to use to pry the bars open. Bowen sighed and a wave of relief overcame him. His body started to shake but the fear of it being because of dehydration was what threatened his sanity. One of the men returned with a long heavy bar and the two jammed it into the crack between the grate and the stone wall. They heaved several times and the wall cracked. They jammed the pole in again, and again, heaved until the latch finally broke free and the grate fell with a clatter to the floor. The men quickly climbed inside and tried to pull Bowen off the chair, but his wrists and ankles were shackled.

Bowen could tell they were talking and trying to figure out what to do, but none of the sounds made sense in his mind. He felt his head become heavy and he had a hard time keeping his eyes open. The younger man grabbed the pole and shoved it between the legs of the chair and slammed his foot into the pole. The force popped the legs apart and they were able to release the shackles from the chair and pull Bowen out.

Bowen woke several hours later in a warm bed. The blurry image of a servants' quarters came into his mind and he found his body was free from the restraints he was in. He lifted onto is elbow and scanned the room. A tall pitcher of water sat on the side table with a mug. He reached for the mug and was excited to find cool water inside. He sipped the water and felt the sting of the liquid move down his throat. His body gagged on the liquid, but he forced himself to keep drinking. The rehydration of his throat was a slow process, but he talked himself through it.

The door opened a sliver and then a young woman opened it the rest of the way. Her long brown hair was pulled up and pinned at the back of her head and she was dressed in the clean crisp uniform of a house servant. Her eyes were delicate, and she had a gentle smile which Bowen found profoundly beautiful. The young woman checked the pitcher and found it was still full.

"Where am I?" Bowen asked.

His voice was scratchy and rough, and he gripped his throat as the pain of speaking surged.

"I'm not supposed to talk to you," the young woman said.

"Why?" Bowen whispered.

"Because you are an imposter," the young woman said.

Bowen laid onto the pillow and stared at the ceiling. It didn't surprise him that she would think that, and he tried to think of a way to prove to them that he wasn't. A heavyset man came around the corner and peered into the room.

"That will be all miss," the man boomed.

The young woman hurried from the room and Bowen turned to the large fellow.

"Bowen is that you?" the full-bellied man asked.

Bowen lifted onto his elbow and again and squinted.

"Paco?" Bowen whispered.

"What are you doing here, you aren't supposed to be here, you could have died, and for real this time," Paco said.

Paco lifted Bowen to sitting and helped him sip more water.

"It's a long story. Where is my armor?" Bowen's voice was slowly returning to normal, but his body still ached all over. Paco pointed to the pile of armor in the corner. "In the pouch, there is a small bottle, please get it for me," Bowen said.

Paco removed the bottle from the pouch and pulled the stopper and handed it to Bowen.

"Boo's aren't going to help you know," Paco said.

Bowen rolled his eyes and swallowed the tincture quickly and the magic overcame his body. His head stopped throbbing and the aches dissipated to a soft rumor in his limbs. Bowen nodded to Paco who stared with confused amazement. Bowen smiled to himself remembering when he too was confused about the effects of magic. Bowen pulled the blankets off and put his feet on the hardwood floor.

"What are you doing, you have to stay here. You can't be seen in the castle, you're a wanted man," Paco stammered.

"Wanted man huh?" Bowen said.

"What have you gotten yourself into?" Paco demanded.

Paco stepped in front of Bowen and his large frame was enough to completely block him from getting out of bed.

"Paco, I don't have time to explain, but I will tell you this, things are not as they should be, and the queen is grave danger," Bowen said.

Paco blurted a booming ga-fa but wasn't sure whether he should believe him or not.

"Yeah from you," Paco said.

"Paco, you know me, we have been friends for rotations and have you ever known me to be a dishonest man?" Bowen said.

Bowen stood up and shoved his torso into Paco's round belly. Bowen looked him square in the eye and held his eye contact.

"No," Paco admitted.

"Then you need to trust me now," Bowen said.

Paco stepped aside and Bowen hurried to his gear.

"What are you going to do?" Paco asked.

"I need to find the queen," Bowen said.

"They have already started the procession, there is no way to get to her now," Paco said.

"Here help me with my gear," Bowen said.

Paco helped Bowen put on his chest plate and gaiters and strapped his belts and pouches on.

"If you go through the servant's corridors, you might be able to get to her before she gets out of the castle, but the chances are slim," Paco said.

"I'll take whatever chances I can get," Bowen said.

"You owe me a full explanation," Paco said.

"Deal, and thank you," Bowen said.

Bowen secured the last buckle of his bracer and took Paco's hand in a tight grip.

"You better hurry," Paco said.

Bowen nodded and left the room quickly.

43-I Am Lashi Of The Traveling Performers

A hush rolled over the people that were crammed in the lobby like cattle and a skinny younger gentleman lifted a bugle to his lips. He inhaled through his nose and exhaled into the brass tube-like funnel of the horn. A powerful tune erupted, and a second bugler started and then a third. The horn players finished their song in unison and the crowd broke into cheers. Oladesni tried to keep her breathing steady, but her blood rushed to her cheeks. They suddenly went hot and she knew she was blushing. The throbbing in her hand didn't help, and she tightened her hand but released it as it only made the pain worse.

A soldier stepped out from the wall and held out his elbow for Oladesni to take, and she hooked her wrist around the crook of his elbow. The soldiers finely pressed trousers made a soft swoosh as he escorted her down the steps. She tried to keep her eyes several steps in front so that she would know where she was going as it was inappropriate for royalty to look down. Her heart raced the closer she came to the bottom. The people nearest the stairs stepped back and the men bowed at the waist and the women curtsied. Oladesni wanted to throw up, but she swallowed hard and smiled. The purple velvet runner ran along the lobby and into the throne room and out into the courtyard.

Oladesni focused on the doors at the end of the room nodding to the people without making herself dizzy. The early sun dripped sprigs of dancing rays around the high vaulted ceilings giving it a sense of charm she hadn't noticed before. She smiled when she turned to find the baker and her husband, who worked in the stables, dressed in fine garments. Oladesni had given them an invitation personally and was pleased they were there. The woman's gentle grin and soft wrinkles around her round eyes eased the pit in Oladesni's stomach. Servants dressed in crisp white and purple clothing opened the garden doors and a burst of outside smells bathed Oladesni's senses.

Several shades of flowers were in full bloom and the morning dew on the trimmed grass with a spattering of shrubs and plants reflected the early autumn weather. Oladesni took in a breath but the gown stifled her ability to fill her lungs. Oladesni hesitated as she came to the door. The sun was sitting at the right spot that she blinked a few times and tried to ease herself into the brightness. The soldier waited until she was ready and then continued to move her along the procession.

The site was amazing, people as far as she could see were gathered, all dressed in exquisite clothing and hats and jewels. Her heart skipped a beat and her knees weakened. She stopped again and gripped the soldiers arm tighter. The young man who wasn't too much older than she was reached over with his other hand and put it on hers. Oladesni turned to find him with a gentle smile and warm chestnut eyes. His strong brows complemented his strongly defined chin and jaw, and she blushed realizing that she hadn't even looked at him yet.

She stifled the giggle at the sight of the silly tall furry hat he had to wear, and he gave her a knowing eye. She guessed he wasn't fond of the look either and maybe that would be one of the first things she changed. Oladesni nodded and he took a step and followed him. His grip was tight and secure and Oladesni relaxed a little.

The courtyard was set up in tiers cascading downward with each tier getting bigger as they went, ten in all. The amphitheater-like structure allowed for the sound to carry and was perfect for formal proclamations to be declared from the center point. Oladesni and the guard made their way to the center where a stone altar sat. Oladesni's stomach churned and she gripped the young soldier tightly and tried to wave at the people. She hadn't remembered any instructions on the use of an altar and a dread began to creep into her chest.

Applause and cheers rippled around the courtyard. Specs of red strewn throughout the people caught Oladesni's eye, and she looked harder to determine what it was. At first, she couldn't tell, but after a few minutes one of the red specs moved, and she was able to make out a man wearing a red robe. She waved happily and smiled but noted all the red-robed figures and wondered why so many people had the same cloak.

A sudden burst of dedicated pitch shot over Oladesni's head as a trumpet blared its attention-getting tune. Oladesni turned to search for the interruption and found a string of banners blowing in the soft breeze. A commotion broke out and Lorn waved a hand gesture to a brute soldier who repeated the gesture to another guard. Guards dispatched around the queen and organized into a blockade around the square.

Soft clops of horses reached Oladesni and she searched the distance. At the edge of the main road to the castle, there was a magnificent procession of stunning horses. Horses she had never seen before in her life. The creatures were taller and had beautifully long mains and tails. Strong legs clopped the cobblestone sending an excited shiver through her body. Oladesni's heart pounded with childlike excitement as several men and women dressed in brightly decorated colorful outfits leaped onto the backs of the horses. Half of them stood up and rode bareback while standing and the others were in a mix of positions as they trotted in perfect sync with each other.

Oladesni quickly and eagerly waved her hand to Lorn to release the barricade but Lorn didn't. Oladesni snapped her finger and shot her hand across her chest and shot him a glare of dismissal. Lorn motioned for the men to move and glared at the oncoming obtrusion. The crowd scooted and crammed even tighter against the buildings as the horses continued to clop with precision toward the courtyard. The trumpets began another tout of notice followed by the happy beats of drums.

A host of men carried a drum each suspended onto a strap that hung over their shoulders. The men beat the drums with long sticks with a tatt-tat and a tick that created the need for the people to join in the rhythm. Their outfits were bright colors, colors that no one else had and the crowd's oohs and aahs were mixed with harrumphs and gasps but Oladesni was enamored by their exactness and the shimmering decals they were decorated with. A finely-dressed man stepped out in front of the horses and the creatures slowed to a soft prance. The man led them around the corner and into the courtyard. He stopped and bent to one knee, took off his tall black hat and bowed to Oladesni.

The Queen smiled and nodded and waved the man toward her. The man stood up with a large toothy grin and started toward the amphitheater's lowest platform. He passed Lorn and gave him a cheesy grin and winked. Lorn rolled his eyes and returned with his steely glare.

"Queen Oladesni," the man boomed. The man's voice was strong and carried over the crowds with a slow and steady excitement. He paused to gather suspense and continued, "May I first give my condolences on the passing of your father. I knew him as a child," the man bowed as he took off his hat again. His medium-black hair shone in the mid-day sun and his eyes sparkled. Oladesni nodded with an accepting smile. "I am Lashi of the traveling Performers, I have come to honor the late King, and in preparation for a new beginning, may I and my people perform for you?" Lashi said.

Oladesni took a few steps to the edge of the platform and tried to keep her enthusiasm 'official-like' and nodded and held out her hands.

"The stage is yours, my friend," Oladesni said.

The man jumped in a hop-spin and held out the long-polished cane he was using. The drummers beat on their drums and the fiddler emerged from the crowd and pulled the bow along the strings in a slow and powerful stroke. The sound was exciting and suspenseful and Oladesni succumbed to her excitement and started to bounce a tiny bounce. The guard next to her smiled at her childlike demeanor.

The fiddler moved through the people and his notes became stronger and faster, the people began to clap to the beat and join the exuberant tune and then he suddenly stopped. The drums ceased and the air became silent. The crowd didn't know if they should applaud or not. A row of men among the crowd stepped through and shoved their feet against the ground and leaped headfirst into a somersault-flip and the crowd jumped and cheered. The acrobats crossed the floor in a series of flips, back-handsprings, cartwheels, and tumbles and the crowd erupted. Musical instruments came to life around the square and the performers jumped and leaped to the beat.

Oladesni followed and was soon encompassed with the flash and sparkle of the performers. She swayed and clapped and bounced with the excitement. Several men in dark clothes maneuvered two very tall poles and a bulky stand onto the platform and secured the poles. A man ran a heavy wire from one pole to the other and started to climb the pole. He heaved and pulled the line and secured it at the top of the other pole. Another man climbed the first pole and together they tightened the line until it was taut.

Oladesni's chest heaved as one of the men stepped out onto the line. He held his arms out and balanced on the tightrope. He held his other leg out to keep his balance and slowly started to walk across the line. The crowd quieted as everyone was holding their breath. The feat was amazing but terrifying. A rider of one of the horses clicked his lip and the horse started to prance toward the tightrope. The horse's legs lifted high and pointed which was most remarkable for an animal of that size. The people had never seen the creatures move that way. The long main bounced and swayed with the movement and the rider lifted himself into a handstand as the horse clopped around the platforms. Another horse and rider entered the circle and then another and another.

The horses moved in unison and the riders moved from handstands to standing to flipping to jumping from horse to horse.

The men at the top of the tightrope walked back and forth and then traded places. Soon a new group of people emerged, and the crowd eagerly waited for their trick. The men poured a liquid into their mouths and touched a long baton to their lips. The ends of the baton lit on fire and the crowd jumped. They lit the other end and began to fling and flip the fire around.

The man with the tall smooth black hat directed the performers in a joyful systematic method and the crowd loved every moment of it, all except Lorn and Isot. Isot impatiently waited for the ridiculous show of disgraceful behavior to end. Lorn rubbed his stubbled face and winced from the now black eye and tried to keep an eye on the riff-raft. He motioned for his men to form a circle around them and organize the crowd so that when the ridiculous promenade was finished, they would take them into custody.

****

Gitre took another step toward Amirra and held out her hands. The dark misty servitor that was suspended over the corpse wriggled and shook against what looked like magical chains. The echoed clatter of chains sank into Riddick's ears and he felt his heart jump and the sweat begin to drip down his back. Amirra dipped her finger into the goopy dish again and rubbed her fingers together smoothing out the goop onto her skin. The stench was strong and Amirra's mind flooded with memories from rotations past.

Amirra hadn't realized how much she knew about the art of the dead until now, and that Semias had taught her so much. Amirra snapped her goopy fingers and the chains from Gitre's servitor fell off. An ear-piercing screech slammed into their brains and everyone flinched. Riddick unpicked the last of the links and the chain broke into several pieces and shattered onto the stone floor. Gitre's black eyes filled with terror and she racked her brain to explain how Amirra was commanding her servitor. The Velshari dodged the two of Amirra's servitors and lunged at Amirra.

The fire escaped her palm and sprung into a billowing explosion that threw Amirra backward into to altar. Riddick slammed his hands together and a thunderous force blasted the woman backward at such magnitude that her neck snapped when she hit one of the vaults in the ceiling and she flopped to the ground with a thud. Amirra regained her footing but dropped the dish with a clang. Amirra rubbed her smeared finger along the talisman and the servitors returned to her side.

"I am giving you one last chance, Gitre," Amirra said.

"I'm not afraid of you," Gitre said.

The rigidness of Gitre's posture indicated that wasn't true, but she was going to do what she was going to do. Amirra wriggled her fingers over the talisman and the gold crest opened a murky green conduit. Gitre's motionless expression turned into a frantic panic as she felt a power pulling her toward Amirra. Gitre struggled against the force and tried to turn toward the door but she was being sucked toward the altar. Amirra continued to wriggle her fingers over the talisman and the force intensified. Gitre lifted off the ground and she let out a crackling howl.

The force moved Gitre's body into the misty green conduit but placed her body on top of the corpse. Gitre kicked and thrashed about and Amirra moved out of the way. Amirra picked up the pieces of chains and with each one wrapped it around Gitre's wrists and ankles. Riddick watched but found his stomach was going to expel its contents.

"You can wait outside if you want," Amirra said.

Riddick nodded and crossed the floor. The mid-morning light hit Riddick in the face, and he shielded his eyes and closed the door behind him and sucked in a deep breath but hurled anyway. The pulsing of the dark energy that pelted the door behind him throbbed against his body and his chest tightened. A sudden crack blasted the early morning and then silence. The latch clicked and Amirra pulled the door open with tears streaming down her cheeks.

"I am so sorry you had to be a part of that," Amirra said.

Amirra's body shook and her fair skin was more pale than usual. Amirra lunged to the side of the building and puked and Riddick didn't feel as bad for vomiting himself.

"Are you alright?" Riddick asked.

"No, but I will be," Amirra said.

"What did you do?" Riddick asked.

Amirra wiped her mouth and closed her eyes and tried to steady her breathing.

"I closed the conduit and sent Gitre to the other side," Amirra said.

"How did you learn all this?" Riddick asked.

"Can I tell you later, things are going to start getting chaotic and we need to find Shaz and Serin," Amirra said.

Riddick nodded and pulled Amirra into a hug which she returned. Riddick started to leave but Amirra stopped.

"We need to barricade this door," Amirra said.

Riddick looked around and found a thorn bush a few lengths away. He pulled the plant toward the door and the bush maneuvered through the ground as if it were crawling from its place. The bush slid its thorns and stems into the ground and into the heavy wooden door and soon the door was encompassed by the bush. Amirra nodded and they hurried away from the crypt.

****

The heavy clanking of the chainmail armor under their shiny steel armor echoed through the tall stone passageways. The early-morning sun shone in through a window as he approached, and Bowen liked the warmth it gave. Bowen found a certain glee in the fact that his heavy armor wasn't so heavy anymore since Amirra had enchanted it with runes to reduce its weight. He didn't mind the new look of the rune symbols that were engraved across the chest either. Shouts in the courtyard outside hit the hallway with faintness and Bowen wondered what was going on.

He rounded the next bend which opened to an extravagant ball-room. The décor on the walls and ceiling had been hand engraved and milled to reflect the intricate nature of the times gone by. Bowen was surprised to find that he had forgotten the beauty of the room. Tall-backed velvet chairs in the nation's colors of green and purple lined the walls and the gold trims of the chairs and tables reflected the early sun-light as it sprung from the long windows. Several guards were in the courtyard on the outer edge of the ballroom and Bowen wondered why there were so many.

Bowen came to an abrupt stop as a row of soldiers closed in on him from the entrance on the other side of the room.

"Step down soldiers," Bowen said. A man from the back stepped through the opening and Bowen frowned. "Blast, I was hoping Lorn would be the one to fight me," Bowen said.

"Lorn has other things to attend to, like the queen's coronation. Unlike you who wants to ruin everything," the soldier said.

"Is that what you think is happening?" Bowen said.

"Did you really think that he was going to hand over his posi-tion as the Kingdom General to *you*?" the soldier sneered.

Bowen shifted his sword belt and took a few steps back.

"No, I didn't, but I was hoping it wouldn't come to this either," Bowen said.

"Come to what exactly?" the soldier asked.

The door to the courtyard opened and rows of soldiers entered the hall. Bowen pulled his sword and tightened his grip around the long handle. A ring echoed around the high vaults as the steel of the blade slid against the inner structure of the scabbard. The crossguard was long and sturdy but was a different texture than the rest of the hilt. The leather wraps were smooth and depressed in the shape of his hand.

The brute soldier pulled his sword and threw the dark purple half-cloak off his shoulders. The warmth in the room left Bowen's short tightly cropped hair glistening. Bowen released the latch that held his half-cloak and let it fall to the ground. Bowen stepped back and eyed the guards making a note of how many there were and how they were holding their weapons. He decided half of the men were trained and the other half were new and he wondered if it was for the coronation.

The soldier stepped toward Bowen who sidestepped and rounded the muscular man. This soldier knew how to fight and tightened his fist around his hilt and with a sudden burst slammed the blade in a side-strike toward Bowen. Bowen held his arm out and the blade hit the steel with great force, but the blade nearly bounced off and there was no mark in the bracer. Bowen smiled and glared at the soldier who shook off a surprised look. Bowen's crooked grin mused at the success of Amirra's buff on his armor to resist damage. A spike of adrenaline shot through his body and he found himself excited to try out his newly enchanted swords abilities of speed and critical attack.

Bowen drew in a deep breath and released it as he brought his arm up with his fist tightly against the hilt. The blade swung so quickly that the sun didn't have a chance to bounce off its flat surface and he hit the soldier in the chest. The force shoved the hefty man backward and he stumbled to keep from falling. The other soldiers moved toward Bowen, but the brute soldier held out his hand to stop them.

The group of men looked over Bowen's head and Bowen spun around in time to get a very large Greederick the Towers fist in his face. The sudden pain of his nose breaking shot into his brain and the force flung him across the floor. He skidded against the smooth polished stone for several lengths and came to a stop. Blood poured down his face and he tried to wipe it with his armored gauntlets. Bowen blinked several times as the natural tears flowed and he heard the laughs and snickers from the surrounding guards.

Heat popped into his chest and his blood began to boil under the surface. He came to his feet and studied the room. He took tally of the soldiers and found Greederick the Tower and his dark bearded friend.

"You know, you shouldn't have done that. You're not as tough as you think you are, in fact, you are as dumb as a light post," Bowen said.

Greederick's brows deepened on his round face and he gritted his teeth. Greederick stomped one foot and slammed his other into the ground as he launched himself toward Bowen. The floor trembled under the man's weight and Bowen waited until the bear of a man was close enough then he twisted at the waist and rolled around the man letting the man's force carry him into the wall behind him. Greederick's head careened into the stone and landed under a pile of debris from the stone opening into a large hole.

The guards murmured and gasped and Greederick fell limp. The dark bearded fella was not amused, and his deep-set dark eyes gleamed a kind of glee that suggested he was going to finish the job. Bowen waited until the man, who was only slightly smaller than Greederick, started toward him. At the last-minute Bowen grabbed a tall-back chair and smashed it over the man's back. A loud crack sounded around the room and the man fell silent. The guards who were the added security and inexperienced started to cheer Bowen on but were immediately hushed by those who were under Lorn's command.

The brute leader signaled one of his men and the soldier stepped out into the room. Bowen studied the man's gate as well as how he held his sword. Bowen breathed slowly and calculated the possible moves. He knew he wasn't going to be able to take on every soldier in the room, and he didn't want to. He just needed to defeat the brute in front of them and show he was in control again, but he knew the brute knew this and that was why he was sending other people to take him out.

The soldier gripped his sword and pulled it from the sheath and Bowen sidestepped. The soldier stepped forward and brought his blade up in an upward strike and Bowen blocked. Bowen rolled his blade around and tried to disarm the man, but the soldier followed through the strike and gripped the hilt. Bowen lunged a side attack and the soldier barely moved his blade in front to block. Bowen stepped around the soldier and swung again. The soldier couldn't bring his body around fast enough and Bowen's blade sank into the space between his chest plate and gaiters. The man yelled out in pain and his body recoiled. Blood seeped into his garments and he fell to the floor.

The brute signaled three more soldiers and started for the door. Bowen bent backward and let one of the blades pass over his head and jumped back as another reached for his gut. The enchanted armor was light and easy to move around in and he moved quickly to avoid the third strike. His heart began to pump blood through his veins, and he felt the heat rise as the adrenaline moved through his body. Bowen was surprised to feel the added endurance of the Runemagic. Several more soldiers entered through the courtyard doors and Bowen's heart sank. A fourth soldier and then a fifth entered the fight and soon the only thing that Bowen was doing was blocking and was hardly able to take a swing.

Bowen tried several times to make his way toward the doorway, but the soldiers blocked him. He was now sweating, and his muscles were starting to tire, and he didn't feel like he would keep fighting for too much longer.

44-Shield Your Mind Like I Taught You

Rat gripped the corner of the stone wall and a small section cracked open and a lever on the other side released. He struggled to pull the heavy door open and Shaz helped him. Rat tiptoed across the opening and pulled back a tapestry that covered the entire wall. Shaz was familiar with these now and waited until Serin was inside and pulled the binding close to the wall until he heard the suction sound the weaved fibers made.

"Shield your mind, like I taught you," Shaz said.

Serin nodded but Rat had no idea what he was talking about. Shaz pulled off one of his rings that Amirra had enchanted and gave it to Rat who slipped it on his biggest finger. The ring barely stayed on and Rat admired its shine. They moved along the inner hallways of the castle and Serin scrunched her nose at the staleness of the air. By the stench she was certain no had been in those hallways for a very long time and neither had any fresh air.

"This is where I leave you. You will find your secret lair in that direction, but that is as far as I know," Rat said.

"You have done well, be safe," Shaz said.

Rat nodded and returned down the corridor. Shaz took a minute to reach out with his magic and try to get an image of what the inner structure was like. Serin studied the backside of the tapestry but nothing made any sense since the design was on the other side and all the knots and ties were on the backside.

"Let's go this way," Shaz said.

Shaz pointed and moved quickly. Serin was used to keeping up with him and had to half-run-half-jog just to do it.

"This is it," Shaz said.

The corridor ended with another tapestry hanging on the wall which made it look like a dead end. Shaz pulled the fibers out of the way and a think odor of wet dirt mixed with a plethora of herbs that didn't belong together creased their faces.

"Oooo this place stinks," Serin whispered.

Shaz nodded but studied the ground.

"Be careful the ground is uneven and rocky," Shaz said.

They moved carefully through the mossy slime-covered walls with Shaz stopping every few lengths to make sure nothing was going to jump out at them. A dim light several lengths away illuminated the passage and Serin accidentally kicked remnants of a skeleton and she cringed. Shaz peeked around the corner and then entered the room. The room was larger than he had expected and found an odd curiosity from the bed and living furniture that was in the room.

Shaz snapped his finger and the orange dusting of particles sprang to life and began moving around the room. The magic pointer darted in and out of the scrolls and books and when it was done it returned to the center of the room and fizzled out.

"It's not here," Serin said.

"I didn't think it would be, but I had to make sure. I'm guessing Isot has it with her," Shaz said.

Serin nodded and started back toward the exit.

"Hang on," Shaz said.

He snapped his finger again and the particles jumped to existence.

"Find me everything on Gavin Rhill," Shaz said.

A shudder ripple down Serin's spine and she turned to find the sparkles shoot over to a small book sitting under one of the pillows on the lounge. Shaz crossed the room and picked up the book and a surge of shadow magic pricked his skin.

"I don't know if that's a good idea," Serin said.

"I know, but I need to learn more about him so I can figure him out," Shaz said.

"Be careful," Serin said.

"I will," Shaz said.

Shaz stuck the book under his tunic in the small of his back and they left the room. They slipped through the second tapestry and was in the part of the castle the royal's would live in and instead of going back out the way they came they took a set of stairs that brought them into the main chambers of the castle. Shaz was about to take the left corridor but stopped and turned right instead. The heavy mingling of people began to fill the atmosphere.

"Why are we going this way?" Serin asked.

"I want to get the layout and find out if we can spot Isot," Shaz said. They turned the corner and found a large lobby filled with people who were trying to filter out of the double doors at the other side. Shaz scooted in next to a man with a spiked beard and the man sneered a snobby glare. Serin tried to push her way through too but the man stepped in front of her. She pulled her dagger and poked him in the behind and the man jumped and turned around with wide eyes. Serin held up the blade and glared at him and he scooted over with a hurmpf look.

"The queen was so beautiful don't you think," a woman gushed to another woman as Shaz stepped behind them.

"Oh yes, I hope we can get to the courtyard to watch the coronation," the second woman said. Shaz turned around but didn't find Serin so he backtracked until he found her still trying to push through the people.

"Let's go this way," Shaz said.

He veered to the back left and they managed to get through all the people. They started down the back hallway but Shaz felt a shift in energy and turned around and headed back toward another entryway. Shaz picked up his pace and shot around the corner and nearly plowed into Riddick.

"Oiy," Riddick called.

"Good to see you too," Shaz said.

"Do you hear that? It sounds like the performers are here," Serin said.

"Aye, come on let's hurry," Shaz said.

"Hey, where's your shirt? You trying to start a new trend here," Riddick asked.

Shaz shook his head but realized that was going to be one of the hazards to his fire magic. Shaz cut across an outer path and toward a set of double doors on the far side of a smaller inner courtyard. The doors led to the kitchens and they had to carefully maneuver the throng of servants and bakers and cooks that were preparing for the great feast after the coronation. On the other side of the kitchens, Shaz rounded a corner but stopped letting the rest of the crew nearly slam into him.

"Oiy," Riddick cursed.

"I hear fighting," Shaz said.

Shaz pointed to the next hall and they darted toward the sounds. Shaz shot into the room and watched Bowen go down. A tall guard had slammed his fist into the side of Bowen's head and was about to lunge another strike. Shaz took two fast steps and flipped up and over the ring of men and landed in the center of the guards. Riddick followed suit and landed next to Shaz. Serin and Amirra found the best vantage points at the back of the room and readied themselves to buff and heal as needed. Shaz and Riddick pulled their weapons and all soldiers drew their swords. The man that had hit Bowen turned around with shock and surprise which quickly turned to anger. Shaz lunged at one of the soldiers and sliced through the steel-plated shoulder pauldron nicking the man's skin and he hissed. The blade fell from his grip and he staggered backward.

Riddick swung his ax around and planted the blade into the

chest plate of another guard, who shot backward from the hit. The men that had been standing around the edges moved slowly toward them and closed the gaps and a new group came from the edges with their weapons drawn. Bowen managed to his feet and shook off the rattle in his brain.

"I don't think we can take them all," Bowen said.

"Ah, sure we can," Riddick said.

Riddick flung his hand out and a flurry of medium-sized rocks flew into the room shattering the windows behind them. Riddick whipped his hand around and the rocks quickly formed a vortex.

"Don't be idiots, attack you fools," the brute soldier commanded.

The untrained men hesitated but those in the service ran at Shaz and Riddick. The vortex spun around the room pounding into as many men as it engaged with. With each hit, the rocks were launched out of the vortex and then started to roll back toward the force until they were sucked back in. Serin heard the cheers that rose from the spectacle outside mixed with the clings and clangs of steel hitting steel. Shaz closed the distance on an oncoming soldier so he wouldn't have room to swing his sword and slammed his fist into the man's face. Several men fell to the rock vortex slinging around the room, but another wave of men entered the ballroom. Serin sent a blast of air and slammed the doors shut locking the rest of the next battalion out. Amirra studied their movements and watched them as they fought and noted the small differences, so she could adjust their weapons and gear. Serin sent a gust of wind through the broken windows and blew over the men that were trying to enter that way.

"Has it been like this the whole time?" Shaz asked.

"Pretty much," Bowen said.

"You must be a real threat to Lorn to have him send this many men to kill you," Shaz said.

"Yeah, who knew," Bowen said.

Bowen blocked and sidestepped, took a swing and caught a soldier in the leg. The man fell away and yelled in pain.

"I guess he really wants you dead, dead, and I mean dead," Riddick said.

"Thanks," Bowen said with sincere sarcasm.

Riddick chuckled and slammed his fist into the face of a tall bulky soldier. Shaz swung and blocked another strike and then another.

****

Isot slipped her hand into her pocket and pulled out the medallion she had taken from Gitre. She rubbed her finger around the edges and admired its smoothness. She pulled out the scroll and unrolled the first few sections. The scroll would take a sufficient time to read that she decided she didn't mind the distraction of the nonsense performers. She cleared her throat and softly read the first few words. A tingle tickled her skin as the medallion started to vibrate. The vibration trickled to the scroll and Isot understood that the medallion was now speaking to the scroll.

Lorn shifted his weight back and forth. He was tired of standing in the growing heat of the sun and was getting annoyed with all the cheering and applause. His surveillance moved across Isot's view and his eye caught her lips moving. He searched her face to make sure she wasn't trying to speak to him from across the pathway, but he wasn't able to make out what she was saying. He scanned around again and checked Isot again. This time her eyes had darkened, and her face tightened. A creepy tingle crawled up his spine and he questioned his decisions. Lorn tried to move his eyes around again for his next sweep but they wouldn't leave Isot's eyes. An alarm sounded in the back of his mind to get out of there, but he found his body wouldn't move. Panic raced through him and sweat encompassed his frame. He heard himself shouting to move but his mouth wasn't moving. A dull ache settled at the back of his brain and he winced. The harder he tried the thicker and heavier the pain sat in his head. His eyes blurred and the ache turned to a sharp pain that stabbed at the back of his eyes.

Isot continued to mutter and unrolled the scroll another few lengths. Lorn's face reddened with the heat of the pain and he begged in his mind for it to stop. A rattily female voice, that Lorn recognized as Isot's mixed with another's that he didn't recognize, commanded his allegiance and he agreed. The pain eased and his eyes focused again. Isot turned her attention to the Viziers and the surrounding guards and continued to mumble until everyone around her was under her command.

Isot unrolled the scroll a little more and it was now halfway to the ground. The green mist that surrounded the medallion and the scroll began to ease and waft off the items and sift through the air. Isot spoke a little louder and the mist thickened. Her voice was steady and strong and the sound ripple over the crowds. Isot motioned for Lorn to end the circus and he motioned to his guards. The guards slammed their battle batons against their shields and armor which startled the throng of people. With each thump, more soldiers joined the beat and the performers stopped and looked around.

Lashi eyed Lorn and shuddered at the darkness in his face and signaled for his clan to disperse and quickly. The man at the top of the tightrope hurried to the end and half-fell-half-swung to the ground. The acrobats somersaulted and flipped their way back through the crowds and the horseman gripped the reins of the horses and steered them away. Oladesni and the people cheered and clapped and cried for them to come back. Isot started toward the amphitheater steps and waved one of her hands and sent the mist into the sky. A gust of wind picked it up and carried it over the people. The people hushed as the mist began to take over their minds.

Oladesni turned to the side and found two large men fully dressed in the highest purity of steel armor that clanked as they lifted the long poles that held two Ebassia flags high above their heads. They saluted Oladesni who frowned that the festivities were over and waved for them to proceed. Another drum sounded in the distance but this time it wasn't the energetic upbeat sound of the travelers. The men took a step toward Oladesni and then stopped and then took another step and then continued in the same cadence as the new drums. Another two guards slowly pulled their long skinny blades from the sheath and held them out in front of their bodies.

The four men took a step and stopped and then took another step. Two of the Viziers stepped into place behind the other four in the same rows and clasped their hands together at the front interlocking their fingers together under their over-sized sleeves. The tall square hats were placed on their heads so that the brim was nearly over their eyebrows and Oladesni tried not to feel sorry for them. They were one of the ugliest costumes in the regiment and Oladesni wanted to change them as soon as she had a chance. Their long purple robes draped the ground behind them, and the emerald green trim reflected the high afternoon sun. The decorations were now gently swaying in the warm afternoon breeze and Oladesni squirmed a tiny bit as a bead of sweat dripped down her back.

The General took his place behind the Viziers. Lorn's husky face stood out as his jaw tightened, and he clasped his hand over his chest in the salute. Oladesni nodded but Lorn didn't release his hand. Isot stepped out from under the shade they had been waiting under. Her long purple robe draped the smooth stones and her tall and slender frame moved with near perfection.

Oladesni didn't see Isot's face as the hood of the robe was too large, but she could see the amulet which had a hint of green mist that surged surge around it and twice Oladesni thought she saw what looked like an eye peeking out of it. She shook her head and sucked in a deep breath. The group of leaders continued the procession very slowly, which made Oladesni nervous for some reason. The crowd was enamored with the attire and poise everyone had, but Oladesni was getting tired and her lower back was starting to ache.

The horn players lifted the shiny brass trumpets and sucked in a deep breath. The air was expelled into the shaft and blaring sound ripped across the sky. The procession stopped on the last platform and the first two men lowered the flag poles, so they were resting on the ground. The horns burst a rhythm of sounds as though they were instructions and the two lines of people sidestepped and were now facing each other. They took a step back and the men with the flags rested the poles into a shiny brass holder that sat on the ground. The two men with the swords lowered their arms but held the blades out straight. Lorn finished his salute and lowered his arm to his side and Isot pulled the hood off her head. Isot crossed the last distance to the altar and unrolled the scroll and draped it over an intricately carved bookstand.

****

The hairs on the back of Shaz's neck stood out and his stomach lurched. Serin felt his energy shift and her guts tightened. Shaz eyed the windows and caught a glimpse of a black dot in the distant sky and a thin green haze wafting across the courtyard.

"We don't have time for your little *party*," Shaz said.

"My party?" Bowen asked.

Shaz called the fire element and focused his efforts on the steel of the swords and armor. The blades began to droop, and the men dropped them as the metal became too hot to hold onto. Murmurings echoed around the room as the soldiers wondered what was happening. The weapons on the floor melted and became a pile of gooey ore to the astonishment of the men. Riddick waved his hand over the broken glass and the shards returned to their former shape and turned to stone. Intense heat surged through the armor and the men clamored to take it all off before it scorched their skin. Shaz and Riddick started toward the doorway, but three soldiers stepped in front of them.

"You can't be serious," Shaz said.

"I think they are, just look at those intent faces," Riddick said.

"I don't think they got the note," Bowen said.

"What note, I didn't get a note," Riddick said.

"Maybe they can't read anyway," Shaz said.

Serin rolled her eyes and Shaz smirked and slapped his hands together. The combustion force flung the men like ragdolls across the room. Everyone hurried into the corridor and Riddick made a new wall behind them and they ran.

"I'm glad I'm on your side. This way," Bowen said.

Bowen led them through the last half of the castle and stopped at a side gate.

"I have some unfinished business, I'll catch up to late after I find the scum I'm looking for," Bowen said.

"Aye," Shaz said.

Bowen gripped Shaz's hand tightly and winked at Serin who smiled. Riddick slapped his back and Bowen shoved the gate open.

45-Time Is Taking Back What Was Stolen

A flash of sparkle caught the sunlight and Oladesni recognized the blade Isot had used to slice her palm and a pit formed in her guts. A breeze picked up and brought with it a hint of hazelberry and lavender from the western forest and Oladesni tried to relax. She closed her eyes and tried to focus on her new responsibilities. Her knees started to tremble, and her head swayed. Isot motioned for her to take her place at the altar. The guard escorted Oladesni and smoothed out the overdress as she knelt on the soft padded bench in front of it. The heavily beaded gown gripped the sunlight and sent sparkles dancing around the courtyard.

"Be it known to all the lands, she who lay claim to the throne of Ebassia is the true and rightful heir," Isot said.

Her voice was surprisingly strong and carried over the distance with ease. The birds even stopped chirping and the silence ate at

Oladesni's nerves, but she swallowed the bile that was trying to creep up her throat.

"I approach as is my right. I am Her Highness, Oladesni Okin, daughter of the late King Oliver Okin, and Queen of Ebassia, Heir Apparent to the Throne of Ebassia," Oladesni said.

Lorn stepped to the side of Isot.

"By what right to do you claim this throne?" Lorn asked.

"By birthright of blood," Oladesni said.

Lorn nodded and one of the Viziers stepped next to him.

"By what right do you claim this throne?" the Vizier asked.

"By the grace of the Gods, and by the virtue of my nobility," Oladesni said.

Each of the men nodded to Isot who nodded back.

"We hereby relinquish the throne of King Oliver Okin, to his virtuous daughter of the birthright to be his successor and to rule and reign all the days of her life as Queen of Ebassia," Isot said.

Isot pulled out the small bottle of blood and pulled the stopper. She dripped several drops onto the altar, and then onto the scroll. The blood sizzled as it hit the pigskin of the scroll and Oladesni's head wobbled. Isot held her hand out for Oladesni, and she rested her hand in Isot's. Isot's cold skin surprised Oladesni, and she flinched. All the people wearing the red robes before covered their heads with the hoods and one of the men near Isot began a low hum. The hum traveled across the distance as every member of the Velshari joined in the chant. The mist thickened and the force propelled the people to lower themselves into a bowed kneeling position.

Isot blinked and her dark eyes vanished into complete emptiness. Oladesni tried to jump back, but she couldn't pull her hand from Isot's grip. The stronger she pulled the tighter Isot gripped. The ache in her hand turned to pain, and she was about to cry out but as the sound started to form in her throat it was seized by a power she had never experienced before.

Oladesni shook her head to clear the misty fog but her head was becoming very heavy, and she wanted to lay down and fall asleep. A deep pounding at the back of her head surfaced, and she winced. Oladesni tried to fight the pain but it only increased. Isot removed the medallion from her neck and placed it in Oladesni's hand and wrapped her fingers around it. The sting the metal made added to the pain in Oladesni's head and the tears flowed down her cheeks. Isot adjusted the scroll and picked up where she left off.

The words she spoke were nothing like Oladesni had ever heard but all she could think of was the pain. Oladesni felt her body lift off the ground and level into a lying position. The cold hard stone of the altar bit at her senses, and she tried to wriggle out of the grip of the green mist. Her attempts were in vain, and she sank into the despair of the shadow magic. Isot rested Oladesni's hand with the medallion in it on her chest and removed the scroll from the stand.

****

The mid-day sky quickly shifted to a dark eerie-green. The black dots Shaz had seen earlier dipped under the heavy cloud cover and circled in a wide pattern.

"What's going on?" Serin asked.

"The conduit has opened, and we have sqwall circling," Shaz said.

"Blast," Serin said.

"I can't go with you," Amirra said.

"Why not?" Shaz asked. Amirra held out her hand. The long pink scar was bright red and swollen. "What does that mean?" Shaz asked.

"I am bonded by the Pact, and there is no grantee I won't be able to fight it this time," Amirra said.

Her voice was shaking, which hadn't even stopped since the crypt.

"Alright, you do what you need to do," Shaz said.

His tone was urgent but kind, and he understood the complexity of her situation.

"I can keep buffing your mental shields from here," Amirra said.

Shaz nodded and Riddick searched the small courtyard. He pulled the elements and arranged a shelter made of stone for her to hide behind. A blast of force careened across the atmosphere knocking everyone off balance. They turned to see a pillar of green light shooting into the sky. Dark clouds churned around the force and then the sound hit them. The thundering crack pelted their senses, and they covered their ears. Amirra ducked behind the shelter and covered her head.

"I'll be safe here, go," Amirra said.

Riddick kissed the top of her head and Serin cast her air spell on them. They shot across the distance and maneuvered the last alleyway. They rounded a corner and slowed to a stop. The energy was so thick it stifled their lungs. Serin popped her air bubble over them which helped but not entirely.

"Shadow magic," Shaz said.

The aggravating pulses ate at her nerves and Riddick scratched and the ickiness.

"Is this what you feel all the time?" Riddick asked.

Riddick shivered with the idea that Shaz had to carry this agitation all the time and appreciated how much energy he spent keeping a calm demeanor.

"Sort of, but this is different somehow. Come on, let's hurry but keep your guard up," Shaz said.

They stopped at the throng of people kneeling in the streets. Serin touched the shoulder of a woman, but she didn't respond then Serin touched another and then another.

"They seem to be in some kind of trance," Serin said.

"Aye," Shaz said.

It was difficult to weave their way around all the people and the pit in Shaz's stomach surged. They finally made it to the square which was considerable with several layers of large stone platforms. Every platform was covered with people that were kneeling and bent over as though they were praying, except the throng of Velshari who were standing and swaying to their obnoxious hum. They could now see Oladesni laying on the altar and Isot standing next to her with her hands stretched out and her face lifted to the center of the green pillar.

Shaz spotted the scroll but there was still a bit of distance before he could reach her. The green pillar encompassed the altar and the force whipped Oladesni's hair around in a cacophony. Isot's frame was ridged and her high cheeks left dark shadows on the lower half of her face, and she looked deformed like her face was a bare skull. Isot's mouth was moving through the incantation, but they couldn't hear anything.

"Give me the missing page," Shaz said.

Serin slung her backpack off her shoulders and threw open the flap. She pulled the old parchment out and handed it to Shaz.

"What are you going to do?" Riddick asked.

Serin looked into Shaz's blue eyes which now had a tint of the eerie green. Serin grabbed his arm and shook him, but he didn't stir.

"Shaz, what is going on?" Serin demanded.

The tone in her voice ripped through his being, and he blinked.

"I'm going to retrieve the scroll," Shaz said.

"Are you sure you're alright to do this?" Serin asked.

"I have no choice and I have a feeling this is going to hurt like a bugger," Shaz said.

"I'll do my best," Serin said.

"Aye, I'm sure of that," Shaz said.

Shaz pulled Serin to him and kissed her. The strength in his grip surprised her, and she melted as his energy encompassed hers. She kissed him back and imagined her lights energy surround him. He pulled away and looked deep into her green eyes.

"I love you," Shaz said.

"I love you too, and your kind of twigging me out," Serin said.

Shaz took the parchment and read through the script.

"Here's the plan, I need to get close enough to interrupt the trance so when she gets to this missing page, I can make my move. You stay here," Shaz said.

Serin nodded and Riddick gripped Shaz's shoulder.

"Any sign of the Minca or the council?" Riddick asked.

Shaz shook his head.

"I hope they are far away like they are supposed to be," Serin said.

Shaz climbed a few terraces and started across the next one, but a prick of anxiety stabbed at the back of his head, and he halted. He searched the surroundings but didn't find anything that stood out. He took a quick inventory of the sqwalls above him, and they were still flying in a holding pattern. Shaz moved a few terraces closer to Isot and her voice came into his mind but didn't quite make out what she was saying.

Serin's anger gripped her heart and the blood heated under her pale flesh as she spotted the Velshari standing around the area all humming a haunting vibration. She sent a blast of wind at the nearest members, but it swooshed around them, and she realized the members were being protected by the green mist, and she stomped her foot. The light beam grew more and more intense the longer Isot spoke, and the pulsating of the chaotic energy wreaked havoc on Serin's nerves. She tried to push it aside, but the sting of the shadow magic ate at her skin. Isot's words were now clear and Shaz understood every word.

Serin scanned the amphitheater and found an old man with long silver hair nearing the top platform. Her heart sank, and she threw her hands out to grab the man with her air magic, but it fizzled into the shooting force of the pillar. She screamed at the top of her lungs, but it was drowned out but the rushing of the conduit.

Serin's cry sank into Shaz's chest and he turned to see her whip her hands through the air. He searched for what she was trying to do and saw Grandfather only a few steps from the altar.

"NOOOOOOOOOOO" Shaz yelled.

Shaz ran as fast as he could but Grandfather stepped into the beam of light. The energy encompassed Grandfather's body, and he instantly faded into the beam which ricocheted around the night sky and sent a blast knocking Shaz several lengths backward. Serin's entire body tightened, and she sucked in a deep breath. Shaz leaped to his feet and saw Grandfather's old and battered body slowly moving toward the clouds. The sqwalls were closer now, and he feared they would strike soon. Isot's words hit his brain with a sudden force he wasn't prepared for, and he gasped and took a few steps backward. Serin blasted him with as much energy as she could. Her body lifted off the ground as her light force left her being. It shot across the sky and lifted Shaz into the air and carried him to the top terrace.

The new concoction of hydro-light magic lifted the weight from Shaz's body, but it didn't cure the dread in his heart. The words of the casting rang in Shaz's ears, *And, with this ultimate sacrifice of purity, I trade these lives for the Binding of the Crypt.*

Tears crested the edge of his eyes and his rage peaked to a new level. He was so angry the fire element billowed from his entire body and evaporated the surrounding air. Waves of flames heaved from his chest and arms and his hair flung around with the force of the ensuing combustion.

"Sharona re mi china charera no'ha latenta, Ma'rray mi china ma no ha. Tarren menin shelt la noshari tere mea'aha. Tay nada' no'halla toma nosh vi say na moha. Potenta stoma nome ha'la'tay kina nara sto'mae'ah'ha."

Shaz spoke the words of the secret page of the Biding of the Crypt spell with a power and force which cause the light beam to ripple and sway and become unsteady. Serin sent a steady stream of wind to feed his inferno and the flames grew bigger. She was just as angry and wanted to give him as much energy as she could. Riddick steadied Shaz with a barrier of earth magic which created a wonderful array of wavy patterns through the green mist. The hum of the earth's magic soothed Shaz's mind and encouraged his rage. Riddick grew the pulsing energy and slapped his hands together and shot all the Velshari off their feet. The humming stopped and Isot blinked.

Serin feared the heat would consume Oladesni, and she sent a shield to cover her. Riddick reinforced it with his and Oladesni's hair settled. The unique metal hovered in the air in front of him and Shaz took his piece of the Time Tablet and rubbed it between his fingers.

"No'halla te narato. Shatyoha re mevina charera no'ha. Latenta somella ray narra anoto chari lataya ha no soma tom'me. Toshchari san ate te narato."

Isot turned toward Shaz, her sunken face barren of expression. The Time Tablet began to spin and Isot flinched. The tablet spun faster and faster and with each rotation Serin's chest tightened. Serin couldn't understand why it was affecting her the way it was, and then Serin's body lifted off the ground, and she hovered toward Shaz. The combustion of the fire element and her healing and light magic melded together. Serin felt a new kind of pain, and understood that she would also have to sacrifice herself with Shaz. They were bonded and what happens to him, happens to her. Tears filled Serin's eyes and her heart ached with the added stress. She found it very difficult to separate his emotions from hers and the pain in his heart was about to overload her and she cried out. Shaz heard her, and knew he needed to make his move. Shaz stepped into the pillar of the billowing green light.

"Shido'ah ray machina chada'rrha. Menin shelt la noshari No'ha la tenta no somalla shento," Shaz said.

Shaz's body arched backward and his body absorbed the pillar of light. He let out a cry of pain that deafened the surroundings. Serin's body arched too as she shared his pain. The glyphs that had been engraved in the stone of the castle were now being burned into the skin on Shaz's back. Serin's body trembled, and she closed her eyes and focused on the light. She imagined the brightness of the sun pouring into their bodies and the strength eased their pain.

Isot stared in horror as Shaz hovered in front of the altar. Isot's body convulsed and twitched.

"Sterami forte, de su shento'at'tayo," Shaz said through gritted teeth.

Shaz finished the incantation and the pillar disappeared. Shaz allowed his energy to dissipate, and they lowered to the ground. Serin gasped at the red-hot etching of the scroll's new resting place. Shaz's back was nearly covered by the intricate ensemble of glyphs which now was a combined symbol for the scroll. Serin's hair stuck to her face as her body was covered in sweat, and she breathed heavily.

"What have you done!" Isot shouted.

"The scroll is now mine, and you will never be able to have it, neither will the shadow. Even if I die, it will die with me," Shaz said.

"How did this happen, I recreated the scroll," Isot said.

"Not all of it, there was a page that was torn out of the original scroll. That's why the magic took you instead, making you part of the castle, but now it is time that you gave back the time you used that didn't belong to you," Shaz said.

A surge of pain shot through Isot's body, and she jerked with the sudden force. The wind forced from her lungs stung her mind and panic swelled her expression. She held her hands in front of her and watched the skin begin to age rapidly. She felt her face and found her soft skin was beginning to crack and wrinkle. A series of cracks rippled through the castle as the stolen age eased into the crevasses.

"What is happening to me?" Isot begged.

"Time is taking back what was stolen," Shaz said.

Isot's body shrunk and hunch over and her hair fell out in chunks. The now white hair sat on the ground and her skin sagged off her bones while the whites of her eyes turned gray. She struggled to move as she tried to run, but her body was rapidly turning into dust. She cried out, but her voice faded quickly. Even her clothes began to deteriorate. Shaz blew as she became a fine dust and then evaporated into nothing. The flames of the fire element burning on Shaz's body rippled through the now dark night and gave a warm glow to the terrace. Shaz dropped his flames and sank to the ground. The night overcame the surroundings and Serin collapsed to the ground. Riddick fell to his knees and panted for breath and Shaz sank onto his knees and breathed heavily.

A sqwall seized its opportunity and dove straight for Shaz. Shaz sensed it coming but his body didn't respond to his commands. A glint flashed in the bird's eye as it closed its distance. All Shaz could do was flinch a second before an enormous charcoal gray wolf leaped over him and slammed his mighty fangs into the sqwalls round belly. The sqwall screeched and tried to flap its long skinny wings but the Ukari gripped tightly and snapped its spine. The sqwall fell limp in the Ukari's jaws as the mighty animal landed quietly on the other side of the terrace.

"Shaz are you alright?" Merrick asked.

Shaz turned and found his father's warm brown eyes and he fell into his father's large arms. Intense emotions overcame him, and Shaz cried into Merrick's shoulder. Merrick stroked Shaz's hair and held him.

"Where is Serin, is everyone alright?" Shaz asked.

"Valida has her," Merrick said.

"Why did he do that?" Shaz asked.

"Grandfather was also on borrowed time. It was time he moved on to his next journey," Merrick said.

Shaz allowed his body to shake for a few moments then sucked in a deep breath. Merrick helped Shaz stand, and they turned to find Serin still laying on the ground. Valida waved to them to come quickly and Shaz's heart skipped. Merrick helped Shaz to where Serin was laying and Shaz fell to his knees and scooped her into his arms and cradled her. Oladesni stirred but found it hard to move and Amirra ran to her and helped her sit up. Oladesni blinked and rubbed her eyes and tried to assimilate what had happened.

"Who are you?" Oladesni asked.

"I'm Amirra the Runecaster," Amirra said.

"The what?" Oladesni asked.

"Are you alright?" Amirra asked.

"I think so, what happened?" Oladesni asked.

Amirra opened her mouth to explain but realized it would take hours, so she shook it off.

"We'll explain later, but for now you're safe," Amirra said.

Amirra helped Oladesni stand and they started toward the others. A hushed murmuring now enveloped the courtyard and Amirra held onto Oladesni's hand and half-dragged her around the throng of people. The Velshari hurried out of the courtyard and Bowen barked orders to the soldiers who obeyed this time and started after them, but they stripped themselves of their cloaks and started to act dazed making it hard for the soldiers to know who they were chasing.

"Is she alright?" Riddick asked.

Shaz listened to Serin's shallow breathing and wiped the hair from her face. Serin blinked but didn't stir. Ladtwig and Turkill burst out of the crowd and huddled down next to Shaz and Serin.

"We need water," Shaz said.

"There's a fountain over there," Valida said.

Ladtwig jumped to his feet and hurried through the crowds who were moving about in disarray. The lampposts began to come on one by one illuminating the terraces showing the effects the pillar had on the gardens and vegetation. Several large trees were spilt in two and there was debris everywhere. A group of street performers came from one of the side alleys and Lashi held his hand to keep them from getting too close. Bowen stood above Lorn and waited until he came to. Lorn's eyes widened as the understanding encompassed his mind, and he stood up. Bowen plowed a full fist into his face, and Lorn recoiled and fell backward. Oladesni winced and then smiled at Bowen with a nod of approval. Ladtwig returned with a man's top hat full of water. Shaz dipped his hand into the liquid and dripped it onto Serin's lips. The cold moisture seeped into her skin and the energy the water gave her body eased into her chest. Shaz continued to drip water on her lips and wipe the water around her face. She stirred and opened her eyes.

"Are you alright?" Shaz asked.

Serin found his eyes full of fear, dread, and pain. Serin nodded and tried to sit up. Shaz helped her sit up and she found the hat.

"This must be Ladtwig's doing," Serin said.

Ladtwig beamed with pride showing all his bright white teeth and Turkill patted his back with a brother's pride and everyone laughed.

"You're supposed to be with the travelers, lengths away by now," Serin said.

"Silly girl," Turkill grunted.

Another sqwall dipped from the sky and aimed its beak. Shaz sensed the creature coming but didn't worry. As soon as the beast was close enough a solid-black Ukari lunged from the shadows and snagged it from the sky. Turkill jumped in triumph and threw his fist in the air and hooted and hollered at the magnificent beast. Riddick ducked and Amirra jumped. Shaz stood and helped Serin who was still a bit wobbly. Jagwynn rubbed her large hide against Serin's leg and Serin leaned down and rubbed her face and Jag purred loudly.

"You must be Serin," Merrick said.

Merrick's warm brown eyes were surrounded by gentle wrinkles and his smile was soft. Serin nodded and held out her hand to shake his, but Merrick pulled her into a snug squeeze, and she felt right at home. Bolgan padded quietly up the cobblestone terrace and people gasped and rushed away. Riddick pulled out the Sistine Moon and held it out for him. Amirra took the pendant and held it toward the bright moon that was nearing the center of the sky. Bolgan stopped and bowed his head and a huge pack of Ukari emerged from the shadows around the courtyard. They lowered their heads and Amirra caught the moons beam with the shiny surface of the blue stone.

Amirra directed the beam toward the Ukari and gently placed it in the center of Bolgan's forehead. The beam shined a bright blue light that mimicked the design on the jeweled necklace. The magic of the moon illuminated a replica of the marking under his long gray fur and then one by one the symbol illuminated under the fur of every one of the Ukari. Bolgan raised his head high and pursed his lips over his sharp fangs. A strong howl rang into the night and the other Ukari followed. The sound was both astounding and frightening and many people scurried away from the courtyard.

"Thank you," Bolgan said.

"It was our pleasure," Riddick said.

"We owe you a great debt," Bolgan said.

"You owe us nothing, but I am proud to call you a friend," Shaz said.

"You have earned the Ukari's eternal allegiance," Bolgan said.

The glistening steely eyes of the large Ukari pack filled the night. Bolgan nodded to Shaz and Riddick, and bent a knee to Serin, Amirra, and Oladesni, who stared with the widest eyes a person could have. Jagwynn moved to Bolgan and he rubbed the side of his head on hers and she rubbed her head on his and purred. Shaz wasn't sure but it seemed like they knew each other in a different time and place as something, or someone else, and that their relationship was a deep and long one. His chest pounded with a sense of its truth and he wondered just how big this universe really was. Bolgan turned and ran out of the castle courtyard and his pack followed.

Shaz felt a little tug on his pants and he looked down and found Nix's big eyes shining up at him. Shaz knelt and Nix threw his little paws around his neck. Shaz patted his back and smiled. Serin knelt and Nix gave her a hug too. Nix pulled away and held out his paw, three Gray Tailix's hesitantly half-crawled-half-walked toward Nix.

"This is Nix's family," Nix said.

Nix's female was a lighter shade of gray and her eyes were slightly narrower and more delicate than Nix's. Her long furry tail was thick and bushy, and she had a puckered smile. The two smaller ones were obviously children and their eyes were huge for their overall size. Serin held out her hand to shake the tiny paw but she leaped onto her neck and gave a squeeze. Serin laughed and the little ones snuggled into her. Shaz smiled at Nix who was beaming with pride and joy.

"I'm happy for you," Shaz said.

"Is the mean lady gone," Nix asked.

Amirra knelt.

"Yes, she most certainly is, and she will never hurt you again," Amirra said.

Nix hugged Amirra who giggled at his long furry ear that tickled her ear. Nix pulled away.

"Nix's is thankful, and forever Shaz's friend," Nix said.

Serin gave Shaz the 'see-I-told-you' look and Shaz rolled his eyes but smiled. Nix slapped Turkill and Ladtwig's hands in the gesture of thanks and the four little critters scurried into the darkness.

"Can anyone tell me what is going on?" Oladesni asked.

"Now that is a loaded question," Riddick said.

Everyone laughed and Bowen barked orders for the soldiers to start getting the people back to their homes, escort the queen and lock down the castle grounds.

46-They Are Under The Care OF The Sun Goddess

Motavo slipped passed Lashi and hurried to Shaz, Serin and the others.

"Is everyone alright?" Motavo asked.

Everyone nodded and Motavo relaxed a little. He pulled Serin into a hug and went to hug Shaz who winced and pulled back. Serin's chest heaved when his pain hit her conscience, and she turned him around and gasped.

"Oh, my!" Serin exclaimed.

Blood seeped from the deep gashes that formed the new giant Binding of the Crypt symbol and was dripping down his back. Serin waved her hand over the burn and a thin covering formed and stopped the bleeding. She swirled her hands over the wound and sent her healing magic into it, but nothing changed.

"This is going to take a bit more time for me to heal, if I even can," Serin said.

"Come, let's get you out of here," Motavo said.

Motavo motioned to Lashi who nodded and waved over his head. A brightly colored wagon pulled by two of the majestic horses trotted toward them. The man in the driver's seat pulled the reins and the carriage stopped in front of Motavo. Motavo opened the door and Shaz climbed inside followed by Serin, Riddick, Amirra and the Minca who squished into one seat. Motavo closed the door and Asher walked up with two more horses.

Asher handed a set of reins to Merrick and Motavo climbed in next to the driver of the carriage. Merrick mounted the large steed and helped Valida onto the back and admired the horse's size and beauty. It fit him just right, and he didn't worry about sitting on its back. Asher climbed on his horse and took the lead and the wagon and Merrick followed him out of the city and into the night. The steady clop of the horse's large hooves and the gentle swaying of the wagon created a hypnotic effect, and everyone slipped into a half-asleep daze. All except Shaz. The pain in his back wasn't only the severed skin or the heat of the burn but his mind was now filled with the intricacies of the scroll, and he found his mind was as disorganized as it was when he first received the sword. The night passed and Shaz guessed they were headed to the highlands. Shaz couldn't relax, he couldn't lean against the soft padded bench because of his wound, so he hunched forward and stared out of the window. The stars twinkled in the night and a trail of white sparkle shot across the sky.

His thought returned to just how big the universe was. His mind ran in circles from the events of the last few days, memories of Grandfather, the time in the Minca Realm, Azrack and the gryphtons, and more. He rubbed his face and tried to shake his mind clear, but it was useless.

Images of the Lavari came in and out of Serin's mind and the language of her people eased into her understanding. She watched in amazement at what she thought was a dream. The amount of healing knowledge they had was astounding and she wasn't sure if she would be able to learn it all. Serin stirred and found Shaz with his face in his hands that were propped up on his knees. She touched his arm and he turned to her. She watched the chaos in his face, but a sensation of understanding crested her awareness and she smiled.

"I know what to do," Serin whispered.

Shaz gave a slight grin and nodded, but his mind was far away. Serin sent another boost of her hydro-light magic into him, but she knew it would take time for him to process everything. She leaned over and kissed his shoulder, and he gripped her hand and interlocked his fingers with hers. The night sky was slowly being pushed away by the upcoming sun, and the wagon slowed and the stopped. Merrick came up next to the wagon and let Valida off and climbed down.

Motavo climbed out of the wagon's front driver's seat and opened the door to the wagon. Riddick helped Amirra and the Minca and Shaz and Serin climbed out after. Shaz ran through his usual scan of the surroundings and a calmness sank into his mind. The jade-green hills rolled for lengths and lengths and the breeze was fresh and cool from weeklong rains that had cleaned the air. Several men and women hurried toward the wagon one being Mergita and Amirra hugged her tightly.

"We have preparations, come, come," a woman said.

The group led them all to separate tents and gathered wood to start a fire. The early morning stillness quickly turned to a quiet bustle of noises as the travelers took care of the crew. A young man pulled the flap open and Shaz and Serin went into the tent. The boy lifted the lantern which hung on the peg next to the doorway.

"We'll take care of that, thank you," Serin said.

The boy nodded and closed the flap behind him. Serin helped

Shaz to the bed across the tent, and he laid onto his belly. Serin found a large wooden dish in the section of the tent that was used for cooking and clapped her hands. A tiny rain cloud formed and drizzled into the bowl. Serin rummaged around the cupboards and found a cloth that would work and returned to Shaz. She dipped the cloth into the water and set the bowl on a table next to the overstuffed cot-like bed.

Serin pulled the large cloth bandage from the dish and wrung the water from it. She gently placed the magic-infused linen on the burned flesh. Shaz winced under the cold but sagged into the mattress as it took the pain. Serin gently placed her hands on the cloth and closed her eyes. She pictured the brightness of the sun emerge into her mind and wrapped the glow with a wave of water and air. The energies merged and became a swirling power of magic. She pictured the ball of force leave her mind and travel through her heart and it picked up the new magic she had learned from the Lavari. The heart magic was a soft pink and it wrapped around the energy ball and continued on its path. Serin had learned from the Chief, that one of the most powerful magics was that of love, but the Lavari taught her how to use it as part of her healing. Serin opened her eyes and the bright wobbly sphere hovered over the bandage.

Serin took off the cloth and the energy moved over the large symbol. Serin wriggled her fingers and the ball moved into tiny threads and began to stitch and sew the open skin of each word and symbol the scroll now left in his skin. Shaz breathed slowly and intently to keep his mind still while Serin worked. The coolness of her magic soothed the red skin and it started to move together. Serin instructed her heart magic to soothe Shaz's mind and he allowed it to take way the chaos. The process was long and Serin stayed focused on the details of her magic mending the wound, which encompassed more than just his skin.

Shaz began to feel the effects of the love magic and his mind stilled, all except for an image of the black figure of Alisdair. The man's blue eyes stood out from the warm tan of his skin but this time Shaz wasn't sure if they were only human. He didn't know what kind of eyes they would be and then the image transformed into the face of a wyvern. The wyvern was deep black and the light that came from somewhere shone off the ultra-smooth scales that framed its face and head. The wyvern had small spikes that ran along the outer edge of what would be its cheekbones and grew until they came to a peak at the back of its head. The lower lid blinked over the same blue eyes and then the upper lid. Shaz stared at the wyvern as it stared at him, and he wanted to talk to it, but there was a barrier this time that only allowed them to see each other.

Serin had to soak the cloth a few more times and apply it to the wound while she formed more energy spheres. The bright light escaped the nooks and crannies of the tent and the people marveled at the site. Riddick and the others had retired to their tents for some much-needed sleep. A good portion of the morning had passed and Motavo and Merrick were getting nervous that it was taking so long. Motavo peeked through a crack in the flap and was amazed as Serin worked. His heart sank as he realized just how much Shaz had done to keep the people safe. He closed the flap and gestured to Merrick that she was still working, but it didn't really ease their nerves.

Serin closed the last of the torn skin and examined the wound. The red skin had softened to a light pink, but the mending left the lines slightly raised which she knew would settle over time. She let her magic dissipate and relaxed her arms. Serin sat back and breathed out a deep sigh.

"How do you feel?" Serin asked.

Serin's soft voice brought Shaz from his encounter with Alisdair and he lifted his head.

"Much better, what was that new thing you did?" Shaz asked.

"The Lavari taught me how to use the power of love," Serin said.

Serin looked at her armlet and watched the inscriptions shift again. She now understood the armlet as like a small conduit of its own that allowed her to stay connected to the Lavari. It gave her heart a kind of peace, but a new sadness crept in and she longed for her mother and father. Shaz rolled over and motioned for her to come to him. Serin climbed in the bed and Shaz wrapped his arms around her. She sighed heavily and his warmth was soothing, and they quickly fell asleep. Late evening settled on the camp and Motavo and Merrick began to pace.

"They are under the care of the Sun Goddess and will sleep for a few days," the Choovino said.

Motavo turned to the old man and sighed.

"I guess I just can't stand to think what they have gone through," Motavo said.

"It is true, they have been through a most intense time, but they have the strength to do it," the Choovino said.

"How can you be sure," Merrick asked.

"Because I am old and see things," the Choovino said.

"I'm going to go check on them," Motavo said.

He left the Choovino and Merrick and made his way to their tent. He peeked the flap open and saw them both sleeping peacefully, and relaxed.

"Let's get some sleep too, we have a lot we need to get cleaned up, and we'll need everyone at their best," Merrick said.

Motavo nodded and they made for an early retirement. The next morning the sun rose as usual and Motavo and Asher rose early. They quickly made a fire and discussed ideas on what to do about the Jaduuk. Riddick pulled back the flap and ducked in under the top of the door.

"Oh good, you're awake, how are you doing?" Motavo asked.

"Alright, where is Shaz and Serin?" Riddick asked.

"Still asleep, the Choovino thinks they might sleep for a few days," Merrick said.

"Aye, I can relate," Riddick said.

His stomach grumbled and he rubbed it.

"Here eat," Motavo said.

He pointed to the trays of fried meats and biscuits and Riddick made himself a plate.

"What do you think the Jaduuk are doing?" Motavo asked.

"Tracking us here," Riddick said.

He popped half the biscuit into his mouth.

"That's what I was afraid of," Motavo said.

Jagwynn crept into the tent and rubbed against Riddick who reached down and stroked her back.

"What do we know about the Jaduuk," Merrick asked.

"They hunt in packs, usually small between eight to twelve, there is a leader to the pack that they follow, and they have impeccable smell and hearing. They are hard to poison but fall easier to the blade and fire. I personally like to drop them into holes in the earth and bury them," Riddick said.

"We don't have enough men to attack them all," Motavo said.

"What about Bowen's forces, I am sure his army can do something," Riddick said.

"Aye, I bet they would, a city of that size should have a formidable sized army," Merrick said.

"What I can't figure out, is how are they getting here. Shaz told me that they are underworld creatures, so where is the portal that brings them from the underworld to our realms. There were thousands in the Minca Realm, so where are they coming from?" Riddick asked.

Jagwynn circled Riddick and sniffed the fried meat.

"They come from the Velshari Temples," Jagwynn said.

Motavo chocked on his bite of breakfast and Merrick dropped his utensil.

"Is there one in every realm, and how do we shut this one down?" Riddick asked. Motavo and Merrick stared at Riddick who popped the last bite of meat into his mouth and licked his fingers, and then he realized they were shocked Jagwynn had spoken. Riddick's brow scrunched in the center, and he knelt and was eye to eye with the enormous cat. "It won't be like the last one will it?" Riddick asked.

She licked his face and he laughed.

"Most realms have one, but I do not know if each one is active and usable, but I can show you where this one is, but Shaz is the only one that can close the temple," Jagwynn said.

"Valida and I will return to the city and get Bowen to organize a hunting unit to finish off the last of the horde, and then we can set out to close off the temple when Shaz is better," Merrick said.

"Amirra and I will come too, we have a little unfinished business to attend to," Riddick said.

Merrick's brow raised but didn't ask. They finished eating and then prepared to travel back to Ebassia. Riddick woke Amirra who ate and helped. Motavo had a few young men saddle the horses and Merrick picked the one he rode the night before. Motavo sent half-a-dozen men with to round up any lost travelers. The days' journey was nice and the wind in his hair and face was refreshing, but Riddick wished they had Serin's wind-walk to make the journey faster. Amirra felt the sting in her tookus and was starting to get frustrated with the ride.

They rounded a bend and topped a hill. The atmosphere and the soft drifty clouds were broken by the majestic buildings of Ebassia. Riddick could now make out the layout of the city. Ebassia was an impressive city with as many palatial high-rise buildings as small modest timbered buildings, tightly squeezed together with small byways that moved about in a labyrinth-like nature through the city. Bright white stones decorated several high rises as light reflected from glass panes that hung delicately into the decorative arches throughout. The panorama excited Riddick's mind until he spotted the pier and his eyes gazed across the horizon and into the sea.

He missed the open sea and especially his home of Turob. He knew it wouldn't be the same ever again and his heart mourned the loss of his childhood. They pushed through the last several lengths and came to the large city gates that were now closed. There were twice as many guards at the gate and around the watchtowers on the outer wall and Riddick wasn't sure if they would be able to get back into the city.

"We are here to see the General," Merrick boomed.

A soldier opened the man door of the main gate and stepped out.

"What is your name?" the guard asked.

"Riddick," Riddick said.

The guard waved to the men at the top of the portcullis and they heaved the handles on the gate irons and the giant wood gate lowered.

The chains clicked in the groves as the men rotated the levers allowing the release of the chains. The portcullis hit the ground with a thud, and they kicked the horses forward. They made their way through the city's main drive and people stopped and bowed as they passed.

"I wonder if they even know what could have happened to them all," Amirra said.

"Aye, but I'm glad that they don't," Riddick said.

The gatekeeper at the entrance to the castle grounds recognized them and signaled for the next portcullis to be lowered. Merrick nodded and the guard saluted. The horses trotted with grace and beauty and it was hard to ignore their presence. The stable boys hurried around the corner, and they handed them the reins as the climbed down. Oladesni stood at the top of the three rows of stairs that lead to the main lobby and waved to them with an eager but sophisticated wave.

"It's a pleasure to meet you, You're Highness," Merrick said.

"The honor is all mine. Please come in. I am glad you are here, there is so much to discuss and I could really use your help," Oladesni said.

Merrick and Riddick entered the doorway and Amirra and Oladesni hugged as she entered. The officials of the city rose a brow knowing that was not the custom, but they tried to have an open mind.

"Where is Shaz and Serin," Oladesni asked.

"They are resting, but you will meet them soon," Riddick said.

"You're Highness, I am sorry to be blunt, but I must speak to Bowen right away," Merrick said.

"Yes, of course, is there something wrong?" Oladesni asked.

"I am afraid so," Merrick said.

Oladesni turned to the doorman and gave the instructions to send Bowen to the council room, and then they quickly hurried to the council rooms in the west wing of the castle. She snapped her fingers and the doorman opened the door. The room was filled with a sizable table surrounded with chairs and several people were sitting throughout them. Oladesni offered them a chair, but they preferred to stand. Bowen threw open the door and Merrick turned around. Riddick was near the door and Bowen and he slapped shoulders.

"Bowen, we have an urgent matter," Merrick said.

"What is it?" Bowen asked.

"We need to assemble a large unit and go after the Jaduuk," Riddick said.

"Jaduuk! Where, how many?" Bowen asked.

"A hoard attacked the outer edges of the city two nights ago and are tracking Shaz toward the highlands. There were hundreds of them," Riddick said.

Bowen turned to the soldier at the door.

"Assemble the first and second brigades and put the third on standby," Bowen said.

The soldier saluted and hurried down the hall.

"Where is Shaz and Serin?" Bowen asked.

"They are resting in the highlands," Amirra said.

"Are they alright?" Bowen asked.

"Aye, but they need time to rest," Riddick said.

"How long will it take for your troops to be ready?" Merrick asked.

"Not long, an hour at most," Bowen said.

"Good," Merrick said.

"I'm sorry, I don't think we have met yet," Bowen said.

"This is Merrick, Shaz's father, and a Ranger," Riddick said.

Bowen's brows raised, and he held out his hand. Merrick took his hand and gripped it in a firm handshake.

"It's an honor," Bowen said.

"What is a Ranger?" Oladesni asked.

"A myth, until now," Bowen said.

Merrick chuckled.

"We will have time for all that, but first we need to get this situation under control," Merrick said.

Merrick gave Oladesni a sparkled wink and followed Bowen and Riddick out to the barracks. They quickly apprised the men of the mission and set out toward the Jaduuk.

47-You Have My Allegiance

Shaz stirred and felt Serin's soft skin next to him and he blinked and rubbed his eyes. There wasn't much light and Shaz wasn't sure if it was early morning or late evening. He scooted close to Serin and wrapped his arm around her and listened to her soft breathing. He wanted so badly to stay there, in that moment, holding Serin close, but the image of the black wyvern entered his mind, and he remembered the Timeless Plains. He lifted onto his elbow and pulled the hair out of her face and kissed her temple and slipped out of the covers.

The cold ground sent a shiver up his spine, and he searched for his boots. He didn't bother looking for a shirt since he evaporated his last one, and he didn't have any more. He started toward his boots across the room and found a small pile of clothes folded on a lounge chair. Shaz sifted through them and slipped on the clean tunic and trousers. He pulled on his boots and laced them and secured the sword on his belt. He slipped through the flap quickly and sucked in a deep breath.

The sun was just coming up in the east and the three moons were starting to fade away into the soft purplish-blue sky. Shaz stretched and enjoyed the solace of the quiet morning. He made his way to the large fire pit the travelers loved to have and found the last night's wood in the center. He shot a burst of flames onto the wood and it bit into the fuel and quickly encompassed the surface. He knew the Ukari would take care of the sqwall and felt a comfort there. Serin came up behind him and wrapped her arms around his waist.

"You're awake," Shaz said.

"It suddenly got cold, and I found that you weren't there," Serin said. She was wearing the tunic and leggings that were left for her, but she didn't have her cloak. Shaz wrapped his arms around her and Motavo crossed the clearing.

"You're awake, how do you feel?" Motavo asked.

"Much better, thank you," Shaz said.

"I would hope so, it's been three days," Motavo said.

"That would explain why I'm so hungry," Serin said.

Shaz and Serin weren't exactly surprised. It seemed that sleep was one of the things that helped them replenish and Serin already knew how much Shaz could sleep if he was given the chance.

"Where is everyone," Shaz asked.

He had already scanned for them and knew they were gone.

"They've gone to get Bowen and an army to go after the Jaduuk and I received a message that Amirra and Valida are staying at the castle to help get things organized, but has asked for us when you awake," Motavo said.

"And the Minca and Jag," Shaz asked.

"They have gone into the city to get supplies, something for their dart guns," Motavo said.

"We can leave after we eat," Serin said.

They quickly made food and ate and Motavo instructed Barsoli on the plans and gave him instructions to send Asher as soon he got back. Serin buffed the horses with wind-walk, and they hurried toward Ebassia.

The portcullis was lowered, and they slowed to a fast trot through the lower sections of the city. The people cheered and hooted as they passed and Serin saw little groups of the street performers mingling with the people. People genuinely seemed interested, and they were laughing and having a good time. It was a much happier place with the shops bustling and the carts and wagons were gaining more business.

They reached the castle's inner portcullis and the drawbridge was lowered as they approached. The stable boys ran to meet them, and they dismounted. The steward at the main entrance opened the door and escorted them to the council room. Amirra entered the room and nearly ran to Serin and pulled her into a tight squeeze. She hugged Shaz and nodded to Motavo.

"Shaz, Serin, I'm so glad to see you. How are you doing," Amirra asked.

"We are good, thank you," Serin said.

"Oh, goodness, have things been just crazy around here," Amirra said.

"In a good way I hope," Shaz said.

"Oh yes, of course, things have changed so much in only a few days, but we still have a lot to do," Amirra said.

"Any word on Riddick and the army?" Shaz asked.

"Not yet, but no news is good news, right?" Amirra said.

Serin could tell she was trying to convince herself, but it wasn't working. Oladesni came into the room and Serin noted her features were a little bit older than she seemed a few days ago. Oladesni rounded the table and held out her hand to shake Shaz's.

"It is an honor to have you as my guest. The Realm of Ebassia owes you a great debt, and I didn't even know about the realm," Oladesni said with a little chuckle.

Shaz took her hand and shook it gently and Oladesni went to shake Serin's but Serin gave her a hug and Oladesni smiled.

"I don't think I have been hugged so many times in my life until I met Miss Amirra here," Oladesni said.

"You can blame Serin for that one, she's the one that taught me the joy of friendship," Amirra said.

The ladies shared a slight giggle and Oladesni turned to Motavo.

"You must be Motavo, King of the Travelers," Oladesni said.

Oladesni curtsied a deep curtsy and bowed her head. Motavo waited for to stand and bowed his formal greeting in return.

"I am pleased to be here," Motavo said.

"As am I. I can't tell you much I adore your people and how much my heart hurts for the way they have been treated for so many rotations. It is my solemn pledge to change that as quickly as I can, but that is where I will need your guidance and council, for I do not know how to incorporate them as you think I should," Oladesni said.

"You are wiser than your rotations Queen Oladesni," Motavo said.

Oladesni blushed, she wasn't sure what to say.

"Thank you, but I am nowhere close to being the queen I need to be," Oladesni said.

"That my dear, will never go away," Motavo said.

His smile was gentle, and he gave her the fatherly gaze and she nodded with a smile. Trumpets sounded in the distance and Shaz instinctually rested his hand on the hilt of the blade.

"Oh, that means the army is returning, come," Oladesni said.

They followed Oladesni through the castle to the back where the army's barracks and grounds were. They stopped on the steps and Serin watched as Amirra tried to see into the distance. Shaz could see Riddick, Merrick, and Bowen leading the rows of soldiers on horseback.

"I see them," Shaz said.

Amirra squinted harder but still couldn't see them and Shaz chuckled. They waited until they were close enough for the rear portcullis to open, and they met them in the courtyard. Riddick jumped off his horse and with his long strides gripped Shaz in an embrace. They rejoiced at their return and then Riddick turned to Amirra who was trying to keep both her feet on the ground. She leaped into his arms and he spun her around. Merrick climbed off his horse and Shaz embraced his father. Bowen rounded a row of soldiers after attending to a quick matter and greeted them all happily. Merrick and Motavo slapped each others shoulders and Oladesni watched from the steps.

The afternoon was filled with story swapping and food. Oladesni was notified of more guests and she gave instructions to bring them in. The Minca, Jag, Asher, and Deagan entered the room and the noise increased with the happy reunions. A few hours later Ceros, Valida, Patriza, and Mrs. Bailey arrived. Oladesni admired how much everyone meant to each other. It was something she had never known, being the only child and raised in the castle by herself. The next several days were filled with meetings and councils and planning for a grand event. Riddick and Amirra took some time and returned to the crypt where Amirra finished the ritual and released the servitor. They returned the remains of the King to its proper place and Amirra added more security to the crypt.

Deagan was elected to be the new castle decorator, and he took to his responsibilities quickly. The first thing Oladesni wanted him to do was to remove the silly hats which he did diligently. He also took on the job of the event planner and was so at home that he didn't miss his gondola.

The council decided Ceros would stay on to keep helping the council in Ebassia and act as an ambassador to help the government. Merrick would return to Turob and make sure things were alright there, but Shaz was certain he was going after Garrison, and Motavo would become a member of the parliament as the King of the Travelers, but would first return with Asher to finish some business in the underground.

The hustle of the day's events was now quiet as the night overcame the sky. The crew stayed in the castle for the last few night as Oladesni's guests, but Shaz and Serin would have preferred to stay with the travelers. The evening breeze was gentle, but a chill sat in the middle signaling the season was about to change. Shaz rested his hands on the cold stone handrail and looked out over the city. The lights popped into existence, and he knew there was still an element of the old magic that once coursed through the realm. Shaz ran his hands through his hair.

"I know what that means," Serin said.

"Aye, after the ball tomorrow, we need to be moving on," Shaz said.

"We headed to the Timeless Plains?" Serin asked.

Shaz nodded.

"We need to make a stop at the castle first," Shaz said.

"Oh?" Serin asked.

"I want to find out if the castle has a portal to the Keep," Shaz said.

"I see," Serin said.

Shaz sucked in a heavy breath.

"I hate having to keep doing this," Shaz said.

"Doing what?" Serin asked.

"Making the people that mean the most to me leave these happy times, and for what?" Shaz said.

"I know you feel bad, but try not to," Serin said.

She touched his arm, and he looked at her, and she smiled her 'I love you' smile. Shaz breathed in heavily and Serin knew he would try but that was one of the things that plagued his mind, self-doubt. She knew how amazing he was and what he was willing to do, but she also understood that people are usually their own worst enemies.

"Let's enjoy one more night here and then let things be as they may," Serin said.

Shaz pulled her into a hug and held her tight.

****

Deagan pined the last bit of hair off Serin's neck and stood back. He put his finger on his lip and scoured the swoops and beaded jewels strategically placed with them. Serin amused at how much detail he was spending on her appearance and thought that she was just going to meet Shaz and the others. It wasn't like they hadn't seen her covered in mud, and muck, and blood, and who knows what else, and they still loved her. Deagan had made her try on over a hundred dresses in the city's finest clothing stores before he settled on this one. Deagan's lip twitched, and he moved one of the jewels and smiled with acceptance.

"Alright, now look in the mirror," Deagan said.

Deagan shoved his finger in his mouth and started to chew at his fingernail. Serin stood and stepped in front of the long mirror that was propped against the wall next to the powder table she was sitting at. Serin gasped at how exquisite the dress was and how well it fit her frame. Deagan blushed but gave a slight jump of excitement.

"Oh, Deagan, it's beautiful. I don't even have words," Serin said.

Serin twisted and turned and examined the details of the delicately beaded glass stones and gems that were organized in elaborate images of flowers over the fern-green chiffon fabric. The neckline plunged just enough to hint to her soft curves but without divulging more than Serin's modest nature. The waist was snug to the hips and the sheer overskirt wafted carefully to the floor.

"You'll need these too," Deagan said.

He pulled a box from the bed and opened the lid. Serin lifted a delicate shiny silver shoe that had a narrow heel and fine straps that weaved over her foot.

"Am I supposed to wear these?" Serin asked.

Deagan chuckled but shooshed her and sat her on the chair and slid the shoe on and latched the buckle at the side. Serin wriggled her toes and decided that they weren't too bad. Serin stood up and was instantly a small length taller than without them.

"Now walk," Deagan said.

"Without killing myself?" Serin asked.

"What, a strong and powerful mage like you can't wear heels?" Deagan teased.

Serin gave him a sideways glare and slapped his arm. Deagan

shooed her, and she walked toward the door and found they weren't as bad as she expected. She turned to Deagan and he clapped eagerly.

"You're ready," Deagan said.

Serin kissed Deagan's cheek, and he blushed, and he shooed her. She pulled open the door and left the room. The shoes made a tiny click sound, and she noted she needed to take smaller steps to keep them from slipping on the polished stone. Shaz milled about the grand ballroom observing all the people and Turkill walked around the room with his warrior swagger and nodded at a group of young ladies in the corner who giggled. Shaz searched for Ladtwig and found him in another grand room where the desert tables were. He chuckled and shook his head as Ladtwig carefully maneuvered a group of people with the largest pile of food on one plate Shaz had ever seen. Oladesni was mingling with the new 'old' Grand Vizier and Motavo, Barsoli, and Lashi. Shaz looked for Merrick and found him in corner with Asher in a discussion that made Shaz wonder who was going to be pummeled next.

The traveler men were wearing a mixture of the bright colors of the travelers customs, mixed with the muted silks and weaved fabrics of the higher-class people. The necktie was bright colors and the jacket and pants were darker with the sparkle of golds and silvers in the buttons. A group of street performers rounded the corner from the other hall and gasped at the incredible décor of the grand ballroom.

A prick at Shaz's heart notified him Serin was close, and he turned toward the door. Serin rounded the corner and Shaz's stomach lurched. Serin looked around the room as she took a few steps into the brightly decorated hall. Shaz started toward her, and she found him moving around a group of people near the back left. Shaz's heartfire surged, and he smiled his amazing grin.

His dark blue silk tunic brought out the deep blue of his eyes and his medium-length wavy hair was smooth around his strong chiseled features. Shaz refused to wear the common dress pants that tucked at the knee, so his trousers were tailored close to his legs and rested on his slipper-like leather shoes which Serin found both interesting and appealing. The Honor Blade was strapped to his belt and thigh and

Serin could see the fang he kept tethered under the silk shirt. The rings he now wore gave him a sophisticated look, but Serin knew what they were really for. Serin met him in the middle of the room, and he held out his hand and bowed at the waist. Serin smiled but gave a little curtsy and then laughed.

"You look stunning," Shaz said.

"Thank you, what do you think of these shoes?" Serin asked.

Serin lifted the gown and showed off the shoe.

"They aren't even half as beautiful as you are," Shaz said.

"Just don't let me die from falling in them," Serin said.

Shaz chuckled. Riddick and Amirra moved around a group of people and Serin smiled and waved. Deagan had also helped Amirra pick out her champagne silk dress which accentuated her lean but curvy figure and Serin admired her long cinnamon hair. Riddick's long curly red hair was pulled back into his usual bun-like feature but this time Deagan had convinced him to use the hair glop he used and so the natural frizz of his curls were tamed and polished giving him a more sophisticated look which Serin, and by the looks of it Amirra, liked.

Oladesni turned to see the couples and nodded to the musicians. The crowd hushed and the musician lifted the fiddle to his chin. He gripped the bow and pulled it against the strings and the vibration radiated the room. Serin turned to see the familiar face of the travelers in the musician's pit, and her heart swelled. Shaz pulled her close and held out his hand. Serin gripped his hand, and he swung her around with a delicate strength and Serin eased into the steps of the formal dance. The tune of the travelers 'lovers' song filled the air and a few other couples including Riddick and Amirra joined the center of the room.

Shaz stared into Serin's eyes, and they were locked on each other, and the familiar radiating of shared magic encompassed their frames. The music danced in her ears, but the people faded away as she stared into his eyes. Shaz moved around the floor holding her tight with one arm and leading her with the other. He was thankful now that Grandfather had insisted, he learn to dance, but remembered how mad he and Riddick were when they had to dance with each other.

Shaz eyed Riddick who led Amirra around the floor with equal passion and his heart swelled. The music changed and Shaz moved Serin around to a new beat. He didn't want the night to end because that meant they would have to leave. Serin finally convinced Shaz that she needed a break, and they made their way to the dessert table.

"Shaz, Serin," Barrick's voice boomed over the noise.

Shaz and Serin turned to find Barrick and Helen. Serin screeched with joy and hugged Helen. Helen rubbed her growing belly and Serin shared her excitement and Shaz congratulated Barrick. The performers danced and performed around the castle halls and grounds and people mingled everywhere. Soldiers stood at alert and everyone enjoyed their time together which made the night pass quickly and Serin found it hard to stay awake. She and Shaz said their goodnights and returned to their rooms and sleep overcame them quickly.

****

The sun warmed the atmosphere which heated the salty water of the ocean releasing an array of scents that Serin couldn't decide if she liked. The newly formed council joined them on the pier and the Mirabella rocked gently with the tide that was about to swell the port. Yerild stood at the top of the gangplank and waited for Merrick. Jag-wynn waited in the shade of the forest near the pier and Shaz anxiously waited for the Queen and Bowen. Shaz paced the pier and Riddick distracted himself with a little rock golem who kept chasing Amirra and Ladtwig. They finally arrived and made their way down the pier. Bowen held out his hand and Shaz gripped it tightly.

"If you ever need anything, you have my allegiance," Bowen said.

"And mine," Oladesni said.

Serin turned to Motavo who was trying very hard not to cry and hugged him. Asher was plagued with a hurmpf look that rivaled Tur-kill's but swallowed her into his embrace. Shaz went to shake their hands, but they pulled him into an embrace as well. Merrick pulled Shaz to the side of the plank and gripped him tightly.

"I am proud of you son," Merrick said.

"Thank you," Shaz said.

"There is a task I need to attend to, but I will keep in touch," Merrick said.

"Aye, when you find Garrison, punch him for me," Shaz said.

Merrick blurted a ga-fa and nodded.

"Will do," Merrick said.

Merrick climbed the plank and Yerild waved at Shaz and Rid-dick as he barked orders to set sail. Shaz and the crew left the pier and headed for the forest. Serin stopped at the edge and turned around. Oladesni raised onto her tiptoes and waved over her head. Serin waved and then disappeared into the shadows.

The End

www.ingramcontent.com/pod-product-compliance
Lightning Source LLC
Chambersburg PA
CBHW071729110726
47908CB00006B/1549